M000281518

Wildflower ON THE Prairie

HEARTS of the MIDWEST • BOOK TWO

TASHA HACKETT

ELECTRIC
MOON
PUBLISHING

Wildflower
ON THE
Prairie

©2023 *Wildflower on the Prairie: Hearts of the Midwest, Book Two* / Tasha Hackett

Published by Electric Moon Publishing, LLC

Copyright 2023 by Tasha Hackett

Paperback ISBN-13: 978-1-943027-63-7
E-book ISBN-13: 978-1-943027-64-4

Electric Moon Publishing, LLC
P.O. Box 466
Stromsburg, NE 68666
info@emoonpublishing.com

All rights reserved. No part of this publication may be reproduced, distributed, or transmitted in any form or by any means, including photocopying, recording, or other electronic or mechanical methods, without the prior written permission of the publisher, except in the case of brief quotations embodied in critical reviews and certain other noncommercial uses permitted by copyright law. For permission requests, write to the publisher.

This is a work of fiction. Names, characters, places, and incidents either are the products of the author's imagination or are used fictitiously. Any resemblance to actual persons, living or dead, businesses, companies, events, or locales is entirely coincidental.

The opinions and quotations of the author are not necessarily those of the publisher or its affiliates/contractors/printers. Author retains all intellectual property rights. Contact author for questions or disputes.

Editing by Electric Moon Publishing Editorial Services
Cover and interior design by D.E. West, ZAQ Designs, www.zaqdesigns.com
Electric Moon Publishing Creative Services, www.emoonpublishing.com
Cover images courtesy of www.PeriodImages.com & www.iStockPhoto.com

FICTION / Christian / Romance / Historical
FICTION / Romance / Historical / American

Printed in the United States of America

www.emoonpublishing.com

For Ben

Chapter 1

Nebraska, June 1, 1879

"P**sst**."

Hannah Benton jerked awake at her mother's hiss and the sting of the accompanying pinch.

"Don't make a spectacle of yourself." Mother motioned for Hannah to sit up straight. "Bobbing your head like a regular layabout. You may be exiling yourself to the frontier, but you needn't neglect your upbringing the moment we cross the river." She snapped her fan open and eyed the other passengers on their train.

"We crossed the Missouri hours ago, Mother." Hannah yawned, but she closed her mouth before adding that her up-bringing hadn't done her any favors yet. She fidgeted on the not-so-soft bench she shared with her mother and smoothed her gloved hands along the lap of her stifling green travel suit.

"Bridle your tongue, child. If I could turn this train around I would. It's bad enough your father agreed to this, and it's only by the grace of God himself your brother hasn't been kicked to death by his oxen or pigs or whatever he's playing with on his homestead." Amanda Benton sat perfectly still, aside from the twitch of her wrist that kept her fan moving. "I don't need your prattle with the rest of my pains today."

Hannah turned her face to the aisle to hide another yawn. "Hiram isn't playing homestead." She shook her head, chiding herself for speaking aloud. *He isn't playing at anything. He's finally escaped your clutches and will do whatever it takes to stay out from under your thumb.*

Words tumbled from Hannah's mouth before she could lock them up. "He has sheep anyhow." *Which you would know if you paid attention to anything we've been telling you.*

The vibrant June grass and rolling landscape seemed to hold Mother's interest outside the window for the time. She ran a fin-ger along the high collar of her charcoal suit. "With Hiram gone, I prayed your sharp tongue would settle. Why God cursed me with twins, I'll never know. If you survive the winter together, it'll be a surprise. You'll find soon enough that books can't be eaten." She muttered the rest. "You with your distractions and he with his animals. Neither one of you with a care for reality."

Her mother's suit was impeccable. Somehow, it didn't reveal the evidence of their two-day trip as Hannah's did. Mother's dark hair with a few silver highlights was swept into a simple chignon with a neat straw hat fastened to the side. A deep burgundy ribbon and a plume of feathers accented the hat, dyed gray to match her suit. Hannah wore one of her own in green pinned atop her mess of hair, black as ink.

Down the aisle, men in suits read the paper. A mother with a toddler sprawled across her lap rested her head against the window, hat askew. The father, arm around his wife and child, slept with his head at a sharp angle. Another son sat facing his parents, lost in a copy of *The Hunchback of Notre Dame*. Hannah's own copy nestled between *Frankenstein* and Shakespeare's *Hamlet* in her trunk a few cars behind with the luggage.

"Farming." Her mother's fan flicked open and shut, joining the rant Hannah heard every week since Hiram left Des Moines in February. "I would never have dreamed it for my children. Son of a surgeon, the world at his feet, mere months from taking his own practice, and he throws it away to live in a dusty, barren field."

Outside the window, the telegraph wires, drooping and rising, drooping and rising, pulled Hannah's gaze. What important messages zipped back and forth? Hannah saw it all in her imagination. A little man with round glasses jumped in alarm when the warning came through his wire: *Enemy advancing west of fortification. Send immediate reinforcement.* Men and women scrambled to arms, hoisting shields and swords. Only a few of the trained warriors remained. The war against the mountain trolls—no, prairie ogres—the war against the prairie ogres had been too fierce, too long. A woman in leather trousers and a tunic slung a water skin over her back and grabbed her spear. Originally trained as a rear guard, she was their battalion's best scout. She ran along the leeward side of the army. Was *leeward* a nautical term? Could she scout leeward on land?

Her mother tapped her fan on the window. "How much longer do you suppose? This car is beginning to sway again. We can put a man into a drug-induced sleep, remove his appendix, and he lives to brag about it, but we haven't discovered traveling in comfort. What would it take to knock some heads together and insulate this car? The dust that blows through is insufferable." She gently stretched her shoulders up and slowly relaxed them with her breath as if it took every ounce of willpower to sit another minute through the torture. "It all comes down to money. They'll charge whatever they like to poor folks like us and stuff their pockets. Never you mind how it should be spent to increase the passengers' comfort."

Hannah lifted her gaze to the ceiling and rolled her neck, breathing through her own rising tension of a different sort. They were likely the wealthiest passengers in the car, perhaps the whole train, since the major cities had been left behind on this spur.

A sleek, shiny rail car took shape in Hannah's thoughts. No, scaled. A machine with scales like a serpent. Yes. Hannah closed her eyes. A graceful dragon taking flight with a mere leap into the air and then only wind. Rushing wind? A gentle breeze. The dragon flight surpassed all forms of travel. Soaring high enough to drown her mother's voice, Hannah clenched her fists in her lap. She'd packed her drawing book and pencils away. They were safe. Hidden. Drawing fanciful creatures or machines in flight in front of Mother would never do. Not when she must be on her absolute best behavior. Hannah was finished after all. Eight years of finishing school had taught her how to hide her personality if nothing else.

"Sit up, child." Her mother flicked her fan against Hannah's knee.

How to hide it most of the time. "Yes, Mother." Twenty-one. She was twenty-one years old, and her mother treated her like a mischievous ten-year-old. If this was a self-imposed exile to Hiram's homestead, so be it. But no. She was not being exiled. Nebraska, though vast, could hardly be considered the frontier. After all, it was admitted to the Union twelve years ago. More than enough time for civilization to take root. However, neglecting her upbringing was her favorite daydream. What good would it do out here?

Des Moines wasn't exactly a metropolis. Nothing like Chicago had been, but it was growing faster than it could keep up. She had no qualms removing herself from the odor of the expanding city, no matter how many fancy shops were added downtown.

Ten years ago, Hannah's father moved his family of four to work as the head surgeon for Saint Mary's Hospital. Her mother fussed about the slums on the edges of town with the tents and shacks of the multiple coal mining operations, but she quickly found her place in high society at the city center. The whole lot blinded themselves. Especially the insurance giants of the business district who pretended they weren't drinking the same water as thousands of coal miners. Mother's days were filled with social engagements, from charity board meetings to dress fittings, and Hannah wanted no part of it.

A smile tugged the corner of Hannah's mouth, but she suppressed it. *One more day.* In mere hours, Hannah would be delivered to her brother Hiram and revel in the distance from her mother. If letting a sleepy head bob on a train made her a spectacle, she looked forward to the motherless possibilities of the West. Perhaps she'd venture into the sunshine with her face fully exposed to the warm rays and let her bare feet dig into mud. Hannah wiggled her toes in her pinched shoes, and a giggle slipped out.

Mother glared with puckered lips as if she'd bitten a lemon.

Turning away, Hannah watched the family across the aisle. The bleary-eyed father adjusted the angle of the sleeping child on his wife's lap before his own eyes fluttered shut again.

"Don't. Stare." Her mother hissed through clenched teeth.

"Yes, Mother." The recurring fear that Mother would attempt to keep Hannah from staying churned in her stomach. The plan was simple. Hiram would meet them at the depot, and their mother would refuse to visit his homestead. Hannah ignored the small measure of guilt from letting her assume Hiram lived in a sod house a full day's ride from town. After one night in a hotel, a tearful goodbye—joyful tears—they'd plop Mother on the eastbound train.

Hiram would bring Hannah to his homestead two miles from town.

And then freedom.

Glorious freedom.

Hiram insisted all would be well, so Hannah forced her fists to open and relax as the reassurance from his letters ran through her mind again. Focusing on her posture, she slowed her anxious breathing. Now was not the time to prod her mother but instead, to encourage the belief that her upbringing was fully intact.

Hannah pulled from her satchel *The Poetical Works of William Wordsworth, Volume 1,* a gift from her mother on her last birthday. Though what she really wanted to finish was the published work of Anna Leonowens and her adventures in Siam. If Mother saw her reading Wordsworth, it might soften her disposition. One could dream.

"Hannah, dear, I'm worried about you and Hiram. I don't understand why you can't settle in the city with the rest of us. Mrs. Preston says they don't even have piped water in most of the state. Whyever would you give up the city for this wasteland?"

Mother's whining was unbecoming to a lady of her stature. Hannah squeezed her hand before offering the book of poetry. "Here, Mother. Read something nice. Take your mind off the stress of the day. There's a lovely poem on the second page, just there."

The soured look on her mother's thin face deepened, but she took the book nonetheless.

Hannah blinked her eyes shut, but the telegraph wires continued to travel through her mind, drooping and rising, until Mother slapped the book shut and thumped it on Hannah's lap.

"You're giving up piped water to keep house for Hiram, who gave up piped water to play with pigs. Will someone please explain the logic behind this nonsense?" Mother refused to acknowledge her children didn't want to live under her rule anymore and jumping states was the best way to go about it. "The excuses you crafted the past year are not convincing anyone."

Hannah built an imaginary bronze shield to protect the back of the man's head in front. He would need something to block the arrows shooting from Mother's expression.

"Nobody in their right mind desires the adventure of self-sufficiency to the point they willingly dig in the dirt for their own food. If Hiram needed to prove himself self-sufficient, Nicholas would have let him the guest house until he was established enough to buy a place of his own." Her fan sped faster and faster in time with her rant. "Both of my children. Turning their backs in the same year. There won't be anyone suitable for the two of you to marry so far from proper civilization. A blessing in that, at least. I don't care what you've said about Ockelbo—"

"It's *OH*-ckelbo, Mother. With the long O. *OH*-kul-boe. Ockelbo. It's Swedish."

For her troubles, Hannah's knee received a smack from the fan.

"I don't care if it's Swedish, English, or Turkish, with barely a thousand in populace, it can't be anything worthwhile. It doesn't even have . . ." Mother turned her face to the window releasing a shuddering breath.

"Have what, Mother?"

"Oh! Piped water among other things. Why would you choose it?" She snapped the fan open and immediately shut it again.

One more day. Hannah would be on her best behavior for one more day. And then . . .

Well.

And then she would *live*.

Chapter 2

Large oak desks pretended to be a friend, but right when a man let his guard down and settled into the idea of the thing, they turned vicious, gobbling important documents and spitting them out half-digested. Tobias Franklin, otherwise known as Boss, sat at his monstrosity of a desk and picked through a pile of papers on the left corner. "Jenkins, Jenkins, Jenkins—aha!"

A smear of dried clay covered the last paragraph of the half-filled-in contract. No matter. The important bits were still there. Tobias muttered as he proofed the page. "Arnold Jenkins . . . three crates of bricks from Franklin Brickworks . . . delivered no later than—" He pushed aside the timekeeper's ledger and uncovered his calendar. "No later than the . . . second of June." He shook his head slowly and whistled low. "Busy, busy, busy." He smiled. Busy was good. Busy meant continued success from five years of hard work since he'd taken over the company.

He found the pen straightaway but locating the ink bottle proved more of a challenge. He patted the stacks of receipts, opened and shut a few drawers, and scratched an itch above his ear. Crouching next to his desk, he picked through the machine repair toolbox. He was in the process of dumping the whole thing out on the floor when shouts came from outside.

He stepped to the window, and forgot the ink hunt. Tobias hunched his shoulders and craned his neck low, but dirt caked the windowpane. Using an elbow, he cleared a small hole.

A group of men gathered around the mixing equipment, and Charles Grady stood on the back of Pokey the mule. Tobias laughed as the man lost his balance and leaped backward, falling toward the others, who made no move to catch him but scuttled out of his way instead.

A knock came at the door.

"Come." Tobias stepped to his desk.

Soot covered Roy Swenson's hands and arms to his elbows and sweat lines cleared paths through the black smudges on his face. "Boss? We have another problem with the second kiln. You best come look."

"Where's Dee?"

"Haven't seen him." Roy pulled a bandanna from his pocket and wiped his face, smearing the streaks horizontally across his face.

"It's half-past nine." Tobias cocked his head. It wasn't like his foreman to be late.

Roy shrugged. "Think it's the baby?"

"No, when the last two came, he sent word with the oldest or Ezra maybe. No matter. Let's have a look."

Not so secretly pleased to leave the papers brooding in their piles, Tobias followed Roy into the sun. He pulled out the key attached to the long chain hooked to his vest and locked the door. "I'll meet you there, Roy. Finish sweeping the inside if you haven't yet."

"Yes, sir."

Tobias nodded and turned to deal with the men congregating by the mixer.

Charles, his auburn curls dancing wildly and the morning sun highlighting his spray of freckles, attempted to stand on Pokey's back, but as he found his footing the animal stretched her neck and nipped at Jonas. Charles lost his balance and tumbled off the hind end to a round of cheers and applause. Tobias clapped with the others, loud and slow, and ambled to the front of the group. They went silent at his presence.

"Morning, men. Interesting new way to make bricks." Mumbles of apology drifted his way. "I've changed your timecards to reflect your work ethics." Most had the decency to look ashamed. The cards hadn't been changed yet, but they would be as soon as he returned to the office. And found the ink. "Charles, a moment. The rest of you back to work."

Charles snatched his cap from the dirt and slapped it against his thigh. "Boss?"

"You can choose. A day off to consider if you'd rather find a traveling circus or dig clay in the pit for the remainder of the day." Tobias scanned the horizon. "On half a day's pay."

"You can't do that to me." Charles adjusted his cap, angry daggers shooting from his eyes.

"Why not?"

Charles sputtered. "I've got board to cover, and meals, laundry, and—other things. How'm I supposed to take care of myself if you drive me like a slave with no pay?"

Tobias smiled amiably. He knew Charles couldn't stand it when Tobias stayed calm. "I hardly think that's a fair comparison. If you were my slave, I'd be feeding you and covering board. But I'm not. What I'm also not doing is paying you to play dangerous games on my property with my animals and my equipment on my time."

"It ain't right." Charles spit in the dirt at Tobias's feet.

Tobias breathed in, and his domineering six-foot-one turned to steel. "I've rescinded the offer. You're dismissed. If you want to return tomorrow and reapply with Dee, I'll look over your application—" Tobias held up a hand to silence Charles's interruptions. He spoke softly. "No, you listen. We work in a dangerous line of business. I cannot have the safety of my men compromised over a few laughs. If you want to play circus, go find your own mule. I will not have it."

"Yes, Boss."

"Go home. Come back tomorrow."

Charles kicked a dirt clod and grunted.

"Good," Tobias said. "See you then."

After a curt nod, the offender stormed off. Tobias clapped his hands once and rubbed them together while turning a slow circle, careful not to move into Pokey's nipping range. Old Kevin loitered in the shade of the small office building, spinning his hat.

When Charles strode away, he shoved the hat on his head and jogged to Tobias. "I'll take her, Boss."

"She didn't even notice, did she?"

Kevin chuckled. "Nope. Mayhap she noticed she wasn't walking in a circle no more, but she's well used to the noise and antics of this crew." Pokey never tried to bite Kevin, who'd been around as long as Tobias could remember. Longer than Pokey. Kevin was hired by Tobias's father the first season Franklin Brickworks was in operation. Kevin had always been old, but he never seemed to get any older.

Tobias slid his thumbs into his trouser pockets. "Has he been in the habit of stunts like this?"

"Who'd'ya mean?"

Tobias jerked his head toward the rise where Charles disappeared toward town.

"Oh." Kevin tempted Pokey with one of the sugar cubes he kept in his pocket and eased her into the harness.

"I see," Tobias said. "How have I not noticed?"

"You can't be everywhere, Boss."

"But what about Dee? Surely he would have crushed this behavior before it got to this."

Kevin finished with Pokey and shrugged with a smile. "Charles is a fool. You'll know what to do." He clicked his tongue at Pokey.

Two hours and a bucket of sweat later, Tobias was blackened with soot. He'd discarded his vest and rolled his sleeves to his elbows. Inside the second kiln, he reached above his head to shove clay into the crack that ran almost the entire length of one side.

"There you are." Dee Williams leaned his head inside.

"The man lives!" Tobias scraped a pile of clay from where it'd plopped near his boots. "What took you so long, dearest? Aches and pains this morning?"

His foreman was a solid Swede with a strong work ethic. "Right as rain. Why are you in here?"

"I'm working. What's it look like?"

Dee stepped in all the way and took the trowel and bucket from him. "Let me do that. You don't have to do everything."

"Watch me."

"No, you have more important work. Jenkins is in your office. Says she was to sign the contract."

"Jenkins! Right. She?"

"Arnold sent his daughter. Caroline."

Tobias wiped a chunk of clay from his hand on a dry wall of the kiln. "Do you know where my inkpot ran off to?"

"Devil if I know."

"Don't let your mother hear you speak like that."

"If she hears me all the way from the fatherland, we have bigger problems, ja?" Dee chucked clay at Tobias, who dodged it. "Go meet Jenkins and look in the second drawer on the left. I might have seen the ink there."

"My lunch is there."

"I know. I sampled a slice or two of Zeke's bread. Eloise still in good supply?"

"Yep. If I didn't like Zeke so much, I'd think my sister is only with the guy 'cause he works at a bakery. You take all you want. I know where to get more."

"Jenkins." Dee shoved Tobias's head down and through the entrance of the beehive kiln. "Get back to your desk where you belong. Let us real men do the dirty work."

Tobias spun around. "Wait. Is everything all right on the home front? With Louisa and the baby?"

Dee studied the trowel and slowly mixed the clay in his bucket. "Louisa has done this before. She'll be fine."

"That's not an answer." He snatched his vest from the ground and shoved his arms through. "We all know she's done this before. Six times before. But you're not in the habit of arriving later than me. A man begins to worry."

Dee nodded and resumed filling the crack. Tobias took it for the only answer he'd get at the moment.

"I sent Charles home. He's pushing the line, and I need you to watch him when he returns tomorrow."

"I'm not a nanny."

"What do you recommend? He's one of our best when he does the job."

"I'll shame him until he changes his behavior or cries." Dee scraped the trowel along the brick wall.

Tobias blinked, honestly not sure if Dee was serious or not.

Dee chuckled. "Get going."

Tobias shook his head and took off to find Caroline Jenkins. She and another woman stood near his office wearing a yellow dress, which complemented her red hair. The other woman hid beneath a pale-green bonnet. They both hugged what little shade the building offered against the wall.

Tobias raised a hand in greeting just as Caroline spoke to her companion.

Maribeth Collier.

Tobias stumbled, then jogged a step to cover for it. He'd been courting Maribeth for months, but she'd never come to the brickyard. She worked with her parents at the mercantile, and he sold bricks. Unless he made excuses to frequent the mercantile, they didn't cross paths during the day. In the past, he'd been able to sneak a kiss on the cheek in the dry-goods aisle, but the store was crowded with busybodies. Maribeth didn't appreciate the gossip that followed. What was she doing here?

Tobias was acutely aware of the soot on his arms, hands, and likely, his face. The sweat dampening his clothes and the state of his attire in general was one that he'd rather keep from creatures in pale-green bonnets.

A lady should give some kind of notice before showing up at a place like this. Least aways when a man was courting, he shouldn't be forced to be seen in such a state. Of course, Eloise popped in almost daily with Tobias's toddler, Luke. But that was different. Eloise was a sister, not a lady exactly or a potential, well, a potential someone he wanted to impress. Good impressions didn't happen with sweaty dirt behind his ears. He stopped moving toward the women and considered going back to the water pump to freshen up. But they'd seen him.

This was his domain. He pushed down his irritation and replaced it with a show of confidence. He'd walk around however he pleased and not be cowed by a couple of women. He rolled his shoulders back and strode closer. Caroline was here about the contract for her father, while Maribeth was here for . . . never mind why she was here. It was a business meeting—about bricks. If there was one thing Tobias was good at it was making and sell-ing bricks. He smiled at the women and pulled out the office key. "Sorry to keep you ladies waiting. Fine spring day, isn't it?" He shoved the door in and motioned them into the office. It wasn't much cooler inside, but it was out of the direct sun.

"Are we still calling this spring?" Caroline led the way and stopped before his desk. "The thermometer outside the livery read ninety degrees when we walked across town."

"According to my calendar, it's spring until somewhere in June. I don't make the rules. Here, sit." He grabbed a stack of papers and a toolbox from the extra chair and dumped them on top of the safe in the corner. "Maribeth, you take my chair." He moved it to the side of the desk near Caroline and waved her to it.

Maribeth smiled gently. He smiled back. His heart beat a little faster as he thought about inviting her to lunch in town. After he changed his shirt and cleaned up. Better yet, since she was here, he'd convince her to share his lunch in the office. Not the most romantic offer, but it'd save time. For propriety's sake, they'd leave the door open, but the men would be sprawled under the shade of the cottonwood, the ones who didn't run home for lunch. They were all but guaranteed to leave him alone and ensure he and Maribeth enjoyed an intimate lunch hour.

Caroline cleared her throat.

He flicked his gaze to the desk. He hadn't meant to stare at Maribeth so boldly. He quirked a smile. "Excuse me. I'm not used to having two such beautiful distractions in my office." Digging through the mess of papers on his desk kept him from noticing if they appreciated his compliment.

Arnold Jenkins's contract was on the top of a pile where he'd left it a few hours ago. The pen had rolled to the floor, but still, there was the matter of the missing ink. He slid open the left drawer. Sure enough, it hid behind his lunch. He snorted. His foreman was a snoop.

Tobias signed and dated the proper lines.

After Caroline meticulously read the thing, she slowly nodded without taking her eyes off the page. "This section here." Caroline pointed toward the middle paragraph. "About damaged bricks. Are not all bricks inspected before delivery?"

"They are. But should something happen between here and delivery, we take responsibility."

"Something like what?"

"Nothing has ever happened. Let's say Pokey is stung by a hornet and runs through town and overturns the cart. Bricks fall off the wagon. Maybe some break, maybe some don't. Either way, Franklin Brickworks would make it right. Let's say they're delivered fair and square, Mr. Jenkins will sign for that too, and after they're delivered and signed for, you come outside during the night and throw them across the road. Franklin Brickworks isn't responsible for that." He turned to wink at Maribeth, but both women stared at him with furrowed brows.

"Why would I throw bricks?" Caroline may have asked why he'd eaten worms for breakfast in the same tone.

"You wouldn't. I'm explaining the contract." He pressed his palms to the desk. Business meetings weren't usually this confusing. "Never mind." He schooled his face into a pleasant smile. "I'm responsible for anything that happens to the bricks until they're with you, then I don't hold anymore ownership of them. Say they're stolen from your property? That isn't my responsibility."

"Has that happened before?" Caroline looked at Maribeth with wide eyes.

"It has. A few here and there, but nothing for you to worry about. I'm sure your father has everything worked out." He held out his hand for the contract, hoping to end any more discussion.

"Very well. It looks fine to me." The women stood, adjusted their skirts, and walked toward the door.

It was on the tip of his tongue to ask Maribeth to stay. To say something, anything to keep her attention. He'd not had a full conversation with her since a Sunday drive over two weeks ago. Or was it three? He rubbed his hands together and stared at the calendar. Caroline slipped out the door, and Maribeth did not. Instead, she pushed the door shut and turned to Tobias, her gaze on the floor.

Now he wished he'd stopped long enough to wash up. He couldn't even stand near her without spoiling her clothes with soot. Most days he worked in and around the office, and though he was often outside with the crew, his work didn't usually have him rolling around the blackened inside of a kiln before noon.

"Hello, Tobias." Her gaze didn't lift past his chest. She was acting far too reserved. Formal.

"Hi, Maribeth." His girl had shut the door on the two of them in close quarters and now wouldn't look at him. Strange. "Sorry I'm in such a state." He motioned to his blackened hands.

"Trouble with the kiln again?"

He nodded and moved closer.

She put a finger against his chest when he leaned in for a kiss. "You stop right there, sir."

"Was there something else you had in mind?"

"Even if your hands weren't soiled, I wouldn't have you nearer. It's not proper." Maribeth looked between her lashes and teased him with a pout.

Tobias pushed against the pressure of her finger on his chest and pecked her on the cheek before backing away. "If you're so worried about 'proper', don't shut the door. Where's Caroline going in such a hurry?"

"She's waiting outside. I told her I needed half a minute."

"Ten seconds left. What'll we do?"

Her gaze avoided his and sought the floor again. "We need to talk."

"Sure, I like to talk." He rested his hand on the doorknob by her hip and slowly turned it. "What do you want to talk about for eight seconds?"

"Can you come by the store after closing? We can sit on the bench out front and discuss it."

The knob stuck three-quarters into the turn as it always did, and he pulled and twisted the other way as he always did. "After the store closes. Yes, I'll meet you after dinner."

"Good, it's settled. I'll see you tonight." She eyed his hand on the doorknob. "Are you going to open it?"

"I am." He turned the knob, pushed it forward, and jiggled until he felt the *click* before gently rotating the knob clockwise. "After you." He pulled the door open in front of her. Perhaps lunch another day. With Eloise bringing Luke to him by the late afternoon, he'd need to work through lunch anyhow to finish the books.

Tobias tossed the pen aside and rose to his feet. Arms up and bent at the elbows, he twisted his torso back and forth. He'd finished checking the timekeeper's notes. *Hallelujah.*

Jedidiah Wilkins, possibly older than Kevin, kept track of the comings and goings of all the men. His calculations were always correct, but his numbers were beginning to wiggle about on the lines, which made it difficult to read. Tobias opened the safe and made a mental note that he'd need to get to the bank before quitting time tomorrow. He pulled out his timepiece. Eloise would arrive any minute with Luke.

He found a bucket of water outside with the pump. Warm. He pumped until cold water ran free and splashed it on his face. With his handkerchief, he scrubbed his neck, face, and arms to his elbows before he rolled his sleeves down to his wrists and buttoned the cuffs. After filling the bucket with fresh water, he walked around playing water boy for the crew until the top of his buggy came over the hill.

Luke, not yet two, was wedged between Eloise and her beau, Ezekiel James. Luke knocked his cap off with enthusiastic waving, and his blond hair stuck straight up in the wind. Tobias left the water bucket on the ground and jogged to meet his family. They stopped outside the office, and Luke scrambled over Zeke's lap and jumped to Tobias. "Dada!"

"Hi, son." Tobias closed his eyes for a moment and breathed in the child's embrace. Luke was better than any tonic, and Tobias instantly felt the tension roll off like excess clay from the press.

"Yuke come! Ehwie an' Eek come." Luke pushed away and pointed at Eloise and Zeke. His face shone, and he bounced with excitement.

Tobias laughed at Luke's declaration. "Eek, is it?"

Zeke grinned. "Not the worst I've been called." Zeke leaned over and tickled Luke under his chin. "I'll answer to it same as anything else."

Luke slapped Zeke's hand away, squealing.

Tobias wrapped him in another hug, but Luke wasn't having it. He wiggled to get down. "I work."

"Oh, no, you don't. You'll stay with me." Tobias swooped him high in the air until the toddler quit trying to get away. "He give you any trouble today?" Tobias looked at Eloise.

"Always." She adjusted her wide-brimmed, floppy bonnet over her brown hair and smiled. "Though nothing out of the ordinary. He napped well, so he'll be in good spirits for you."

"Have her home before sundown." Tobias tried not to enjoy bossing Zeke around too much, but the gangling twenty-year-old with coffee-brown hair in his green eyes begged to be picked on.

"Honestly, Tobias. I'm not a child." Even as Eloise said it, her round cheeks turned pink.

Tobias chuckled, wondering what she was thinking. "Zeke is."

"Hey!" Zeke clubbed Tobias's shoulder, and Eloise snagged his other arm to keep him in the buggy.

Tobias didn't flinch. "We don't hit our elders, boy."

"We do when they deserve it." Zeke smiled. "Don't we, Luke? We'll hit anyone we very well please and ask questions later. That's what I always say." He leaned back and draped an arm around Eloise. "Isn't that what I always say?"

"I'm sure it is, darling." She looked at Zeke with affection, and Tobias didn't miss the way Eloise relaxed into Zeke's hold. It was odd to see his sister so comfortable there.

Tobias hunched over and gagged until Zeke slapped him on the back—which required him to remove his arm from Eloise. "Sorry." He wiped his mouth with the back of his hand for show. "I thought I heard my sister call you a darling, and my lunch suddenly decided to come up."

"I answer to *darling*." Zeke tapped Eloise on the nose. "Especially when it's in agreement with me." He lowered his voice and looked at Tobias. "What you've got to look out for is when they say, *dear*, with that bite on the end of it. You know the one."

"I know it well." Tobias patted Luke on the back when he tried to wriggle down again.

"If you boys are about done shooting the breeze . . . I wouldn't mind sitting a while longer, but Dan's falling asleep." She motioned to Tobias's dappled gray.

"Have fun." Tobias waved Luke's hand at Zeke. "Don't do anything foolhardy."

"Thanks, Boss. What'd we do without your sage advice?"

"Get outta here."

Eloise tapped her hand on Zeke's and leaned toward Tobias. "You'll be all right for dinner? I honestly don't know what's available. I haven't spared a single thought about your dinner. I'm so sorry."

"We'll figure it out." He jerked his head back to keep Luke's finger from going up his nose. "Maybe I'll take him downtown for a treat."

"Oh, I'm sorry to do that to you." She looked between Zeke and Tobias with concern.

"He'll be fine, Chipmunk." Zeke used his pet name for her.

Tobias never had gotten a straight answer for how it came about. "He's a smart guy. He's never depended on your culinary skills."

She narrowed her eyes but didn't argue. Zeke spoke truth.

Tobias opted to change the subject. "It's fine. Have to stop by the depot and sign for a shipment of coal anyhow. It'll be fun. Luke likes to see the trains come through. What are you two eating?"

Zeke glanced at Eloise. "I tossed in a basket of leftovers from the bakery. You grabbed the bottle of cider?"

Luke wrestled against Tobias's hold, desperate to play, when Dee Williams came their way, tugging his hat lower to shade his pale skin.

"Välkommen," Dee said.

Luke's botched attempt at the word was cause for laughter all around.

Chapter 3

The Ockelbo depot greeted Hannah and her mother with a large sign that hung from roof. "Välkommen." Hannah whispered the Swedish word, not needing a translation. *Welcome.* The sign was painted a cheery yellow with the word scripted in blue letters. Pink wildflowers were painted above the word with a leafy green fringe branching out from the petals. From its chains, the sign almost waved at her as the train jostled, screeched, and bumped to a stop.

Amanda Benton surged to her feet and passed her daughter to be the first down the steps, leaning heavily on the porter's hand. Frantically waving her fan in her face, she looked around with squinted eyes and a downward turn of her mouth.

The depot wasn't large in comparison to the others they'd passed through. The wooden platform extended far enough to access the luggage car behind them, and an awning reached from the ticket counter and covered most of the platform. A couple of storehouses and a corral completed the station.

Hannah approached her mother's side. "Mother, find a bench in the shade. I'll see about my luggage."

"Fiddlesticks, I've been sitting for hours." She snapped her fan shut.

"Of course."

"You see about your luggage. I'm going to find water that doesn't taste like the inside of a boot."

"Yes, Mother."

"And Hannah, hold your satchel tight. Don't stand too close to anyone. Keep away from the porters." She sniffed. "I don't trust these people."

Only a handful of passengers exited the train with them, but plenty of men moved around the station. Nobody was interested in her satchel. They all had work to do.

"Hannah!" Mother glared, waiting for an answer.

"Yes, Mother."

She left Hannah alone and waltzed through the open double doors of the building.

Butterflies flipped in Hannah's stomach. Alone. She was almost there. She turned to the luggage car to find her trunks. The porters were already busy unloading and had collected quite an assortment of boxes and crates on the platform. One of her trunks—the heavy one with most of her books and other private things—sat at the top of the ramp. She'd packed this one secretly without Mother nosing into it. Shakespeare and Homer were inside among her other book friends.

"Careful! It's full of—" Her warning was too late. The man below caught the full weight of her trunk when it slid down the ramp. He scowled at his partner inside the rail car, who laughed in return.

A blast of smoke clouded her vision. She stepped closer to the growing pile but stayed well out of the way. Men swarmed the depot like ants. Focused. Quick and busy. She gripped her satchel with one hand and dug her handkerchief from her sleeve to hold against her nose and mouth.

My, but it's smoky. The dirt clinging to the faces of fellow passengers didn't give her much hope for her own appearance. Were there bathtubs this far west? She'd need one after this sweltering heat. Before she left Des Moines, a friend had shared dire warnings of the shady characters she might encounter, but most of that knowledge was gleaned from her friend's kid brother and his dime novels. The truth of those stories was nil.

Surely not all the men visited saloons, spit tobacco, or frequented gun fights . . .

She was beginning to sound like her mother. *Blimey, I'm not frightened, am I? No, thank you.* She tucked the handkerchief up the cuff of her sleeve, straightened her shoulders, and drew in a deep breath. A new cloud of something hit her, and a fit of coughing ensued.

The man attempted to lift her trunk, but another crate slid down the ramp, crashed into him, and threw him off balance. He straightened and gestured for the other man to come and assist. Hannah ignored the words he yelled, glad that Mother wasn't within earshot for they were not fit for her ears.

The two porters hefted her trunk. Hannah leaned forward with her weight on her toes. She wouldn't breathe easy until the last of her possessions were off that train.

A small form with a blond head flew past her skirts.

Gaining on the toddler, a tall man raced toward her. "Grab him!"

Hannah was too startled to obey his barked command.

The child rushed between the porters and stopped underneath her trunk. His laughing eyes connected with hers before he spun away. Clearly aiming toward the ramp into the luggage car, he collided with the porter's legs instead.

Suddenly the danger was very real indeed. Hannah gasped, dropping her satchel, as she covered her mouth. The porter tripped on the boy he couldn't see at the same time the man in pursuit swooped into the mix. In two blinks, all three men landed on the ground, her trunk upended, and the boy crawled away squealing.

With the end of her trunk over his legs, Tall Man snatched the boy's foot before he ran off. His gray cap had flown off and hair the color of polished oak flopped over his forehead. "Luke, stop it!" He commanded with a voice that suggested he wasn't used to being ignored. The man extracted himself from the mess and dangled the child by his ankle.

Books spewed forth among her nightgowns, stockings, and an emerald corset embroidered with flowers. The corset rolled a foot from the rest of the mess to display itself on the ground. It drew everyone's attention.

Tall Man swung the child through the air and hooked him under his arm. The two other men tried to side-step Hannah's books and intimates as they disentangled themselves.

28

"What's this, boys?" Tall Man waved his hand over the mess. "Plunder a library?"

"Don't you have work to do, Boss?" The first porter righted the trunk and threw in her small boxes of drawing pencils, paints, and notebooks. The second porter stacked books. They avoided her intimates and pretended the glaringly obvious corset didn't exist.

Hannah stood stock still as a trickle of sweat beaded along her temple. Maybe nobody suspected it was her trunk. She eased backward, thinking she'd get away unnoticed, but Tall Man looked up, catching her. His laughing smile matched that of the child. And then he winked. With one hand he gathered a few of her intimates and tossed them into the trunk. A porter jerked his hand back as if burned when the lace from her nightgown brushed against him.

For once, it wasn't the heat of the sun that flushed her face red.

Since she'd been discovered, she rushed into the mix, facing the embarrassment to save her things from rough handling.

"I'll do it." She snatched a gilded copy of *The Iliad* from the first man, and he seemed only too happy to let her take over. He and the other porter disappeared into the luggage car without a word.

"I'm sorry." Tall Man handed her *The Adventures of Tom Sawyer.* "Not the welcome-to-town ritual you'd anticipated?"

Hannah knelt by the trunk, and she layered books along the bottom, shoving the clothing to the side.

"Name's Tobias Franklin."

Hannah nodded but focused on repacking as quickly as possible. Mother could not see this mess.

She twisted at the waist to grab another handful, and Mr. Franklin passed her the corset and a pair of purple and white striped stockings.

"Oh, dear." Hannah's hand moved of its own accord and slowly reached for the garment.

"It's a beautiful article of clothing." He spoke as one commenting on the weather.

"Thank you. I think so too." Hannah widened her eyes and swallowed. Did he . . . did he just compliment her undergarments? And she thanked him! She tucked it discreetly into the corner of her trunk and turned to find Mr. Franklin crouched beside her. With a handful of books in one hand, he tucked the tow-headed boy against his side with his other.

"You've read all these?" He listed the titles as he passed them over. "*Sir Gawain and the Dragon, Emma, The Odyssey.*"

"Yes." She bent over the trunk and arranged the books.

"*Midsummer Night's Dream.* I skipped that one in school." It joined the others along the bottom of the trunk. "Still wrote the essay for it."

Hannah paused her frantic repacking. "How did you manage it?"

He smiled, handing off another book. She studied his face for the first time. His eyes weren't simply blue but ringed with a thin circlet of midnight. Smooth skin, with the barest hint of stubble on his strong chin. He was mid-twenties at best, which was much younger than she'd first assumed. A playful wink brought her attention to his eyes. "A friend of mine did the reading and shared the key points."

"Oh, that's a shame." Hannah blinked, firmly, and forced herself to quit staring into his eyes. "You missed the heart of the story and the humor." When she glanced at him again, his smile broadened. She patted her hair to make sure it hadn't come loose on one side.

"I've told you my name, but you've neglected to share yours." Momentarily breaking eye contact, he stopped the boy's hand from opening a pencil box and passed it to her. His hand brushed against her gloved fingers at the exchange.

"Is this your son? He's the mirror image of you, differing only in hair color."

"He is. Meet Luke. He's, ah—" Mr. Franklin chuckled. "—undomesticated. His mama didn't live long enough to teach him the obedience to go along with his cherub face."

"Oh, I'm sorry."

Mr. Franklin dipped his head in acknowledgment and roughed Luke's hair.

"How old is he?"

"He'll be two in October." He flashed a smile and passed her *Journey to the Center of the Earth*. "Are you visiting or here to stay?"

"Hannah!" Her mother screeched from across the platform, and Hannah's heart about burst her laces.

She leapt to her feet and walked across the platform as quickly as she dared. Mother already wanted to pack her on the train and cart her all the way home. As if Hannah's—as Mother said, "outlandish"—book collection wasn't enough, the green corset would throw her into a tizzy. It *was* a beautiful article of clothing. It shouldn't matter if she wore beautiful undergarments. They had to be worn, whether white muslin or green silk. Why not wear green silk? Nobody saw it either way but her.

Correction. Nobody had seen it before today.

Mother clutched Hannah's arm. "One minute in the wild West, and things are already unraveling. Isn't that one of your trunks?"

"Did you have any luck with the water?" *Distract. Distract.*

"It looks just like your other trunks."

"I'm parched. Would you show me where it is?" Hannah pulled her farther away from the luggage pile, but Mother looked over her shoulder. "Have you found Hiram? I can't wait to see him. It's been so long." Hannah refused to turn and see any more laughing and winking eyes.

"Excuse me, Miss Hannah Benton?"

When Hannah and her mother turned, Mr. Franklin strode toward them with Luke hooked under his arm. He held one of her books.

Was it possible to feign ignorance? *You child. You can't pretend your name isn't Hannah when Mother is standing next to you.* Hannah squared her shoulders. "Yes?"

Her mother glared between the two of them. "You know this man?" Her head swiveled like a snake charmer's pet, eyeing him with a sense of wariness and hatred, poised to strike. "How do you know my daughter's name? Are you acquainted with Hiram? Did he send you? What have you done with my son and why didn't he come himself?"

Mr. Franklin swung the boy into a proper hold against his chest and held the book up. "There's a name written inside the cover, ma'am. Hannah Claire Benton." He ignored her mother's other questions and smiled at Hannah. "You must be Mr. Benton's sister. We met at church this winter, and he spoke of you joining him." He wiggled the book in the air between them. "Here."

Hannah glanced at the title, *Frankenstein,* then gave the tiniest shake of her head, widening her eyes.

The blond toddler grabbed for the book, but Mr. Franklin tucked it behind his back out of the boy's reach. He didn't seem to notice Hannah's fear and kept babbling, pushing her closer to danger. "I hate to say it, but after our tumble, the cover of this copy tore along the spine. I apologize for the damage. Maybe it was already like this, but I'm afraid it was our fault." Dodging the toddler's hand, he held the book between her and Mother.

Hannah froze. Like a silly, useless child, she froze.

Her mother finally read the title. Hannah knew this to be so when she turned on her with lips pinched together and nose flared. With no other warning, Mother's hand came up and slapped Hannah across the face.

At first the shock stung more than the physical pain, but in a heartbeat, tears sprang, and her cheek burned. Hannah turned her gaze to the ground and covered the side of her face with her hand.

Mr. Franklin sucked in a breath and took a small step toward Hannah, but his muddied work boots shuffled back again. Luke whimpered and burrowed his face into his father's chest.

Hannah turned from them both.

"This isn't my daughter's book." Mother spoke in clipped, tight words. "A daughter of mine would never read such filth." She snatched the book and threw it on the ground where the hardback cover flopped open at an angle. "And you should be ashamed of yourself. Letting this child run amok around a train? I knew we'd be stepping into a new world out here, but I didn't think I'd have to keep my wits about me for fear of unattended wild boys. This boy should not be at a train station. What if he'd fallen onto the tracks? Or climbed aboard a departing train at the last moment? I saw the whole thing unfold. You weren't even watching him while you gabbed at the ticket counter. He ran right around you and onto the platform. This boy has no manners or training in obedience. If it were my boy, he'd be over my knee this very minute. Where is this child's mother? I would have a word with her."

His jaw muscles clenched before he answered. "I'm afraid that's not possible." Mr. Franklin's large hand covered the side of Luke's face, keeping him tucked against his chest, as if shielding him from the onslaught.

Hannah met the man's eyes a moment before closing hers and hiding her shame. She turned away and walked toward her trunk, leaving *Frankenstein* where it lay. Mr. Franklin had finished repacking and latched the lid.

Her mother wasn't finished. "Very well, you may report that due to her poor training and your negligence, her boy was almost killed twice over and caused a scene."

Hannah's cheek smarted, but she refused to bow under it. She hoped it left a mark. Let Mother look at that for the rest of the day. *One more day.* Now that she was here, there was nothing her mother could do, save physically dragging Hannah onto the train and tying her down, to keep her from staying.

Chapter 4

Tobias sat in his shirtsleeves and rocked Luke in the front room. He'd scraped together a few bites for dinner with leftover ham and a healthy layer of butter on Zeke's bread. Luke rested with his back against Tobias's chest and sucked his thumb. He wasn't asleep, but neither was he attempting to tear down the house. One little hand tugged his ear, and a bare foot kicked at the air anytime Tobias slowed the swing of the rocking chair.

"Maybe she's right, Luke . . . in a way. You oughtn't to run away all the time." Tobias rocked in big swooping waves. "But dad-blame-it, if that's the way she treats her grown daughter, I wouldn't take her advice for a new team o' horses and a shiny buggy."

Luke sat up and popped his thumb from his mouth. "Toys?" He waited for Tobias to nod and slipped to the floor. He ran around the sofa to his tin can of blocks and tried to pick it up. Grunting and breathing hard, he pulled the can to the rug in the middle of the room and dumped the contents on the floor.

Tobias lifted *Frankenstein* from the end table and flipped the cover open to the title page. He read the inscription again.

For Hannah Claire Benton,

May this sate your imagination for another week.

Love, Father

Hannah's flushed cheeks and covert glances as they worked together over her trunk flashed through his mind. Then her fear, the flinch, and dejection after her mother's outburst. What kind of mother took such measures over a book? And so publicly? A book given by the girl's very own father.

Tobias knew her brother, Hiram. Not well but knew who he was and that he sang a strong baritone on Sunday. The sheep farmer was quiet but friendly. Lived a couple miles from town in a white board house. A beautiful spread he'd been lucky enough to snatch from a line of previous failed attempts to turn a profit.

Tobias didn't know anything about Hiram's family except he'd been anticipating a twin sister to join him this summer. Looked just like her with dark, elegant features. Though before today, Tobias had never attached the word *elegant* to Hiram's face. There was no other word he'd use to describe Miss Benton. Elegant. Her dark hair was a strong contrast against skin as pale as it comes, even with the rosy flush on the apples of her cheeks. Tall for a woman. Intense gray eyes, pink lips, and—

Movement from the large window facing the street interrupted his musings. Zeke and Eloise were back. Tobias glanced at the clock on the shelf. Luke should be in bed by now, but Tobias remained in the rocker, slumped and brooding, too exhausted to move.

The couple eventually made their way to the porch. Zeke teased, and Eloise laughed. Both disgustingly in love. If they weren't perfect for each other, Tobias wouldn't have put up with their nonsense.

Zeke threw open the screened door, and Eloise skipped inside. He dashed behind her and slapped at a mosquito that flew in with them.

"You'd better get it." Tobias didn't budge from his slouch except to rest *Frankenstein* on the end table. "There was one here yesterday that buzzed in my ear all night long."

"Hi, Boss." Zeke stalked the mosquito across the room. "Did you wait up for me?"

"I figured I ought to. You likely wouldn't find your way home if you strayed off the road again, and I know Eloise isn't any help."

The couple shared a look, and Eloise giggled.

"Tell me." Tobias lowered his eyebrows.

Eloise flopped on the rug next to Luke, who immediately snuggled into her lap, blocks forgotten. "We didn't get lost, exactly."

Tobias eyed Zeke, who still chased the mosquito, clapping his hands and slapping at the wall. "Zekey James, you inventing a new folk dance?"

"I've almost got it—don't distract me." He clapped his hands again. "And watch your mouth. Nobody but Ma got away with that Zekey James business. This little bloodsucker will not spend the night in the same house with my girl." He smacked his hands together once more and *whooped* when he saw the dead bug in his palms.

Tobias stretched out his legs and intertwined his fingers over his stomach. "You got lost on the prairie?"

"Oh, it wasn't quite like that." Eloise stood with Luke on her hip. "We left the road, sure. We were looking for a bit of shade for our picnic, and you know how it is along the creek there on the east of town."

"I guess I don't because I've never been lost. There's a creek, road, and house every mile." He pressed the tip of his tongue to his side molars, tension pulling along his jaw.

Zeke pushed off the wall where he'd been reclining and sauntered into the kitchen. "Relax, old man. As she said, it's not like that. We left the road and turned one way and then the other and had a fine time of it. There was only a moment or two of mild confusion before we spotted Layton working his spread. He pointed us straight again." The cupboard creaked opened and clipped shut. "I know I brought two loaves over yesterday." Zeke hollered from the kitchen. "Crumbs! You left me nothing but crumbs. You ate all of it?" He stepped into the room, holding the empty breadbox upside down.

"Honestly, Tobias. We weren't really lost." Eloise swayed with Luke snuggled into her chest. "We're home before dark anyhow. You needn't fuss so. It wasn't a big deal."

Tobias looked between the two of them with his heel tapping a rhythm on the floor. "It *is* a big deal." He pointed at Eloise. "You should know better. You're not little children anymore. What if you'd been hurt and needed help in a hurry? Zeke, you have work in the morning. Early. What time do you start at the bakery?"

"Four." Zeke returned the breadbox to the kitchen.

"See? That's early." Tobias stood. "I don't believe this. El, you've gotta keep your head on." Heat rushed into his face, and his voice rose. "You can't be running around on the prairie all hours of the night. You're smarter than that. If I can't trust you for a few hours out of my sight, then—" He snapped his mouth shut when Zeke stepped in front of Eloise, pushing her behind him with an arm. Eloise side-stepped his protective posture, shoved Luke at Zeke, and fled upstairs.

Great. I've offended my baby sister again. "What did I say?" He was ready for this day to be over.

Zeke hitched Luke a little higher. "I don't think it was the *what* so much as the *how*." He backed to the sofa and sat with Luke. "I've never heard you yell before, and I'll have to say I don't like it." He tucked Luke into the crook of his arm.

Tobias stood in the middle of the room, taking up space like an uninvited guest. "I wasn't yelling."

"You were yelling."

His jaw ached from how hard he clenched his teeth. "Was not." He cut the air with his hand. "I was . . . passionate."

Zeke snorted. "Shut it, Boss. You overstepped, and you ruined her evening, and now she feels like she's in trouble even though she's done nothing wrong. Quit acting like she's one of your employees because she's not. I can't go comfort her because then we'd kiss and forget all about you being a bully." While cradling Luke, he stood and grinned. The fool man. "Actually, on second thought. Here, take your kid. Eloise needs comforting."

Tobias glared at Zeke. "You've made your point. Si'down." He growled the words and slowly advanced until the know-it-all stumbled back to the sofa. "You won't be stepping one foot into El's room until a preacher signs off on it."

He left the baby with Zeke and found his sister sitting on her bed with the door open. She sat on the edge, staring at the lamp on the washstand while brushing her long, brown hair. The pins were in a pile on the stand. She ignored him when he knocked on her door frame. And she ignored him when he stepped into her room and sat in the small wooden chair by the bureau. He crossed his arms and waited.

She pulled the brush through her hair in smooth, tedious strokes.

After twenty repetitions she spoke. "I'm sorry I caused you to worry."

He dipped his chin. "Forgiven. Sorry for yelling."

"You weren't yelling."

"Ha!" He uncrossed his arms and pointed. "I knew I wasn't yelling. He said I was yelling."

She looked at him sideways without turning her head. "He's never seen you worked up, I guess. That wasn't yelling. If you'd been yelling, I would have brought Luke with me and shut you out of my room. Luke would be crying, and I'd be crying—instead of sulking. You're frightening when you yell."

"Hm." Not a great character reference from his sister. "I don't often, do I?"

"Twice since, well, since you grew up and got scary."

"Twice, as in twice ever?"

"Sure. Once after Jessica and I spilled that bottle of ink on your desk a few months after Mom and Dad . . . after you'd taken over the brickyard." She smoothed a hand down the full length of her hair. "We deserved that one."

"No one deserves to be yelled at." He leaned forward and scrubbed his face in his hands. May as well dig into the wound while it was open. "When else?"

"Oh, let's not talk about it." She put the brush on the washstand and stared at the pile of hairpins. "Tobias?"

"Mmm?"

The pins proved more interesting than whatever she wasn't saying. She straightened them end to end and made two parallel lines before laying her hands on top, covering them. "How did you know it was time to move on?"

The tiny chair was too small for him and creaked when he adjusted. "From what?"

"Philip's been dead more than a year. A long time in a way, but also not at all. Even though we were only married a few months, we were sweethearts for almost five years. Now with Zeke—" A hairpin dropped to the floor, but she didn't move to pick it up. She gathered the rest into a pile and left them there. Finally, she turned to look at him. "Zeke's been in town for two months. Two months! But I, honestly, I can hardly even say it." She lowered her voice to a near whisper. "I really like him."

Tobias crowed. "You don't say?"

"You know what I mean." She watched her finger absently tracing patterns on her blue skirt.

"Maybe I do, El. Maybe I don't. I like ostkaka, but I don't care to eat it every day. You and Zeke are together more than I eat ostkaka."

"Zeke isn't a pudding."

Tobias leaned forward. "You don't think he's trying to butter me up for his old job at the brickyard, do you?" Zeke worked for the brickyard less than a week digging clay before he was let go for assaulting Tobias, his boss. It was a misunderstanding, one in which Zeke might have been justified in his actions—if he hadn't been dead wrong.

"Be serious. How did you know it was time to move on? That you were ready? After Katie died, within months you were courting Maribeth."

"Oh, dash-it-all!" Tobias lurched to his feet. "Maribeth. What time is it?" He clenched his fist but didn't hit anything. "El, put your hair up. I've got to go."

Her eyes grew wide at his outburst, and the color had all but drained from her face. "Why do I need to put my hair up?"

"Because Zeke is downstairs." There was no time for explaining. Didn't she understand this was urgent?

"You're the one walking around in your shirtsleeves with a guest in our home." She stood, placing her hands on her hips.

He gripped the door frame. "Zeke's not a guest. Don't look at me like that. It's not the same! I say put your hair up because I know what it does to a man when he sees his girl with her hair down." He didn't have time for this. "Never mind. I haven't even put Luke to bed yet." He fled downstairs but halted at the base of the steps when he saw Zeke and Luke both asleep. Zeke's leg stretched the length of the sofa, and a decorative pillow propped the side of his head against the armrest. Luke curled between Zeke and the back of the sofa, sucking away at his thumb.

A high-pitched whine came from behind Tobias. Eloise was there with her hair tied in a ribbon. Both her hands covered her mouth under big puppy-dog eyes. "It's the sweetest thing I've ever seen."

Tobias growled. "Knock it off. Doesn't he have his own bed to sleep in?"

She placed her hand on Tobias's forearm and whispered, "Don't wake them up."

"I have to! You don't understand. I told Maribeth I'd meet her after work, *and I didn't.*"

Eloise's jaw slacked. "Shame on you, Tobias."

"Yes, well." He rolled his eyes. "That's why I need to go."

"Then go." She grabbed his overshirt and vest from the back of the rocking chair and shooed him toward the door.

"I am not—" He pulled the shirt on and stuck his arms and head through. "—leaving him alone with you."

"Honestly, Tobias. What could possibly happen? He's asleep."

"Then he should be in his own bed." Tobias shoved the tails of his shirt into his trousers. "And it's not proper. At all." He snapped the suspenders into place over his shoulders. "Get the baby. Zeke's coming with me."

"Very well." Eloise bent over the two on the sofa and gently brushed the hair from Zeke's forehead.

Tobias hissed as he donned the vest. "I said, 'Get the baby.' Come on, El. I've got to go."

She only smiled. Zeke awoke and looked at Eloise with love-sick eyes. Tobias finished with his vest and pushed Eloise out of the way. Luke still slept when Tobias pulled him to his chest.

A quick kiss for the toddler, a transfer to Eloise, a tug on Zeke, and finally, *finally,* Tobias was out the door.

Only ten after eight according to his timepiece's judgmental face.

Chapter 5

*S*he wants to talk. It's no big deal. 'Sit on the bench out front.' *She can't be too mad about me forgetting that. It's not like I left her high and dry for a dance.*

Tobias stumbled. *When's the next dance? I'll invite her to that. Let her know I've got time this weekend.*

"What's the rush, Boss?" Zeke jogged to catch up with Tobias marching down the street.

Maribeth and the rest of the Collier family would still be up, but would she be pleased to see him? *She might be angry. I've never seen her angry . . . I've never stood her up before.*

"Boss, why are we running?"

Tobias slowed. Though he hadn't been running exactly, it wouldn't do to arrive out of breath. He stopped. Smoothed his hair under his cap. Tugged his vest. "I'm late for a thing with Miss Collier. Missed it, actually. Completely forgot about her." He turned to Zeke and rubbed his palms dry on his trousers. "I think she'll be mad. How do I look?"

"Like a middle-aged father who's late for a date."

Tobias flashed a hand toward Zeke's shoulder and made contact on account of Zeke being in the middle of a yawn. "Shut your mouth."

"A grumpy, middle-aged father," Zeke said, rubbing his shoulder.

"I'm not middle-aged," Tobias muttered. The two walked across the town square to Rose's Mercantile, above which was the Collier apartment.

Zeke's room at Anderson's Bakery was on the same street. Oscar and Agnes Anderson rented the room on the main floor to Zeke, and they lived above the store in the larger apartment.

Zeke and Tobias split ways.

"And Boss," Zeke said.

Tobias pivoted but kept walking backward.

"Just . . ."

"What?" Tobias immediately regretted his tone when Zeke's face fell. He was more irritated with himself than Zeke.

"Never mind."

"Sorry." Tobias stopped walking. He forced himself to relax his posture and look at his friend. "What is it?"

"I was only going to suggest you try groveling." Zeke smiled.

"I don't grovel."

"We know. You lead, command, protect. Might be time to grovel." Zeke lifted his gaze to the sky for a heartbeat, and his smile broadened.

Tobias tightened the back of his throat, trying hard not to growl, and dug his hands into his pockets. "You got a verse for that one?"

Zeke only cocked his head and chewed the side of his lip for a moment, then smirked. "Psalm 25. 'Pardon my iniquity, for it is great.'"

Tobias grunted and turned his back.

Rose's Mercantile was a large store that sold everything a person needed for home life. And if they didn't have it, they would order it. Catalogs heavier than his bricks lined the back counter. Since specialty stores had popped up all over town, they didn't overstock like they used to, but business remained steady.

Tobias stood at the top of the stairs outside Maribeth's apartment tugging his vest. He rolled his shoulders and blew out a breath.

He knocked.

Brent Collier, her fourteen-year-old brother, opened the door. "Hiya, Boss." The whole family was in the main room. Mr. Collier read *Scribner's Monthly* and Mrs. Collier sat on the sofa with ten-year-old Felicity, working with a needle and brightly colored thread. Maribeth was in the rocking chair reading *McCall's Magazine*. She glanced at him briefly when the door first opened but returned to her magazine without so much as a how-do-you-do.

So, it was going to be like that. "Good evening."

Mr. Collier put down his magazine and waved Tobias inside. "Mr. Franklin. Now there's a man who will back me up. Sit." He pointed to the only vacant chair in the room. Far from Maribeth.

The room was well lit with multiple oil lamps, and it had a homey atmosphere about it. Tidy but lived in. Parents and chil-

dren all settled for an evening of reading and handiwork. Eloise
and Tobias often sat together in the evenings, but it was different
here. Louder. Maribeth's blatant avoidance to look at him was
sharper than Eloise's conversation could ever be.

Pardon my iniquity, for it is great. He mentally brushed aside
Zeke's annoying advice.

Tobias went to the empty chair by Mr. Collier. "How's the
mercantile this week?"

"Good, good." Mr. Collier rolled the cover of the magazine
and flashed Tobias the article. "What do you think of this telephone business in Boston? They're installing new lines every day."

"Exciting, isn't it? Someday we'll be able to pick up a receiver
and communicate with whomever we wish from our own office.
I had a man who was late today, due to trouble at home. Would
have been nice to get a message about it."

Maribeth made a rude noise from across the room. Tobias
looked at her, but Mr. Collier wasn't finished.

"Rubbish." He laid the magazine on the side table and leaned
forward. "A lot of money and resources being thrown into this
new device. What would you say on this telephone that you can't
send in a telegram or a letter? Too much money flowing into it,
if you ask me."

"And the operator?" Brent joined the discussion from where
he sprawled on the rug with his schoolbooks. "Ever think they
might be listenin'? Same with the telegraph operators, I s'pose.
But what's there to say anyhow? People talk too much."

"True." Tobias didn't feel like arguing about electronics.
"Maybe it'll never take off."

Collier went back to reading, and Tobias watched Maribeth, plotting how to best start his groveling. First, she had to look at him.

She didn't, but Felicity did. When Tobias smiled at her, she giggled. Maribeth narrowed her eyes at her little sister and turned her focus to Tobias. He took his chance and mouthed, "Can we talk?" He jerked his head toward the door.

She blinked once as if he weren't sitting across the room from her and went back to *McCall's.* There was probably an article she needed to finish with line-by-line instructions on how to handle a truant lover. Fine. Two could play this silly game.

"Felicity, show me what you're working on. It looks intricate." Tobias leaned forward and motioned her over with one flick of his finger.

That's the only invitation she needed.

"Oh, thank you." In a moment, she bounced from the sofa and stood by his side. "I'm making it for Grandma, and you mustn't tell."

"Grandma Joan?"

"The other one back east. She says she doesn't believe in winter—"

"Everyone believes in winter," Brent said, nose still buried in his book on the rug.

Felicity shrugged and leaned close to Tobias. "Grandma Dora doesn't believe in winter."

"She does so! She doesn't believe in *dying* in the winter. There's a difference." Brent threw his pencil at her, and Tobias jerked his hand forward and caught it before it hit Felicity in the face.

"Brent." Mrs. Collier murmured from the sofa without looking up from her sewing.

"Where's Grandma Dora live?" Tobias guided away from winter to diffuse any more flying objects.

"Missouri someplace." Felicity turned her back to Brent and shoved her needlework under Tobias's nose.

He made all the appropriate *oohs* and *ahhs,* and soon she leaned against his knee, enthusiastically explaining the details of the project. A quote would go in the middle with a border of vines and berries. The animated conversation with the ten-year-old was almost big enough to block the non-glares from Maribeth. With a few pointed questions, he had Felicity expounding on the happenings at school, and they both laughed over the trouble with the boys when a frog climbed from Samuel's pocket during the First Class recitations.

Tobias easily kept her talking until the clock crept along to nine o'clock. To the second, Mrs. Collier put down her own sewing.

"Bedtime, children." She stacked Brent's books and straightened the room while the younger two went down the hall. Soon, Maribeth was the only one left in the sitting room with Tobias.

He moved to sit on the sofa nearer her chair. "I'm sorry." He kept his tone near a whisper. "I'd like to talk about it, please."

She turned the page in her magazine.

"Unless you'd rather keep ignoring me."

The magazine fell to her lap, and she buried her face in her hands, shoulders shaking.

He clenched his stomach. "Are you . . . crying?" He hadn't had much practice with groveling.

She lifted her face, and though it wasn't exactly tear-streaked, it wasn't the happiest he'd ever seen. "You should go."

"I'm sorry. I had Luke with me at work, and he was, and they—" *Pardon my iniquity, for it is great.* "No, I don't want to make excuses. How can I make this right?"

"I don't wish to speak of it any more tonight."

"Tomorrow?"

"I'm not of a mind to make future plans with you."

"What's that supposed to mean?" What kind of future plans was she concerned with? He certainly didn't have any future plans. Dadgum.

"It means I want you to get out of my house because I'm upset with you, and I don't want to talk about it." She fidgeted with the cuff of her sleeve.

"Because I forgot to come sit with you after work?" It wasn't like he'd been twiddling his thumbs all evening.

"No."

McCall's wasn't going to be any good for reading the way she intermittently crushed and smoothed the pages throughout their conversation.

He reached to pull the magazine from her lap. "Maribeth, help a fellow out."

"I told you. I don't want to talk about it tonight."

"Then when?" They both worked at least a half-day on Saturday. Sunday would be okay for a drive. He could take her out then. She probably expected him to.

Her hand tightened on the page and tugged against his pull until he released it. "When you're ready to figure out what you want from me."

"What I want from—" Tobias slumped into the back of the sofa. "You're not making any sense, Maribeth. Is this still about Zeke and that night? You know he didn't mean it. We've been over this. It was all a misunderstanding. I know he gave you a fright, but I'm fine—he's fine. Things are great between him and Eloise. He's now one of Luke's favorite people."

"Oh, Tobias." Here she wept in earnest.

Tobias managed to coax her out of her rocking chair and moved her next to him on the sofa. Now, at least, she snuggled into his side while she cried. It was better she wet his shirt than sit two feet away while he awkwardly watched her. He dug a hand-kerchief out of his pocket, gave it to her, and wrapped his arm around her while he waited. After a time of trailing his fingers across her shoulder, her sniffling stopped.

"Is there something bigger going on that I don't know about? I tell you what, Maribeth—I've put out a dozen fires today. The crew keeps me spinning. Eloise is doing better, but you know I still worry about her. I can handle a lot of things, but I can't read your mind." He chuckled. "I found Luke climbing into the cup-boards yesterday."

Wrong thing to say. A new wave of convulsions preceded more tears and more sniffling. Maybe it was better he didn't open his mouth.

The clock across the room ticked slowly around, and it did little to help the cramp forming in his shoulder. When she lifted her wet face, he kissed her forehead. She didn't pull away, so he pressed his lips to her temple.

She stared at him when he pulled back, serene and unblink-ing, her eyelashes glistening with tears. "Why do you kiss me?"

"Because I, um . . . kissing is . . ." What kind of trick question was this? He dipped his eyebrows. "Should I not?"

Maribeth extracted herself from his arms and paced the rug. "Tobias, when is my birthday?"

He beat his thumb on his thigh. Cleared his throat.

"You don't know, do you?"

He shook his head.

"Do you know my favorite food?"

He smiled, relieved he wasn't failing the whole test. "Chicken-fried steak."

"No." She knelt in front of him and placed her hands on his knee. "That's *your* favorite."

"You order it every time I take you to the diner."

"It's faster to get two of the same meals rather than two different orders."

"Why would you do a fool thing like that?"

"Because I know how limited your time is, and if it's not Eloise, it's Luke. If it's neither of them, it's something at work or church or Zeke or you just plain forget."

The door to the washroom opened down the hall, and Mr. Collier crossed to his bedroom. A moment later, he padded his stockinged feet into the main room. "Have you seen my—ope, there they are." A pair of spectacles hid underneath his magazine by the lamp. He dipped his head to the couple and padded back to his room.

"Come for a walk with me."

Maribeth took a shuddering breath and stood, pulling her hands from his. "We moved into town only weeks after your wife died. How long ago now? Over a year?"

Tobias blinked and quickly did the math from Katie's April funeral. "Fourteen months."

"There. Over a year. I met you as a widower. A bereaved man with an expanding company to manage, a baby to care for, and a sister who never left the protection of your home. I marveled at your strength, Tobias. How a man could shoulder all of this and still be—still be everything that you are. But we've been courting for five months, and your son doesn't even know my name." Her lip trembled. "I've never been invited into your home, though it appears Mr. James all but sleeps there. And—and I don't think we're progressing."

"What's that supposed to mean?"

"For one, it means you don't have the right to kiss me when you have no intention of marrying me. I'll not be a placeholder anymore."

He wanted to cover her mouth with his right now just to keep her from talking. Things were great as they were. "Do you want to get married?" His mouth was dry as a desert, and his skin prickled with goosebumps. Was there a draft from the window? If he was so cold, why were his hands clammy and drops of sweat beading on his forehead? Finding himself short of breath, he stood and paced away from her.

"Tobias." His name came from her with a sob. She stood at the edge of the room, looking as small as a little mouse. A hand-kerchief materialized from her sleeve, and she wiped her nose. "I told you I didn't want to talk about it tonight."

Tobias faced her, standing tall. Drawing in a breath, he prepared to say the words. Only they wouldn't come out. *Maribeth, will you marry me?* Wasn't that the goal of this courting business?

To get to know someone better before marriage? Five months was plenty of time to know someone. Tobias blew out his breath like extinguishing a flame. *Pardon my iniquity, for it is great.*

He collapsed in her father's upholstered chair. "I've been a cad."

She neither affirmed nor argued.

"I really do like you, Maribeth." A small string of the upholstery from the worn chair came loose, and he rolled it between his thumb and forefinger.

"I like you too. But liking each other isn't . . ." She delicately blew her nose. "Judd asked if I would go riding with him next week." Her voice was almost too low to hear. "I said I would like it very much."

Tobias swallowed. And he swallowed again. "What kind of name is Judd?"

"Please, don't make light of him. It's a perfectly fine name." She folded and refolded the handkerchief. After a time, she cleared her throat with a dainty sort of cough. "I think it's his mother's maiden name."

He was almost grateful this conversation hadn't occurred on the public bench outside the mercantile. "So, that's it then?"

"I'm sorry to hurt you, Tobias."

"No." He waved a dismissive hand. "You've been nothing but sweet since we met. Any man would be lucky to have you."

Tears dripped from her eyes when she ducked her head. It was time for him to go. He stood and pulled her into his arms for a last embrace and kissed the top of her head from habit. "Give my regards to Judd. I'm sorry I've been a fool."

He quietly pulled the door shut and stood on the balcony with his hand on the doorknob. When she turned the lock from the inside, he made his way down the stairs. His walk home was a solemn affair.

He'd failed. Hands deep in his pockets, he nudged a rock loose from the crack in the boardwalk and kicked it in front of him. It popped up and bounced against the side of the building. By the time he made it to his street, he was ready to escape indoors, where at least the mosquitoes wouldn't plague him.

He'd failed at work, he'd failed with Luke, he'd lost his temper with Eloise, and now he'd lost Maribeth.

Failure welcomed him when he opened his front door.

Tobias tripped his gaze over the front room of his house. It was exactly as he'd left it. A mess. Luke's blocks stretched across the floor, and his crumbs from dinner trailed in from the kitchen.

Eloise had left a lamp burning low for him on the end table by the sofa. He walked through the mess, turned the flame higher, and surveyed his home.

Each item out of place waved to another one of his failures.

Katie would be appalled at his current habits. Her Swedish heritage influenced her housekeeping standards, and the house never fell into this state when she was alive. When she lived here, the windows sparkled, the floor was scrubbed daily, and even the exterior of the house showed a clean face.

Tobias wasn't a complete slob. Most of the time. Katie simply kept the house at a level of cleanliness he and Eloise had never mastered. Something about being a Swede demanded nothing less.

Well, Luke was only half-Swede, and Tobias's ancestors got off the boat so long ago that he didn't claim to be anything but

American. He wouldn't go to war against the dust on the windowsill tonight.

He lay on his back, arms splayed out to the sides, and discovered the rug wasn't as soft as it looked. He was exhausted. But not the kind that sleep would do anything about. He'd been trying to hold everyone afloat, and he was sinking.

The time he'd been given with Katie was a blip of peace through the past five years since his parents' deaths and inheriting the company. Having someone to share the bed with each night made the days easier. A companion.

He missed the friendship.

He wasn't even sad about losing Maribeth. That piled on even more guilt. How long had he been stringing her along? Had he truly been using her? Nothing but a warm body to hold and kiss? A placeholder, as she'd claimed? He covered his face with his hands and lay on the floor like a clod of dirt scraped from his boot. The longer he thought on it, the sicker he felt.

There was nothing wrong with Maribeth. She didn't fret, didn't nag. She didn't hound about anything. She was sweet and always had a kind word for him. Her concern was for the welfare of others, and she was certainly easy on the eyes.

So why did he let her go? Why couldn't he find the spark to make it work? Why didn't he take the next step? Why did the words clog his throat?

He should have let her go the moment he realized he wasn't going to marry her . . . except he hadn't thought two whits about it.

He'd gone on with life. Home, family, work, and kissing Maribeth.

Tobias tossed a handful of blocks into the tin can from where he lay. The least he could do was put his house in order. After half an hour of tidying, he picked up *Frankenstein* with its busted cover. Another failure.

He tucked it under his arm and blew out the lamp, curious to read the cause of such a ruckus.

It was well past midnight before he set the book aside and tried to sleep. He didn't feel any better about what he'd done with Maribeth, but he was thankful he hadn't released a murdering monster to ravage the prairie. That was something at least.

Chapter 6

Hannah stood across the hotel lobby from her mother, who pestered the poor clerk at the desk.

The evil queen strutted about the castle, lashing at all who dared to cross her path. Servants scurried in her presence. They each had one mission: obey the queen's orders in all haste and then keep far away. Falsely, they believed if they remained out of sight, they could avoid her wrath. Hah! She knew where to find them and would exercise her vengeful powers regardless.

"Hannah." Hiram put a hand on her shoulder and Hannah startled, returning to the present. Her twin was tall, thin boned, with short black hair. He was practically a male version of herself—in looks, if not temperament. "I'm glad you're here." He spoke the same words he'd given her last night.

Hannah smiled and threw her arms around him, trapping his arms at his sides. "You've mentioned it a time or two." Her grasp on him threw them off balance, and they stumbled like a drunken four-legged creature. They were both laughing before he wrestled his arms free and gained his footing.

It was enough to draw Mother's attention. *Drat.*

"Attention, soldier." Hannah dropped her arms and brushed her hands down her skirt. "The queen returns."

Hiram didn't seem afraid. The opposite, in fact. He relaxed his expression and tightened his arm that he'd wrapped around Hannah in the most nonchalant yet protective kind of way.

The queen advanced. "I see the west hasn't improved your manners. You're like little children, causing a scene everywhere you go."

The twins shared a flat look and bit back laughter. Amanda Benton caused more scenes than the two of them ever did. True, they were prone to rowdy behavior, but that was mostly Hannah's fault. Hiram knew better when he was on his own. He was so serene, possessing a clear head and determination that Hannah lacked. She was more inclined to fancies. Frivolities, her mother would say.

Hiram tugged her closer. "Mother, I trust you straightened everything?"

"Of course. He was willing to offer a complimentary breakfast. It's not much, but it's something. I've left him with a proper list for preparing rooms in the future. The buffoon would do well to take my advice. The amount of dust I found under the bed." She visibly shuddered.

"Under, but not . . . in?"

"Heavens, son. I, sleep in a soiled bed? Mercy, no. Underneath looked like it hadn't been swept in days. I could go on, but we have breakfast to attend. For all it may be as bad as the rooms, but we'll need the sustenance. Come, children."

Mother led the way, Hiram followed, and Hannah tripped along behind like an energetic puppy.

The eggs were too dry, the potatoes too soft, and the coffee too weak. For Amanda Benton. Hannah didn't taste a thing, for she was too busy holding back giggles. She was almost there. Almost free. She fairly squealed with excitement. Filling her belly was of minor importance, but she went through the motions.

Hiram interrupted their mother's list of complaints. "It really is a shame I couldn't show you the homestead. The little house isn't so bad. You're sure you won't be able to stay another week?"

Mother clicked her cup on the saucer. "Couldn't possibly. Don't make me say it again. I've heard too much about these frontier homesteads. Nothing but hovels. Sod shanties or claim shacks, outlaws running about and jumping claims at their convenience." She waved her hand as if pestered by a fly. "And my—" She sighed dramatically. "My very own two children, my only children choose this . . ." The coffee was no longer of interest. She traced the edge of her plate with one finger and swallowed.

Hannah shared a look with her brother and almost felt sad for their mother. Not very sad, but a bit. As one might feel sad for a possum left out in the rain.

"Your train doesn't leave for another forty-five minutes." Hiram took Mother's elbow and guided her away from the table. "Let's have a walk about town before you go. You can take in a few shops. You may find something that sparks your interest."

Hannah loitered outside Abigail's Dress Shop, waiting to signal Hiram when he arrived with the wagon. Blessedly, Mother deemed the fashions up to date with the same styles offered anywhere else back east. *Back east, back east, back east.* Hannah was tired of hearing it. She wanted to scream and stomp and lash at Mother. It wasn't like Hannah was leaving the country or wearing buckskin in the wilderness. She was a mere two-day trip from Des Moines.

Two days of the relative comfort of train travel could plop her back in the disgusting city with too many wagons and coaches rolling down the street, too many horses, and too many fancy men with fancy titles in fancy suits.

The village of Ockelbo wasn't a frontier town by any means. It supported a population close to one thousand and offered its resources and shops to all the farms spread throughout Polk County. Why, it boasted not one but two cigar shops. She didn't turn circles in the wildly free spin her feet yearned for. Only looked, taking it all in. *Don't give Mother any fodder. Don't give in to her qualms.*

Hannah's first morning in Ockelbo. She closed her eyes and breathed it in, soaking up the smells and sounds. The bakery two shops away sent a pleasant aroma her direction. Coffee, yeast, cinnamon, and another earthy spice she couldn't place.

She leaned against the hitching post. The creak and rattle of wagons, crows of roosters still asking their hens to wake up, and the bustle of people greeted the morning. Boots on the boardwalk. Children's running feet. Bells jingling as shop doors opened.

Nearby conversation floated her way.

A woman's voice. Soft and light, though urgent. "We don't need to speak of it anymore."

A man answered. "Really and truly, I need to tell you I'm sorry. I behaved badly."

"I have to go back to work. It's . . . it is well. Please, be at peace."

A cart rattled, and Hannah lost the rest of the conversation when Mother burst from the dress shop with a new hat box. Hannah abruptly turned her head aside just as a young woman came from the alley between the dress shop and the mercantile. Trailing behind her was the tall man from the depot yesterday, Mr. Franklin. The man who'd so confidently handled her corset and undergarments. The man with the wild toddler, and the one who hadn't caved under her mother's attacks. Hannah did hope he hadn't left her book to be trampled at the depot.

Mother noticed the couple and paused her march across the boardwalk. Hannah prayed she wouldn't speak.

"Ah, you two." Her mother gestured with the hat box as an executioner might show off his sharpened ax. "Was the child dealt with?"

Mr. Franklin stepped in front of the woman.

Commendable. He knew danger when he saw it, but Mother barreled closer.

"Where is the boy now? Left to his own devices again, I'd wager."

The man squared his shoulders and stood taller, blocking the woman behind him. He was a warrior preparing for battle. Hannah could almost see his shields being strapped into place.

Hannah's fingers curled into fists, and she willed him to stay strong.

He thrust his hand toward Mother, and the idiot man smiled. It didn't reach his eyes, so perhaps he wasn't a complete dolt. But still. Smiling? What battle tactics were these? His outstretched hand hung between them, palm slightly up. "We've not been properly introduced. I'm Tobias Franklin."

Mother didn't acknowledge his hand. Instead, she sniffed.

Mr. Franklin's smile deepened. He rallied his troops and commanded his elite forces into the fray. "Pleasure's all mine, I'm sure." He glanced sideways and raised his eyebrows when he noticed Hannah watching him. Nodding once, he plunged his hand into his pocket before redirecting his attention to Mother. "Are you staying in Ockelbo, then?"

Mother pursed her lips.

He motioned to the hat box. "We boast that Abigail runs the finest dress shop in the county. I'm glad you found something you liked."

Hannah sensed an ambush but couldn't determine from which angle. The woman behind him slipped into the mercantile, and Mr. Franklin visibly relaxed. He breathed easier, and his shoulders released some of their tightness. He still maintained a strong defense, but he directed his troops into the main offensive line of attack.

Hannah's mother finally opened her mouth. "I wish to speak to the child's mother alone."

"Not possible, ma'am." He lifted his cap and smoothed his hair under it before pulling it back into place.

"Quit being obstinate."

"Of course, ma'am." He smiled again.

"I can march in there myself and speak to her." Mother said as much, though she hadn't made one move toward the mercantile. She was clearly out of her element with this man.

"What questions would you like answered first? You asked if the child was dealt with." He raised an eyebrow. "Yes, I carried him home, saw to his dinner, let him play where he is safe and loved. He was still asleep when I left this morning, and my sister will care for him when he wakes. May I clarify your interest in my son?" Mr. Franklin rocked back on his heels. "Are you applying for a nanny position? I may have need of one soon. If you have viable references, I can take you into consideration." He clapped his hands together once and rubbed his palms. "Of course, I'd need assurance you'd handle Luke with temperance. A character reference or two to confirm you'd never strike a child in anger."

There it was. His elite team of soldiers burst from the trees and dropped around the enemy forces in great numbers.

Mother sputtered and yet didn't have the decency to retreat. "I asked to speak to the child's mother." She flicked her gaze to the mercantile as if she could route his entire army.

Mr. Franklin stepped into her line of sight. "If you're looking for Miss Collier, she is no relation to Luke and, as it happens, has no connection to me either. Not that it's any of your business."

His troops began a controlled retreat, but Hannah saw cracks forming. He was wearing thin. The muscles along Mr. Franklin's jaw clenched.

"It's my business because I make it my business. As one mother to another, I have the right to speak to her."

He shot an arm to the side and pointed. Tendons rippled in his neck, and his shirt pulled tightly along his arm. "Three blocks down and one over. You'll find Luke's mother in the cemetery six feet underground. Katherine L. Franklin. Loving wife, mother, and daughter. I'd love to hear what she has to say back to you. By all means, let me know how it goes." He nodded once. "Good day, ma'am."

Hiram arrived then with the wagon, and Mother wasted no time in climbing aboard, not even waiting for Hiram's help. But Hannah didn't remove her gaze from Mr. Franklin's back until he disappeared around the corner. Controlled strength. Determination. A man unafraid of speaking truth to the royal Amanda Benton.

Now, there was a man Hannah could set her cap for. And he came with a ready-made family. Mother would choke on her mid-morning tea when she heard the news of their engagement via telegram. Hannah wondered if she'd have time to settle it by Christmas.

Hiram placed his hand on the small of her back. "What are we looking at?"

"Freedom," she whispered.

He helped settle her on the bench with their mother between them, and the three sat in silence for the short drive to the depot. Mother ignored Hiram when he dismounted and reached for her hand. Instead, she turned to Hannah. "I've changed my mind. You're coming home with me."

"Mother, no." This couldn't be happening.

"I can't bear to leave you in a town full of uncouth men and all the dangers of the west."

"Hiram needs me, Mother." A weak excuse. "We haven't met anything dan—"

"Let him come home too. Without you here to enable him, he'd never stick it out, and we'd all be together again."

They'd never been together the way Mother implied. Father was always working, Mother at social engagements, Hannah in boarding school, and Hiram busy with his own school and medical training. There was nothing to return to now that she was of age.

"Mother, please."

"We came as arranged, but I've seen enough. I can't let you stay here alone." Mother looked her so squarely in the eyes that Hannah had to avert her own or be burned. Hiram stood by the wagon, mouth in a thin line.

It wouldn't do any good for Hannah to tell Mother she was an adult for Pete's sake and had been one for years. Her age didn't hold any bearing on Mother. Hannah had used up her entire storage of excuses to get as far as she'd come.

"She won't be alone," Hiram said. "Come off the wagon, Mother. We'll talk about it."

Hannah did not move, but Hiram managed to get Mother down on his side. Hannah couldn't speak. She could hardly swallow. *I knew this was too good to really be true.* Her eyes drifted up. The sky was a vivid blue and cotton clouds filled the horizon. The show-off kind. Too happy. Too free. Tauntingly beautiful. Yes, Hannah could simply refuse to get on the train . . . and then Mother would cause a scene and there was no guessing what would happen then. It wasn't worth the risk. Hannah's mind ran in circles, searching for a solution. It was like finding her way out of a labyrinth that rearranged itself every time she thought she'd figured it out.

Hiram talked softly to Mother, too low for Hannah to hear, but Mother started blubbering into her handkerchief.

If Hannah were married, Mother would have no more power over her. Mother wouldn't be able to demand a thing—and if she did, it would go through Hannah's husband first. If Hannah had a husband from the West . . . over a hundred miles from Mother's reign . . . Hannah merely needed a chance. A window. A few months to make it a reality. To ensure her freedom.

"Six months." Hannah interrupted whatever Hiram was whispering. "Mother, let me stay for six months."

Their mother whipped her head around and narrowed her eyes, all pretenses of crying evaporated.

"Six months." Hannah tugged her glove and dipped her eyes from Mother's penetrating glare.

Mother lifted her chin and brought it down oh-so-slowly. "Three." She drew out the word.

"Very well." Hannah schooled her features to hide any sign of her jubilance. Mother thought she'd won.

"And you'll write home twice a week."

"Yes, Mother."

"After which, I will send your father to personally bring you home where you belong."

"Yes, Mother."

June. July. August.

Would it be enough to secure a husband? It didn't leave time to dilly-dally.

Hiram cocked his head, no doubt confused why Hannah had given up so quickly. Hannah never gave up the high ground if there was any chance of keeping it. But three months was a start. It was the crumb she needed.

All she truly needed was to get Mother on that blasted train.

Hannah and Hiram could figure out what to do later. They always did somehow.

The train let loose a shrill whistle, and Hannah fought off the panic that tried to claw its way from her chest. Hiram steered Mother toward the platform while Hannah climbed off the wagon and hustled after them with Mother's satchel. In a matter of minutes, for what felt like the first time in her life, Hannah would direct her own steps.

Chapter 7

"Oh, do let me drive, Hiram." Hannah reached over and grabbed the reins from Hiram a mile out of Ockelbo.

Her brother laughed and handed them over. "Suit yourself."

The grass, the wind, the sky—clouds and all—danced with Hannah in her delight. "I can feel them!" The energy from the team of chestnut quarter horses came down the lines through Hannah's gloved fingers. "I think they're talking to me."

"I can hear them too. Sometimes." Hiram stretched his arms overhead before resting them on the backboard.

"What do they say?"

"The usual. Horse stuff. 'Hiya, Sal. Get enough to eat this morning? The master only brought me half a carrot.' Sal answers, 'Sure thing, Speck. I got the other half of your carrot, which you'd know if you weren't too busy eating to pay attention.'"

"Oh, no." Hannah nudged him with her elbow. "That's not it at all."

"Is too. They're my horses, and I oughta know."

"Sal and Speck is it?" Hannah flicked the reins once, trying to tease more speed out of them. "Come on, girls. I know you want to."

"Don't do that, Hannah." He knocked his fist on her knee. "You'd don't want to run them with your trunks in the back. You'll get'em all jostled up."

"But they want to! That's what they're saying. Sal is actually descended from the great Pegasus, and at night when you're sleeping, she uncurls her wings and takes flight. I can't believe you didn't know. She soars all over the country looking for treasure."

"What kind of treasure?"

"The kind that pirates bury. Chests of gold and pearls."

"No."

"Why ever not?'

"You've got it all wrong. How would Pegasus fly and see buried treasure?" His eyeroll came through in his tone. "Pirates, for one, never ever come through Nebraska, and if they did, sure wouldn't've carried chests of gold and pearls all the way with them." He laughed. "If you're going to tell stories, at least get it right."

"How's this for a story: once upon a time there was a prince and a princess. Twins. They lived happily together in the castle and played and frolicked—"

"I don't frolic."

She shushed him with a raised eyebrow. "Frolicked. Doing whatever caught their fancy until the prince grew up, and then they were separated by the evil queen, and the king sent him away on a special quest. While he got to go adventuring, the princess was sent to a terrible prison."

"I've heard this one before." Hiram flicked her earlobe. "And the handsome knight never came, and the princess was never rescued, blah blah, and boarding school was purgatory."

"Quiet." Her muscles strained against the leather pulling her hands. "So the prince was gallivanting and frolicking about as he pleased. Questing and such."

"And such as medical school. Both a quest and an adventure, but never frolicking."

"The princess remained locked in her tower—"

"The one full of other princesses?"

"Yes, Hiram! Boarding school was purgatory. Dreary. Boring. You can't imagine the drudgery of it. The dancing was swell, and music and art and history was okay if you could skip the lectures, but the professors and their rules. Did I mention the lectures? I don't know how I ever made it out alive."

"Hannah, you've been out of school for years, and yes, I can imagine the drudgery because you wrote me pages and pages of it with enough pictures that I can still see your professors in my sleep—even with your embellishments. Thanks to your letters, I probably learned more than you did. Get to the point."

She smiled, loving the easy conversation her brother afforded. Nobody put up with her the way he did.

"All right, school wasn't great, but it was better than home, and now Mother is the worst, and I can't go back to her ever. I need your help."

"Always." He pressed his shoulder against hers.

"If Mother forces my return to Des Moines in three months, you'll be a bachelor again."

"Still a bachelor, Hannah. Living with a sister doesn't make one not a bachelor."

"You'll be cooking your own blasted meals and washing your own smelly clothes again. So there. If Mother gets her way, I'll be a spinster, serving tea for committee meetings to organize political fluff nobody gives a rat's knee about for the rest of my life."

"You could do worse."

"Hiram, listen to me. I need your help."

His hands covered her hands on the reins, slowing the team she'd unconsciously encouraged, until she let go and slipped her arm through his elbow. "We worked on the parents for months to convince them to let you keep house for me once I moved away." He took a deep breath. "I will not allow you to go back to Mother. Her temper has grown worse over the years. Now that you're here, we'll keep you here. Three-month agreement or not, you won't be going back to her alone."

Hannah raised her free hand to her cheek, still tender from yesterday's slap. "You promise?"

Hiram's chest rumbled, and she felt it through her arm. It was a rather scary sound. "I am through tiptoeing around that woman," he said through his teeth.

"How far does 'honor your father and mother' reach?"

"I don't think we ever outgrow that one, but 'Children, obey your parents' is one we could wrestle with. *Honor* doesn't mean you have to curl up and die." He thumbed his wide-brimmed hat farther up his forehead and looked at her. "You can learn to be respectful—*kind*—without tucking tail and bowing to her every whim."

Hannah pulled closer to her twin. Her first friend, companion, confidant. His bicep tensed when he pulled on the line, angling the team around a knoll. "Pray with me?"

He cleared his throat. "You start."

She tightened her grip on his arm. "Father, the rocks would cry out if we ever stopped praising you." The breeze swept across the prairie and bent the grass under its weight. "You, the creator of the skies and the prairie, shepherd your people with gentleness. I boldly come to you with a plea for freedom. For a clean break from Mother and Father. For this reason, a man and woman will leave their parents and cleave to another. I'm asking to be Tobias Franklin's wife before three months have passed."

Hiram choked. Once recovered, he shouted at the team. "Whoa!" He pulled on the reins and set the brake, lips drawn in a tight line. Looking at her with eyes wider than silver coins, he opened his mouth and shut it, head shaking. "Hannah." He rubbed his chin. "God isn't your personal fairy godmother. That's—that's not how this works. You can't simply demand what you want and wait for it to manifest. 'Dear God, please make it rain. Today. At 10 o'clock. That'd be great. Thanks. Amen.'"

She grinned. "Why not? 'Ye have not, because ye ask not.'"

"No, ma'am. You put that verse back where you got it."

Hannah blinked and offered her sweetest smile.

Hiram worked his mouth some more. "Tobias Franklin? That's so . . . specific. Do you know him? How do you even know the name?" His voice trailed off as he muttered. "You've not been in town half a day." He released the brake and slapped the reins.

The team kicked up their hooves in a mesmerizing rhythm. Tails swishing and ears attentive.

Hannah rethreaded her hand into his elbow. "Are you mad?"

He bit the tip of his tongue and rocked his head slowly to one side, thinking. "You're being silly, and you shouldn't play games with God. I enjoy your stories and drawings. I think you've got real talent." He briefly glanced at her. "Your imagination is something wonderful, but marriage isn't a game. To pick a random man and demand God set it up for you is presumptuous."

"Do you know Mr. Franklin?"

"I do."

"Dreamy, isn't he?"

"He's got a girl, I think."

"Nothing I can't handle."

"Hannah." He shrugged out of her arm and scowled at her.

She laughed. "Sorry, you're right. That was rude of me. But I don't see any harm in asking. God can set it up any way he pleases. Do you need it to rain? I'll tack that on for you." Hannah clasped her hands to her breast and looked up at the deep blue sky, dotted with quick-moving clouds. "God? Thank you for hearing my earlier petition about Tobias Franklin. I'm adding a caveat, please."

Hiram grunted, and she elbowed him.

"If Tobias is a good man, and if I wouldn't be ruining another gal's dream, I'd like to be married to him. Soon. And while you're at it, if you could bring the rain for Hiram. We'd like to eat this winter and not starve. Thank you. Amen."

Her brother tightened his lips and shook his head. "Feels wrong."

"Shall I say it all again more professionally? I could write it in a composition. In academic prose."

"Just stop."

"Mrs. Hannah Claire Franklin . . . rolls off the tongue nicely."

"That's enough, Hannah."

"Don't you think I'd make a fine wife for him?"

"You don't even know him!"

She clapped and bounced her feet on the floorboard with the vision of walking down the aisle to meet Mr. Franklin at the end already forming. "Oh! Tell me everything you know, and I'll add together what I know and what you know, and we'll see how he fares."

Hiram muttered something incoherent, and Hannah dug her shoulder into his. He was a solid boulder, which became a rolling boulder when he shoved back. She squealed and grabbed the bench.

With one finger she poked him in the soft spot between two ribs.

"Hey!" He arched his back. After transferring the lines to one hand, he pulled on the trailing ribbon from the bow of her straw bonnet. The wind played favorites and snatched the hat from her head and tossed it to the grass.

"Blimey!" Both hands went to her hair, already being abused by the wind. "Man overboard. Avast!"

"Still doing the pirate thing, are we?" He pulled the reins. "Whoa."

"Listen to this new one I've learned: 'Scupper that!'" Hannah snatched Hiram's hat and flung it to the grass on the other side.

He squinted in the mid-morning light and deliberately set the brake, never taking his eyes from hers. "Scupper . . . that?" While climbing over the wheel, he repeated the phrase to himself a few times. "Scupper that." He waded through the grass and called to her on the buckboard. "Is it specific to hats?"

"Nay. It's meant to be said in anger whilst commanding items to be thrown overboard. Which I have done."

Hiram swiped his hat from the ground. "Aren't you going to fetch yours?"

"The rapscallion that sent it flying may fetch it," she said with her nose in the air.

"Rapscallion?" He marched behind the wagon.

"It means a scoundrel or a mischievous—oh!"

Hiram grabbed her arm and yanked her over the side. "I know what it means, wench." She squealed with laughter and tried to fight him off, but she fell into him, and he deposited her in a heap of skirts on the grass.

He stepped over her and climbed into his seat.

Hannah strode behind the wagon where her bonnet lay partly buried in the waist-high green grass. A cold wind blew across the prairie, pushing her forward and rolling her bonnet farther away. The breeze was in full contrast with the sun heating her face. The mixture of the cool wind and the heat of the sun was heavenly.

Ten feet ahead, a cluster of fiery orange blossoms caught her attention. Hannah skipped over to pick them, and a dozen white butterflies took flight and spun around her. "Beautiful," she whispered in delight. Turning with arms wide, she danced with them around and around. One landed on her sleeve and slowly fanned its wings, as if undecided about where to go. It made its mind, however, and went in search of friends. Hannah chased it through the grass and discovered more of the orange blossoms. In no time she'd picked a bouquet of them.

"Giddy-up." Hiram called to the team and the wagon lurched forward. Without her.

Hannah sprinted back to her bonnet. Flowers in one hand and bonnet in the other, she hustled to catch up, but Hiram only increased his speed.

"You scalawag!" She ran behind the wagon, but with her pinched boots and heavy skirts, the gap continued to widen. "Bilge rat!"

His laughter reached her, but he didn't stop.

Hannah planted her feet and held the flowers aloft like a sword. "Thou mewling clay-brained barnacle!"

The wagon slowed while Hiram turned to face her. Then he stood, placing one boot on the bench, and looked every bit the Shakespearean ruffian. One hand on the reins, the other cupped around his mouth, he shouted, "Keep up, thou beslubbering idle-headed lewdster!"

Hannah's cheeks already ached from so much smiling this morning and now tears threatened to spill over with joy. "Hiram, thou tottering toad-speckled measle, I suspect I've never felt happiness my whole life until this moment." She ran to him.

"Get in the wagon, thou paunchy milk-livered harlot." After setting the brake yet again, he leaned down for her hand, but she passed him the bouquet first. "Oh, hooray . . . You found weeds."

"Flowers."

"Weeds."

Now that both hands were free, she replaced her bonnet and tucked her dark hair up under the brim. "Wildflowers?"

He smirked, still holding her bouquet. "Precisely. Weeds."

"They're not weeds simply because they bloom wherever they want and cannot be contained in man's cultivated world."

He stuck his tongue to the side and raised his eyebrows in a silly I-win-and-can-we-please-go-home-now face. "Get in the wagon. I'm leaving." His hand closed around her wrist, and he hauled her into the seat beside him.

Even as he flicked the reins, she wrapped her arms around him.

"It's good to have you here but get off me so we can go home." He patted her arm with a free hand. "Only a quarter mile at best."

"Is that all? Why didn't you say so? I could have found my way."

"Leap out again, but I'm not stopping. Speck already doubts my authority."

"Not Sal?"

"Sal's not much of a freethinker. She follows Speck and doesn't mind much of anything as long as she's fed and curried."

A rumble of thunder rolled across the sky. Not especially close, but deep and drawn out, the type that made Hannah wonder if it wasn't thunder but in fact a growling beast from the deep. The wind pulled her bonnet, but she pressed the top down and clung to Hiram's elbow. "Hiram? Only a quarter mile, you said?"

He looked at the sky with her, watching a dark column of clouds roll from the north. "We'll make it. It doesn't look too foreboding. Only a good spring rain, maybe some wind." Nevertheless, he pushed Sal and Speck faster than he had previously.

The wind grew stronger, gusting in waves. Hannah marveled at the prairie rippling under its pulse. Grass and flowers danced to a wild tune across the landscape.

A single drop darkened the lap of her green travel suit. A heartbeat later it was joined by three more. "Hiram?"

"Looks like we're going to get wet." He grinned and tugged his hat lower. "Welcome to the country, my lady."

She dug in her pocket for her gold-enameled pocket watch. Popping open the cover, she gasped at the time. "Hiram, look." She shoved it in front of his face.

He jerked his head back and swatted her. "Stop that. What?"

"Look at the time."

He held her arm steady a moment. "Ten o'clock on the dot. So?"

"So? It's raining!" She giggled. "At ten o'clock, just as requested." Hannah clenched her fists level with her shoulders and squealed. Tilting her head to the sky, she closed her eyes and let the rain wash over her. It came down much heavier now than even moments before. They would both be wilted kittens after a bath before they reached the farm.

"Therefore, Hiram—thou villainous fly-bitten miscreant—I'll take it for the sign that you're seated next to the future Mrs. Hannah Claire Franklin. You're at leave to begin practicing."

The rain fell in sheets the next few minutes, and Hiram was clearly too busy with the team to acknowledge her claim on the future.

By the time he'd pulled into the yard in front of the house, the storm had worn itself out.

"Hiram, it's a dream!" The house, the barn, corrals, and fields lay before her. "It's everything I imagined it would be. Only, wetter." She reached for him, but he swung his leg over to the wagon bed to untie her trunks. "Can you show me the lambs straightaway? Please, please, oh, please. I've never held a lamb ever in my whole entire life, and I might burst if I wait another minute."

Hiram ignored her while he pulled and shoved her luggage to the end of the wagon. "You going to help with any of these? Let's get them inside before they soak through."

"And then we can see the lambs?"

"Whatever the princess wants. The day is yours." He hopped down. "I'll also show you how to feed the chickens, weed the garden, and where to find the coffee grinder." The heavy trunk with her books came first. "Come on, Hannah."

But Hannah stood still in the wagon, gazing at her new home with tears streaming down her cheeks unchecked, mixing with the rainwater. *Thank you, God. Thank you, thank you. Thank you for bringing me home safely. I was so afraid it would never happen. But you did it. I'm here.*

The house was a simple one-and-a-half story boxy white square with peeling paint and a south-facing porch, sporting three little steps up. The barn stood nearby with the driveway going between the two. Corrals and fenced pastures lay in one direction for the sheep. A chicken run, large garden, milk cow, and a sow rounded out the homestead. Hiram's main income rested on the sheep's wool. But the lambs were all that interested Hannah at present.

A small corral with a shelter nearest the barn held a handful of ewes and their young. She pointed toward them. "Are those the babies?"

"The last of them. The others have rejoined the flock."

"The rain is over." She wiped her face with her sleeve. "Leave the trunks. Lambs first, brother dearest, and then chickens, weeds, and coffee." She clambered down the wagon and splashed through the puddles, heels sinking into mud.

She was home.

Chapter 8

"Dada! Dada!" Luke hollered from his crib across the hall on Sunday morning.

Tobias yelled back. "Luke! Luuuke!" He tossed the quilt aside and scrubbed his face with both hands.

"Daaada!"

"Tobias!" Eloise yelled from her room. "Tobias? Can you get the baby?"

"I'm coming." He flopped one foot to the floor.

The bars of the crib rattled as Luke shook them. "Daaada!"

"Tobias?" Eloise's voice turned sharp. "Are you up?"

"I'm up!" The other foot thumped on the wood floor, and he slid off the bed.

"Okay, because it sounds like Luke is up, and you're not."

"Mind your own business. I'm up." Tobias eased to his feet, each muscle in his thighs and back complaining. Helping the crew load yesterday's shipment was fun, but his body wasn't regularly put through an hour of squats. He'd been on the ground team—bend, grab, stand and toss to the man on the cart. One brick at a time in a smooth rhythm. The swinging motion was repetitive, and watching the brick soar through the air to be caught by the man above was enthralling. But unless it was done every day, the body was gonna fuss like—

"Daaadaaa!"

Like a toddler trapped in a crib in the morning.

Tobias eased a pair of trousers over his flannel drawers and stumbled bare chested to the boy's room.

Luke's blond hair stuck out in all directions. With hands clutching the side of the crib, he squealed when he saw Tobias. Even in the dim morning light, the toddler's blue eyes sparkled.

"Hey, son. Do you have any idea what time it is?"

The boy smiled. It was impossible to stay irritated with that chubby face.

"Morning time," Luke said. "Eat food?"

"Eventually. Can we wake up first?" He pulled Luke close for a squeeze and planted a kiss on his head. "It's barely five o'clock, son."

"Morning time!"

Tobias winced as he lowered himself to the floor and pulled the chamber pot from under the bed. "That's what I'm telling you, buddy. It's not hardly morning. Just because the sun shines earlier in June doesn't mean you need to. You sleep until seven any day of the week, but today on the Lord's Day, you insist on waking with the sun?" He helped Luke remove his diaper. "Good job, buddy. Still dry. Here, have a seat." A large yawn stretched over Tobias's face, and he rested his head against the side of the crib.

Luke finished his business and ran out of the bedroom. Naked. Doors opened and slammed.

Tobias chuckled, waiting for his sister to holler at him again.

There it was. Another squeal from the boy, another call from Eloise.

Tobias still sat on the floor with his head against the crib when Eloise, in a blue wrapper, marched the naked boy back into his room. She glared at Tobias. "What are you doing sitting there? Get up."

"Can't." He flopped his arms once like a stringed puppet.

"Dada! Eat food?" Luke patted either side of Tobias's cheeks.

"Yep, we'll eat."

"Keep him here." Eloise pointed, and Tobias smiled at her tone. "Get him dressed. I'm busy."

Tobias lifted an arm. "El! Come baaack."

She spun and looked at him with raised eyebrows. "What?"

"What are you doing up and dressed already? Am I missing something? Why are you snippy?"

Eloise stared at Tobias while a red blush creeped up her neck and cheeks until it spread from ear to ear.

Tobias coughed to hide his laugh. "Please don't tell me the whole house is awake because of Zeke." He liked Zeke. He did. Liked him quite a bit, actually. Despite their misunderstanding weeks ago when Tobias ended up with a black eye, and Zeke in jail. Since then, Zeke hung around the house almost every day. In all likelihood, before the summer was over, they would be brothers.

Until then, Tobias must endure his sister acting like a silly girl. He smoothed his expression. "He'll be here for breakfast?"

She nodded.

"Is he at least making the breakfast?"

She nodded.

"Good." He clapped his hands together once. "There's that then. What's on the menu? Cinnamon rolls? Tea rings? Cheese Danish?"

"I think he's going to try Swedish pancakes since he can make them here. He heard your complaints the last time I burned the whole batch." She fiddled with the tie around her waist. "I told him it's my ornery stove, but he's not convinced."

"Hallelujah." The crib dug into his back, and he leaned forward. "Go on with you. Braid your hair, rouge your cheeks, or whatever you're about."

"Jessica lent me her curling iron. Haven't had a time to try it until this morning."

"El, it's fine." Tobias smiled at Luke attempting to tug his blanket between the slats of the crib.

"Sorry he's awake. He must have heard me moving around."

"He's picked up extra skills he didn't learn from me. I didn't hear anything until the both of you were caterwauling at me."

She smiled. "It was some time after that started before you answered." Eloise lingered in the doorway, her face softening as Luke continued to struggle with his blanket. "Feels like I haven't seen you in days. Everything all right at work?"

Tobias shrugged.

"Anything I can do to help?"

"Let a man sleep in on a Sunday." He winked to take the edge off the complaint.

Luke exhausted his efforts to extract the blanket. He sat on the floor, hugged a corner of the soft cotton, and put a thumb in his mouth.

Tobias pulled on Luke's big toe until he looked up and giggled around his thumb. "El, have you ever heard of *Frankenstein*?"

Eloise tipped her head. "Is that the book about the monster?"

"It is, but it's not what you think. Well, it wasn't what I thought." He heaved himself off the floor. "Come—I'll show you."

She followed him to his room. "Your son is still naked."

"Yep." Tobias picked up the book from his washstand and turned to hand it to Eloise, but she balked at the door with a crinkled nose.

"You could at least make an effort." She toed a pair of trousers that had missed the hook where he'd tossed them last night.

"Why? Might offend the wife I don't have?"

"You have a sister it offends and a son watching and learning. Maribeth would be shocked to see this other side of you."

Tobias tossed his pillow to the head of the bed and jerked the gray and white quilt until it was smooth—sort of. "Maribeth will never be in this room, so you needn't worry yourself." Why had he waited to tell Eloise? Now it festered like an ill-timed confession. "I didn't say the other day, but you'll find out soon enough." He grimaced at Eloise who stood in the doorway. *Just say it.* "Maribeth and I aren't . . . anymore."

"Aren't?" Her eyebrows soared. "Aren't what?"

"Aren't anything. We're not." He sat on the edge of his bed.

"What did you do?" Apparently her compassionate personality overwhelmed her desire to stay outside making a statement about the room. She wrapped her arm around his shoulder, no longer nagging. An improvement in one area. "Oh, Tobias. I'm so sorry. Can I help? What are you going to do to fix it?"

He chuckled. "No, sis. We don't want to fix it. I should have ended things from the beginning when I realized I wasn't ever going to—wasn't ready to—oh, you know. It's obvious to me now that I didn't love her like that, but I was so busy enjoying the, well, anyhow." He stood to get away from her hand that stifled him like a restraint across his back. "It's clear enough I'm not ever getting married again, so why pretend?"

"Says who?"

"I do!" He waved a hand to highlight the mess of his room. "Who wants to put up with this? The real Tobias Franklin."

"The real Tobias Franklin might be a slob, but he's a sweetheart." She chose a shirt from the floor and tossed it to him. "He loves his son and is a doting father. He works hard. He manages his employees fairly, and he's an outstanding brother. Just last week you helped hang the sheets on the line!"

"Put that on my obituary when you send it to the *Omaha Bee,* will ya? Look here." He tucked the shirt under his arm and knocked his knuckle on the hardback cover. "*Frankenstein.*" Tobias shoved the book at Eloise and shuffled to the bureau. "Dr. Victor Frankenstein is a scientist of sorts who somehow brings life back into a human. Well, a dead human."

"Ew. Why?"

"He took the best parts of different dead bodies and sewed them together to create a more elite human, or, I'm not sure." The shirt going over his head muffled his words. "There wasn't much detail on that part, and I haven't finished it yet." He grabbed a pair of mostly clean trousers and pushed them into the bottom drawer. Two pairs of dirty socks landed in the empty basket in the corner.

"That's appalling, and how is this 'not as bad' as I thought? It's every bit as bad. Worse, maybe. How does Victor get the bodies?"

Tobias sniffed an undershirt, and it joined the socks in the basket. "It's not important. But the story doesn't make sense. He spends all this time making the monster. Years. Then doesn't do anything with it? With him. With it? Him, I guess." Tobias cocked his head, thinking. The monster wasn't precisely human but was made from dead men. That would be a him. He nodded.

Eloise hadn't changed her expression from her initial shock of disgust.

"Regardless." He finger-combed his hair. "Dr. Frankenstein stays in bed, sick and afraid of the thing he made, gets better, and goes home to attend the funeral of his kid brother who'd been murdered." He leaned toward Eloise while buttoning his shirt. "Guess who murdered the kid?"

She leaned away from him. "I don't want to know."

"His monster. Though a friend of the family is accused and hung for it instead, and Dr. Frankenstein says nothing." Tobias swiped his hand in the air, chopping an invisible opponent.

"Heavens." Eloise shivered and touched her fingers to her lips.

"Victor is the most pathetic man I've ever read about." Tobias scooped a pile of coins from the top of his bureau and dropped them into a small tin cup.

"Why are we still talking about this? Hey, who's Hannah Claire Benton?"

"It's her book." One of his drawers was stuck open a couple of inches, and he worked at jamming it back on its track. "Dr. Scientist doesn't say, 'Oh, no! It's my fault! I created a disgusting monster,' because he thinks nobody will believe him. But I say he's wrong. I don't even want to finish it because I'm so mad. What a lousy excuse of a man."

Eloise kicked her bare foot against his calf. When he looked at her, she held the cover open. "I know it's her book." She tapped on the inscription and rolled her eyes. "But who is she, and why do you have it?"

He shrugged. "She was at the depot at the same time I was scheduling to have the coal delivered for the brickyard. Her trunk upended when Luke ran into the porters."

Eloise sat up straighter. "You didn't tell me any of this."

"I don't have to tell you everything."

"You met this Hannah the same day you ended things with Maribeth?" Eloise gasped and hugged the book to her chest.

"I didn't end things with Maribeth. She—" He growled and forced the drawer until it broke loose and slammed shut. "Things ended."

"And now you have Hannah's book." Her eyes grew wide. "When you return the book, you will both fall madly in love and live happily ever after." By the time she finished, her voice was pitched an octave higher.

He snatched the book from her death grip and popped her on the top of the head with it. "Stop that nonsense."

"No, Tobias. This is perfect. Just you wait, and I'll set it right up for you."

"No, you won't." He used *Frankenstein* as a scepter and pointed it at her nose. "You'll leave it alone. What do I need to get married for anyway?" He tossed the book on the bed. "I've got you and Luke."

"If Zeke proposes, I'm saying yes and then what?"

Tobias snorted. "You mean, 'when'?" He crossed his arms and leaned against the wall. "Obviously. And then he can live here, and we'll all be one happy family." Tobias showed his teeth. *With free, freshly baked bread for life as a bonus.*

Eloise was clearly biting her cheeks to keep from smiling, but it wasn't working. Her eyes smiled all on their own. Finally, she burst into a giggle, feet dancing on the hardwood floor. "You think he'll propose?"

"I didn't say nothin'."

"He asked you about asking me?"

Tobias mimed locking his lips and threw the key over his shoulder. He caught Eloise just in time when she launched herself into his arms, squealing into his ear. Good grief, apparently he'd brought Christmas early. *Sorry, Zeke.*

Luke shuffled into the room with his legs through the arms of a shirt. "Helpy?"

Tobias laughed. "Get offa me, woman. I have work to do. Look at that boy, would ya?"

Luke's serious little face remained focused on his task, and he struggled to get his feet pulled through the shirt's arms. When he noticed their smiles, he paused his work and grinned back. He showed all eight of his teeth, squished his eyes closed, and did a wiggle dance. This demonstration pulled the desired effect from his dad and aunt. When they laughed at him again, he clapped his hands. He then tripped on the tangled shirt and fell into a heap.

Eloise rushed to help him. "Oh, po' baby."

"Don't 'poor baby' him. He'll grow up expecting his knee kissed every time he falls."

"And I will." Eloise made kissy noises and pitched her voice into baby talk. "I will kiss his wittle knees forev'ah an' ev'ah."

Luke laughed, and she swung him up at arm's length, passing him to Tobias.

He kept his face sullen, and pretended to disapprove. El used to fret that she wasn't a good enough mother for Luke, but Tobias knew better. Luke was loved beyond reason, and that would always be enough.

"Now." She tapped her finger against the patch of stubble on Tobias's chin. "Put clothes on him and get ready. I have company coming, and we have to get to church *on time* today."

"He's hardly company if he's making breakfast."

"He's company enough for me to wear more than this wrapper over a nightgown, wouldn't you say?"

"Valid."

A flash of lightning with a thunderclap on its heels startled the three of them. As a group, they rushed to the window. The sun had risen an hour ago, but the sky had since darkened. The tops of trees across the street whipped back and forth and drops of rain splattered the windowpane.

Luke bounced in Tobias's arms and pointed down the street at a large leather ball rolling toward the house. It lost its momentum after it bounced off a hitching post but soon found a rut in the street and rolled with the wind again. The drops on the glass grew angry, and the wind pulsed like the breath of a beast, blowing in and out with force.

"Eek!" Luke smashed his tiny pointer finger against the window. "Eek come!"

"That son-of-gun." Tobias elbowed Eloise's shoulder, and she was already blushing. "He must really want to feed me breakfast."

Head down, hands buried deep in his pockets, Ezekiel James pushed against the wind toward their house. The three at the window cheered when the ball rolled near, and Zeke pivoted to kick it far down the street.

"We should get dressed." Eloise spoke with a hint of a smile.

"I suppose we should." Tobias looked forward to a day of rest. Even if they were rained out of getting to the church building, his family surrounded him, and a good breakfast was imminent. God could be praised from these walls as well as from across town. Everything was as it should be. Absolutely perfect.

Chapter 9

This was absolutely wretched. Hannah pressed her nose against the cold glass of the windowpane and sighed. The puff of air fogged the glass and obscured her view even more. The gray weather matched the ache in her soul at missing her first opportunity to socialize. Torrents of rain. Floods of rain! This must be how Noah's wife felt on day one of her voyage. Trapped. All her plans ruined.

From the red blob of the barn to her window, little brown rivers flowed through the yard. A wet, muddy mess. One she wouldn't mind exploring if she hadn't spent the past two hours leisurely putting together her ensemble. Not to mention the arduous task of curling and coaxing every dark ringlet to its proper place.

She'd been up before dawn, and the morning had greeted her with a cheerful sunrise. She'd sat on the porch railing with a steaming cup of coffee, pale with cream and sugar, and watched the sky turn from its mauve and corals to a rich scarlet before it eased to a calm robin's egg blue. The perfect dawn of what was to be the perfect first Sunday of the summer.

Before dressing for church, she'd tromped around the barn with Hiram and introduced herself to the animals again. The lambs begged for attention but ignored her and ran to Hiram when he came near. The sun emerged to play with the fluffy white puffs of clouds across the horizon when the horrid weather flew in like a banshee and destroyed her Sunday morning dreams. Devastating, ill-timed, and unwanted. Stupid rain.

Hiram sat at the kitchen table, ignoring her laments and woeful sighs.

She blinked long and hard, willing the clouds to clear. "I'd feel much better if you'd change out of your work clothes. If it stops in the next five minutes, we could still make it."

"It won't." He sipped his third cup of coffee. She knew because she'd poured it. He'd filled multiple sheets of paper with his small, neat handwriting. She hadn't bothered to ask what he was working on. Why should she care? Her misfortunes were too great.

So engrossed in his writing, he didn't spare her a look. Even after another noisy sigh. Didn't he understand how dire her situation was? Her first Sunday in town, washed away.

"You can't say for sure." She marched across the kitchen, through the living room, into her bedroom, and stopped in front of the mirror. Yes, her hair was gorgeously in place. She put on the new hat she'd purchased the morning she'd arrived. A fashionably small hat. Deep blue with red flowers along the brim, accented with the colorful ends of three peacock feathers. After pinning it so thoroughly in place that a tornado wouldn't pull it off, she frowned.

Of course. It was sublime. It was the perfect hat for this dress, and she looked every bit as wonderful as she thought she would. Sophisticated, proper, elegant, and—

"I can say without a doubt." Hiram called from the other room.

"What?" She sashayed one way, then the other, enjoying how her pink skirts swished over the toes of her boots. The reflection in the mirror pouted, mourning the wait of another week to wear the hat.

Hiram called louder. "I can say without a doubt."

"I heard what you said." She offered her hand to an invisible prince in the mirror and curtsied. "What are you talking about?"

Chair legs squeaked against the floor. Hiram entered the living room and stood in front of the window. "I'd forgotten you have the attention span of a kitten."

She waved goodbye to her prince and joined Hiram at the window. "Very possibly, but I don't know anyone who doesn't love a kitten."

"Until they climb behind your neck and stick needle-claws in your flesh."

"I believe you've taken this analogy far enough."

"Wearing the hat for dinner?"

"I will if I want to." She curtsied for him. "Especially if you insist on ruining my morning. Maybe if you changed out of your work clothes, the rain would stop, and then we'd be on our way in no time."

"You'll quit nagging?"

"Yes." She crossed her fingers behind her back.

"You'll stop sighing like you're on your death bed?"

She rested her palms against her cheeks and fluttered her eyelashes. "Yes, dear."

"I'll change. You pick a passage for us to read, and we'll sing. You, me, and that bird on your head'll have our own church."

Hiram changed into clean trousers, and the rain did not stop. Not in five minutes. Not even in ten minutes. But halfway through a delightful rendition of "God Moves in a Mysterious Way," one of God's smaller creatures joined the service. The gray furry animal with a tail bolted from under the sofa where Hiram sat and stopped in the middle of the rug.

Hannah didn't scream. Though the noise her breath made whooshing so quickly down her throat was nearly indescribable. She pressed a hand to her chest. "Hiram," she whispered. "A mouse."

"Sure enough." He didn't seem worried.

"I'll thank you to get it out of my house." She didn't move.

"My house."

Hannah snapped her gaze to him. "Our house. Get it out of our house."

Hiram clicked his tongue. "Heeere mousey, mousey, mousey."

"For crying out loud, Hiram. Get it out."

"I'm handling it." He chuckled. "It's afraid of your hat. If he doesn't move, he thinks that bird won't eat him."

"Oh, blarney."

Hiram sighed as he stood. The mouse was clearly more afraid of a grown man than the hat, and it streaked across the floor ahead of Hiram into the kitchen.

"What are you going to do?" Hannah wasn't frightened but held no desire to participate in the capture. Mice weren't friends. They were best handled by those with stronger dispositions. Kittens and the like.

"I'll surrender him to the barn cats."

"Such violence on a Sunday."

"That'll teach him to stay out of my house." Pots rattled in the kitchen.

Hannah grimaced, though she didn't argue with his methods. She stayed in her upholstered velvet chair with her feet pulled up, unwilling to witness the demise of the poor creature.

Sunbeams poured again through the window. The rain had let up. Streaks of sunlight highlighted the dust particles floating in the air. If she angled her head a smidgen to the left, the shadow of her hat cast a picture on the rug.

Hannah giggled. It really did look like a bird's nest sat directly on her head. The bird ruffled its wings when she gave her head a little bob. She smiled again when it appeared to settle back in its nest. Raising one hand and then the other, she made shadow hand puppets of talking birds until she'd moved one in connection to the hat-bird. There it was. The shadow bird was complete with a beak, wings, and nest.

"I'm going out. I'll be gone for a while. I need to check on the . . ." Hiram stood looking at her from the opening to the kitchen with a pail in his hand.

She ruffled her shadow bird with a wiggle of her head. "Tweet, tweet." Her hand snapped its beak.

He expressed no outward emotion but simply nodded and left.

With Hiram in the barn, the rain stopped, but with nowhere to go, Hannah slumped in her chair and twiddled her thumbs. *Bugger.* Read, sketch, paint, sew, write? Bake?

Read first, then bake.

No. Mix the dough, then read, then bake.

The plan formed, she dug her apron from her trunk of random things yet to be unpacked and assembled ingredients for bread.

First, a cup of tea.

While the tea steeped, she returned to her room and brought out her sketch pad and pencils and set them in a basket in the living room.

She returned to make the bed, tucked Austen's *Emma* under her arm, and headed back to the kitchen. "Kitten indeed," she murmured.

She rolled up her sleeves and made short work of mixing the dough out of the sponge she'd started last night. She kneaded until her arms ached and plopped it in a greased bowl to rest. Then she sprawled on the sofa in unladylike fashion and smiled when no one told her to sit up straight. With a sigh, she flipped to the final chapters of *Emma* and read aloud.

Hannah had reached the height of the romantic tension and stood to read Mr. Knightley's confession with greater passion. "'My dearest Emma,' said he, 'for dearest you will always be, whatever the event of this hour's conversation, my dearest, most beloved Emma—tell me at once. Say "No" if it is to be said.' She could really say nothing. 'You are silent,' he cried."

Hannah stopped her dramatization when she noticed a stick poking out from under the sofa. *How odd.* Then the stick flicked its tongue.

Hannah screeched and suddenly found herself standing on the chair opposite the sofa. *Emma* was on the floor, pages still fluttering from its flight across the room. The snake was green with two yellow stripes flowing down its back, and it flashed a red tongue.

She concentrated on breathing after noticing her faculties had momentarily ceased. "Hiram!" The window showed an empty pasture. "Oh, heavens." She gripped the back of her chair, and her heart thumped against her sternum. "Hiram! I say, Hiram! You have a snake in your house!"

The three-foot-long reptile took no notice of her and began a slow migration across the living room. It paused in a sunny spot on the wood floor, tasting the air all the while.

Hannah yelled for her brother a few more times, but help did not arrive. Not in the form of her brother, not in a dashing young hero on a white steed, and certainly not from Mr. Knightley.

"I can do this." She patted her chest. "I can very well do this. It's only a little—huge—garden snake. Harmless. Perfectly harmless." With her hand directing the air, she calmed her breath, in and out, until her pounding heart relaxed. "Besides, I'm not Hannah Claire Benton. I'm Sir Benton, snake wrangler from Australia come to entertain his Grace, the Duke of—" She inched off the chair, thankful she yet wore her boots intended for church. Breathing slowly through pursed lips, Hannah made her way to the offending serpent. "—the Duke of Canterbury." Her voice came out in a breathless whisper. "I arrived at the opportune moment, fully prepared for the challenge, because the Duchess would faint dead away at even a glimpse."

She wiped her perspiring hands on her hips and edged closer. "Dead away. Even the talk of snakes is too much for her disposition. Of course, everyone in court is duly impressed by Sir Benton's prowess and finesse, and how in heaven's name a black mamba made its way to court is a secret to all but me."

Hannah bent at the knees, preparing to grab the creature by its tail, when it turned and hissed at her. Snake wrangler or not, she was no fool and retained some sense of self-preservation. Therefore, she released another scream—or three—and jumped back, hands to chest. But in the next moment the snake turned from her and undulated across the floor toward her bedroom.

"Oh, no, you don't." Heart beating wildly and breath panting, Hannah lunged before her courage gave out completely. She grasped it tightly by its tail and yanked it from the floor, shrieking like all the damsels in all the distress combined into one screaming contest.

The fiend tried to curl around her arm with its mouth open, but she held on and shook her hand. It stiffened and curled in a downward spiral, unable to sink its fangs into her.

Still screaming, she threw open the door and flung the snake out of her hand and directly toward one Mr. Tobias Franklin racing up the porch steps.

Evidently, there had been a hero on his way to answer her call. The concern on his face quickly morphed into one of relief and then shock as the snake blasted his way. Hannah could do nothing but watch her would-be hero arch his back and slap the snake away from his face. He jumped backward into the mud behind his gray horse untethered at the rail.

The trespassing serpent ricocheted from the latest impact and fell in a coil under the horse's nose, which startled and kicked the man in the side, knocking him to the ground.

The snake slithered under the porch, the horse whinnied and galloped away, and Mr. Franklin lay motionless in the mud.

"Lord, have mercy," Hannah whispered.

Chapter 10

Hannah ran to Mr. Franklin, sprawled on his side with his arm twisted at a sharp angle behind his back. The cheerful, cloudless sky mocked her, and the cold wind blew away any of the sun's intended heat. Shaking from terror and adrenaline, Hannah stood over him, unsure of what to do. For fear of broken bones, she dared not try to move him.

Hesitantly, she adjusted his head to turn his mouth and nose out of the mud. Her hand came away covered in blood. "Mr. Franklin? Mr. Franklin? Oh, Mr. Franklin, please don't be dead."

He must have knocked his head against the corner of the steps on the way down. She knelt closer and pressed a hand to the soft flesh under the corner of his jaw. A strong pulse thrummed against her fingers.

Thank you, Lord. With her hand still at his throat, she screamed toward the barn. "Hiram!"

Gently, she lifted Mr. Franklin's head and let her fingers comb through his thick, brown hair, looking for the source of blood. It oozed from a gash above his right ear. At least two inches long and bleeding profusely.

"Hiram!" Hannah craned her neck and shot her gaze to the second story where she knew Hiram hid his medical bag. "Stop the bleeding. Stop the bleeding." She closed her eyes. "Oh, God in heaven, please, stop the bleeding."

His head weighed heavy in her hands, and she pulled his shoulder to roll him on his back to keep the gash out of the mud. Aggravating a broken bone would be better than mud in his head . . . maybe.

She ran inside the house and up the flight of stairs to Hiram's room. The wood floor banged against her knees next to his bed, and she stretched her arm far underneath. Her fingers grazed the edge of the black leather bag, but her arm was too short.

"Agh!" An unbidden scream of frustration scraped against her throat. Lying flat on her stomach, she inched under the bed until she clutched the handle.

She opened it there on the floor of his room. It was fully stocked with bandages and everything else Hiram might use for an emergency house call. "Bless you, Hiram."

For the moment, Hannah snatched a roll of cotton and packing, pressed the bag to her chest, and ran down the stairs. Tossing the bag on the table, she continued to the door with the bandages. With the door half open, she remembered the dinner bell. She hadn't been here long enough to make use of it because Hiram was nearby around mealtimes. She wrapped her red-tinged fingers around the wooden handle and brought it to the porch.

She rang it again and again, calling for Hiram as she crossed the porch.

She blinked. Mr. Franklin was no longer passed out at the foot of the steps. The bell slipped from her hand and hit the porch with a terrible thump.

She dropped the bandages next to the bell. "Mr. Franklin?" Thankfully, she didn't need advanced tracking skills to follow him through the mud. A clear path of footprints led her around the side of the house.

He stood, leaning one hand against the white siding, the other pressed to his head.

"Mr. Franklin?" She sprinted into his line of sight, though he appeared to look through her.

"Where's Luke?" He slumped against the wall but then gasped in pain. His eyes focused, and he seemed to see her for the first time.

"He's not here, Mr. Franklin. We need to get you into the house." She put a hand on his shoulder when he swayed. "You hit your head. And the horse—oh, Mr. Franklin, wake up. Wake up! I can't carry you. I don't know where Hiram is." The weight of him pushed forward against her palm. "Dear God, where is Hiram? No, no, no. Mr. Franklin, wake up."

His knees, which had begun to buckle, straightened again.

"Good. Here, put your arm around my shoulders." She tucked herself against his side. "We're going to walk together and get you inside. We can do this."

The blood from his head flowed around his ear. It left a bright trail along his neck before eagerly soaking the collar of his shirt. She turned her focus to the muddy ground in front of them. *God, stop the bleeding. Send help.*

He kept one hand on the wall, and she bore more of his weight than she'd prefer. She envisioned herself in warrior garb, dragging a wounded comrade off the battlefield. An incoherent, lumbering giant of a comrade. Somehow, they navigated their way to the porch, managed the steps and door, and stumbled into the kitchen. She sat him in a chair, and he slumped forward, resting his head on his crossed arms on the table.

"Can you sit? I need you to stay here. Please, don't go to sleep. I don't want you to fall." Her hands hovered a moment over his shoulder, waiting to see if he was steady. "Stay here."

Hannah rekindled the fire in the iron stove and dumped the few remaining cups from the water pail into the largest pot she could find. She'd need to get more water, but she couldn't leave him.

He didn't move, and a rivulet of blood dripped off the edge of the table and puddled on the floor near his boots.

Hannah blinked. Swallowed once. *God, I need help.* She gave herself two seconds to gather strength then shook off her fear. She pulled a new length of cotton from Hiram's bag. "Mr. Franklin? I'm going to wrap your head temporarily until we get someone here to put you back together."

Pushing the skin together best she could, she pinched it closed with one hand and leaned across the table to the packing. Her fingers were smeared red.

He jerked his head aside, and his eyes flew open. Wild and afraid. He feebly attempted to push her away while holding his head.

She knelt beside him and put her face level with his. "Mr. Franklin, please hear me. You're bleeding. Bleeding all over the place. You need to be still so I can wrap the wound."

"Where's Luke?" His gaze roamed her kitchen before landing on her.

"Luke is safe." Working quickly, she pressed the packing against his head and wrapped the bandage around multiple times before he could argue.

He stayed awake, tracking her with unfocused, unblinking eyes. Pupils dilated. His complete silence was unnerving.

Before she finished securing the end of the bandage, a button-sized crimson circle had soaked through the bleached cotton and was spreading. "Mr. Franklin, you must stop this bleeding. I tell you—enough is enough."

His head drooped to his arm on the table, asleep.

The screened door creaked, and Hiram took a step into the kitchen. Rolls of bandages and the dinner bell filled his hand. He stopped.

His gaze followed the muddy footprints on the floor to the wide hem of her formerly pink dress that was damp and brown. Blood covered both of her hands and ran along one sleeve. A mixture of red and brown coated the entire front of her dress. Wayward strands of hair tickled her cheek, and she cocked a shoulder to rub an itch near her ear.

"Hiram. You're back." She smiled, even as her lip trembled, and her nose began to burn. "I've gotten myself into a bit of trouble." A sob choked her, and she dared not wipe the tears. "I need your help."

Hiram twitched an eyebrow. "Found a horse in the east pasture. I put him in the barn."

Mr. Franklin shifted, and he started sliding out of his chair.

Hannah stepped forward and braced her hip against his shoulder, but his bulk was almost too much for her. "The horse brought you back?"

"Wasn't my horse."

"I rang the bell. I called and screamed and yelled for you."

He lifted one shoulder. "I heard nothing."

"You came back because of the horse?"

Still in the doorway, Hiram nodded to the table. "Who is he?"

"He needs your help." She adjusted Mr. Franklin's head so Hiram could see the blood soaking through.

"Tobias?" Hiram pushed against the door. "I'll go for the doctor."

"No, Hiram. He's lost too much blood already."

"Don't do this to me, Hannah. Let me fetch someone else."

"At least look at him, please. That's all I ask. Please, help me." *If not for him, for me.*

Hiram stepped inside, shaking his head.

Hannah knew some of the events leading to Hiram's dismissal from medical school. She knew about the meeting with the hospital board, and how Hiram and her father had fought. There was more to Hiram buying a farm than his desire to raise sheep. But right now, that didn't matter.

What mattered, whether he liked it or not, was that Hiram Benton was the closest thing to a surgeon the small town of Ockelbo, Nebraska, could boast. She wasn't about to let him ride off for help and leave her here alone with a bleeding, unconscious man.

Hiram absently picked at his top button.

She stepped back, and when Mr. Franklin began to slide, Hiram caught him.

Something switched in her brother. No longer hesitant, he handled Mr. Franklin with the firmness and confidence of a well-trained doctor.

After checking Mr. Franklin's pulse, he adjusted him so he'd stay at the table and moved to the sink after fetching warm water from the stove. "What happened?"

"Horse kicked him. Knocked his head on the steps."

Hiram grunted. "Man ought to know better than that."

"I threw a snake at him."

He wiped his hands on a clean towel. "I'm not even going to ask. Here, help me with his head. I'm going to check for injuries from the kick." Hiram beckoned her, but when he saw the state of her dress, he grimaced. "You're as disgusting as he is. A little more mud won't make any difference. Stand behind his chair. I'm going to lift him up, and I want you to hold his head steady."

She cushioned his head to her chest, braced it with both hands, and then let it tip sideways to cradle in the crook of her arm. "I never knew a head could weigh this much."

Hiram chuckled. "Dead weight. If he hadn't walked, I would have had trouble getting him inside. An unconscious, six-foot man is not easily moved. I'd like to get him up on the table, but he's too tall." Hiram laid out a clean cloth and lined up a row of medical tools near his bag. "How did you know where to find this?"

"I snooped yesterday while you were out."

Hiram shook his head without looking at her. He didn't appear surprised.

"I was disappointed." Hannah leaned over to scratch an itch on her nose, then thought better of it. She couldn't think of a time her hands had been this disgusting.

"Disappointed?" Hiram used the dipper to fill a bowl with hot water.

"I didn't find any love letters in the entire house. Not a single one. I was desperately looking for incriminating evidence. Something to wave in your face and say, 'Aha! Now I know all things.'"

"We need more water."

"I know. There wasn't much left." She'd rather joke with Hiram than live in her current reality. Mr. Franklin hadn't so much as twitched, although his breath was steady. The bandage she'd hurriedly wrapped around him partially covered his eyes. He'd have trouble opening them even if he were to wake.

Hiram unbuttoned Mr. Franklin's jacket, his vest, and his overshirt. "Keep his head steady. We're going to lean him forward enough to pull these off."

They settled him back against her once his outerwear was removed. Hiram used a pair of blunt scissors and sliced the front of Mr. Franklin's undershirt.

The cotton fell open, revealing a tight stomach and a fine layer of brown hair across a muscled chest.

Hannah gasped and almost dropped Mr. Franklin's head.

"What is it?" Hiram jerked his face toward her, concerned.

She swallowed and shook her head, suddenly very warm. How she wanted to pull at her constricting collar.

"You've seen a man's chest before. Surely."

She shook her head in tiny, quick movements, looking directly at Hiram and not at the man within her arms.

Hiram raised his arms in surrender. "Well, scupper that, Hannah! You're the one who didn't want me to find help." He blew out a breath and laughed. "If you're going to be a surgeon's assistant, you might see a little more than a bare chest. Now, lift him up again so we can get this off."

With Mr. Franklin naked from the waist up, Hannah found the room much smaller than it was moments ago. She could look neither at Hiram nor Mr. Franklin. The kitchen had exploded. Muddy tracks even led through the living room. She stood by Mr. Franklin's side, holding his head tightly against her chest while Hiram felt along the man's back and sides. A growing pile of soiled clothes filled the floor at her feet. There weren't that many more layers left to—

"Look here." Hiram's command brought her gaze down. He pointed to Mr. Franklin's back. Below his shoulder blade and partway under his arm, a rose-red half-circle the size of her hand was already spreading with deep purple bruising.

"Here, feel this." He grabbed her hand and pulled it down to cover the bruise. "Can you feel it?"

She shook her head, unable to speak because her corset squeezed the air out of her. *Why was it so tight?* She'd had no trouble with it this morning. She breathed in shallow bursts through her nose. "What am I supposed to be feeling?" She only felt hot skin under her fingers. So much exposed skin. *As someone's wife, I'd see this much and more of a husband every day. Goodness. Even touch it if I wanted.* Goosebumps ran along her arms. *By default, it would go the other way too. Would he undress me? Or wait outside the room for me to change into a nightdress?* She blinked. Do married women see their husbands with the lamp still burning in the bedroom? Would he ever undress like this in the middle—

"You can't feel that broken rib?" Hiram removed his hand from hers, and she snatched it away. He chuckled, and she feared he could read her thoughts. Unbidden thoughts about summer weddings and honeymoons and no chaperones. Damsels and knights and—

"Poor sucker." Hiram pressed ever so gently around the area. "Though he's lucky enough. Best I can tell, no internal injuries. Lift him up again. I'll bind him, and we'll see about his head. It'll be easier to set the stitches in before he wakes up."

Chapter 11

This was the end . . . or maybe the beginning. Tobias waited for the light to appear so he could follow it home. Would his parents await him? Were the streets really paved with gold? Gold streets. What a laugh. The wear and tear on them would be exhaustive. Perhaps there was a layer of solid brick underneath. That's a maintenance crew he'd volunteer to work. Heaven's Highway Maintenance.

Though, he figured God could design it however he liked. If the Big Man wanted gold streets, the gold oughta hold up for eternity.

Beyond Tobias's musings, a dreadful pounding pulsed through him. Was there supposed to be this much pain in the afterlife? Once a fellow crossed over, he rather thought the pain stayed behind.

He wiggled his toes and fire seared between his shoulder blades. He froze. More pain enveloped him. He was being consumed by it. An immense weight pulled him under, drowning him. It was easier to go with it. He let the blackness cover him.

Talking. The incessant sing-song rhythmic talking drew him out of sleep again. Why wouldn't she let him sleep? That voice had trailed him throughout his dreams. They were only dreams. They must be. Dreams of deep clay pits where he was buried alive. Smothered. Lost in dark forests, hunting someone or being hunted. Looking for Luke. And that voice. Always there, but far off, kept him from believing the lie of the dreams.

Bits of her words came to him, but they didn't make sense. No matter. Sleep was still good, despite the dreams. If he slept, he didn't hurt. Better to sleep than be ripped apart.

The next time he awoke the pain had shifted. The radiating oppression was gone. It was precise now—localized to his side and his head.

The voice washed over him like a soothing brook. A gentle cadence already familiar. Peeking his eyes open, he found the room cast in shadows.

A figure nearby glowed faintly. She was only a silhouette with the lamp behind her. With a book balanced in one hand and a teacup in the other, she read aloud. "By this time the Queen had reached her towering castle. She stood before her mirror, dressed in her finest, and commanded, 'Mirror, mirror on the wall. Who's the fairest one of all?' And the mirror spoke as before. 'Queen, though your beauty is most rare, Snow White is lovelier and more fair. She dwells in a cottage near the glen with seven little bearded men.'"

The woman paused to sip from her teacup, looking at Tobias over the rim of the china.

He tried to smile, to speak. Only a croak escaped. Was that his own voice?

She was at his side, and a cool cloth bathed his forehead. That didn't hurt so much. It was rather nice, actually. His eyes drifted closed once more, too heavy to hold open.

Her hand slipped into his, and he tightened his grip around her slim fingers.

She laughed, a harpsichord playing the scale. "He lives. He doesn't wake. But he lives."

He didn't attempt to open his eyes. After another minute of rest, he forced out the ever-present thought: "Where's Luke?"

"Shhh, I can't understand a word of what you're saying. Rest now. You're going to be just fine." She brushed her thumb along his knuckles.

The invisible weight pushed him under, and darkness crept through the corners of his mind. This wasn't right. Being here was wrong. Eloise was alone . . . she wouldn't . . .

He cracked his eye a sliver, and the woman wavered. A triple outline of her face danced before him. He focused on the one in the middle. "I must go home."

"You will." Her hand squeezed his again.

"No." He struggled with the word, surprised by the gravel in his throat.

She pulled her hand free of his even as he tried to hang on. Darkness swept over him when she disappeared from view. It wanted to bring him under, and he couldn't remember why he should fight it. As it tightened around him, the cloth was taken from his forehead.

"Can you take a sip? I have water."

A drink would be good. His tongue was dry and filled his mouth. A sip was all he could manage, and even half of that dribbled across his face. "I . . . need to go home."

"Rest now." She replaced the cool cloth.

She didn't understand.

"Where's Luke?" He needed to make her listen. She needed to . . . needed to . . . he had to get home. Didn't she know where Luke was? And Eloise. How long had he been here? Were they in the forest? Did they come with him through the forest? He wouldn't have left them there. How did this happen?

Eloise must be at home with Luke. They were home. They wouldn't have come with him into—into . . . no. There was no forest. Was there? There wasn't a cave or a pit. Eloise was home with Luke.

He tore his eyes open again. He was delivering that awful, troublesome book.

The woman leaned over him, replacing the rag on his forehead. The cold brought almost enough relief to send him back to sleep. "Can you take another drink of water?"

"El can't be alone. I have to get back to her."

"All is well," she crooned. "Please try another swallow of water." Waves of ebony hair spilled over her shoulder when she offered the cup to his lips.

He drank, getting more down his throat this time.

Hannah Claire Benton. That's right—he knew her. She was funny. She had a lot of books and pretty clothes. She was pretty. He wanted to protect her. And meet her again. That's why he had the book.

She pulled her hair together in a thick twist and tossed it over her shoulder as she settled into the chair beside him. She didn't know about Eloise. She didn't understand. Why didn't she understand? He'd been telling her.

He had to get home, but he was . . . tired. Getting more words out of his head and through his mouth was taking more effort than it should. He thought carefully for a long time before attempting to explain in the fewest words. "Eloise is afraid. I cannot leave her alone in the dark."

There. Now this woman would understand.

The pain in his head pulsed with each heartbeat until its intensity spread throughout, as if he were slowly being dipped in lava. If a steel rod had been shoved through his temples, he didn't think it would hurt any worse.

Fighting off the wall of darkness only fed the flames, and with the release of the next breath, he stopped struggling and sank into the cycle of dreams again.

Hannah pushed off her toes to set the rocker in motion next to her bed. Mr. Franklin was asleep again—at least he'd stopped trying to speak and no longer responded to her coaxing him to drink.

She rocked in big, swinging arcs and enjoyed the whoosh of each downward fall as it fluffed her hair. It was dry now after her bath. The water had turned three shades of murky by the time she was done washing off the events of the day.

She'd figured for sure Mr. Franklin would wake up this last time, but after two sips of water and a few incoherent mumbles, he'd conked out again.

His breathing calmed, and his face relaxed—signs that he wasn't dreaming, as far as she could tell.

She'd been at his side most of yesterday and now half the night.

Sometimes his face tensed, and his breath turned shallow and rapid. During those moments, she replaced the cool cloth on his forehead, held his hand, and sang a hymn until he resumed a restful sleep.

Each time he stirred, she'd tried to offer water, but he'd been mostly unresponsive.

Since her bedroom was the only one on the main floor, and he was too tall for the sofa, it made sense to put him here. Besides, he might be with them for a few days. It didn't seem charitable to stick him in the living room.

The door at the foot of the stairs near her bedroom squeaked, and she checked her pocket watch. A quarter to three. She smiled at Hiram's mussed hair. "Good morning, Captain."

"How is he?"

"The same. Mostly. He's not fully awoken yet, but he's getting closer. The last time, he mumbled about his family again. I think he's worried about them, but I can't make out half of what he's trying to say." She rested her head against the back of the chair as Hiram watched Mr. Franklin from the doorway. "I offered water. Though I'm not sure he swallowed any." She ticked off the list on her fingers. "No fevers to report, no seizures, no convulsions, and no blood seeping out of his head."

Hiram nodded. "My turn?"

"If you'll wait here while I stretch my legs and see to a matter of importance, I'd appreciate it. I'll sleep tomorrow, for Eloise said she'd be back again in the morning to sit with him. I'm younger than you, you know, so I've got more energy to spare."

A slight narrowing of the eyes was Hiram's only reaction.

Hannah clapped him on the shoulder and made her way outside. She twirled in the fresh night air, and it did wonders for waking her spirits. She was tempted to stay out longer and enjoy the moonglow. Alas, she couldn't spend the whole night stargazing when there was a half-naked, unconscious man laid out on her bed. Her not-a-doctor but 99.98 percent surgeon-trained brother said Mr. Franklin needed to be watched. So she watched.

When she finished her business in the outhouse, she was ready for another shift at her post. After splashing her face with cold water, she sent Hiram back to bed.

The room didn't feel like her own yet. After all, she'd slept in it only one night. The shelf Hiram had installed for her on the wall held most of her books. Those she'd unpacked straightaway. Nothing spoke of home like seeing her books arranged in their proper order. She returned the collection of fairytales to its place on the shelf, brought her teacup to the kitchen, and settled into the rocking chair by her bed.

The prayer she'd spoken the morning after her arrival haunted her. Had she invariably caused this? Did God deliver Mr. Franklin on a simple whim of her fancy? Surely not. Surely her audacious request hadn't been answered so swiftly. She hadn't mentioned it again to Hiram and hoped it'd slipped his mind—unlikely.

If Mr. Franklin was sent by God to be her husband, she'd rather avoid any hard feelings between him and her brother. The fact was, her request nagged her incessantly.

What have I done?

With her head firmly against the back of the rocker, she swung it forcefully into motion.

God knows better than to satisfy the impulsive whims of my mouth. Doesn't he? Blimey, I'll crave sweet bread one minute and salted roast the next. She'd prayed for anything and everything through the years, and nothing like this had ever happened before.

She snorted, remembering the time she'd prayed for a hailstorm to ruin Mother's flower garden. *Thanks for ignoring that one, Lord.*

Mr. Franklin's arrival smarted like a slap from her mother. It loomed over her like a consequence more than a blessing. Her mother's voice rang in her ear, *What have you done, child?*

If God had sent Mr. Franklin, had he also sent the mouse to get Hiram out of the house? And the snake to orchestrate the accident? Had he sent the horse to fetch Hiram home again?

Was Mr. Franklin sent to her for marriage, a divine rescue from Mother, a salvation from the tiresome life of duplicity among her mother's circle of friends, or did God send him just to show off that he could? That she was out of her mind for demanding such a specific and outlandish thing?

What if Mr. Franklin was a wife-beater? Oh! He could be a common drunkard or a card player. Perhaps he swore or kicked puppies. For all she knew, the man wasn't a believer, couldn't read, and had no personality.

Her rocking chair tipped backward, and in the moment of free fall, she sucked in a scream. She crash-landed on the back of the rocker in the open doorway. Holding still as a bean, she waited for signs of alarm from anyone else in the house.

All was quiet except for the pounding on the back of her head where she'd hit the floor.

There was no solving this mystery tonight. Perhaps Mr. Franklin would marry her. Perhaps he wouldn't.

Hannah lay as a forgotten pile of laundry on the upturned rocker and pressed her hands against her flushed cheeks . . . if he did marry her, would it be by his own free will?

Oh, God, what have you done? I don't want a man who is forced into marrying me.

It would be better to go home to Des Moines than to live the rest of her life never sure of a husband's true love. She'd never be able to confess what she'd done. He'd resent her forever!

Forever and ever until death do us part.

She rolled her head back and forth and whimpered. *Of all the scrapes I've gotten into, this may turn out to be the very worst of them all.*

Hannah extracted herself from the chair, put it to rights beside the bed, and stood looking at Mr. Franklin, hands on hips and hair wild about her shoulders.

He groaned, clenched his fist, and jerked his head to the side as he'd done numerous times during the night. "Luke?"

She knelt at his side and took his calloused hand in hers. "You're all right," she said. Humming first and then finding the words, she softly sang "All Creatures of Our God and King" until his face relaxed and his breath returned to normal. Only then did she release his hand and return to the rocking chair.

She dug out her pocket watch.

A quarter to four.

Chapter 12

Today was a special day. Today Eloise and Zeke brought Luke. It was Tuesday. Day three of nursing Mr. Franklin. Thankfully, Dr. Farley had come Monday morning and given a positive report. He'd only prescribed extensive rest and left a packet of headache powder. Rest was the easy part. Getting Mr. Franklin to wake up enough to take in fluids had been the challenge.

Hiram agreed that it was a good idea for Mr. Franklin to see for himself that Luke was fine—even at the risk of the extra excitement the child would bring. Hiram cautioned that as long as the child stayed off the bed, he'd allow the visit.

Hannah leaped from the porch steps to meet Eloise in the buggy.

Despite her reassurance, Mr. Franklin incessantly asked about Luke. His anxious questions resurfaced each time he opened his eyes. Though his widowed sister and her new beau joined in assuring him that everything was being managed, Mr. Franklin continued to fret.

Hannah didn't believe he suffered memory loss, but he was overly concerned about the well-being of his toddler. Understandable. There was nothing wrong with a father interested in the care of his child. Commendable, really. *If the man asks me one more time where his son is, I might be forced to accidentally shove the pillow over his face.*

Clearly, he wasn't used to being away from his family or letting others take over. When Hannah pried, he shared that Eloise had moved in with him after her first husband, Philip, tragically died a few months after their marriage. He confessed she'd never spent the night alone since, and she always kept a lamp burning when he was out. In Hannah's opinion, Eloise depended a little too much on her brother. It would do her good to spend a few days taking care of herself for a change.

Regardless, what Hannah wanted to see was this baby Luke. All she'd seen last week was a flash of blond hair and a cheeky grin—she'd been a little distracted by the boy's father.

Hannah waved to the trio in the buggy.

Luke sat between Mr. James and his Aunt Eloise, and as soon as the wheels stopped, he attempted to scramble over the side. His itty-bitty finger pointed to the nearest pasture. "Baa! Baa!"

"Hold it, sir." Mr. James wrangled the boy to the bench.

Hannah took hold of Dan's bridle—the same dappled gray Mr. Franklin had ridden to the house on Sunday.

"Good morning, Mr. James." Hannah swiped at the hair blowing into her mouth.

He hopped to the ground and tipped his wide-brimmed hat. "Miss Benton." He offered his hand. "Friends call me Zeke. Just Zeke."

He helped the others to the ground and nodded to Eloise. "I'll be back after a while to pick you up."

"I can bring them home." Hannah would enjoy the ride and getting out of the house. "It's no trouble. I'll have Hiram hitch the wagon for us."

Eloise and Zeke looked at each other for a moment, and Eloise nodded.

"Come inside." Hannah led the way to the house. "Mr. Franklin will be glad to see you."

"Oh, my. You don't need to call him that—nobody does."

Hannah paused with one foot on the porch. "What do people call him?"

Eloise spoke in a calm, soft voice. "Mostly I hear 'Boss' around town. Though I don't go many places. And do please call me Eloise, and Zeke, well, Zeke. I do hope we can all be friends." She tugged on Luke's hand when he tried to pull away toward the barn. "I'm very sorry he's laid up here. If we padded your wagon with enough hay, I'm sure we could get him moved." She pulled Luke into her arms when he refused to walk.

"My brother, Hiram, has extensive medical training, you know, and I think he secretly enjoys putting those years of school to good use. We could move him . . ." Ticking off the list on her fingers, Hannah squinted toward the sky. "Broken ribs, a long row of stitches, blood loss, concussion, and head trauma doesn't necessitate the continual eye of a surgeon. The fact is, we feel responsible for him. After all, it was our snake that caused this whole ruckus. Please, let us keep him a few days more."

Hannah put her hands out for Luke, and he went to her without question. "Well, hello, dearest. Aren't you just a peanut?" She smiled at Eloise. "Just between the two of us, I enjoy the company of having someone else here. I wasn't sure how I'd spend my time this summer. I like the sheep, but you know, I've never lived in the country before. How does one manage it?"

She opened the door and continued through the kitchen. "I was almost in tears Sunday when we were rained out from going to church, having only the wagon for getting to town. Were you able to go? I almost made the trip anyhow. Snooty Hiram wouldn't hear of it. Wouldn't that have been a scene? Wilted and dripping." She laughed. "Their first impression would be the sound of my drip, drip, dripping all through service. Still, I was so looking forward to meeting everyone."

Hannah stopped in the living room and lowered her voice. "Luke, dearest, Daddy is having a little nap, so we're going to be very quiet and sneak in to say good morning." She eased the door open.

Eloise went in first and laid a hand on Mr. Franklin's forehead.

He smiled at her, but his expression changed to pure relief when he noticed Luke at the door. His eyes flitted across to Hannah's face, his smile deepening, and then all his attention reverted to the child.

"Hey, buddy. C'mere." Mr. Franklin raised his hand to Luke.

Luke chewed on his thumb. "Daddy owie?" He reached for Eloise.

Eloise cuddled him while he examined his daddy. "Daddy is tired. He has an owie on his head. See how it's all wrapped up?"

Mr. Franklin tried to sit up, tightened his eyes, and settled on lifting a hand to Luke's leg instead. "Can I hold you, son? I've missed you."

"Daddy owie?" Luke pulled closer into Eloise, seeming afraid that Mr. Franklin wouldn't be able to answer.

Eloise sat on the edge of the bed. "Give Daddy a snuggle. He needs one of your special hugs."

Hannah stepped forward to stop the child from hurting Mr. Franklin. She didn't get there in time, and Luke curled into the man's side and was immediately cocooned in his father's arms.

Mr. Franklin and his son both closed their eyes and took a deep breath together as one. The moment drew on and neither she nor Eloise interrupted.

Hannah eased out of the room and let the family continue their visit.

Later that evening Tobias listened with half-lidded eyes. Miss Benton's voice dramatized each character, and she brought Tom Sawyer's story to life with expressions and hand gestures he'd miss if he let his eyes close all the way.

"Huck, I wouldn't want to, and I don't want to—but what would people say? Why they'd say, 'Mph! Tom Sawyer's Gang! Pretty low characters in it!' They'd mean you, Huck. You wouldn't like that, and I wouldn't."

Tobias smiled but had learned better than to laugh, for his body didn't thank him for the jostling.

She stopped reading and peered over the top of the book. "You never formed a gang, did you?"

"Of course I did." His voice had more gravel in it than usual. "But I was never as ornery as Tom. I had both parents around and a baby sister who followed me everywhere. I didn't have the time for mischief."

"Hmm." The sleeves of her cream blouse were rolled to her elbows, and he was pretty sure he'd caught a glimpse of bare feet the last time she'd walked into the room. "I can't imagine the kind of freedom Tom enjoys. Forming gangs and sneaking out at night?"

"You never snuck out?"

"Blimey, no."

Blimey. He smiled again. *Aye aye, matey.* "You should, sometime. It's good fun."

She put her finger between the pages and rested the book on her lap. "What would we do?"

"It doesn't matter. Walk around mostly and talk about all the wild things you want to do, then sneak back inside and go to bed."

"The risk, in my case with my parents, wouldn't be worth a turn about the park walking and talking."

"What *would* be worth the risk then?"

"Something more exciting than walking and talking, I'd say. You can do that very well in daylight hours."

He rested his eyes and grinned. "If you've never done it, you wouldn't know. Ho-hum, now you've missed your shot because you can never go back to being twelve. There'd be no point because no one would stop you."

Miss Benton snorted. "My mother is Huck's worst nightmare. She'd stop me yet."

"You forget I've met your mother." He held up two fingers without opening his eyes. "Twice."

"Oh, dear, yes. I've blocked our first meeting from my mind." The familiar squeak of her rocking chair punctuated the conversation. "And the second . . ."

"I'm sorry about your trunk . . . and the books."

"I'm not. Well, I'm a little sorry for the porters." She snorted again, possibly the cutest snort he'd ever heard. "You were such a cad, gathering handfuls of unmentionables like you've handled them your whole life."

"I have been married before." He peeked at her face to see if she was embarrassed. "Someone had to pick them up, and I was only trying to save your dignity."

She giggled, no sign of shame in her expression. "What was left of it."

"I am sorry about . . . afterward." Shoot, he'd brought them full circle to her mother.

"Yes, well." She worried the corner of the book with a finger. "It wasn't the first she's behaved so, and I doubt it'll be the last."

"Why not stay?" He tipped his palm open, thinking to take her hand. *Behave yourself.* Before she noticed, he turned it inward and made a fist.

"She won't let me."

He brought his hands together over his chest and farther from trouble. "You could simply say, 'I'm staying here.'"

"It's *simply* not that simple." She pulled her watch from her pocket and fiddled with the cover, popping it open and clicking it shut. "She's still my mother and I . . . listen." Hannah stood. "I've never ever in my life set out to displease her on purpose, but it turns out that way, regardless."

She shoved *Tom Sawyer* on the shelf and ran her finger down the line of books. "Did you read *Frankenstein* while it was in your possession?"

Hmm, and now you're avoiding. He could play along if she didn't want to talk about it. "Hated it."

"Bugger," she said, her back to him. "And we could have been such good friends."

He barked a laugh, and pain coursed through his side. "Dr. Frankenstein is the most whiny slug of a man I've ever read about."

She spun toward him, skirts swishing about her ankles. Yep, barefoot. "You are well-read, then?"

"For Ockelbo, I'm well-read enough."

She lifted her nose.

"What're you looking hoity-toity about?"

"Are you a believer?"

He narrowed his eyes. "I believe a lot of things."

She lifted an eyebrow. "Don't be smart with me. Jesus, God's Son?"

"Born a human with the Spirit of God, died, and came back? Yes, ma'am."

She snapped the cover of her watch and dropped it into her pocket.

Strange woman, this one. He gathered a slow breath. "All right, then. Excuse me. Nurse, please fetch the doc. He and I have a personal matter to discuss." Dignity wasn't something he had in excess this week. Asking for help to the outhouse was better than an emergency rescue after falling over on himself, or worse, letting her deal with the chamber pot.

"Very well. It's past time you were asleep for the night anyhow."

He grinned. People weren't generally in the habit of telling him what to do, much less when to go to bed.

"I'll heat some water, and you may wash if you've a mind."

He lifted a finger as a farewell. "Mmhm. G'nite."

Chapter 13

Thursday morning, Tobias opened the door to the outhouse. The sun in the eastern sky blinded him, and he covered his eyes with the crook of his arm. Any other time he'd enjoy the picturesque pastures with fluffy dots of sheep grazing in the spring-green grass of June. By the end of July, each knoll would be burned dry by the unrelenting sun, and haying season would begin. The prairie came alive this time of year with new flowers opening their buds each week.

Every part of him ached, and the sun was his nemesis. His unplanned convalescence couldn't have been in a more beautiful place. If only he weren't trapped here.

Hiram worked near the house, pounding a row of stakes into the yard. Tobias raised an arm to him. With mallet in hand,

Hiram jogged over to support Tobias's walk—rather, shuffle—
into the house in a desperate attempt to put one foot in front of
the other without keeling over.

"I shouldn't be this weak from a couple of broken ribs and a
few stitches, doc."

"Men have died from a horse's kick. You're a lucky one." Hiram didn't rush. He didn't sigh out of boredom or look longingly
at his barn or pastures, where Tobias was sure he'd rather be.

"This doesn't feel lucky." Tobias, for one, would rather be anywhere but strapped to a bed and let out only for personal matters.
"What kind of man is laid up for days from a bonk to the head?"

"Blood loss. You'll heal much faster when you've restored your
supply—which could take up to a week. Ask Hannah how much
you need to restock. She spent hours washing it from clothes and
house. Your headache will lessen with time, rest, and fluids."

"What are you building?" Not wasting the strength to point,
he trusted Hiram to know what he meant. "Looks like a little
fence."

"A paddock for your son."

Tobias stopped moving and squinted at the stakes in the
ground.

Hiram's hand tightened around his waist. "It is your ribs? Do
they need wrapped again?"

"I'm fine." He wasn't fine. "You're building a cage for Luke?"
Tobias took a slow step forward on his own to prove he was better. The ground moved underneath him, and he leaned into Hiram, only until the yard quit rolling.

"It was Hannah's idea. She wants a place to keep a few lambs
corralled for Luke to play with when he's here, and we thought

it would be easier to manage without any of them wandering off, including your son." Hiram smiled at his work. "Clever, you think?"

Tobias waited at the foot of the steps and gathered the strength to lift his leg. "Not a bad idea." He got one leg up without grunting. "Except, I'm going home today."

Sweat gathered on his upper lip, and he wiped it with the back of his hand.

Hiram left him once he gripped the support of the front door.

Perhaps he'd rest a while this morning before making his case again.

Hannah hummed while she carried a plate of toast and eggs into her room. Oh . . . Mr. Franklin's room.

He's got a stronger claim to it than you, you goose.

Hush, it's still full of my things. Still my room. He's sleeping in my bed.

She bit her lips to keep from giggling at the absurdity of it. Was her future husband sleeping in her bed?

Goodness, child, back those horses up a mile or two.

He lay fully dressed above the covers on his stomach. Her white pillow trimmed with her hand-knitted lace covered his face. The crisp white contrasted the tanned skin of his hand that held the corner.

"Good morning, sleepyhead. Time for breakfast."

The only indication he'd heard her was a twitch of his two fingers, dipping the muscle along his forearm to his rolled-up sleeves.

She knelt near him and raised the corner of his shield. "Mr. Franklin, are you alive?"

He grunted, eyes closed, but she noted a hint of a smile. "Are the curtains shut?"

"Yes, and I rigged the quilt over the whole of it while you were snoring, so it's dark as a moonless night in here. At least, it will be when I close the door."

He didn't move. "I don't snore."

True, but she wouldn't tell him that. "I'll leave the food on the washstand. If it's not eaten within the hour, we will have words about it. Serious words."

He snorted. "Coffee?"

She started to tug the pillow down his back.

He gripped the other corner and kept it in place. "Mine."

"Actually, sir, it's mine. The bed is mine, the blankets are mine, and the lace on this pillowcase was stitched by my own hand." She had the urge to flick his forearm. She went so far as to form the circle with her thumb and middle finger.

He pushed the corner away from his face enough to look at her. "Is the coffee yours too?"

She flinched like she'd been caught being naughty and dropped her hand out of his line of sight. "Yes."

"Wanna share?"

Clearly, Luke learned from the very best. Father and son smiled and expected to get whatever they asked for.

Hannah rocked back on her heels, putting distance between them. It might make things uncomfortable for him if she acted on her impulse and ran her fingers through his hair. "Well, now, I don't know. I'm a bit put out this morning."

Hannah, dear, are you flirting?

She pushed down her mother's voice and carried on. "Hmm. I suppose I can make arrangements for coffee. I'm related to the head chef, you know. Second cousin thrice removed. It's hard to say. The family details are fuzzy. But just between you and me, she's a little hot-headed and hates having her kitchen imposed upon. Whiny, snoring patients asking for favors after the pot's been scrubbed and put away . . ." Sighing as if the world were ending, Hannah made a show of standing up. "I'll have to call in a favor to get another pot brewing."

He cracked an eye and barely lifted the corner of his mouth. "Thank you, Miss Benton. I'm honored you'd go to such lengths for me."

She *hmmph*'d with her nose in the air. "For you? No. But Hiram's going to town and will return with your sister in about an hour." The ruse over, Hannah relaxed and spoke normally, clasping her hands together at her waist. "Eloise is a dear, which you already know. I love her to death, and I've decided we're going to be the best of friends." Funny how her knee-jerk judgments of Eloise changed so quickly. "Our morning visits over a cup of coffee on the porch are the highlight of my days. I'll brew another pot soon and be sure to save you the dredges at least."

He dropped the pillow over his face and mumbled something about a toddler in a cage.

"What's that?" She leaned over and lifted the whole thing off his head.

He squinted, though the only light in the room filtered through the doorway. "Turn off the sun."

He was a whiny baby.

She smothered him again and closed the door. "You can come out of your cave. The doors are barred, guards posted, scouts are running the perimeter. It's safe." Hannah dared not move lest she trip in the darkness. "Can you see a thing?"

"I can." The bedframe squeaked. He gasped and slowly released a breath.

"Are you well?"

"Yep."

"You don't sound well."

"Miss Benton, it feels like a steel rod is jammed through my skull, and each movement and sound and thought jiggles this rod until a wall of darkness threatens to overtake me." He slowly moved to a sitting position against the headboard. "In the meantime, the very act of breathing, though necessary, is in itself trying to kill me. Rows of newly sharpened knives are being tested along my rib cage."

"Oh, is that all?" Her eyes adjusted somewhat to the bedroom interior, so she eased her way to the rocking chair.

Mr. Franklin rested his head against the wall and balanced his breakfast plate on his knee. From the looks of things, he hadn't bothered to lift a bite to his mouth. He angled his face toward her. "I'm sorry I don't have an appetite. Will you convey my apologies to the chef?"

"No, sir." She put her hands on the arms of the chair and rocked. "I'll do no such thing. Pulling strings for coffee is the length of my influence. If I return with a report of low appetite, she's apt to kill the messenger."

"I'll send a letter." His whining hadn't imposed on his sarcasm at least.

"Perfect! I'll slide it under her door when she's not looking."

"We could send it through the post. Save any suspicion of your involvement." Mr. Franklin dropped his knee and returned the plate to the washstand an arm's length away, no longer making a show of pushing the food around. The poor man must be in a world of pain.

Hannah stood, retrieved her drawing pad and a pencil from her bookshelf, and perched at the foot of the bed. "Take two bites, Mr. Franklin, and I'll be sure to put down your precise dictation."

"My dear Miss—" A forkful of eggs went to his mouth. He rested his head against the wall, and his eyes slid shut. After a moment, his Adam's apple bobbed. "Let it be known, though your food is so-so and does a fair job of filling the stomach, I shall not be partaking of it henceforth." He cracked an eye open at Hannah as she chewed her pencil. "You getting that?"

"Mmmhmm. A good, strong letter. You have experience letting people down easily?" The room was so dark that Hannah couldn't make out a single streak of lead on her paper. She scribbled a design along the edges and let her pencil go where it might with swirls and curlicues. She arched her back and adjusted her position until she rested against the footboard of the bed frame and pulled her knee all the way on the bed to sit in a more relaxed posture, sure to tuck her bare toes under her skirts.

"Furthermore." Mr. Franklin put the plate aside and scooted down until he lay flat on his back. "Until I get a sip of coffee, I refuse to play any more games. Forever yours, Mr. Tobias M. Franklin."

"What's the *M* for?" Hannah scratched unseen patterns on the page.

He dropped the pillow over his face, so his answer was barely audible. "Nothing—it's just an *M*."

"You jest." She signed his name with a flourish.

He said something else, but she couldn't make it out.

"What's that?"

He raised the edge of his pillow. "I said, 'I never jest. Wastes energy that'd be better spent sleeping.'"

"Shall I leave you to it? I thought I'd keep you company until Eloise arrives, but if you'd rather sleep, I'll go."

He rocked his stockinged foot on its heel and tapped it against her hip a few times where she sat on the end of his bed. *Her* bed. More mumbles came through the cotton and feathers over his face.

She put down the drawing pad and stood to leave. When she collected his plate, he exposed his face and spoke clearly. "How about it?"

"How about what?" She curled her toes, annoyed. "I don't enjoy speaking through pillows."

"You could crawl under here with me, and we'd hear each other quite well."

"Why, Mr. Franklin—" Her heart thrummed erratically.

"Stop." He chuckled, though his expression was hidden in the dim light. "That's not—" He wheezed, holding back more laughter. "I'm hiding from the light, is all."

She waved her hands around. "What light?"

"All of it. Phantom light . . . it doesn't hurt less under the pillow, but somehow it hurts more without it. Regardless, I ask, through a pile of feathers—my apologies—if it's all the same to you, would you mind reading aloud from one of your books again?"

Her stomach did a little flip-flop all on its own. Now, wasn't that interesting? She'd held his hand on and off during his fitful dreams the first night, she'd been in his presence for days, and she'd seen him in varying stages of undress. Doubtless, she'd been intrigued by the familiarity she and Mr. Franklin shared. They were becoming dear friends. Going on five days, and she was completely comfortable around him.

The stomach, and the flip-flopping . . . that was new. Why did this request to read feel more intimate than anything he'd asked of her yet? She'd been reading to him for days.

"Forget it." He dismissed her with a wave.

She'd been silent too long.

"You've got better things to do than entertain me. Let me rest, actually. You can post the note to your relation thrice removed. Be sure to tell her I'm going home today, and she needn't worry herself about tomorrow's breakfast."

"You're not going home today." Hannah absently straightened the blanket under his legs. "Hiram says you can't go until— I can't say any more, else you'll do something stupid." She cleared her throat. "What would you have me read?"

"Hiram says I can't go until I can what? When will I be released?"

"It's not important." She felt along the edge of her bookshelf.

"It *is* important. I have a job, woman." His pillow hit her in the back.

She'd not even heard him throw it.

"I have an entire company to run. I have a son. Do you know, this is the longest we've ever been apart? Until this very week, I've been home for his bedtime every single night since his mother died. Haven't missed a one." His voice tightened. "I don't like it. Not one bit. I'm going home as soon as I can. Now, give me that pillow back."

"Your foreman. Mr. Dee Williams? He's visited twice, and he assured me everything's running well, and they're managing fine without you." She picked the pillow from the floor and hugged it to her chest. "Luke and Eloise visit every day."

"It's not the same."

"I'm sure it isn't." If she could offer solace to his pain she would. "You need to heal first, or you won't be any good to anyone. Let me read. It will help take your mind off things. What would you like to hear?"

"Don't bother. I wasn't thinking." He reached out his hand, and she reluctantly returned the pillow. "I'm fine. I'm sure you have other things to do." He was back in his pillow cave.

"I don't, though. I would like to read to you." She sounded more desperate than she intended. "I enjoy it."

He was quiet for a long time, and she wondered if he'd heard her. Then, in a burst of energy, he yanked his face free and snapped at her. "What would you be doing if I weren't laid up in your room?"

Hannah sighed. Maybe she should leave the grumpy man alone. "Let's see. I'd been here a whopping two days before you joined us. I'm only here to play and keep house for Hiram. It's not a demanding job. I've already fed the chickens, and the bread's rising. No laundry until next Monday." She tapped her chin. "Hmm. I could pull weeds in the garden, or I suppose I could scrub the floors again if I had a mind to, which I don't. I've had enough scrubbing after the mess we brought in Sunday afternoon, thank you very much."

Her book friends were familiar to her, even though she couldn't read the spines in the dark. "If you weren't here, I might go to the pasture and see if any lambs want to play with me." Repressing a giggle at the memory of how this week began with Mr. Knightley's proposal and the snake, she pulled a book out of line. "Have you ever read *Emma* by Jane Austen?"

"Sounds like a girly book." He closed the conversation by dropping the pillow over his face.

Her shoulders sank, and she tucked the corner of the book between its neighbors.

"I'll keep this over my face."

She spun toward him, and he grinned, a hand lifting his cave door.

His voice was light, unmuffled. "Then you can bring in as much light as you need. I can hear you fine from under here. Hey, if I snore, just attribute it to the soothing quality of your lovely voice."

She didn't bother to hide her smile. Let him see how happy she was. "You don't snore."

"Wake me when my family gets here. Please. Thank you." Down went the pillow.

She opened the bedroom door, and light streamed in from the living room. It was enough if she angled her rocking chair to keep her back to the door. She cleared her throat and began. "Emma Woodhouse, handsome, clever, and rich, with a comfortable home and happy disposition, seemed to unite some of the best blessings of existence, and had lived nearly twenty-one years in the world with very little to distress or vex her."

"I hate her already. Sounds spoiled."

"Hush, or I shan't continue." She waited.

He waved a finger in her direction and then went still.

"She was the youngest of the two daughters of a most affectionate, indulgent father—"

"Ha! Told you. Spoiled."

Hannah smiled but continued without reproach. She wondered how long Mr. Franklin would put up with this *girly* book. "—a most affectionate, indulgent father, and had, in consequence of her sister's marriage, been mistress of his house from an early period . . ."

Chapter 14

A comfortable, happy, and sturdy disposition, good health, and all-around stubbornness had kept Tobias from the hospital for his own care up to this point in his twenty-four years of existence. After most of a week, his concussion lessened insofar as he no longer saw double, he slept less, and could make his own way to the outhouse. A near-constant pain lingered.

Saturday morning, Hiram deemed him healed enough for the ride into town after Tobias made a few successful walks around the yard and sat through a meal at the kitchen table without any of it coming up afterward. Grateful to be released, Tobias could have done without lying on a bed of hay in the wagon like a dying man. He was glad none of his crew witnessed the shame of it.

Tobias sat on an examining table while Dr. Farley, a large man in his sixties with a fuzzy white beard and thick sideburns, pressed a long funnel to Tobias's back. "Deep breath in." He adjusted the contraption and moved it to another location. "Luke's doing well? I like to see him scampering across town with Miss Eloise." He'd built the hospital eighteen years ago, hired more doctors and nurses who worked with him, made his own house calls, and still managed to keep track of everyone who walked by the window of his front office. "She appears to have a special interest in the bakery of late."

"That's true enough." Tobias smiled. "Thankfully the new baker gives her a discount, or my savings would be thrown out the window at her newfound sweet tooth." He winced when Dr. Farley pressed along his ribs.

He was here to ask if the doctor had any experience with head trauma. If nothing else, a new packet of headache powders would take the edges off now and then and allow for a restful sleep. Since he hadn't been asked to remove anything, Miss Benton stood in the corner like a hovering mother dog taking her puppy out for his first walk. Tobias winked, trying to coax a smile out of her.

Hiram had driven them to town, helped him off the wagon, and saw to other errands. Tobias thought nothing of it when Miss Benton remained at his side, though there was no reason for her to have followed him.

She wore a forest-green skirt and a white blouse trimmed to hug all the right places. The toe of a black boot tapped under her skirt. He hadn't seen her in shoes very often, and she'd done up her hair this morning in a new style. He'd watched her brush out the long dark strands in front of the mirror in the bedroom while he'd waited on the sofa. She'd left the door open while they talked, and since Hiram had been in and out of the house all morning, Tobias supposed it was okay. After all, he'd witnessed her put her hair up, not take it down . . .

"Deep breath out." Dr. Farley reminded Tobias he wasn't here to stare at a lovely woman.

Her expression was very unlike what he'd come to expect over the past week. Since when was she serene? She blinked and released him from the trap of her stormy-gray eyes.

Tobias controlled his breathing to avoid any telltale wincing. Miss Benton would never let him go if he couldn't sit through a simple examination.

He sought her gaze again, but she watched Dr. Farley like a hungry lion. Tobias had gotten used to her being within earshot for a week, and it'd gone to his head. If there was one blessing from his injury it was the friendship he'd gained in the Bentons, but it was past time he returned to work.

Hmm . . . they had a remainder of at least three or four books to finish. He could ask to borrow them . . . no, the pain behind his eyes would never do for reading. Maybe she'd be willing to come over . . .

Grow up, man. You don't need a nursemaid.

Dr. Farley patted him on the shoulder. "Very good. No fluid in the lungs."

Miss Benton stepped forward and put a hand on Tobias's forearm, not unlike a protective mother. "Dr. Farley, if I may." She assumed that regal posture he'd come to recognize. The one where she straightened her shoulders and put on airs.

Tobias smiled, and a warmness washed through him.

She'd often take that pose when reading, depending on the character's persona. This was Emma Woodhouse. He'd put money on it. Dad-blame, but she was beautiful when she did that. Stunning, in fact. Though he'd listened to much of *Emma* from under a pillow, he'd found himself watching Miss Benton read on more than one occasion, paying more attention to the reader than what was being read.

He tried to wipe the smirk from his face. No matter what argument she was about to start with Dr. Farley, Tobias knew from experience that nothing would alter Dr. Farley's opinion once it was set. A calmness always permeated the doctor's interactions. He wasn't prone to fits, but he was a stubborn old dog and rarely changed his mind. The doctor paused in his examination and took notice of Miss Benton.

She wrapped her ungloved fingers around Tobias's arm, and the heat of it spread to his chest. He tucked the fingers of his opposite hand under his thigh to keep from taking her hand in his. That would never do.

"My brother performed a thorough examination and has been closely monitoring Mr. Franklin's condition. We've never had any concern of internal injuries." She neither lowered her eyes nor showed any sign of backing down. "As Mr. Franklin explained when we arrived, we're interested in your opinion as to his sensitivity to light and continual head pain. Is this common for a concussion, or should we be concerned about something more serious?"

Tobias fought the urge to wrap her in a big ol' hug, ruffle her hair, and tell her to have some tea with that sass.

Dr. Farley smiled tightly and shooed her away as one might a chicken. "Step aside, please, Miss Benton, and let me continue."

She didn't move.

Tobias raised his eyebrows. What would his guard dog of a nursemaid do now? What would Emma Woodhouse do?

The doctor's tone turned serious. "Your brother clearly has medical training, but as I am in a hospital with my license framed on the wall, and he is a sheep farmer, I will make my own assessments." He looked pointedly at the corner she'd previously occupied.

She gripped Tobias's arm as she turned to him and pleaded with her eyes, almost begging him to take up the fight. Tobias shrugged but said nothing. She could hoist the banner if she wished, but his opinion was simple. The sooner he passed this examination, the sooner he could go home, be with his family, and return to work.

Miss Benton pursed her lips but dipped her head to Dr. Farley in acquiescence. *Great—now I've let her down by not siding with her.*

Dr. Farley stored the tools he'd been using. "Miss Benton, will you be so kind to fetch my nurse, Mrs. Klein?"

Her eyes darted between Tobias and the doctor. She looked likely to refuse. Silly woman. *Guard dog* wasn't a strong enough descriptor. *Soldier under orders*, perhaps. Tobias nodded for her to go on, and only then did she leave.

Dr. Farley blew out a breath. "Lie down, if you please. We're going to try to bring you relief. You'll be feeling better by tomorrow."

Tobias shuffled on the padded table, slowly lowered himself to his side, and rolled to his back. It was a painful process. He rested his eyes and thought happily of returning to his own bed after this. His upstairs bedroom wouldn't be much of a problem. There would be less lace and nobody to tease him if he snored.

Nobody coming in at all hours of the day to pester him. No, of course not, because he'd be at work. Where he should be.

Miss Benton followed a stern woman with graying temples in a white cap into the room.

"Mrs. Klein, we're going to utilize bloodletting to aid in the release of his lingering head pain." Dr. Farley brushed aside a lock of Tobias's hair at the scalp. "See along the side of his head, he's had a row of stitches put in. They're healing well, and I see no sign of infection, but take care not to disturb them. Bring a bowl and the kit from the supply closet, please."

"Very good, sir."

"Dr. Farley." Miss Benton was on Tobias's other side. "I have to disagree. Respectfully, sir. What do you hope to gain?"

The doctor clunked a bottle of ether on his side table. "Miss Benton, your assistance is not required. Please make yourself comfortable in the waiting room. You'll find a stack of *McCall's* to occupy yourself."

The look of disgust that washed over her face was missed by the doctor, who had his back turned. She moved closer and put a hand on Tobias's shoulder. "You don't have to go through with this." The midday sun streamed through the window high on the wall, glinting off her dark hair. Her focus speared him. "You must know this is a barbaric practice with little supporting evidence—"

"Miss Benton." Dr. Farley snapped at her. "If you please." He held a bottle in one hand and a cloth in the other. "Tobias, if you can't control your fiancée, she cannot remain here."

"I don't aim to control her, Doctor, and she's not my fiancée," said Tobias with a smile, enjoying how her cheeks turned pale and the snap in her gray eyes.

Miss Benton was speechless for once, and the shock displayed across her face was something new. It was short-lived, though, for she pursed her lips and steeled her features. "Dr. Farley, I really must protest." Her hand traveled down his shoulder, and her fingers dug into his bicep.

Out of reflex, he tightened his muscles under her hand.

The two argued over Tobias's prone body.

"If you were undergoing the procedure, you would have some say in the matter. But you're not. And if you are of no relation to Tobias, why are you here?" Dr. Farley looked down at Tobias skeptically.

Before things got any worse, Tobias reached across his body with his free arm and patted her hand. "She can stay."

The doctor said nothing more until Mrs. Klein returned with a bowl. Inside lay a coil of tubing and a long needle.

Miss Benton leaned over Tobias. "Please, don't do this." She lowered herself to mere inches from his ear. "Mr. Franklin, let me fetch Hiram. This has the potential to do significantly more harm than good." Her breath tickled his neck. "I beg of you, wait until you speak to Hiram."

Tobias raised his hand to her cheek. "It's going to be fine." He offered his best reassuring smile, while his thumb caressed her cheekbone.

She stood abruptly and brushed her fingers along the side of her face where his had been a moment before.

"I've known Dr. Farley practically my whole life. He was there when Luke was born, and there at the last when Katie died. If he thinks this is the best course of action, I'll go along with it."

"But you can't!" She wrung her hands and looked frantically between him, Dr. Farley, Mrs. Klein, and the window. Perhaps she searched for a timely appearance of Hiram to support her arguments—hopefully not planning an emergency escape. Her regal posture had slipped, and desperation was now forefront.

He didn't want to hurt her, but this wasn't her battle to fight. "If this can get me back to work and my family sooner, I'm going to try it." Tobias nodded to Dr. Farley. "Please excuse us for a minute."

Dr. Farley didn't appear to have heard him at first, then raised a hand. "Thirty seconds, and I must get on with it. I have other appointments waiting."

As soon as they were alone, Miss Benton immediately took up Tobias's hand and held it between both of hers. "I'm begging you, Mr. Franklin. Don't do this."

The pulsing against his temples strengthened. He wanted this over with. "I'm not asking you to have it done. I'll not even ask you to watch. It's me, not you. Can you let me handle it?" His voice rose, and he gripped her hand. He grew irritated when she pursed her lips and shook her head in defiance. "Why are you so worried about me? I'm not a child in want of a nursemaid."

He pulled his hand free and pointed a finger at her. "If there's a chance this will work, I'm taking it!" He was near shouting by the end of his little tirade, and he almost felt remorse at his outburst until she shouted back.

"What if I'm right? What if it does more harm than good?" Her fists rested on the examining table by his shoulder, and she leaned over him.

Tobias closed his eyes and waited until his pulse slowed so he could speak calmly. "I don't know how that's possible at this point, and I don't think Dr. Farley would suggest it if that were likely."

She dashed a hand over her eyes. "I feel responsible for you."

"Miss Benton, you've paid any debt you think you may have owed." He offered his hand, but she'd turned aside. "I never blamed you for my accident. It could've happened to anyone. You've fed me, kept me comfortable and entertained for days. Consider your job done. I don't know if this procedure will help, but it certainly can't do much harm. Let Dr. Farley do his job."

As if on cue, a tap at the door announced the doctor and Mrs. Klein's entrance. The doctor looked at Tobias and ignored Miss Benton entirely. "Shall we proceed?"

Tobias nodded. He spoke softly, watching Miss Benton. "We shall."

Her eyes met his while Mrs. Klein prepared the room and adjusted his head. The sting of ether bit his nose, and he was about to ask if it was necessary when Miss Benton stepped forward, chin jutted determinedly.

"You can't do this." She addressed everyone in the room.

Dr. Farley dropped the damp cloth over Tobias's mouth and nose. Then he put his large hands on Miss Benton's shoulders and forcefully removed her from the room. The pounding of her fists on the door melded and swirled together with the drums beating inside his skull.

Darkness washed over him.

Chapter 15

Hannah attended her first church service in Ockelbo with a hollow resignation because she knew Mr. Franklin wouldn't be there. He was resting in his own home now, and good riddance to him. She sat next to Hiram near the center of the left section and had trouble listening to a word of the message. This was especially true once Luke spotted her from three rows ahead.

The boy popped over Zeke's shoulder next to Eloise and waved at Hannah repeatedly. Zeke grabbed Luke's arm and turned him around. Luke spent forty-five seconds on Zeke's lap and then launched himself at Eloise, swiping at her hat.

Eloise blocked him without turning her head. Soon Luke squirmed around and peekabooed over the back of the pew at Hannah. He was quiet but oh-so-wiggly.

Hannah did not even try to keep a proper expression on her face. It was a good thing Mother couldn't see her making bug eyes and sticking her tongue to the side at the blond little imp. Hiram elbowed her once or twice when her own giggles slipped out.

After the service, everyone was very welcoming. Pastor Bernas and his wife introduced themselves. She met a handful of men from the brickyard who peppered her with questions about Boss while jostling and winking at each other. Her face warmed at their insinuation that he played sick only for the nurse, but she was hardly able to get in a word before a man with a sassy smile stepped forward.

"May I come a'courting, Miss Benton?"

She laughed. "Oh!"

He was pushed aside by another with untamed copper curls and freckles across his smiling cheeks. "Jonas, she'd never go for a man like you. It's brains she's after. Pleasure to meet you, miss. Charles Grady." He offered his elbow, and the other men scuffed their feet and smiled. None spoke over Mr. Grady.

He was a fine-looking man with twinkling green eyes. He leaned closer, pulling her hesitant hand through the crook of his elbow. "We've been mighty concerned about Boss this week. We're grateful he's been well cared for."

Hannah ducked her chin. This had never happened in the city with Mother hovering and sending evil glares at the men who dared speak to her.

Hiram, the lucky one, was free to walk about and speak with friends, but Mother was never more than a few feet from Hannah when they were out. Few were brave enough to challenge her hawk eyes.

"Very true, Miss Benton." A shorter man spoke up. "Charlie here speaks for all of us. Seeing you in the flesh, you're a vision of a ministering angel."

A blond man with a peeling sunburn jockeyed in front of the speaker. "An angel. Sent directly from God to care for our fallen leader." The group snickered, crowding nearer, speaking over one another.

"I wish it'd been me."

"I'd be nursed by you any day."

Over their shoulders she caught the curious gaze of a dark-haired gentleman in a black suit. A very nice suit. His hair was neatly greased and combed. She smiled at him too, and he lifted a hand with a half-smile.

Mr. Grady tugged her elbow, pulling her tightly to his side. "So how 'bout it?"

"Well." Hannah let her gaze drift over all of them. Perhaps this is what her mother meant by the Wild West. It wasn't so bad. Quite thrilling, actually. Though she knew she should put a stop to it before the boys got out of hand. "I'm flattered. The fact is, you see, I have a prior—"

The man in the suit stepped forward. "Good morning, Miss Benton." That's all it took for the crowd around her to disperse.

Even Mr. Grady dropped her arm and slunk off, mumbling, "We'll talk later."

"Hello. Mr. . . . ?" Hannah was intrigued by the unspoken pecking order the men assumed.

"Johanson." He spoke softly, respectfully. "Were they giving you trouble?" He nodded to the others who were disappearing out the door.

"Oh, no, just a friendly welcome. They've been concerned about Mr. Franklin, you see."

Mr. Johanson's lips pulled to a tight smile, and he shook his head. "With a face like yours, pardon me, but I'd be cautious of their attention. That group is known for rowdy behavior."

Hannah dipped her head. "Thank you for the warning." Her words came out tighter than she intended. *And who's to vouch for your behavior, Mr. Fancy Suit?*

It seemed half the church members descended on her after that.

She answered questions about her plans for the summer, how she enjoyed the country so far, and how Mr. Franklin, rather *Boss*, was improving. There were many looks of horror from the women when she described the snake incident. She scanned the crowd for Hiram. He stood near the door and smiled ruefully when she caught his eye.

Overall, it was a very pleasant first service, despite a certain Mr. Someone's absence.

Her spirits soared by the time Hiram helped her into the wagon. She nodded to him, a queen acknowledging her footman.

"Don't let it go to your head, Your Grace." Hiram bowed. "You're new—that's all."

"Where there is carrion, the vultures will gather?"

After pushing her skirts away from the wagon wheel, he looked up at her. "Precisely."

"I'm meeting with Eloise this evening. She promised to show me her pattern for the quilt she's making for Luke."

Hiram looked at her sideways, settling onto the buckboard.

"I can drive myself if you hitch the wagon. Or I'll walk." She avoided meeting his gaze, not sure about her odd feelings of guilt.

"Around four o'clock, and I'll stay for the evening service at six."

"Don't overstay your welcome," Hiram groused.

"I'll make cookies."

He snorted. "Hannah, he's fine. He'll be weak again for a few days, and he'll recover."

"Do you think he's going to try to go to work tomorrow?"

"He will."

"Men." She lifted her hands. "I'm going. And I'll walk. I'll make a double batch of cookies and leave a whole two dozen for you." Hannah didn't need a bossy brother telling her where she could go. She *was* going to visit Eloise. If Mr. Franklin happened to live in the same house as her very good friend Eloise, that was no fault of Hannah's.

After days, six of them to be exact, of visiting her very good friend, Hannah had still not laid eyes on her very good friend's brother. Not that she was upset about it. *Hmph*, yes. She wouldn't be able to maintain the nonchalance around Eloise much longer. Today, they shared *fika* on Eloise's porch, the lovely Swedish pastime of coffee and a treat with friends.

"I can only reassure you of his health so often, Hannah. Why don't you go see him at the brickyard?" Eloise smiled at Hannah over her coffee on Friday morning. "Calm your fears."

Her last view of Mr. Franklin with a cloth draped over his face made her shudder each time she remembered it. He was wrong. She was right. But that truth didn't keep her from angst, because she knew how the blockhead likely pushed himself.

"He gets himself to work and back every day. He's obviously fine."

Hannah envisioned the stubborn man hobbling home, barely lurching from one hitching post to the next. Mr. Franklin keeled over into the mud, desperately crawling home on his hands and knees, so weakened from blood loss. *Hannah, my love!* Tears pooled and dripped from his icy blue eyes. *If only I'd trusted your wise counsel!* Slumping to the ground, he fainted.

Hannah bounced Luke on her lap, flinging away her depressing daydreams. "I'm not afraid for his health."

I'm terrified that he hates me for interfering and probably doesn't want to see me again. Ever.

Holding her cup away from the boy's reach, she considered Eloise's suggestion. "I wouldn't be in the way at the brickyard?"

"Goodness, no," Eloise said. "Luke and I visit all the time. We used to, anyhow. I've enjoyed our visits with you this week instead." She shrugged one shoulder. "He's usually bent over his desk, buried in paperwork during the lunch hour, scribbling away. He welcomes the distraction. That's what I tell myself anyway."

"He's probably very good at it."

"Paperwork? I thought you'd know him better than that!"

Hannah's cheeks warmed. "I meant running the place. He's cut out for it. The men I met Sunday seemed genuinely concerned about him."

"Hmm." Eloise sipped her coffee. "They were genuinely concerned about something else, I'd say."

"Does he speak of me?" Hannah averted her eyes, knowing how desperate she sounded. "It's just that . . . oh, dash-it-all, our last interaction was strained. You could say we fought. We did.

We fought, and I don't think Mr. Franklin will want to see me again." Hannah waved a fly that buzzed near her plate of day-old cardamom rolls Zeke had brought from Anderson's Bakery. "I don't want to make myself a nuisance, but—"

Eloise cocked her head. "He's not been himself, Hannah. Not since we brought him home. He pushes his food around and goes to his room. Honestly, I've hardly seen him more than you have." She nodded firmly. "One of us should definitely check on him at work, I think."

"He's in a good deal of pain?"

"I believe so, but he doesn't speak of it."

"Oh, blimey."

Luke smacked the table. "Blimey!"

Laughing, Hannah covered Luke's mouth with her hand. "Shush, child. You'll have me in trouble."

Eloise tried to distract Luke with a wooden train, but he wasn't interested. "Did you hear Mrs. Williams had her baby?"

"The foreman's wife?"

"Yes, I haven't been to see him yet, but Dee's stayed home to help with the children. This is their seventh. I guess she wasn't able to get things set up beforehand like she normally does because he arrived early."

"What's his name?"

"Something Old Testament. Johash? Don't repeat that—I'm not sure of it."

"I'm going to name my firstborn Jehoiakim Abimelech."

Eloise coughed into her napkin and waved her hand, choking on a mouthful of coffee. "Hannah, you're a goose."

Hannah smiled. "The second will be Jerusalem Obadiah." She refrained from adding any last names to this game.

Luke busied himself picking apart a roll and dropping the crumbs onto the table. His tiny fingers pinched another crumb and shoved it into Hannah's mouth.

Her muffled cry of surprise goaded him into doing it again. "Stop it, child. If you're going to feed me, at least give me enough to chew." She smothered him with kisses, working her way into the crease of his neck until he squealed.

Eloise rested her empty cup on the table. "We should bring her something. Mrs. Williams."

Hannah let Luke catch his breath. "A pie? A pan of breakfast rolls? Soup?"

Eloise squished up her nose. "Oh, dear. Tobias says I'm not to bake anymore."

Hannah barked a laugh. "Nonsense. He's not the boss of us. I'll help you."

"If you say so. But only if you promise to take all the blame if this doesn't go well. I have a . . . reputation."

Standing with Luke on her hip and shaking off an entire roll's worth of crumbs, Hannah pointed an accusing finger at Eloise. "I promise nothing because it will go well, and you can take all the credit. Reputations can be false opinions of past failures. Let's be about it, then. Daylight's a-wasting. You can deliver it in time for lunch, and I'll check in on your insufferable brother."

Plans in place, Hannah danced into the house. Determination didn't begin to describe her current state. She would discover where she and Mr. Franklin stood, and the wheels were already turning toward the next step. "Eloise, I'd like to stay for dinner. How do you feel about chicken? I'll stop at the butcher on the way back from the brickyard and see what's available."

Chapter 16

The door was open when Hannah arrived, but Mr. Franklin wasn't bent over his desk scribbling or otherwise. Her breath lodged in her throat at the sight of his prone figure on the floor. Frozen, her gaze traveled along his clay-encrusted boots, skimmed over his legs, and jumped to his face—half covered by an arm thrown over his eyes. A moment's inspection confirmed the rise and fall of his chest.

The rustle of her skirts made the only noise when she knelt at his side, which was nothing compared to the cacophony of the work site, but he must have heard, for he lifted a finger toward her in greeting.

Her hands automatically reached for him, though she redirected them to her lap and began tugging off her gloves. "Mr. Franklin?"

A quirk of a smile pulled his lips. "Come to gloat?"

"Never," she said. "I only wish you'd listened. Given yourself more time to rest."

"I don't have time for . . . time . . ."

She *hmmphed* loud enough to make sure he heard how much she disagreed with him.

Instead of arguing, he moved his arm toward her—not the one over his eyes. He rested his hand on her knee, and his thumb casually moved back and forth. He had never done that before. "They told me what you tried to do to Dr. Farley."

"And did they tell you what he did to me?" She gripped her fingers together, not touching him, as the warmth of his hand burned through her skirts to her knee. "Hauled me out and barred the door. Pardon me, but I'll say it again. Bloodletting is a barbaric practice, and I won't stand for it. Not for anyone, and especially not—" Hannah snapped her mouth shut. *For someone I intend to marry.* Had she really almost spoken those words out loud?

"What's that?" His finger tapped her knee.

"Especially not you."

"Hm." He flipped his hand palm up on her lap, inviting her to take it.

She gingerly placed her hand in his, and he curled his fingers, holding tight.

"I heard the commotion before I went under." His voice was quiet. Tired. "Sounded like a wildcat fighting a . . . oh, a big furry whale. You didn't stand a chance."

They were holding hands. What did this mean? If he wasn't going to mention it, neither would she, but, oh, how her stomach flipped, and her heart warmed. It felt *right*.

She forced herself to stay on topic, which wasn't too difficult based on her annoyance with the doctor. "If I have anything to say about it, Dr. Farley will soon be looking for a new profession."

"Good luck. He's delivered most of the babies in this town. He might be older than Kevin."

"How old is Kevin?"

"Ancient."

His hand cradling hers soothed her. This was completely different than when she'd taken his hand while he slept. That offered comfort. This was . . . was what? What did this mean? There was no book of instructions for post-recovery affection.

The man was lying on the floor, blocking the light from his eyes, probably in a good amount of pain, and holding her hand.

Her pulse increased.

"Thank you," he said quietly. His tan, work-calloused fingers were dark against hers. "If it's any consolation, it didn't work. You were right."

"I usually am."

"Head still hurts as bad as ever."

"You need to rest." She pushed because his tired voice worried her. "Rest, fluids, and anything else you can do to encourage healing. You lost enough blood from the accident, for which I can't help but feel responsible." She grimaced at the image of him face-down in the mud. "You lay there, practically lifeless, the blood pouring out the side of your head. I had quite the trouble keeping it in. You know I held you together while Hiram sewed you up? Pushed the skin closed so he could get in the stitches without it tearing."

She lowered her voice. "The experience has only confirmed that, though I enjoy the science and reading of it in journals,

I will not be pursuing a career in the medical field. Then a week later, to have someone bleed cups of it from the back of your head? The medieval logic astounds me. If he was concerned about brain swelling, he should have punctured a hole through the skull. Which could kill you if done wrong or leave you a drooling fool the rest of your life. Dr. Farley is incompetent. You know my father could do it, but he's the only one I'd trust."

Dirt crunched under the boot of a man striding by the door; then all was quiet again.

"Have I told you about the time my father removed the tumor from behind a man's eye? The gentleman was up walking the very next day. The very next day! Everyone was astounded, but not me. No, my father's skill as a surgeon is unparalleled."

Mr. Franklin lay still.

"Sorry, did I say I wasn't going to gloat?" She would have thought him asleep if not for the firm grip of his hand around hers. "Talk to me—I need to know you're okay." Hannah squeezed his hand.

He tightened his hold and hummed an exhale. "I used to replace the oil in Eloise's bedroom lamp with water." The man didn't even smile. "I did it on three separate occasions before she fussed at Mama about it."

"Brothers are terrible."

"They're wonderful. Sisters, now—*pfft*—always running to Mama for every little thing. Tell me something. How did you cope with a brother?" His thumb trailed over her knuckles. "Why do I get the feeling it was you causing all the mischief instead of your twin?"

"It was—is. Hiram is an old, gentle soul." Hannah wanted to continue like this. She wanted to sit in the cool, brick office, holding his hand, and do nothing else. Did he feel the same? Every point of skin-on-skin connection buzzed. She didn't feel his hand but his palm pressed against hers and each finger as it lay against the back of her hand.

"Hiram doesn't cause mischief?"

"Not if he can help it." They'd fallen into the ease of conversation they'd established last week with no hard feelings left over from the argument at the hospital . . . with the minor addition of hand-holding. *What does this mean?*

"But you?"

She opened her mouth to tell him more and shut it again. How far did she trust him? Probably more than anyone. "I dream. I—and this is a secret. You can't go spreading this in mixed company. Promise?"

"Sure, I promise."

"I make up . . . things. Stories. Adventures. When I'm stressed, or bored, or overwhelmed. Most often when Mother is around, I escape into my head, creating elaborate scenarios where I'm— where I'm in control, I guess. I fight dragons or tame them to fly over forests, hunt lions in India, wrangle snakes . . ."

The muffled sounds of the work carrying on outside faded, and all she heard was Mr. Franklin's soft breathing, and all she felt was his hand around hers. "Is that too strange?"

"No," he murmured. "It's beautiful. I hope you let me into your next story. We could defeat the dragons together. Or fly on them." His tone was amiable enough, but he didn't move, didn't chuckle, didn't twitch his foot, didn't sigh.

"You're in too much pain to be here," Hannah said. "Can you call it a day?"

His thumb caressed the valley where two of her fingers met. The obstinate man tried to console her. But his simple touch killed any other admonishments on her tongue.

What would you do if I leaned forward and kissed you smack on the lips?

His lips curled into a smile as if reading her very thoughts, and heat crawled up her neck.

"Just a trifling pain, nothing I can't handle. I was resting before you interrupted. Isn't that what you ordered? Besides, as soon as I finish the books for the week, I'll be done."

"*Trifling* pain wouldn't have you on the floor, Mr. Franklin. The books can wait."

"The men can't. They need paid, and with Williams out for a week—rotten timing to have another baby if you ask me."

"Nobody asked you."

He adjusted the arm over his eyes and peered at her from the shadow. "Pull the curtain, will you? The light."

She released his hand. After darkening the room, she settled next to him on the floor with her legs curled to the side.

Rays of light snuck through the edge of the window. A bright pin of sunshine speared the keyhole, and it flooded under and around the door left open a crack. It was dark enough to be improper. She pretended it wasn't already improper that she'd shown up at his workplace uninvited and entered his office without knocking. With the lack of proper lighting, nobody would be doing the books.

Once her eyes adjusted, she could see well enough. He'd removed his arm from his eyes but kept them closed.

Her hand wanted his again, but he'd buried them both in his trouser pockets. Impulsively, she brushed her fingers across his forehead.

He sucked in a breath, and she froze.

"Sorry." Her hand hovered.

"Do that again. It helps."

Slowly, she traced a path with her fingers from one temple along the smooth skin above his eyebrows and back. The tension around his eyes relaxed with each breath. She combed her fingers through his hair and gently massaged his scalp. His thick, brown hair slid through her fingers. She trailed circles around his temples, careful to avoid the stitches above his ear. A few minutes later, she noticed his eyes were open, watching her with an unreadable expression.

He reached up and took her hands in both of his. "Why are you here?"

She looked into his eyes while fragments of a dozen answers slipped through her mind. *I'm here because I feel responsible . . . because I want to be near you . . . Eloise told me to . . . I miss you . . . I'm sad I yelled at you last week . . . I wanted to see for myself if you were okay . . . I'm falling terribly in love with you, and I don't know what to do about it.*

She blinked. "The same as you."

A sudden smile spread across his face. "You're ensuring the men are paid by the end of the day?"

"Something like that." She tugged against his grasp while avoiding his eyes.

He tightened his hold a moment before releasing her. "Go home," he said gently.

"How often are you on the floor?"

"Only as often as you come to spy on me. It's a ruse to coerce you into making more cookies. Is it working?"

He liked the cookies! So even though he'd been holed upstairs in his room during her Sunday visit, he wasn't unaware. A wash of smugness spread through her.

He sat up, mostly hiding the wince of pain. "See? I'm fine. Off with you."

Maybe another batch of cookies would help turn his heart. "Mr. Franklin, how old are you?"

He raised an eyebrow. "Is this another test? I'm twenty-four. And William Evarts is Secretary of State, appointed by President Hayes, and our minister to Sweden is John Leav—"

"Shush. I know your faculties are in order. There's no call to show off. Twenty-four and running an entire company by yourself."

"Not by myself. There are more than a dozen men working for me."

"I said, shush. They work *for* you. They get paid when you pay them. Stop interrupting. You're running Franklin Brickworks by yourself."

"My foreman, Dee Williams—"

"Just had his seventh baby! His wife felt poorly the entire last month. You said so yourself when you were at my house, and Eloise mentioned it again today that he's less reliable during his wife's confinement. Now, will you be quiet? You've been working diligently for years. Years! You took over when your father died. You were how old?"

He gave her a flat look.

"You were nineteen? Twenty?"

He feigned surprise, mouthing, *Am I allowed to talk?*

"Answer the questions."

"I was nineteen. And?"

"You were a baby." She put her hand over his where it rested near her.

He pulled it away and ran his hands through his hair. "Was not." He sighed, loudly for him. Apparently she'd hit a nerve. "Woman, I don't have the energy to spar with you today." He dropped his hands in his lap and angled to rest his back against the side of the massive oak desk with eyes closed.

She tried to speak with more compassion moving forward. "From what Eloise says, you took over a company of three employees, and in five years you turned it into a full-fledged, thriving business that supports fifteen men full-time with more during peak season."

"Did my dear sister mention how those full-fledged, thriving men need paid, Miss Nosy? If you don't mind, I'm going to see to their accounts."

"You can't possibly."

"Watch me." He opened his eyes and leveled her with a look, daring her to stop him.

"Mr. Franklin! You can't even open your eyes without the curtains pulled shut. How in the blazes do you expect to finish this today?" She paused to catch her breath, realizing her voice had notched up higher than she'd intended. Glancing at the door, she leaned closer and whispered sternly. "I'm trying to convince you that you've handled everything very well, but it's time you put some things in place that will allow you to take a break. You don't have to be the one doing everything. This company could run very well with a few simple—"

His expression stopped her mid-thought with a slow, knowing smile. One that started with just a quirk of his lips before lighting up his whole face. A man had never looked at her like that before. Mr. Franklin had the most fetching smile she'd ever seen. How could she lecture a man looking at her like that?

She coughed in an attempt to cover her stutter but was afraid he saw right through her. Could he hear her heart chasing after him? Beating a quiet rhythm of her hidden confessions? *I love you. I love you. I love you.*

She pressed her hands against her flushed cheeks.

"Are you asking to be hired as my secretary?" He heaved to his feet and reached for her hand. "I've never had one before. I've heard they can be helpful." Once they were both standing, he twined his fingers with hers, which set free a whole passel of butterflies. The white ones that fluttered around the prairie, hardly ever landing.

He stepped closer. "Miss Benton?"

"Mmmhm?" She dared not move. Coherent thoughts evaded her. Speaking was out of the question.

"Come here." He dropped her hand and wrapped his arms around her.

In awkward, jerky motions, she hooked her hands behind his back. She'd never been hugged by a man other than Hiram. Mother and Father weren't even in the habit of it since she'd been a young child.

Hannah *fit* in his arms. She melted slightly, resting her cheek on his shoulder, and his hand was firm between her shoulder blades. He smelled of lamp oil, bay-rum aftershave, and sun-dried cotton.

"I've missed you," he said, his breath warm against her neck. "Am I allowed to say that? I got used to your unconscious humming, your reading. Your incessant chatter."

Laughter bubbled within her. "My incessant chatter?" She pulled back far enough to look at him with a smile. "If you thought that was fun, then batten down the hatches, matey. Just wait—"

"Shush." He placed a finger on her lips.

Hannah nipped the end of his finger.

Mr. Franklin hissed and shoved her head against his chest. "Don't bite me, woman."

Smothered against him, she mumbled. "Don't shush me, Mr. Franklin."

"You've been reading too many Jane Austens, my dear. You needn't keep Mr. Franklin-ing me."

"What should I call you? Boss?" She tipped her head to look at him again. Her face inches from his.

"Goodness, no." He chuckled and pressed the back of her neck until she leaned against his shoulder. "Nobody calls me Mr. Franklin."

"Then I shall."

"Very well, Miss Benton."

"You may call me Hannah if you wish."

The man gave no indication of ending the embrace. In fact, his breathing slowed, and the muscles along his back loosened the longer he held her.

A man's footsteps approached the building, and Hannah eased out of Mr. Franklin's arms.

The door burst open and let in a blast of sunlight.

Mr. Franklin grunted and buried his face in the crook of his arm. "Geez, Kevin. Don't you ever knock?"

An elderly man with a floppy hat, work trousers the color of dirt, cracked boots, and a vest too small for his middle stood in the doorway. "Sorry, Boss. Oh." He swiped his hat from his head, revealing shaggy white hair. "G'day, miss. Didn't know you was here." Kevin looked away, hand on the doorknob, and shifted from one foot to the other.

Mr. Franklin stumbled to his desk and dropped into his chair behind it, waving to Kevin. "In or out, man. Only shut the door." He grabbed the waste bin under the desk and emptied his stomach into it.

Chapter 17

Kevin's eyes stretched wide, increasing the wrinkles on his forehead. He scuttled inside and pushed the door until only a crack of sunlight poured around the opening. They were cast in shadows again. "Is he okay?" Kevin appealed to Hannah while twisting the brim of his hat. "Should I fetch the doctor?"

"No!" Mr. Franklin and Hannah spoke together.

She wet her handkerchief from the canteen slung across Mr. Franklin's chair and laid the damp cotton over the back of his neck. "He'll be fine. It's a *trifling* pain from the burst of sunlight." She muttered the rest under her breath for Mr. Franklin's ears only. "And the natural consequences of foolish stubbornness and misplaced heroism in refusing to go home and heal properly."

He took the canteen she offered and rinsed and spit into the waste bin several times. Pouring water in his hand, he then splashed it over his face, unmindful of the drops he scattered on the floor.

"What did you need, Kevin?" Mr. Franklin didn't move from his position. Elbows on knees, head in hands, breath slow and controlled.

"Oh, right. Oh, Mr. Johanson is, um, here from the bank." Keven spun his hat nervously between both hands, not meeting Hannah's gaze. "Says he was to run the books on Fridays. Says you hired him."

Hannah gasped, slapping Mr. Franklin's back.

"Ow!" His shoulders shook with laughter.

"You . . . you miscreant. Letting me go on and on. Why didn't you tell me? You lily-livered blockhead."

Mr. Franklin sat up and reached for her hand. "I did tell you I didn't want to fight today." He pressed the back of her hand to his cheek. His skin was flushed and warm.

"It was easier to just let me talk?"

Grinning and locking eyes with her, he slowly pressed a kiss to her fingers.

Hannah forgot how to breathe.

His lips brushed her hand as he spoke. "It's safer than trying to shush you."

Kevin cleared his throat. "I should bring him over then? Roy's giving him a walk-about."

Mr. Franklin dropped her hand. "Yes, bring him in," he said, still looking at Hannah.

What did that kiss mean? The long embrace? The hand holding? She breathed through her nose to combat her sudden light-headedness.

Kevin hesitated at the door. "Oh. I-uh, I'm going to open the door again."

"Yep." Mr. Franklin turned his head. "Wait. Here." He handed Kevin the waste bin. "Take this with you."

The man grimaced but didn't argue as he slipped out the door with it held at arm's length.

Mr. Franklin swiped Hannah's handkerchief from the back of his neck and pressed it to his forehead and eyes before looking at it. "This isn't mine."

"Keep it for now. I've got more."

"I'll ruin it, this dainty thing." He pinched the corner and held it up. "What's it good for, being this small?"

"It's good enough to cool the back of your neck and bring a moment's relief."

He grunted.

Hannah threw her shoulders back. "Can I bring you dinner tonight?"

"I don't—I wonder if we . . ." He rested his head against his arm on the desk. "My brain hurts."

"I'll make more cookies. Besides, I've already made plans with your sister."

He chuckled and then winced. "All right. The girls win. Make the cookies. Don't let me stop you."

Before she did anything impulsive like kiss the strip of exposed skin above his collar, she spun toward the door.

"Miss Benton?"

Hand on the doorknob, she looked back.

"Thank you," he said sincerely. "For looking out for me. I'm not used to it. Having someone else see to my needs. I—well." His boot heel repeatedly tapped the floor. "I don't hate it."

Hannah tried not to feel smug. She pursed her lips to keep from giggling. "I'll see you tonight."

It wasn't exactly a confession of his undying love, but it was a start. With what she'd learned about Tobias Franklin, a start was as good as finished.

She turned to go, but the door didn't open. "Mr. Franklin, there seems to be something wrong with this door. Is it locked?"

"No. Turn it clockwise, and then counter, and then push it forward until it catches. I would do it for you, but I've been instructed to rest and avoid work at all costs. I can't be everywhere and do everything, you know."

"Rubbish." She fought the brass doorknob. "You can do whatever you please, you scalawag. You don't need anyone to tell you what to do." *Clockwise.* "Least of all, me. I think you've rigged this door—" *Counter-clockwise.* "—on purpose. You delight in putting—" *Push it forward.* "—yourself in a position of power."

There was no click and no catch.

She started again. "If you'd let people help you." *Clockwise.* "You might find out—" *Counter-clockwise.* "—how much you are cared for." *Push it forward.* Nothing happened.

She stomped her foot.

He came toward her. "Is that so?" His voice was low, deep. Like rich, chocolate frosting. He moved behind her when she didn't step out of his way and covered her hand with his.

She slipped her hand away. "Sorry—that was uncalled for. I let my tongue run amok again. Sometimes I say whatever silly things pop around in there without thought of where they come from. Incessant chatter, you know."

His gaze held hers, swallowing her, and she couldn't get enough air.

Drat these corset laces.

Planting her hands at her waist, she worked on slowing her breathing—a difficult thing with him so close.

He didn't smile, and the intensity of his gaze reeled her in. He leaned closer ever so slightly. Closer, closer.

The latch clicked. Mr. Franklin pulled the door, letting in a crack of sunlight. He dipped his head and let his hand drop from the doorknob.

She stayed rooted to the floor while he toed the door open inch by inch with his boot. Once it was barely wide enough, she slipped through, bursting into the sunlight. Into a bright, noisy world where she could breathe again.

"Good day, Hannah."

She waved a hand behind her as she left, too afraid of what might happen if she turned back. Of what she might do if she looked at him.

Practically running through the brickyard, she passed Mr. Johanson on his way to the office.

His pressed, tan suit was out of place among the laborers, machines, noise, and clay. "Miss Benton, what a pleasure." He doffed his bowler hat.

She skidded to a stop and greeted him. "Hello, Mr. Johanson. Quite a warm day, isn't it?" She pressed a hand to her cheek, sure it was flushed.

"Is it? I'd hardly noticed." He looked down the path toward the office and back at her. "Ah, excuse my bluntness, but may I ask if you're engaged Friday next?"

"Why, no. I don't believe so." Hannah's mind was still with Mr. Franklin. She felt his hand against her back and his breath on her neck. It *wasn't* her imagination that he'd leaned closer at the end. He'd kissed her fingers in front of Kevin . . .

"Ockelbo holds a monthly social, year-round if we can manage it." Mr. Johanson raised a hand to shade his face from the early afternoon sun. "Nothing fancy, mind you, but the band is there, and we dance a bit. It hardly compares to anything you'd be accustomed to in the city."

"Oh, what fun!" Why had nobody else mentioned this? "I do love to dance. Hiram hasn't said a thing, the cad."

"No, he's not one for going out, is he? Boss is usually there with Miss Collier, along with a good amount of these fellows." He waved at a group near the mixer. "You'd like to come?"

"I would very much." She'd wear her yellow dress with the pearl buttons.

"I'll come by for you at seven. I have a comfortable two-seater that will fetch you into town in no time."

She pressed a hand to her chest. "Blimey, you needn't go to all the trouble. I'm sure I can get Hiram to bring us in for the evening. It's not the sort of thing you must arrive in pairs, is it?"

"Nonsense, no need to bother him when he's made no effort to come to the dances before. I get the impression he's the type of man who enjoys a quiet evening. Really, I've been looking for a chance to dust off the rig this season."

"All right then. See you Friday."

Hannah waved and skipped along the path to report to Eloise and help prepare something nice for dinner.

Hiram wouldn't miss her as long as she was home before dark, and with the long June days, she'd have no trouble walking home again after dinner.

Mr. Franklin had almost kissed her. Hannah was sure of it. Another evening in his company . . . well, she'd not think too far ahead.

Eloise was right. Someone had needed to check on the man.

Chapter 18

Girls like candy. Tobias nodded to himself. *Candy is simple. Buy candy. Gift candy. Say thanks.*

Tobias crossed the street as he made his slow walk through town. Miss Benton was going to be at his house for dinner. *Hannah.*

He'd bring her a simple gift for all she'd done and because girls like candy.

Comforting smells assaulted him when he entered the cigar shop. Sharp peppermint mingled with the rich tones of tobacco. Barrels of each lined the wall of the tiny shop. Boxes of imported cigars filled one shelf of the display, and the rest of the store was dedicated to candy, chocolates, truffles, and more. He rubbed his palms together absently as he considered Hannah and the wide variety of treats.

The bell above the door jingled, and Tobias blinked. He squinted at the old cuckoo clock mounted behind the counter. It claimed he'd been standing here fifteen minutes. *Hmm.*

Tobias pressed his thumb and forefinger to the bridge of his nose and leaned into the pressure. *God, fix my head.* He refused to believe his healing had stalled. He *would* return to a pain-free, clear-visioned life again.

After situating Johanson in his office, Tobias had taken a turn around the brickyard, making time to speak to each man. It was good to be back at work. Good for the men to see him on his feet. The walking and talking he could handle if he paced himself. The sunlight wasn't even so bad as long as he warmed up to it and kept his eyes shaded.

It was the written word and numbers that would simply not behave. He could read the same paragraph three times and not be able to repeat a word of it, and that was if he managed to catch the words before the letters blurred and wiggled off the page. Johanson would have to settle the books for a few weeks until Tobias's brain cleared up.

A glass-protected display filled with colored confections judged him. *Just pick one, dad-blame-it.* This errand was supposed to be a quick stop.

Five boys tramped into the shop and filled in the space around him, each with a penny to spend on something sweet. Tobias stood heads taller than all of them, yet they crowded closer, jostling him and each other to get the best view of the candies.

One boy stepped on his foot. That snapped Tobias into focus.

"Boys," he said sternly.

They looked at each other and then craned their necks up at him, as if noticing him for the first time.

"You forget yourselves. Behind me, please. I haven't made up my mind."

Ten round little eyes grew wide, but there were no arguments as they shuffled into a crooked line behind him.

There. Now he could go back to not making a decision. The pain in his ribs and behind his eyes was distracting enough.

Hands in his pockets, he rocked back on his heels. *Perhaps the coconut truffles. They're three times the price, but . . . chocolates are so . . . chocolate.*

"Boss?" One of the sticky boys poked him in the thigh.

"Shh," Tobias said. "I'm thinkin'."

The boys whispered incessantly, invading his space. Could a man not deliberate in peace? There came a tapping on his elbow. He turned, and the whole group inspected him. Samuel Forsberg was among them. Tobias hired the kid on occasion to run errands for the brickyard.

"Is it true?" Samuel said with his eyes round as saucers. "Did you really get bit by a rattler?"

"I did." Tobias narrowed his eyes. Someone had been spreading tales. "A real big one. At least six feet long. I got a good look as it came right for my face."

"And you was passed out for a week?" The boys edged closer, clearly in awe of his heroics.

"Days and nights," Tobias said dryly. "Barely pulled through."

"And Ol' Doc Farley bled out the poison?"

Tobias lifted his chin and turned to the candy display.

Another furtive conference. Another tap on his elbow. "We wanna see it."

"The snake bite?" Tobias gave up choosing candy. He lowered to one knee so his head was level with theirs. "Careful—don't poke me." Tipping his head, he pointed to the line of stitches above his ear.

When the boys had all leaned closer, peering at his wound, Tobias grabbed Samuel just above the knee and hollered. "Boo!"

All five boys screamed while running into each other as they tried to scramble away. They pointed and laughed, accusing the next boy of having screamed the loudest.

Ezra Williams, gap-toothed and freckled, approached Tobias. "How'd you get bit on the head?"

"It all happened in a blur. You see, I went to make a proper acquaintance with our new neighbor in the country. I was doing the gentlemanly thing by returning a book Miss Benton had dropped in town, but as soon as I arrived at her farm, I heard her screaming from inside the house. Miss Benton was screaming and screaming. Not just one little squeak. I knew she must be in trouble for sure. I leapt off Dan and flew up the steps in a hurry, when this massive snake comes flying toward me. Without hesitation, I snatched it right out of the air before I even knew what it was."

Tobias paused for effect and took time to make eye contact with each face in his audience. He lowered his voice. "Shame on me. I grabbed a little too far from its head. I fought as it wrapped around my arm, but before I had time to do anything else, it sunk its fangs into my flesh." He gently tapped above his stitches. "Darkness covered me after that, and I don't remember anything else. And that's exactly how it happened."

A few eyes blinked, and a few feet scuffed the ground.

Samuel cocked his head. "Why was she screaming?"

Tobias stared at the boys until one asked, "Where'd the snake come from?"

"I never heard of a snake flying from a porch before."

"Yeah, whoever heard of that?"

"You're full of stories."

Tobias raised a hand to ward off their accusations. "It was a trained guard snake and had never seen me before. He was only doing his job."

"Yer joshin'," said one boy, pulling his finger out of his nose. "Ain't no such thing as a guard snake."

"Suit yourself." Tobias hoisted himself with a hand on the counter and resumed staring at the candy. "I know what I know." He tapped his fingers on the counter and sighed. "Yes, sir. I know what I know . . ."

Behind the counter, reading a newspaper, Gary Lindberg sat in a rumpled gray suit with a know-it-all smirk around the pipe hanging from his lips.

The whispers of the boys grew bolder, some for and some against the notion of guard snakes.

Tobias spun around, startling them into silence. He steadied himself with a hand on the counter, immediately regretting the quick movement. "Which is the best?"

No answer.

"The best candy." He smacked the counter. "I haven't got all day. If you could have any of these you wanted, which one is the best?"

Five small fingers pointed unanimously to the candy cigarettes.

No help there. Tobias crossed his arms in front of his chest. He should splurge for the truffles.

Mr. Lindberg folded his paper once, twice, and slapped it on the counter. "Come along, boys." Lindberg motioned them forward. "Don't mind Boss. He's been holding up the line for half an hour." He reached under the glass countertop and drew out the box of chalky white sticks.

The boys picked their own.

"Are you out of money?" Samuel asked Tobias, clutching his penny.

"I'm out of gumption, and I'm a coward."

Samuel's gaze flitted along the candies. He was no doubt confused why a grown man with plenty of money would have so much trouble.

"It's like this, Sam." Tobias waved his hand at the display case. "These all have secret messages attached to them. All of them. I'm not prepared to find out what some of them say. If I buy her the peppermint drops, what's that mean to anyone these days? Any bloke can buy a girl a bag of peppermints. Though if I hand over a box of chocolates, she'll want to meet me down the end of the aisle."

"What aisle?" Samuel looked over his shoulder at his friends waiting outside.

"Any of them. I don't want to meet any girls down any aisles," Tobias muttered as he deliberated between the hard caramels and the maple meltaways.

Samuel dropped his penny on the counter and ran out the door. Lucky kid. All Samuel had to worry about was making it home in time for dinner. He didn't have a dark-haired beauty with stormy gray eyes waiting for him. If Tobias wasn't careful, he'd be caught in that storm. He'd almost lost control this afternoon, and he needed to stay at the helm. He'd not misuse a woman again as he had Maribeth.

Nope, he did not need to be kissing Miss Hannah Claire Benton, regardless of her response to him. Tobias smirked a little, pride seeping in the edges, recalling her obvious reaction to his nearness. He cleared his throat and stepped to the counter. *None of that, Boss. For all you know, she simply tied her laces too tight this morning. That happens sometimes. Fool woman.*

Truth be told, he'd missed her this week. For now, he needed candy. Just a simple thanks-for-helping-stitch-up-my-head gift. Which one of these had *that* message attached to it?

Chapter 19

The view through the window halted Tobias mid-step on the porch.

Hannah relaxed on his sofa while reading to Luke snuggled in her lap. The boy popped his thumb out of his mouth and pointed at the page. Whatever he said made Hannah laugh. She brushed a lock of her hair behind her ear, kissed him on the cheek, and turned the page.

He smiled. *Oh, Katie, I hope you see how your boy is loved.*

Tobias opened the front door when his desire to be part of that scene grew too strong.

"Dada! Dada!" Luke came running to meet him before Tobias was two steps inside.

Tobias took a knee to better scoop Luke into a hug without injuring his ribs. Two weeks after the accident, his ribs were much improved, but Hiram was clear in his instructions about what was and wasn't allowed. Bending at the waist to pick up anything—including a wiggly toddler—was not allowed.

Tobias glanced at Hannah. "Hi," he said over Luke's head.

She closed the picture book on her lap. "How's the noggin'?"

"I could use a cup or three of water." He kissed Luke and tried to set him aside. "Let Daddy change, and I have a present for you and the girls."

"Why, Mr. Franklin." Hannah beamed and took Luke, sending heat along his side when her hands brushed against him. "I'd tell you that you shouldn't have, but there's nothing much I love more than presents."

That lock of hair fell into her eyes again, and she blew it out of the way. It settled back where it was before. Tobias shoved his hand in his pocket.

Her slender fingers absently fiddled with the section of hair, twirling it one, two, three times before tucking it behind her ear. She raised her eyebrows expectantly. "Don't wait, Daddy." She bounced Luke in her arms with each word. "We want our presents!"

Holding Luke against her chest, she spun in circles until the boy giggled. Luke's joy was infectious, and soon she giggled too. She stopped spinning and grinned at Tobias, slightly off balance. "It's not even my birthday."

Having Hannah in his house was as if someone had lifted the roof and invited all the warmth of the sun after the rain. With her came the intensity of the new grass, freshly turned fields, and the burst of wildlife that always seemed to appear overnight. How did that happen? The call was sent out, and all at once nature rejoiced as if it knew exactly how many days were left until the first snow.

Sheepishly, Tobias pulled a paper sack from his back pocket. "Don't get too excited, even though I'm told on good authority these are the best." He reached inside and brought out a handful of chalky white candy cigarettes.

Hannah began to laugh. Not a polite smile or a soft sound hidden behind delicate fingers, but a full, joyful laugh, and Tobias knew he'd made the right choice. Whatever secret message was attached to these was the right one. She stuck one in the corner of her mouth, letting it hang out the side, and adopted a terrible British accent. "Well, I say, gov'na, fine weatha' we havin' dis time a yea-ah."

He was about to answer in kind when he noticed his sister standing in the doorway to the kitchen with a bemused smile on her face. "Here, El." He raised a handful of candy sticks. "I have one for you too."

"Honestly, Tobias." She raised her eyebrows. "Offering tobacco to a lady?"

Hannah and Tobias grinned at each other, and Hannah burst into another fit of laughter.

Zeke sauntered through the front door and joined their party, and they soon crowded around the small table in the kitchen. As the meal progressed, Tobias's eyelids drooped, and he contemplated an early bedtime. The ache in his head came and went through the day in waves. He mentally prepared for another crest.

"Do you think the brickyard would help put together a float this year?" Eloise jostled his elbow, and Tobias realized he'd missed the entire last conversation.

"A float? For what?"

"For the parade." Zeke nudged Eloise with his elbow. "Chipmunk's been telling Hannah and me about the Fourth of July. Foot races, horse races, shooting contests, bakeoffs, fireworks, the parade. Tell me—does the band stick around for dancing? I've been hankering for another waltz." He winked at Eloise, and she blushed.

She sported a full face of rosy pink in less than three seconds. Eloise always blushed in an instant. Anytime she spoke in public, was called to attention in front of others, whenever she thought of something she deemed embarrassing, and, of course, anytime Zeke winked at her. It was adorable.

Hannah brightened. "We'll dance next Friday too. I heard something about a monthly social. You'll all be there, won't you?"

"Wouldn't miss it," Zeke said. "Eloise has promised all her dances to me. Ol' Boss might need to sit this one out. And now that Maribeth—"

"I don't know about the parade this year." Tobias glared at Zeke. "It's news to me if the boys built a float. We haven't organized it, so I doubt they've put anything together. It's peak season, and we're working full steam just to fill our current contracts."

"You had a float last year," Eloise said softly.

"We did, but I wasn't in charge of it. That was George's pet project, and they started it by the end of May."

Zeke looked thoughtful. "We'd need a wagon. Lumber, nails."

"Paint," Eloise said.

"Who's Maribeth?" Hannah bounced Luke on her knee and redirected his attention to a spoonful of peas. Since Luke's first visit to the Benton's farm, Hannah seemed to have him on her lap or attached to a hip whenever they were together.

"I bet the Andersons would let me build one for the bakery," Zeke said, his excitement apparent.

Tobias waited for Hannah to look up at him before answering her question. "She's a friend."

Zeke continued on about the parade. "Afterward, we'd set up a table outside the bakery and sell cookies or rolls or biscuits. Maybe those Swedish cracker things? Something easy to grab that can be made little and cheap."

Eloise stuck her lip out. "Oh, but you'd work all day long. What about your holiday?"

"True, it will make for a busy day. But wouldn't it be fun? We can pretend it's our very own celebration. You would ride on it with me. We could get dressed up in the Swedish garb and make a fun show of it." He sat up straight, grinned, and waved his hand near his face.

Hannah leaned closer to Tobias. "A friend you used to go to dances with?"

He nodded.

Zeke and Eloise cut their parade chatter and looked at him, expecting more.

"What?" Tobias took an enormous bite of bread. "Don't look at me like that, El." He mumbled around his food.

His sister narrowed her eyes and told him without telling him that he was in dangerous water and that if he didn't spill it, she would. He stared back with a look that said, *Mind your own business,* and she gave the tiniest shake of her head.

"Heard Maribeth went riding with Judd last Friday." Zeke shoved another bite of chicken in his mouth, oblivious to the growing tension. "Bakery gossip." He laughed and pointed his fork at Tobias. "You wouldn't believe the tidbits I pick up when all the old coots get together. Judd has a matched set of sorrel mares. Word is he's been giving Maribeth honest-to-goodness riding lessons every evening."

Tobias leveled Eloise with a stern glare, willing her to keep quiet. He knew he'd have no luck with Zeke. Hopefully the man would change topics all on his own.

Zeke tapped his plate with the end of his fork. "Hey, did you hear you were bit by a rattler? I started that one myself. Mentioned it to one of our delivery boys, and it was all over town before I could stop it."

"I heard." Tobias continued his stare-down with Eloise.

Eloise turned to Hannah with a slimy smile. "Hannah, did my brother ever tell you about the time Zeke gave him a black eye?"

"Dad-blame it, Eloise," Tobias grumbled.

"Blimey, no!" Hannah glanced between Zeke and Tobias. "But you seem like the best of friends. What ever happened to cause such a thing?"

Tobias muttered vile warnings to Eloise under his breath.

"Oh, it's a fine tale." Zeke took up the story, and Tobias closed his eyes. There was no stopping it now. "When I first came to town, I misunderstood the family relations and assumed Eloise was married to Boss." He put his fork down and raised both hands level with his head. "I know, sounds plumb crazy. I mean, she was living here and caring for his kid. Could you understand my angle? Regardless, when I saw Boss here getting friendly with Maribeth, my own sense of justice for Eloise took over. You could say I took matters into my own hands." He raised a fist, flexing his bicep.

Hannah smiled at Tobias. "Mr. Franklin, how in the world did he get the drop on you? You're a head taller and he's . . ." She shrugged at Zeke apologetically.

"I'm not a beast?" Zeke asked. "We know. Boss is built like a brick. Mostly, I had the element of surprise." He mimed an uppercut, and Eloise scooted his cup farther away from his plate. "I wouldn't have stood a chance if he'd tried to return hit for hit. *Bam, bam,* and it was over. Worst I got was my head knocked against the wall when he tired of me flailing about." Zeke laughed at himself. "Pinned me like a toddler having a tantrum. I mean—" He shrugged. "It could have been worse. He was pretty focused on his, ah, *conversation* with Maribeth." He speared a piece of chicken and wiggled his eyebrows.

Hannah's eyes grew large. "Oh, I see. *That* kind of friend." She gaped at Tobias. "Why, Mr. Franklin, you ought to be ashamed of yourself."

"All right, all right." Tobias was growing increasingly uncomfortable with this conversation. "So Maribeth and I went together for a while, but now we don't. The end. She works at the mercantile. Go ahead and double-check the back story tomorrow."

"And now she's with Judd, and you have nobody to dance with," Hannah said with a twinkle in her eye.

Tobias shrugged to hide his exasperation. "Glad she's happy."

Eloise looked around the table at each of them in turn, ending with Zeke. "Can we? Can we tell them our news now?" She reached for Zeke's hand.

Zeke winked at Tobias and grinned like a fool. "Eloise said, 'Yes.'"

Hannah squealed and clapped her hands. "Oh, I knew it!"

Luke bounced and joined with her clapping.

"Congratulations." Tobias's chest constricted. The room shrank, and the walls crowded closer. The chatter around him echoed. He wanted to be happy for his sister, though he wasn't sure she was ready.

Could Zeke take on the responsibility of a wife? Eloise needed special care. Her heart had been trampled, and he was uneasy thinking of her on her own. On her own, without him. If she were married, she wouldn't be under his roof anymore.

An ache unrelated to his injuries spread in the pit of his stomach. What if Zeke wasn't there for her when she needed him? Who would help her then? What about Luke and his reliance on her? What if—

"Tobias?" Eloise put her hand on his arm. "Are you okay?"

"Yeah." He tried to smile at her. Reassure her. "I hadn't realized the full extent of what this means until now. Of course, I knew it was coming." He nodded at Zeke and gave a half smile. "I've known for weeks." He knocked his fist into Zeke's shoulder. "Way to leave a guy hanging with a secret like that."

Eloise beamed, blushing and full of love for her soon-to-be husband.

Zeke, who'd come to town only this April, had shaken up their lives. In those short weeks he'd become someone Tobias highly valued. There's no way he'd be giving his sister to the man otherwise. Zeke had brought joy back to Eloise.

Eloise began to change the first day Zeke arrived in Ockelbo. She'd slowly returned to Tobias in ways he'd not seen since their parents died. His sister was back. Her laughter, her smiles, her confidence, and Tobias would never begrudge Zeke for that—even if it meant Tobias's relationship with her would change again.

Now that he thought about it, she hadn't woken him with a nightmare in over a month. Perhaps Zeke didn't yet know what it was to be a husband, but he loved her, and she loved him.

Tobias rubbed a spot on his chest and cleared his throat. He swallowed and cleared his throat again.

Zeke slapped him on the back. "Don't cry, old man. I'm not taking her away yet."

Tobias nodded. "I need to put Luke to bed. Excuse me." He wet a rag and slowly wiped Luke's face and hands while the other three excitedly made plans for a late-summer wedding. He took the child from Hannah and carried Luke upstairs, clutching him close to his chest.

Chapter 20

Hannah and Eloise put the kitchen to rights while Zeke stayed busy, drawing a rude sketch for his parade float at the table.

"C'mere, Chipmunk. What do you think of this one?"

Eloise leaned over his shoulder to admire the drawing but never looked at the sketch, for Zeke turned his face to meet hers. With love-sick sighs, they spent far too many seconds staring at each other.

Hannah coughed to remind them of her presence.

Zeke smiled and pecked Eloise on the nose. He went back to his work, but both of their faces flushed pink. Eloise remained behind Zeke's chair and rubbed his shoulders.

Hannah feigned annoyance. "Someone might think the two of you are in love if you continue that nonsense." She took her time drying each plate and stacked them on the counter, though her own thoughts drifted to lunch hour at the brickyard. There hadn't been an exchange of long and meaningful stares because the man had his face half covered most of the time. Though there was that long and meaningful hug . . .

No.

Hannah nodded, resolute. The man was in too much pain this afternoon to think rationally. She'd taken certain liberties that would never be allowed in polite society or even a nurse-to-patient relationship. Hannah's stomach flipped. She'd pulled her fingers through his hair as intimately as a wife might caress a husband. And Mr. Franklin'd encouraged it! That meant something. If only she knew exactly what.

Zeke waved a hand to get her attention as Hannah leaned against the counter, her gaze unfocused. "Need a ride home? It won't take a minute to get the buggy hitched—

Eloise smacked him gently across the back of his head. "Shush."

"What?" he asked, rubbing his head.

"Tobias is a gentleman, so you needn't worry about that." Eloise patted Zeke on the shoulder and left him to go tidy the living room. Zeke, eyebrows furrowed, followed her with his gaze.

Bless Eloise.

She and Eloise had talked about many things, but Hannah hadn't mentioned being sweet on her brother. Had she? Perhaps it was obvious to Eloise. Obvious to everyone but him? *Oh, dear.*

There was no hurry, of course . . . Hannah could wait the rest of the summer to see if he returned her affection. Unless he didn't, and she wasted her time ignoring other suitable candidates. *June, July, August.*

God's answer to prayer wasn't as straightforward as she'd hoped. Why was this turning out to be so complicated?

Zeke was eyeing her with an odd look on his face when Eloise returned to the kitchen and hustled him out the door. Then she turned to Hannah while bouncing on her toes. "Would you like to see my wedding gown?"

Hannah laughed. "I absolutely want to see your wedding gown. How do you have one already?"

"Come see." Eloise grabbed Hannah's arm and pulled her to the stairs. "It was my mother's. I know it's terribly out of fashion— she married in the '50s—but there's plenty of fabric, so we can make it over. You will help me, won't you? I can't believe Jessica's not here for this."

"Who's Jessica?"

The girls tiptoed up the stairs, afraid of disturbing Luke. Eloise whispered, "My main confidant since grammar school. Oh, heavens, I don't know what I would do if you hadn't come. Helen, her mother, is so busy now with the summer boarders, and normally Jessica is here to help me with things like this, but she's just moved out to a homestead with her father for the summer months. They're too far out to come into town very often."

Eloise pulled a cedar box from under the bed and unwrapped the dress from the paper. "I can't bear to wear the same dress I had for Philip's wedding. Just doesn't seem right. So this . . ." She held up a deep-blue silk gown with off-the-shoulder cuff sleeves and enough fabric in the skirt to rig a sail. "It really is too much. Indecent even. When I was a little girl, Mama let me get it out whenever I wanted, and I always told her I would wear it just like it is. She laughed at me. Can you imagine the hoops needed to fill this in? Honestly, I don't know why they bothered. It's like wearing a little house around your waist."

"The things we do for fashion and love," Hannah murmured. "Stand up. Let's put it on you."

"Oh, it doesn't fit me in the slightest," Eloise said. "Honest, Jess and I tried a few weeks ago. But I think you might be thin enough for it, though you'll never be able to breathe after we cinch you in to button it all the way. Want to try it?"

"Could I truly?" Hannah reached for the dress, giddy with the thought of playing dress-up. "I'll be the fairest of them all in this."

The girls fussed and giggled throughout the process, shushing one another for Luke's sake when they were too loud. Hannah grasped the edge of the bed frame while Eloise pulled her emerald corset as tight as it would go. They needed to trim at least four inches from Hannah's waist to fit her into the dress. Through no little amount of work, the dress was finally on with every tiny button in place. Hannah turned slowly, modeling for Eloise.

"Oh, Hannah." Eloise propped her fists beneath her chin. "You're a vision. Hold still." She pulled from Hannah's hair the last pin that had survived the change into the gown. Her hair tumbled about her shoulders in dark waves.

"I can't catch my breath. How did they do it?" Hannah pressed a hand to her stomach. "And so low-cut." Hannah bent at the waist, leaning toward Eloise. "Tell me—do you think I'll fall out?"

Eloise covered her eyes, laughing. "Oh, heavens. You might."

A tap came at the door, and Hannah squealed. She bolted upright and covered her mouth with her hands, though the laughter still burst out.

The door opened a crack, and Mr. Franklin whispered, "May I come in?"

Hannah shook her head and fanned her face, desperately trying to breathe. Then she grasped the edge of the scooped neckline with both hands and tried to pull the dress up. It didn't budge. She dropped her arms and shrugged. She threw a wink at Eloise and assumed a posture of royalty. "You may enter, sir."

Tobias's mind was wiped clean. Nothing remained but Hannah Claire Benton. He stood gaping in the doorway and forgot why he was there. She filled the middle of the room, wearing his mother's wedding gown with her raven black hair cascading around her shoulders, shining in the lamp's glow. Her dark features contrasted with her pale skin and the lace along the top of the dress. His gaze flitted from the excuse of sleeves at her shoulders down slender, bare arms. Her fists planted on her hips highlighted her slim waist. Surely, his hands could span the circumference. His fingers twitched, wanting to see for himself.

The neckline was low. Dangerously low. The tops of her . . . they were exposed. She was trussed up so tightly that she could hardly breathe. Her two rounded curves moved with each breath, and she was fairly panting.

"Good evening, Sir Franklin," Hannah said, and his gaze snapped to her face. "We're dressing for the ball. So sorry you weren't invited. Royalty only, you know. Knights who behave like knaves simply aren't tolerated." She paused to suck in a few shallow breaths. "Our carriage arrives any moment. Miss Eloise, darling, would you be a dear and fetch a shovel? We'll need to scoop your brother's jaw from the floor. Poor man has forgotten to close his mouth." She lifted each side of the dress and floated across the floor on her toes.

She wore no shoes, and he caught a glimpse of her striped white-and-green stockings. She spun toward the window, showing off her back and the wide expanse of creamy skin from shoulder to shoulder. She tossed her hair and turned her face to him.

"Do you like it?" She flashed him a coy grin as she glided closer. When she dipped into a formal, albeit wobbly, curtsy, she revealed so much of herself that he averted his eyes.

She offered her hand. "You may kiss me, Sir Franklin."

Whatever facade of resistance he'd built against her charms quickly unraveled. He was her servant. Her slave. Her knight, if she wished. He'd follow wherever she went, go where she pointed.

Still in her curtsy, she wiggled the fingers of her hand that he hadn't taken. "Hmm," she said, eyebrows raised. "Eloise, bring a physician with that shovel. He's forgotten how to speak along with his manners."

Spurred into motion by her taunts, he grabbed her hand and yanked her to her feet.

She stumbled, and he caught her with a hand around her waist. Before setting her away from him, he curved both hands around her, and his thumbs met in the middle. Yep, sure enough. A jolt of energy shot through him. He shivered but hid behind a mask of annoyance.

"Get out of this thing before you suffocate." He shoved his hands in his pockets. Even he was tempted to cringe at his stern tone. He looked at Eloise. "You're not wearing this for your wedding unless you move some of that—" He pointed to the skirts. "—to cover, uh, that." He waved a finger at the general area of Hannah's shoulder.

Hannah looked at him, preening like a cat. "What's wrong with my shoulders? They're perfectly fine, strong shoulders."

He cleared his throat. "Yes, well. If you want a ride home, I'll hitch Dan. Otherwise you need to start walking before it gets dark."

Hannah curtsied again, and he moved his gaze to the window, blowing out a breath. He swore she did it on purpose that time.

"Oh, well," Hannah said. "I suppose I can go to the ball another night. Eloise, you heard the man. Help me out of this contraption before I pass out."

She fumbled with the tiny buttons along the back, and Tobias fled, shutting the door with a bang.

He leaned against the door, and it took more than a few deep breaths to calm his racing pulse.

Chapter 21

Hannah rested comfortably against the backrest of the buggy. Mr. Franklin hadn't been himself since dinner, and she'd given up trying to pull him out of his hovel. She grimaced. He hadn't even teased her about the dress. Just groused. It must be his head paining him again.

She fluffed her skirt and recrossed her ankles. "I should have walked home. Sorry to trouble you. It's been a long day. Next time just throw me out, and I'll make my own way. I walked the two miles in, and I can walk them back."

He grunted and lifted a shoulder. Adjusting his cap so it came down to his eyebrows took the rest of his attention.

"Mr. Franklin," Hannah said in a mock whisper. "Are you mad at me?"

He sighed and leaned back, and his shoulder brushed against hers. "You've spent a lot of time with Eloise the past two weeks."

"I have. Every day," she said slowly, confused, but glad he was speaking. "We've already made plans for tomorrow."

"Fine. Do you think she's ready?"

"For what?"

"To get married."

Hannah sat up straighter and slapped Mr. Franklin's knee. "This sounds like something from an overprotective beast of a brother."

"No, it's not like that." He ignored her touch. "I'm genuinely concerned about her. You don't know how it's been since Philip died. How El used to—" He speared her with a glance. "I'm not going to tattle, but it's been a difficult year." The wind tugged his cap, and he brought it lower. "So you think she's all right? She talks to you and seems happy?"

"She's stronger than you think, and she's more than all right. You needn't worry because Zeke is the right man for her. And they're the sweetest. You know they've been reading in the afternoons? When Zeke gets off work after the lunch rush and Luke is still napping, they study the Bible together."

"I know, he takes his dinner with us eight out of seven nights. I guess it's a fair trade for all the free bread."

"It's more than free bread, Mr. Franklin. They're very much in love." A cool breeze blew across the prairie. Without thinking, she took the man's arm and snuggled closer. The buggy bounced gently along the road at the slow pace he'd set. "Mr. Franklin, you're not worried about Zeke's ability to take care of her." She rested her head against his shoulder. "You're worried about how you and Luke are going to manage without her, aren't you?"

"I've been thinking about what you said this afternoon." He swatted a mosquito on his forehead.

"I said many things this afternoon."

"About me needing help. With Eloise planning her wedding, and me playing catch-up at work. Do you think Hiram would release you a few hours a day?"

She scoffed. "Hiram isn't my boss, sir. He was doing well without me and will do very well when I leave. I've taken on the garden, the chickens, laundry, and most of his meals. But I'm free to do as I wish."

"And you wish to manage paperwork in an office?" Uncharacteristically, Mr. Franklin sounded unsure of himself.

"If it would help you." She ran a hand along his arm, and he tensed. "And I wish to have daily *fika* with Eloise and play with Luke. Sounds like a dream of a summer."

"By *fika* you mean sit and gossip. Don't assume I don't know how these things work."

"Nonsense—*fika* is a chance to enjoy the company of friends and take a break from the demands of the day. Rest is a wonderful thing. It comes highly recommended. You should try it."

"I've had enough recently for the remainder of my life. Now I'm behind and floundering, and El's leaving me." He sat straight and shrugged his arm out of hers.

Abruptly, he pulled back on the reins and set the brake. He rested his elbows on his knees, removed his cap, and rubbed a hand on his forehead. "Hannah, what am I supposed to do? You're completely right. No matter how hard I try, I can't do everything—as much as I wish I could. How am I supposed to maintain the business, and now run a house by myself, mind the toddler, and still find time to sleep? You know Luke. He must be watched at all times. Bringing him to work is a nightmare, provided I actually wish to accomplish anything."

Wind rustled the grass around them. Dan lowered his head, shook his mane, and stomped a foot. Hannah's heart beat a heavy rhythm before she spoke. "Have you considered taking another wife?"

Mr. Franklin snorted and crossed his arms, leaning back with eyes closed. "Why, you volunteering?"

Hannah didn't answer, and when he eventually looked at her with one eyebrow raised, she felt like the tenth fool. A lump formed in her throat, and all her misgivings came crashing in around her.

What sort of man was Tobias Franklin? How much could she know about a man she met two weeks ago? Talking, talking, talking for a week of rehabilitation didn't put her in a position to know if a life of love was possible. Was she forcing an Ishmael when she needed to wait for Isaac?

Yes, he'd demonstrated qualities of restraint and kindness in response to Mother's quick insults. He was a devoted father and brother. His employees treated him with respect. He was a high achiever and not one to shirk responsibilities.

Based on what she'd seen, he would make a great husband. She would agree in a heartbeat if he truly asked. Not only did his character shine, but he was tall, strong, and handsome. He was clever and easy to be with. Would that be enough?

She wanted to be loved. In the confines of his office, he'd confessed that he'd missed her . . . but what else? The intensity of her fears drew out the moment, and she turned her gaze from his and fiddled with the hem of her sleeve.

She wasn't Hannah Claire Benton; she was a runaway princess with a knight at her side. He was merely a hired escort to the next kingdom. One couldn't travel between kingdoms unescorted in this day and age—what with the trolls on the loose. Along the ravine there was a creek—no, a river—fed by magical springs. Any moment a wild beast might lumber out of its lair. Though she'd been trained to carry a sword, it was foolhardy to assume—

Mr. Franklin knocked his knee against hers until she looked at him. With a soft smile he whispered, "Are you flying with dragons?"

She shrugged and looked down at her hands, whispering back, "It's safer than responding to your flippant question."

"Hannah." He murmured her name before the gentle brush of his lips on her cheek stilled her frantic thoughts. He leaned away to look at her, questioning.

In answer, she closed her eyes and leaned toward him.

His arms wrapped around her, and his mouth covered hers. He kissed her hungrily, with a sense of urgency and desire.

She'd never been kissed before and hadn't thought it would be like this. Raw, full of need. She moved against him, angling her head and grasping the collar of his jacket, pulling him closer. There was nothing but Mr. Franklin and her. *Tobias*. No knights. No princesses. No dragons or trolls. No pirates or robbers, no highwaymen or flying contraptions. None of it was needed.

There was only the warmth of his lips, the scratch of his chin, his hand pressing against her back, his fingers threading into her hair. The scent of smoke and machine oil lingered on him, and the taste of apple cider was on his lips.

His lips were firm yet pliable, guiding her own until she let escape a soft moan, and he tensed.

As suddenly as it began, Tobias stopped. He pushed her back, breathing heavily. Releasing the brake and taking up the reins, he cleared his throat and set the buggy in motion with a harsh slap across Dan's back. With a jolt, they moved forward.

"I'm sorry." He wiped the back of his hand across his mouth, as if erasing her touch. "I didn't mean to do that."

"Oh . . ." Hannah worked at catching her breath. "I don't believe you're allowed to say that. From over here, it felt like you meant it very much, and don't pretend you didn't." She grazed her fingertips across her burning lips. "Whether you *should* have or not remains to be determined."

Pushing down a flash of anger, Hannah folded her hands in her lap to keep from attacking the beast. "Kissing someone with that kind of fervor doesn't happen by accident, Mr. Tobias M. Franklin. If you didn't mean to do it, perhaps I won't mean it when I slap you for taking liberties."

Chapter 22

Tobias had let himself kiss her. His heart thumped wildly against his sore ribs, beating in triumph or trepidation—he wasn't sure.

Wind whispered through the grass, teasing it to one side and then the other. A hawk soared overhead in lazy circles. A family of deer bolted across the field to his left.

It must be his head injury messing with him. It must be. Otherwise, he was fairly sure he'd accidentally asked Hannah if she'd volunteer to be his wife, and when she didn't answer, he kissed her in a manner reserved for husbands. The kiss was greatly influenced by the vision of her in the low-cut, too-small silk gown, but he was no kind of man if he used that as an excuse.

If his sister hadn't been standing as witness, God knows what he might have done . . . *God? I could use a little help here. Ah, sorry*

I didn't ask for it three minutes ago. I messed up again. I like Hannah, and I do need a wife to care for Luke, to bring stability to my home and life. Hannah and I suit very well. Is this . . . is this your plan too? Two weeks is a little short notice. If you had something like this in mind, a warning could have been arranged.

On second thought, did Maribeth walk away because God prompted her? He realized he hadn't given Maribeth much thought until this evening at dinner. And why was he bothered about Hannah learning about her? Well, any guy might be ashamed to be exchanged for a Judd.

'*Cause you're so perfect, Boss?* He blinked and clicked his tongue, mentally apologizing.

A gentle tug at his heart told him his attraction to Hannah was more than needing someone to watch Luke, more than his desire for a physical connection. He *liked* Hannah. Maybe liked her enough to spend every day with her.

God? Am I crazy? Kissing Hannah made everything feel less crazy.

Perhaps a box of chocolates wasn't such a bad idea. Aisles and meeting her at the end of one wasn't quite so scary after holding her in his arms. His arms wouldn't take any time at all to get used to that.

"Nothing? You have nothing to say?" Hannah let out a humorless laugh. "Let me out," she snapped. "Just stop the horse. I want out."

He did not stop the horse. "Hannah, do you like coconut truffles?"

She stilled beside him.

He kept his eyes on the road. "Caramel pecans? Mint nougats? The confectionery options are vast, but I always figured chocolates to be the best. The elitist of candies."

"Mr. Franklin, I will climb over the seat and jump out the back of this buggy if you do not stop the horse in five seconds."

In response, he slapped the reins across Dan's back, increasing their speed. And five seconds later, Hannah spun and began climbing over the seat. "Whoa." He quickly pulled the reins. Their buggy jostled to a stop, and he grabbed Hannah to keep her from tumbling off.

She yelped as his arms circled her middle, and his cap was lost somewhere in the tussle when she landed on his lap. Too many delightful ideas engulfed him for how this could end. Namely, with her remaining on his lap, and his lips on hers.

Her elbow made sharp contact with his ribs, and he released her with a grunt.

"Oh, Mr. Franklin." Rolling off his lap, she turned and began fussing over him as usual. "Did I hurt you?" She crouched near his legs and retrieved his cap from the floor, smoothed his hair, and rested a palm against his cheek.

He was fine, but he held his side and curled into a posture of agony. He leaned into her hand, and she brushed her thumb along his bottom lip. The sensation caused him to inhale sharply. Her lips were before him, slightly parted. Concern for his well-being reflected on her face, but she studied his mouth, not his eyes.

"If I confess that I meant it," he said, still hunched over with an arm wrapped around his side. "Does it still warrant a slap?" He covered her hand with his own.

She licked her lips and pressed them together, and he groaned—not brought on by any pain in his side, real or exaggerated.

He brought her hand against his lips. "If I ask . . ." He moved to the inside of her wrist. "If I mean it . . ." Her palm. "If I'm not sorry . . ."

He cupped her cheek and guided her nearer. "May I?" His lips hovered over hers.

She closed her eyes, and it was all the permission he needed.

This kiss was soft, slow. He took his time and kept his hands safely entwined in hers to protect them from roving.

She shifted onto the bench next to him. "I have something to confess." She broke the kiss only long enough to speak. "I'm not sure if you'll ever forgive me."

He planted three quick kisses along the side of her jaw. "You're promised to someone else?"

"Gracious, no." She tried to pull away, but he followed her. "But I've—wait. 'Promised to someone else' is the first thing that comes to your mind?"

"I can't think of anything else I'd have trouble forgiving you for." He freed a hand to guide her mouth back to his, but she pushed against his chest, spreading a tingling sensation through him.

"I—I don't know what to say. Do you—are you proposing marriage?"

"I'm . . . not sure. My mind is muddled." Muddled with whether he should have splurged for the chocolates, among other things. He already pictured her in white, or in nothing but that embroidered corset he'd seen at the train station. He wondered if she wore it now. A husband would be allowed to think about something like that. He blinked and shook his head, unable to halt his thoughts.

"Then wait." She pulled her hand, but he held it until she relaxed. "Listen to me first. After our first two encounters, when you stood against my mother and I glimpsed my first chance at freedom, my promised land, so to speak, that's when she changed her mind and told me I could only stay through August."

She'd told him as much already.

"She doesn't like it when she doesn't get her way, and I think she believed Hiram and I tricked her into letting us go. Which maybe we did by neither of us mentioning in earnest how all we wanted was a chance to make our own way. To be free from her and Father. And the simple fact that we don't enjoy being with them. With the commotion at the depot—and all of my silly books shoved in her face. But, oh, Mr. Franklin, you don't know how it is at home. Since Hiram left, it's me alone with her. She's not happy and makes everyone around her miserable. Father escapes to the hospital every chance he can manage because even he can't bear her constant—" Hannah shook her head, a fierce look in her eyes. "I can't go back and I . . ." She swallowed.

Tobias traced along the back of each one of her fingers until she shivered.

"I can't think when you do that," she whispered.

He smiled but covered her hand and stopped moving.

"Mr. Franklin, please look at me."

He did, and she appeared to be in anguish.

"I've just gotten to the heart of it." Her yellow bonnet hung down her back, and the wind played with the tendrils of hair framing her face. Moisture filled her eyes, but she blinked it away and raised her chin. "I brazenly demanded that God send me a husband by the end of summer so I wouldn't have to return to the city with Mother."

Tobias made no comment, only smiled, thinking how perfectly beautiful this woman was and how he'd like to keep kissing her. "I haven't heard anything from this confession of yours to turn me away." He sure didn't mind being the answer to her prayers. Actually, he wouldn't mind strutting around a little to be so chosen. She was everything a man could ask for in a wife.

"It gets worse—I prayed specifically for you. I asked God to set things up for me to be Mrs. Tobias Franklin." Her voice dropped to barely a whisper. "And then Hiram mentioned another girl, and then the snake, and the horse, and—and then you kiss me like this, and it's all happening so fast. I don't know what to do. I like you, but what if I've cursed you, and I've lost my mind, and maybe I should go back to the city right away before it all falls to pieces—"

He put his finger over her lips to quiet her, and she jerked her head back, sputtering.

"What are you doing?" She swatted his fingers.

"It's my turn." He grabbed her hand. "You are amazing, Hannah. If this is a curse, I can't wait to see the blessings because I've entered the outer fields of heaven."

He chuckled when she rolled her eyes. Growing serious, he squeezed her hand. "First, you cannot blame yourself for Maribeth. It's clear to me now that we weren't a good match, and I'm glad she broke it off when she did. I misbehaved. I'm actually incredibly grateful for Judd, and I hope he treats her better than I did."

Tobias held up another finger. "Second, you cannot blame yourself for my injury. I don't believe God kicked me with a horse, but he may have thickened my skull to take the hit. Third." He cleared his throat. Here goes . . . *Pardon my iniquity, for it is great.*

"I should not have kissed you, but, yes, I meant it. I'm sorry only because it threw us into this conversation, and I don't know if we're ready for it yet."

She averted her gaze.

"I promise not to put you in a compromising situation again. Based on your decision to stay, your prayer, your desire for freedom, are you open to a marriage of convenience? Because I do need help at the house with Luke, and you need a husband's protection from your mother. We suit, and there's clearly passion between us. Hannah, it's not my imagination. You were on the other end of that kiss."

A smile twitched her mouth, and she glanced at him.

He waited for the cold chills, the sweaty palms, for his chest to squeeze the breath from him.

Nothing.

A slow grin spread across his face, and he drew in a healing breath. "People have married for less, Hannah. When did she say you would have to go back?"

"Three months. June, July, August."

"We're only halfway into June. Hannah Claire Benton, may I court you?" A mosquito buzzed around his head, and he waved it off. "We have time to get to know each other before your mother returns."

"You don't hate me on the chance God stripped away your freewill?" Her expression was so earnest—not a flicker of humor to be found. This woman truly believed she'd cursed him.

Tobias tossed his head back and laughed and nearly forgot his pain next to his joy. He wrapped both arms around Hannah in a rough, brotherly sort of hug and rumpled her hair in the process.

He was still chuckling as he took up the reins. "Now, a few ground rules." The grass waved around the buggy wheels, and dragonflies flew out of the way before them.

"We have rules?" She settled next to him, leaving a scant half-inch between while she tucked a wayward lock of hair under a pin.

"Most definitely. You've tempted fate tonight, sweetheart, beginning with what transpired in my office over lunch. I promise it won't go so well for us next time because you might be one of the most beautiful creatures I've ever laid eyes on, and I cannot be trusted in the slightest to keep my hands to myself." *There.* May as well get that off his chest. He was a shameless cad.

"Oh, Mr. Franklin. You can't be serious."

"Aha, there's another rule. You start calling me Tobias."

"Nonsense. It's my own little game, and I shan't change it."

He tried to sound very domineering. "Hannaaah."

"Mr. Fraaanklin." She wasn't cowed in the slightest.

"You're going to go the whole summer Mr. Franklin-ing me?" He rolled his eyes. "*Pfft.* What a mouthful."

"If you behave, I'd consider *darling* or *sweetheart* when I'm feeling especially generous."

"Dearest mine," he said.

"Honey," she answered.

"Sugar."

"Rogue."

He smirked, reaching for her hand, and brought it to his lips. "Temptress."

"Pumpkin."

Tobias laughed so hard he was forced to hold his ribs against the pain. He whined like a sad puppy, willing it to pass. "Dear

Hannah, promise you'll never call me pumpkin in public." He wheezed, trying to stop his laughter. "I will lose all my authority."

They approached Hiram's farm, and he slowed again, willing the farm farther away.

"Do you have any other rules, darling?"

"You never answered if I may court you. Let's get that one answered."

"You may."

"Whew." Truly, he felt a certain level of elation difficult to contain. The dull ache behind his eyes and sore ribs kept him in his seat. Otherwise, there'd be nothing to stop him from standing and throwing his cap in the air.

"I think we've unmuddled the situation? I feel better already. This is good. This is great!" He looked and found her returning his giddy smile. Desire burned his chest. He needed to lay some ground rules. Quickly. "Sugar honey, here's rule number one: you keep your hands out of my hair." He shook a finger, and she wrapped her slender hand around it.

"You told me you liked it." She blinked and stuck out a lip. "You said it helped with the pain."

"Don't play innocent. I do, and it does. And it also makes me want to do things to you I'm not allowed to do. Yet." When he glanced sideways at her, she had the decency to blush. He shook off her hold on his finger and threw an arm over the back of her seat. "Now, rule number two: no more kissing." Enjoying her nearness, he rubbed a thumb on her shoulder. "I like you, Hannah. I really like kissing you. But I want us to get to know each other without any distractions, as delightful as those distractions may be." He sobered, serious about his proclamation, though he wished he'd asked for one last souvenir before blurting out his oh-so-necessary rules.

She shifted closer to him. "Do you play cards, Mr. Franklin? Or drink spirits or swear?"

"Not often, no, and sometimes," he said.

She nodded, as if he'd answered correctly. "Have you ever struck a woman?"

"Heavens, no," he said, squeezing her shoulder. "You wouldn't believe the turmoil I was in watching your mother have her way with you."

"How do you feel about puppies?" She scooted another half-inch nearer.

Chapter 23

Rule number two already pained him. But this was good. Boundaries, cut and clear, would keep his mind on more important things. Like getting to know this fantastic woman snuggled next to him in the buggy. "Puppies? I don't believe in them. Let someone else deal with the chewing and jumping, the whining and soiled rugs. Maybe I'll reconsider if I have nothing better to do when I'm old and lonely." He brought both hands back to the reins and directed the buggy to the front porch. When it came to a stop, he made no move to get out. "My turn to ask nonsensical questions." He cleared his throat. "I've been mulling this about for months. The deadliest animal in the world: tiger or flea?"

"Tiger, clearly." She answered without a moment's hesitation.

"Wrong," he said. "Fleas have caused the deaths of millions in cities across Europe, especially during the Middle Ages, and who knows where else." He waved at Hiram exiting the barn, hands full with a bucket of milk and a wire egg basket.

"True," Hannah said thoughtfully, "but with today's medical advances—provided you aren't attending the hospital of a barbarian—"

"Noted."

"—the flea poses an infinitesimal risk compared to a ferocious beast with claws and fangs."

"Millions, Hannah. The flea has killed millions of people. The tiger? So few we don't bother keeping records. They haven't been rampaging across cities, slaughtering millions in their wake since the beginning of time."

Hiram managed the screened door with one finger and went inside. The evening sounds of the farm filled the air. A rooster settling down, sheep bleating, mosquitoes buzzing.

"But one could argue that the flea," Hannah said, "in and of itself has not actually killed anyone, but merely transferred an illness that did the actual killing. Nobody says, 'Killed by a flea.' Your millions died of the plague, Mr. Franklin. One swipe from a tiger and you have little hope—"

"Over the years." Tobias raised his voice. "If millions have died because of the flea, wouldn't that make them deadlier than a tiger?"

"So are we speaking specifically about how many people have died? Just the facts and death records? Or the present danger of the creature? Are we speaking clearly *tiger* versus *flea*, or is this a question of deadly versus danger? State your terms."

"Yes, all of that. Don't twist the argument. If millions have died from a flea, wouldn't that make it more dangerous than a tiger?"

"Hardly." Her posture straightened on the seat next to him as she matched his volume. "You give me two doors; behind one is a wild tiger and another is a wild flea. Ha! I'll take my chances with the flea. Now, a plague and the infestation of fleas upon a household poses an honest risk, but if that's our scenario, then we must account for a horde—a pride?—of tigers."

Tobias's blood ran hot with excitement. He felt more alive than he had in a long time. This gorgeous woman was willing to debate. "What if you knew for certain that the one flea behind the door carried the black plague in its blood? What if the tiger was sleeping behind his door, and you had a rifle? Now, what if *you* were asleep and the doors were opened at the same time and the flea came along on its own, skippity hop, over to your neck." He grazed a finger along a vein on her neck. "But the tiger was well-fed and then you would—" He was cut off when Hannah put her fingers over his mouth. He stuck out his tongue and licked her hand.

She snatched her fingers away. "You're disgusting." She laughed and wiped them on the front of his jacket.

"It was either that or break rule number two." It would take all his willpower to keep it too, especially when she beamed at him like that with the sun about to dip over the horizon, casting her fair skin in its soft, orange glow.

She leaned in, tauntingly close. "You'd kiss me even if I choose to run from the tiger and suffer the plague?"

He held his ground and wrapped his hand around hers where it gripped his jacket. "Even then, pumpkin. Because I'll save you,

Tobias's medical needs. But now, with Hiram looking between Hannah and him that way, Tobias would have rather taken his chance behind the door with Hannah's tiger. Misgivings rolled over him, as if he'd been doing something disobedient. Which he hadn't. Much . . .

"Hannah, what did you do?" Hiram glared in a fashion that beat all big-brother glares. Their twin connection was strong—both with their defined, gray eyes outlined in thick black lashes that challenged the other with raised eyebrows and the upward tilt of the chin.

Tobias might have snickered if he wasn't busy cowering with the tiger.

"Nothing." She slipped her hand out from under his relaxed grip and threaded it through Tobias's arm. "He came to it all on his own. Didn't you, Mr. Franklin?"

Came to it? The passionate kiss? The request to court?

Hiram narrowed his eyes.

Tobias didn't have anything to hide. He reminded himself of a few important life details. Like the fact that he was a grown man, completely responsible for all areas of his life. He met Hiram's stare. "My intentions are completely honorable. Hannah and I are good friends, and well, we'd like to get to know each other better."

"She told you she's going back to the city in three months?"

"That came up, yes," Tobias said.

"And you're not jumping head-first into a convenient marriage on both ends?"

Neither Tobias nor Hannah made any comment. They fidgeted, not looking at each other. And Hiram continued to stare at them. Sooner or later, Hiram was going to hurt himself with that face.

Tobias cracked first. "Well, like I said, that's why we're going to get to know each other better before we sign any papers. Can't it be convenient as well as mutual, ah, appreciation?" *Passion* almost slipped from his lips. Honest to goodness, pure passion.

"Hiram, stop being a blockhead." Hannah chided her brother. "You and I both know you like Mr. Franklin, and you're only playing at being a bully. You should also know I've gotten myself a little job at the brickyard, and I'm helping Eloise with Luke so she can prepare for her wedding. Now, help me out of this buggy so the man can rest before work tomorrow."

"You're working Saturdays?" Hiram asked Tobias while handing her out of the buggy.

Tobias nodded. "Peak season we do. We have the kilns firing around the clock when we can fill them."

"How many do you get out of each firing?"

"We aim for ten thousand. We can fit near eleven thousand in each kiln, but the ten percent overage gives us a solid cushion to account for breakage, ill-formed bricks, accidents." He spoke to Hiram, but with Hannah smiling at him so sweetly, talking bricks wasn't forefront in his mind.

"Goodnight, boys," she said, and they both watched her enter the house. Hiram tapped Tobias on the knee and brought his attention back to earth.

"You know what it is to be a big brother," Hiram said, and Tobias nodded. "But you don't know what it is to be Hannah's brother. She's never needed my protection because our mother kept her under lock and key. I'm her passage to freedom. I promised her as much when she joined me, and I'm not going to prevent her from going out, making friends, and having fun this summer, but I don't know how to keep her safe in the process." He knocked off his wide-brimmed hat and mussed his hair. "As kids, she was the one getting us into trouble."

Tobias laughed. "I suspected as much."

"I trust you well enough, but I worry because I know Hannah. I'm worried she might jump into something for the fun or for the freedom of it and not have the sense to know when she's gone too far."

Tobias grunted at the twinge of guilt that washed over him. Was he too excited? Too sure of himself again? Had he thought this all the way through?

"I'm serious when I tell you, if you mess up, my father has the means to make your life miserable."

"Even as far as here?"

"Even so." Hiram sighed. "I'm not threatening. I'm asking you to think carefully."

Chapter 24

Hannah breezed into the brickyard the following Friday morning with a handful of flowers she'd picked on her walk to town. "Morning, Kevin!"

The old man smiled before he ducked his head while leading two mules from the stables. He still hadn't adjusted to her role as secretary.

Mr. Franklin spoke with a group of men near the mixer and stepped out of the way when the mules arrived. He'd been a different man this week than she'd previously known. Very driven. Focused. Absolutely no time for long and meaningful stares. He was invested in every facet of the brickyard, from overseeing the men to repairing machines and closing sales. He wasn't always the one physically doing the work, but Hannah trusted that he could. She was confident that he could mold, burn, and load a warehouse of bricks by himself.

When she walked nearer, he left the group while pulling out the office key attached to the long chain on his vest. She turned sideways to squeeze past him as he held the door open and loved the familiar smell of his shaving soap.

"I didn't think." She stopped in the doorway, trapping him there, and held her bouquet between them. "You have anything handy to put these in?"

"In the shed?" He edged around her, clearly in no mood to play. "You can poke around inside. It's unlocked for the day." He rapped his knuckles on the desk. "Thanks for retrieving the post yesterday. If you have time, would you order more billing forms from the printer?"

"Sure. They're across from the livery?"

"Near enough."

Sidling next to him, pretending to look at his notes on the desk, she touched the toe of her boot against his. "First, I'm dealing with the dust in here."

He didn't appear to notice her touch. "Suit yourself."

"How are you feeling today?" She reached to brush a lock of hair out of his eyes, and he jerked away.

"I'm fine. Be sure to let me know if any of this doesn't make sense." He moved a page of his chicken scratch notes atop a disorganized pile of papers on the desk. "Here—I'll find a jar." He gathered the flowers and left a path of dirt clods and white phlox petals in his wake.

She unhooked the broom from its peg. The swish and scrape of the straw bristles against the wood floor channeled her annoyance into action and eased her into the morning.

Since Monday, she'd walked to town after breakfast and back home again before dinner to catch up on chores for Hiram. The morning walks were perfection; the afternoons, blazing, but both full of wildflowers, foxes, rabbits, buzzing insects, and blustery gusts of imagination. Her interactions with Mr. Franklin had been about the same each day. He was usually more polite than today, yet he always left her wanting more. After a week as his secretary, she discovered that the charming man who'd asked to court her had been replaced with a no-nonsense company manager.

Thankfully, Hannah's afternoons were pleasant with Eloise and Luke. While Hannah entertained the little tyrant, Eloise made use of the time to prepare for her upcoming wedding. They'd scheduled the big day for the first Sunday in August and were busy putting things together to set up their new home. Zeke had bought a tiny, one-bedroom cottage on the edge of town.

Though Hannah didn't mind the work and loved her games and naps with Luke, she looked forward to the dance that evening. Finally, something just for fun. Funny that Mr. Franklin hadn't mentioned it. She'd excuse him on account of his head trouble—based on what he employed her to do this week, he still avoided reading. He limited his writing to the terse notes left for her on his desk.

She forcefully swept. Mr. Tobias M. Franklin need not have bothered with his rule number one and rule number two. Since their delightful ride in the buggy, they hadn't spent more than a moment alone. He was never in the office except for a cursory good-morning-and-here's-the-list. It was just as well that she'd agreed to let Mr. Johanson take her to the dance. It would give her a chance to go out while Mr. Franklin rested.

Hannah swept a pile of dirt through a convenient crack in the floor. The dust from the worksite had a way of sneaking under the door but keeping this office clean wasn't impossible.

From the broom's crooked handle and the bits of straw that kept dropping off, Mr. Franklin clearly cared little about the state of his office, so she'd assumed that chore on her own accord.

The man's bedroom was the same. Tuesday afternoon she'd lost the battle against her curiosity and peeked inside. Regarding his bedroom, she would leave well enough alone, but it brought her pleasure to see the office come to order. Not to mention the surprise on the crew's faces whenever any of them noticed the difference.

Hannah stood at the desk and surveyed today's damage. She whistled a jaunty tune and rolled up her sleeves. No sense in stalling any longer. So far this week she'd made lists, run errands about town, taken stock of the nickel-and-dime expenses, and filed everything in its proper place. She tackled today's tasks, along with the mess on the desk, full steam ahead.

On a stretching break an hour later, she paused at the window to clear a smudge that hadn't been there yesterday. Outside, Mr. Franklin strode toward the office. Her heart's acceleration betrayed her, and she smiled. He'd been meeting with potential buyers all morning. Maybe now he'd be in a better mood to discuss the evening's dance. Depending on what he decided, she could set Mr. Johanson straight soon enough when he came in later to settle the payout ledgers.

The door crashed open, and a burst of summer wind raced through to play in her hair. Mr. Franklin didn't glance at her by the window. All his attention was on his desk, and his eyes narrowed. He yanked drawers open and slammed them.

"Good morning again," Hannah said. "I was hoping to speak with you before I left today."

A grunt was his only reply, and after shoving another drawer shut, a mix between a growl and a sigh escaped.

"What are you looking for?" She pushed the window curtain aside, letting in more light.

He was now on one knee, rifling through files in the bottom drawer. Smacking his hand on top of the desk, he turned to her. "I had everything I needed right here. Last night, I'd laid everything out so I'd have it ready. Now—"

She put her hand on his arm. "What are you looking for?"

"Dad-blame it, Hannah. I left it right here." He fisted his hair with both hands, and his cap fell to the floor.

"I can't help you if you don't tell me what you're looking for."

"The contract! The contract. What do you think I'm looking for? It was on my desk. Where I'd left it. Where I always leave them, in the spot where I know I can find them when I want them."

The contract was filed alphabetically under Drafted Contracts. A new and necessary category she'd created. Gently, she moved him out of the way, opened the large bottom drawer, flipped to the correct file, and pulled out the contract. "For Mr. Rhys, I assume?" It had been left on the desk, along with a handful of inquiries, bills, yesterday's lunch crumbs, a broken pencil, and not one, but four, oddly shaped bricks.

He put his cap back on his head and stood. "I hired you to help, not take over." He skimmed his finger over the contract. Then he paused and held his thumb and forefinger against his closed eyes. "Leave things the way you found them." Fiddling with the papers, he made his way to the door and stopped. He opened his mouth and closed it. His Adam's apple bobbed. But his attention remained on the contract, and he didn't speak again. Eventually he nodded to himself and walked out, pulling the door closed behind him.

Carefully, deliberately, she closed the two drawers he'd left open. Controlled. Poised. She was queen of the brickyard, not to be mistreated by mere knaves.

"*Decem, Novem, Octo, Septem . . .*" Counting backward in Latin didn't stop the tear trailing down her cheek. She seized the broom and swept with renewed fervor until every clod and speck of dirt he'd tracked in disappeared down the crack in the floor. Everything else that could be handled was handled. She hung the broom on its little hook and put on her bonnet and gloves.

Sadly, the doorknob had other ideas about her departure. Blast it all. No matter how many times she turned it one way and then the other, pushed, pulled, and jiggled, the door wouldn't open. Going to the window, she watched the men like busy worker bees at each station. On the far edge of the brickyard with his cap pulled low on his forehead, Mr. Franklin stood with Mr. Williams in deep discussion. Soon, they walked away together toward town. Hannah knocked on the window, hoping someone would look her way, but with all the other noise of the morning, nobody did. The window had been painted shut and would not open.

Hannah spun and yanked open the top drawer of the desk. She made herself comfortable with a sheet of stationery. Gloves and bonnet discarded for the time being.

She wasn't Hannah Claire Benton; she was an indentured servant working the remainder of her sentence for an ogre in a cave.

In due time the ogre would return for lunch, and when he did, she would be released to see to her needs until the morrow.

In concentrated silence, Hannah drew a scene of the moss-encrusted entrance to a cave. Toadstools peeked from the rocks and a whimsical weeping willow concealed part of the cave's door. The ogre was off stage for the moment, and Hannah placed a medieval version of herself in the center. She wore a dress with long, flowing sleeves, and hair that fell to her waist with intricate braids piled atop her head. She added a jeweled belt and a small side knife. Always handy to carry one of those.

The minutes ticked by, and she added more details to the ink drawing. Smoke through a crooked stovepipe peeked from the roof of the cave-dwelling. A mouse with a wedge of cheese. Birds taking flight overhead. A myriad of flowers along the path that led away from the cave. For good measure, she placed a secret cache of weapons behind a boulder. A bow and quill full of arrows and a broadsword. A slingshot found its way into the maiden's hand.

With a sigh, Hannah set the page aside and took out another sheet of paper. Her heart's frantic pulse had calmed. This time, she focused on the ogre. Without much premeditation, she drew him crouching before a stack of bricks. Counting them.

A brick miser. A brick miser of an ogre.

With warts.

If he happened to be wearing Mr. Franklin's vest and cap, it was mere coincidence. Not sure if she needed to laugh or cry, she ended up doing both. She dashed away an uninvited tear and stored the ink pot.

She returned to the window. While she stood waiting, Charles Grady happened to walk near, and she knocked and signaled for him to come around to the front.

"Miss Benton?" He knocked on the door.

"I can't get the door open," she yelled.

The handle turned and jiggled. "I think it's locked," he said, voice muffled.

"Locked?"

He was mistaken.

She tapped her toe against the door. "It's not locked. Only the latch is jammed."

"No, ma'am. It's locked for sure," Mr. Grady said. "Dee and Boss have the only keys. We'll get you out."

The door was not locked. She knew for certain it wasn't. Rotten old doorknob was jammed again, just like last week. Mr. Franklin wouldn't have locked her in the office moments after speaking to her.

She banged her knuckles on the wood. "Mr. Grady?"

He didn't answer.

She worked on the doorknob again. Finally kneeling, she saw for herself, sure enough, the deadbolt went crossways into the door frame. At first she was too shocked to feel any emotion.

Mr. Franklin had locked her in the office.

He had locked her in the office and walked to town with the key.

She backed away from the door. *The villain. The fiend. The yellow-bellied, vile, wart-encrusted slug!* A growl purred from the back of her throat, and she fumed while stalking back and forth in the small space.

Somewhere in the back of her mind, reason and logic tried to remind her that it must have been an accident. He was preoccupied. His head still troubled him. For all his bravado, she knew he was in pain. By no means would he lock her in the office intentionally. There would be nothing to gain from it and everything to lose. But the little voice of reason was not nearly loud enough to silence the fit of anger that had been simmering all day.

Reason and logic were trampled. And flogged! And thrown out with the rubbish, burned in a bonfire, and the ashes were thrown into the wind.

Hannah swung her arms as she paced. Insults and curses from every book she'd ever read fueled her rants about the ogre of a man who'd locked her in this cell. Her tongue tripped on a few of the more vulgar accusations, until she sank into the corner with her knees drawn up to her chin. The two walls pressed against her. The tight space quieted her mind. Remorse crept in for her wicked thoughts, and she wondered at her temper. *Lord, forgive me.* There she remained until a knock sounded on the door.

"Hannah?" The muffled call of Mr. Franklin jolted her upright. "Miss Benton?"

Chapter 25

Tobias's head rang like the anvil at a smithy. He hadn't believed Charles when the man came running with the tale of Miss Benton locked in his office. But yes, it was definitely locked, although she didn't answer his call. He slipped the key in and threw open the door.

She stood at his desk, methodically donning her gloves.

He paused at the door with an arm wrapped across his ribs, heaving breaths of air from his rush across town, and watched her pull on the second glove and then tie the ribbons of her bonnet under her ear without looking at him. "Hannah, I'm so sorry. You have to know I didn't mean to do it."

She smiled tightly, but her gaze wouldn't meet his. "Add this to the growing list of things you didn't mean to do, Mr. Franklin." She brushed past him but pulled to a stop outside the door.

Most of the crew gathered nearby with lunch pails in hand. No doubt, Charles had alerted them to the commotion. She spun on her heel toward him and greeted Tobias with a false smile. Too bright to be earnest. The anger festering behind it wasn't something he wished to encounter.

He lowered his voice so only she could hear. "Hannah, please. Habit. I wasn't thinking straight—"

"If the weather holds, won't it be such a fine night for dancing?" She surveyed his crew, smiling at each in turn. "I expect each of you to save one for me. I'm counting the hours, you know." She clasped her hands together. "I haven't been to a dance in ages."

Tobias ground his teeth and stared at his men, warning them to ignore her offer. Before anyone could answer, she grabbed Tobias's sleeve.

"Poor dear, so afraid of your employees walking off that you lock them up to keep them safe." Her eyes flashed fire, though her mouth smiled. "You needn't worry so. I'll be back next week to sweep away the muck tracked everywhere you step." She patted a hand against his cheek, and he curled his fingers into fists. "Oh, it must have slipped my mind. I forgot to tell you that Mr. Johanson offered to bring me into town tonight so you needn't worry your little head about it." She looked him square in the eye before she lifted on her toes and planted a loud, smacking kiss on his cheek. "Good-bye, pumpkin."

His men did a poor job of holding their composure as she strode across the brickyard with her ribbons flying in the wind behind her. As soon as she'd entered the field that separated them from the edge of town, the men were slapping each other on the back, hooting at him, and making kissing noises. Tobias slammed the door shut and locked it. On purpose. He adjusted his cap and stalked after her, ignoring the catcalls of his employees. He'd deal with them later.

When he'd left the edge of the brickyard, he called to her again, and she slowed to allow him to catch up. "What's this about Johanson?"

She bent and picked the head from a blood-red prairie rose, spinning it between her thumb and fingers, ignoring him.

He placed his hand over hers to stop her distractions. "Hannah, I thought we had an understanding."

She jerked away and threw the flower to the side. "What did you do with the flowers I brought in this morning?"

He closed his eyes. "I think . . ." Raising his arms out to the side, he shook his head. "I think I left them on a shelf in the barn. Jonas called for help, and I forgot—" That word again. "—about them."

She pursed her lips, nodding slowly. "Oddly enough, Mr. Franklin, I forgive you for locking me in the office. It's plausible your mind was elsewhere, and, as you say, force of habit compelled you to pull the key from your pocket and turn the lock without any thought of me."

"Just so." He answered warily, but from her stance and stern features, she didn't hold the posture of one who was in a forgiving mood.

"When you asked if you could court me, I thought you meant it. We did have an understanding, and I thought it implied you gave a rat's knee about me. You said lovely things and that you looked forward to our getting to know each other better—"

"And then I lock you in an office? What are you getting at?"

"Ha! If that were the half of it. Mr. Franklin, you've hardly acknowledged my existence for a week."

"I've been working!" Indignant at her accusations, Tobias was silent for some moments before speaking again. How could he possibly tell her that he hadn't thought of her because he simply hadn't? He'd thrown himself into getting caught up at work and set aside any and everything else for the time.

She crossed her arms, and her attention was aimed at boring the toe of her boot into the ground.

"When I'm at work, I work." He stalked a few steps one way, and then the other. "Hannah, what you did back there, belittling me in front of my men, was uncalled for. Be upset with me if you want, but public disrespect isn't necessary, and furthermore, you shouldn't invite the attentions of those you don't know and have no reason to trust."

"I can take care of myself." She swiped her sleeve under her nose.

"Can you?" His volume rose. "How's that work with throwing me down in their presence? You wish to align yourself with them over me? You think one of them will bow at your royal feet when I don't measure up? You know nothing about those men. Just because I pay them to make bricks doesn't mean I want their hands all over you."

"Jealous, sir?" She sneered at him.

He growled under his breath. "Listen to me, Hannah Benton. Most of them are fine, but if you prance around here throwing out smiles and invitations to every male who makes eye contact, you'll find yourself in a compromising situation where you don't want to be. I don't need to be jealous to tell you when you're being a fool. Not to mention petty, childish, and spiteful."

"Don't you dare turn this around on me." She took a step closer with a finger pointed at his face. "I'm the one mad at you for treating me like a servant all week long."

He couldn't believe this. "I pay you to work here. I hired you!"

"No. You ignored me, Hannah, your friend, all week long. I'm the one you locked in the office because *you forgot about me.*"

"I said I was sorry."

"And now you're pouting because I have a prior engagement with Mr. Johanson that you'd know about if you happened to speak to me once in a while!" Her shout rang in his ear, and he let out a breath.

He darted his gaze to the brickyard, hoping the machines were louder than they were. "Hannah," he said sternly, "if you wanted to spend time with Mr. Johanson, I deserved to know about it."

"You don't own me, sir."

He threw up his hands and turned from her. This conversation went wrong ten miles back. He no longer felt like apologizing, and he sure didn't feel like going to a stupid dance. It was just as well she had an escort. He turned back to the brickyard and stalked down the path, or he would have stalked if the jolting pain in his head didn't caution him to step lightly. He ambled with determination down the path.

"Mr. Franklin," she called. "I—if you've changed your mind about me—about us." She fiddled with her hands at her waist. "I'm sorry we've quarreled. That's the whole thing I'm trying to tell you about. I don't *want* to spend time with Mr. Johanson. I wanted to spend it with you. I meant to tell you before today, but prior to our, um, our understanding, I already agreed to let him drive me to town for this event. Nothing more has been promised. I believe him to be honorable. If you have no objection to him—if I allow no advances—if you need to rest tonight." She blew out a breath and put her hands on her hips. "If it's all the same to you, I plan to attend and enjoy the evening with friends. And we can speak more—" She waved her hand, pointing at him and herself. "—about us, and this, when we're both in a better frame of mind."

He nodded once. "Fine."

Chapter 26

Hannah enjoyed the breeze against her cheeks while dressed in her butter yellow dress with half sleeves, square neckline, and pearl buttons, and wrapped tightly in a wool cloak to ward off the evening's chill. Mr. Johanson drove a smart black rig that fairly flew over the grass.

Hannah tried not to let a little thing like a lover's spat get in the way of her evening of fun. If one could call it that. She'd never had a beau before. Is that what Mr. Franklin was? She'd thought that was his intention when he asked to court her. What with the kissing and the rules. Their relationship was more official than that of a simple gentleman caller. Blimey, her friends from school had accepted multiple callers a month until they'd landed the one they wanted. She and Mr. Franklin had only gone about it backward. They'd spoken of marriage. Marriage was the intended end. He'd asked to court her on the grounds of their getting to know each other better before summer's end. He needed a caretaker for Luke, and she needed . . . she needed Mr. Franklin.

Although the last week produced dismal results in regard to getting to know Mr. Franklin, she thought fondly of their time together at her house. He'd been a friend like one she'd never had, and he'd left behind a void when he returned to his own home.

No, she didn't wish Mr. Franklin to be in pain, but when she'd read to him for hours on end and he relaxed in her presence, they'd enjoyed each other's company in his moments of respite. The stories they shared, the laughs, and silly arguments. A unique connection drew them together. She'd thought.

She wasn't in the habit of guarding her tongue in Mr. Franklin's presence. Hannah never once put stock in any of her mother's condescending warnings to bridle her tongue around men. Why wait until after the wedding to find out if her husband hated half of what she thought and said?

So she said what she wanted, and Mr. Franklin did too. The result was a lively friendship built on frankness and honesty. Until the words came out too quickly and people were hurt . . . Perhaps saying whatever she willed had its limits. Even a friend needed kindness. She *tsked*, tucking stray hair behind her ear. A friend especially deserved kindness.

Mr. Franklin's apparent disinterest and preoccupation throughout the week still didn't sit well. If she married the man, she wouldn't tolerate being ignored six days of the week. Better to return to Des Moines with Mother.

Goodness, no. She chuckled out loud at the ludicrous thought. Not that. But . . . would it be better to search elsewhere for a husband?

Mr. Johanson looked sideways at her, smiling when she met his gaze.

"What's so funny?" he asked.

"I was laughing at myself, thinking Mother would be a better option than remaining here." Hannah gave him a tight smile, realizing this man knew nothing of her situation, her mother, or her need to marry.

He raised an eyebrow. "You're unhappy at Hiram's farm?"

"No, sir." She gazed out at the fields of swaying grass dotted with bright yellow flowers closing up for the evening. "You misunderstand me. I do not wish to return." The sun neared the horizon ready to dip below the prairie. A cloudless sky left little for it to play with, and it slowly sank without its heavenly entourage. Unwilling to ruin her evening, she turned her thoughts to Mr. Johanson.

Before long she had him talking about his work at the bank and plights of mischief he shared with his two brothers. In good spirits they arrived in town, ready to join the others. Since he'd made no forward advances, either by his actions or words, she didn't think it necessary to bring up her precarious and as-yet uncertain understanding with Mr. Franklin. No reason to muddy the waters.

A true community dance. *This* was what she'd been missing for so many years. A variety of dances were taught at her boarding school, and since coming of age, she'd attended a number of events with dancing. Of course, with her parents in tow at all the formal gatherings, Hannah never experienced the same joy and freedom as this night. Who wants to dance with a girl with a badger for a mother?

Hannah found herself spun around the floor from one dance to the next. She'd lost count of how many different men, some only boys, invited her back to the floor. She laughed until her cheeks hurt as she tripped over some of the unfamiliar steps.

Hannah did her best to learn the Swedish *schottische* and *hambo*. Thankfully, there were enough regular waltzes, two-step, polka, and a goodly amount of country dances she knew.

Eloise and Zeke were in attendance along with a few of the couples she'd met at church, but mostly the hall was filled with single men and women like herself. She'd even had the pleasure of meeting a certain Maribeth Collier.

Maribeth was a sweet girl of which nothing bad could be said. She was especially welcoming to Hannah, and they took a rest together on a side bench. Maribeth asked Hannah about Hiram and family in the city, and she hesitantly asked after Tobias's health. Everyone knew he'd spent a week recovering from a head wound at Hiram Benton's homestead. News traveled quickly and efficiently.

A man who introduced himself as Judd Clydale brought her and Maribeth a cup of pink lemonade. Formalities were lost in the evening, and Hannah couldn't keep track of the names. She'd danced a two-step with a schoolteacher, Simon Oakfield, another with Layten, a homesteader near town, and a polka with Isaiah, the new blacksmith.

And square dancing! It was her favorite of the evening. All the men from the brickyard had taken a turn or two with her. Charles, Jonas, Thomas, and even Bob O'Hara, though Hannah did try to avoid another round with him. The tobacco stain in his white beard was certainly not something she wanted to look at any longer than required.

Long into the evening, Hannah took herself to the side and stood breathing heavily, hands on hips. Before she'd caught her breath, Charles Grady was by her side.

"You look flushed," he said. "Having too much fun?"

"Unimaginable, but my feet beg to differ. A short rest, and I'll hop back in."

"How about some fresh air?"

"What?"

"Air." He motioned to the side door standing open. "Let's get some fresh air."

"Oh, that would be heavenly. Let's." She let him take her elbow and guide her through the hall and out into the night. The door opened to an alley between buildings, and the light from the streetlamp hardly reached halfway. The breeze that blew about her face immediately cooled her. She spread her arms out and tilted her head to the sky, drawing in a deep breath. "Oh, what a night." She spun in a slow circle. "Mr. Grady, look up at those stars. It's simply magical. Isn't it the most beautiful thing?"

"Sure is," he replied. "Come with me. I'll show you a place you can see the whole sky without these buildings in the way."

He took her hand, and she ran with him down the alley and around behind the building. He brought her to a staircase that led to a second-story entrance of the long brick structure. "Come on." He tugged her arm when she paused.

"We're allowed to go up there?"

"Sure, sweetheart. Nobody lives up here; these are city offices. They wouldn't prevent you a view of the sky. Come on. You don't know what you're missing 'til you've seen it from there." He was on the second step and beckoned her to follow.

And she did.

Leaning over the railing at the top, she found he was right. Not a building or a tree to block her view and not a cloud in the sky to hide a single star. "It's glorious," she murmured. But instead of adding to the evening, she felt slightly homesick. She wished Hiram would have joined her, and the barricade she'd built to set aside her quarrel with Tobias Franklin collapsed.

If she'd calmed herself and worked out the issues with him today, would he be standing here with her instead? With a dry chuckle, she realized she hadn't even seen Mr. Johanson since the second dance of the evening. She swallowed, thinking of her father and how she would miss him if she stayed in Ockelbo. Their relationship wasn't much, but at least he was pleasant to be around and bought her lovely presents.

"Thank you for showing me this view, Mr. Grady." She wished to launch and fly across the sky. "We should return before we are missed."

"How about a kiss for your rescuer? If it weren't for me, you'd still be locked up." He leaned casually against the wall, blocking her path at the top of the stairs.

"You're in jest, sir. Let me pass, and we'll dance another round before the evening's spent."

"I'm looking for something a little softer. Something sweeter for my reward."

Breaking out in a cold sweat, she gripped the side of her skirt with one hand, but she smiled at him, hoping to disarm him. "I was never in any real danger. I am grateful you happened to be nearby, and I do appreciate your speed in alerting Mr. Franklin of my predicament, but you flatter yourself, Mr. Grady."

He scowled and took a step closer. "Mr. Grady is my father."

She eased a step backward, bumping into the other corner of the balcony.

"Miss Hannah Benton," he crooned, "the first to get away with mouthing off to Boss."

"What do you mean?" She whispered as he inched closer to her.

"You're on the same payroll as me, aren't you?" He raised a hand and brushed it along the side of her face. When she moved her face away, he scowled and grabbed her arm, pulling himself against her. "Tell me, Hannah—what else does he pay you for?"

She gasped and struggled against him, but his entire body pressed her against the brick wall. Her legs were trapped in her skirts where he pinned her with his, and he somehow managed to secure both of her wrists in one of his strong hands. "Mr. Grady—Charles." Her voice came out in a whimper. "Charles, let me go. You don't need to do this."

"Shhh, shhh. Don't be frightened." He spoke softly against her ear as if calming a skittish colt.

She closed her eyes and tried to breathe. Just breathe. But her lungs wouldn't obey, and she was unable to fully draw a breath. *Oh, God, help me. Save me. Help me. I'm sorry, I'm sorry, I'm sorry. Please, God—help me.* She squirmed against him as his lips tried to claim her own. She twisted her head, but her efforts were no more than an annoying fly to his iron grasp. Hannah tried to scream for help, but his free hand came under chin, locking her jaw closed and forcing her head up to his.

He crashed his lips against hers and forced his tongue in her mouth. She bit down on his tongue, and he reared away and backhanded her, knocking her face to the side.

She slid to the ground at his sudden release. Shielding herself for another blow, she cowered behind her raised arms. Spots clouded her vision.

"Ungrateful whore." He spat flecks of blood on her.

Around the corner below, someone called her name. Charles cursed and ran down the stairs. The sound of his boots running on the boardwalk quickly faded.

"Miss Benton, are you out here?" Mr. Johanson called from below.

Lying on her side, Hannah curled tightly around her knees and began to shake. She gulped air and prayed. *Thank you, thank you, thank you.*

"Miss Benton?"

Hannah struggled to sit up and pulled against the rail post. Mr. Johanson stood just outside the alley with the side door to the dance hall. He turned to go back.

"Up here," Hannah said, voice catching. "I'm up here." Her legs shook so badly she could hardly stand, but Mr. Johanson was soon beside her, offering his hand.

"Are you ill? What are you doing up here alone?" He gently took her elbow and led her down the steps. All she could do was put one foot in front of the other and lean on his arm. At the bottom of the stairs, she sank to the ground again, numb. He knelt before her. "Miss Benton, what do I do? Do you need medicine? A doctor?"

She held the side of her face where it throbbed and turned her gaze away from his. It was then she noticed the rip on her dress. One shoulder seam was torn, exposing an inch of skin, and a lock of hair fell in front of her eyes.

"Miss Benton, has someone . . . tell me what you need."

She swallowed and allowed him to lift her to her feet. "Mr. Franklin."

"Boss did this to you?" He gripped her arm so hard it hurt.

"No!" She turned to him, pleading. "No, please. Please, take me to Mr. Franklin." Her throat felt too thick to talk, and she tried again. "I need him to take me home. I must speak with him. I need to—" She wiped a hand across her eyes. "—please, will you take me to him?"

He searched her face in the darkness, eyebrows lowered, but eventually he slowly nodded.

Chapter 27

Pounding on the front door woke Tobias. He sat up quickly on the sofa and groaned. He paused as the pain washed over his head. The pounding continued, both on his door and through his skull. "I'm coming," he muttered. Pulling his suspenders over his shoulders, he shuffled to the door. A spike of fear shot through him as his thoughts immediately jumped to his sister, who hadn't returned yet from the dance. This may have been the first time he'd ever fallen asleep before she was safely home. Negligence on his part. Jerking open the door, he found Johanson standing on his porch.

"Boss, I'm sorry to wake you—"

"Hannah?"

Johanson stepped aside, motioning to his rig with Hannah huddled in her cloak, a small figure in the dark. "She won't talk to me, but something's happened, or she's taken ill. I think some-one, ah, she went outside—" He coughed. "She only asks to speak with you. I don't know what to do with her. I can't tell if she's sick or hurt. Maybe both."

Tobias brushed past Johanson and climbed into the seat next to her, but she didn't acknowledge him.

She'd wedged herself in the corner of the bench with her head turned away.

"Hannah." He placed a hand on her shoulder, and her entire body trembled beneath it. "Hannah, what is it?"

"Will you take me home?" She whispered without looking up.

Johanson spoke quietly on his other side. "I asked if we need-ed to alert the sheriff or find the doctor, but she kept insisting I bring her here."

Tobias released a slow breath, and a silent moment passed between him and Johanson.

Hannah begged again to be brought home, and he turned back to her.

"I will," he said. "It will take a few minutes to hitch Dan, oh—" He remembered his sleeping son. "I can't, honey. Luke's dead asleep. Until Eloise returns—"

"I can sit at the house," Johanson offered, looking relieved to be out of the picture. "And take the rig with Silver. He's ready to go. I'll stay 'til you return."

Arrangements were made, and if Johanson knew anything more than he let on, Tobias wasn't privy to it. Once they were out of town, Tobias slowed the buggy and set the brake. Han-nah hadn't moved, aside from the trembling as she burrowed in her cloak.

"I'm here," he said. "Want to tell me what's going on?"

Sniffling was her only response.

He sighed and took hold of her, pulling her against him. How many times had he played this game with Eloise? Someone had probably said something to upset her. Eventually, she'd talk. Women usually did.

She wasn't Hannah Claire Benton; she was a child. A small, disobedient child without any sense. An evil, wicked girl who knew only how to fall into trouble. She rested in the arms of her friend, and her body shook in violent, uncontrollable spasms.

He rubbed his hands along her back and spoke soothing words, but only because he didn't know of her wickedness.

When he found out what she'd done, he'd throw her out with the other orphans. With the dogs and the beggars and—he sang to her. Softly he sang a familiar hymn with words of promise and holy praise that warmed her and slowly chased away the shaking in her limbs.

Wrapped in her cloak and snuggled against his chest, she was safe. The fear was banished for the moment, and with her eyes closed, she relaxed, feeling only the warmth, comfort. Peace. A heaviness settled over her, and her breathing slowed.

This is what it felt like to be at peace, to know safety. Dare she say, to be loved? Growing drowsy, she wondered faintly why he didn't take her home, but it was a fleeting thought. Surely he'd be furious when he found out, but for now she rested in his arms.

His touch was gentle, firm. His strength was a shield, a rock to hide under. Not a weapon or a cage. How could he hold her with such gentleness after their fight this afternoon? His song faded, but he didn't press her for answers.

Surprised by how lethargic she felt after her muscles stopped trembling, she didn't fight the wave of drowsiness that washed over her.

With only the moonlight and the stars lighting their seat, Tobias was pretty sure she'd fallen asleep. Hannah Benton, asleep in his arms, was an alabaster figurine. The paleness of her face fairly glowed in the moonlight. He'd held her until her shaking ceased, intending to question her again once she was over her episode of whatever ailed her.

He'd weathered Eloise's fits of hysteria over the years, but Eloise usually soaked his handkerchiefs with her tears while spilling the whole story. Usually some fear from a nightmare, a resurgence of grief, or painful memories. Hannah neither cried nor spoke a word. An unease picked at him. Johanson seemed to think something unsavory had happened to Hannah, but if that was so, why didn't she tell him?

Tobias didn't know why Hannah had asked to come to him, but if it was for this, he would give it to her. The thought of Johanson holding her in his arms or any other man brought heat to Tobias's veins, and he tightened his grip around her. She'd turned in her sleep, and he cradled her against his chest.

Crickets took up the chorus around him, and he sat silently, letting her rest. He watched a fox slink across the road along a game trail. He smoothed her disheveled hair from her face, and she scrunched her nose in her sleep. Rationalizing that rule number two referred only to lips on lips, he pressed his own to her forehead. "Hannah," he murmured. "Wake up, my love."

She opened her eyes and looked at him. Her posture was in a state of rest, and he brushed his hand along the side of her face to push her hair back. Hannah whispered, "Does God answer the prayers of a sinner?"

"He must, darling, for we're all sinners."

"But the prayer of a righteous man availeth much."

He smiled. "There is none righteous, no, not one, and all have fallen away from the glory of God."

"You can't marry me, Tobias Franklin."

He laughed at her proclamation. "No, I'm sure the pastor's gone to bed tonight."

She turned her face from him, exposing a bruise on her opposite cheekbone.

"Hannah." His voice was strained, barely audible. "Did someone do this to you?"

"Please, take me home."

"Not until you tell me what's going on."

She sat up and glared at him with her chin raised. "Then I'll walk." Standing, she moved to step out of the buggy, but her cloak caught under her shoes and fell away from her shoulders revealing the full state of her ensemble. Her skin was raw and scratched along the back of her arms, half her hair was still in its pins with one side hanging near her waist, and the moon highlighted an inch of skin at her shoulder through a rip in her dress. All that he tallied at first glance.

Hannah stood, ready to jump from the buggy and run all the way home, but Mr. Franklin's soft intake of breath threw another layer of shame on her exposed shoulders.

He'd seen. He'd seen the mark on her face and the state of her dress. She refused to look at him and witness how much he hated her and crumpled to the seat. "I did everything I shouldn't have done," she confessed. "I danced with everyone who had a notion, I smiled, I laughed, and I had the best time in the world." She began to cry, truly cry, for the first time this evening. "But I didn't stop to think, and I did exactly what you and my mother and everyone has always told me not to do. We were alone on the balcony for only minutes. It was gorgeous, and all I wanted was to be there with you, and then, and then—and he—" The words wouldn't come out, and she buried her face in her hands, sobbing.

Mr. Franklin shifted, and she fell against him as the buggy rolled forward. She shivered in the wind, and he reached down at her feet and shoved her cloak into her lap, not even sparing her a glance. His face was chiseled of stone, and he spoke not. He made a wide turn in the empty prairie, and they were again on the road to town.

"Where are you taking me?"

"To the sheriff," he said.

"Oh, don't. Please, don't. I couldn't bear it." She took his arm and pleaded. "Please, take me home. Just bring me home. I don't want to speak to anyone or see anyone. I just want to be home."

He all but growled like a wild beast. "Hannah, did he have his way with you? Have you been . . . ?"

"No," she said. "No, nothing like that, exactly. I'm only shaken."

He pulled back on the reins and sat staring ahead. He scrubbed his hands across his face and blew out a breath. "Tell me who did this." But when he turned to her, she cowered from the anger pouring out of him. "Who touched you?"

"I wasn't thinking, and he—"

"Who, Hannah?"

"Mr. Grady," she whispered.

"I'll kill him," he ground out. "The bloody fool. I'll kill him." He shook his head. "We're still going to the sheriff. One look at you and he'll have reason enough to incriminate Charles."

"On what grounds? It was all over in ten seconds. He could claim I fell down the stairs, and it will be his word against mine. I did go out alone with him, let him lead me to the balcony. I don't know how many dances we shared. Perhaps I gave him the idea that I wanted his—his affection."

Mr. Franklin's eyes jumped from her hair, shoulder, and face. "Pardon, Hannah. But this was not affection."

Chapter 28

Hannah sat across the kitchen table from Sheriff Milton while his wife bustled around filling coffee cups. The lazy steam curling from her mug was at least something to look at. Each time she glanced at Mr. Franklin, she wanted to melt into the floorboards and slink away. His earlier sweetness and charm had been replaced with a steel ferocity just as she knew it would, and she dared not come any closer to it.

Standing tall, towering over the proceedings with his arms crossed, he snapped at anyone who spoke to him. He'd had her remove her cloak when they arrived and showed the scratches on her arms. She hadn't even realized the brick wall had scraped her when she'd struggled against Mr. Grady. In the light of the dining room, she was overly aware of her disheveled state. She wished only to have a few minutes to pin her hair in place, but Mr. Franklin insisted she present herself as she was.

The lamps in the kitchen were obnoxiously bright, and her mind began to buzz as it had in the moments after the incident. She mumbled another round of answers to the sheriff's questions and let the men discuss, uninterrupted. Lost in the tendrils of steam rising from her mug, she imagined the dungeon she would live in. It would probably have rats. *God, I'm sorry. I was so stupid. How did I let this happen? I've lost everything good that you put in front of me. I really didn't deserve any of it . . .*

Mr. Franklin draped her cloak around her, and they were off again, bouncing in the buggy toward home.

It was a silent two miles home. But she welcomed it, grateful he wasn't shouting in his anger. She kept her eyes on the horse's proud head, black in the night, and listened to the pounding of his hooves on the packed dirt road.

Mr. Franklin made the briefest of contact while helping her from the buggy. He led her forward, and his hands were feather-light against her elbow as he guided her up the steps and into the house, but nothing more. Was he repulsed by her?

Hiram was where she'd left him, though his book had fallen to the floor, and he curled against himself on the too-short sofa. He jerked awake when Mr. Franklin slammed the front door.

Hannah stood in the middle of the room, and her trembling returned.

"Hiram," Mr. Franklin barked, "we have a situation."

"What's that?" Hiram sat up, rubbing his eyes.

"Your sister," he spoke through clenched teeth, "found herself alone with Charles Grady, and he—show him." Mr. Franklin exhaled and tugged at Hannah's cloak, but she held it firmly about her shoulders. "Fine, he can see your face very well on his own. Have fun explaining away that shiner. She's a bit tight-lipped about it, but we already spoke to the sheriff and nothing irreversible happened. I have to get back." He kicked a chair out of his path on his way through the kitchen. "Stay away from the brickyard until you hear differently from me." And he was gone.

Hannah stared at the rug.

The sounds of the retreating buggy faded until all that was left was her own jerky breathing.

"What's this about Charles Grady?"

She squeezed her eyes shut and shook her head.

"Hannah . . . ?" Hiram's compassion-filled face tore at her soul.

Her lips curled around her teeth to staunch the inevitable tears.

"You're not going to talk to me?"

If she spoke, she'd fall to pieces.

He eased up from the sofa and came toward her. Gently, he ran a finger along her cheekbone. "Anything else need tending?"

When she shook her head, he huffed out a breath.

"I let you have all the space you wanted to play and enjoy your summer, and then this? Charles Grady? Everyone knows he's a cad."

She nodded, and the tears leaked out, trailing a line down each cheek.

"Hannah, how did this happen?"

She ran from him and fell to her bed. She didn't need his words to confirm her own incriminating evidence. The receiving end of her brother's disapproval was almost worse than Tobias's anger.

Tobias Franklin was disgusted with her. She knew it in the way he avoided her touch and how he sat like a stone the whole way home. His abrupt departure made it obvious how he felt.

She'd ruined everything. He would never choose to be with her after this and especially not after her disrespect this afternoon. God had only teased her with a bit of happiness before reminding her of her reality. Freedom wasn't to be so easily obtained.

She shoved her encounter with Mr. Grady far away in the lowest recess of her mind. The swirls of fear about what could have happened were worse than what did. That counted for something, didn't it? But her hands still shook, and her knees felt like pudding while she undressed and readied for bed.

She left the lamp burning and buried herself in the blankets. With too many doubts and fears stalking her mind, Hannah lay awake for hours.

When she did sleep, Mr. Franklin filled her dreams. Silly dreams in which they lay on a blanket in the tall grass surrounded by wildflowers and butterflies. A delightful vision from a fairytale, but in one dream after another Mr. Franklin turned away from her.

He walked away. He grew horns and breathed fire. He turned to stone. He disappeared.

No matter how many times she tossed, half awake, she found herself on the prairie with him, and they all ended the same way. Her offending and him angry.

At last she awoke with the sun pouring through the window. Turning her head, she discovered little Luke staring at her, sucking his thumb. When he noticed her eyes open, he leaned against the bed and patted her face. "Shhh. 'Annah seeping."

"Not anymore," she whispered.

"Wake now?" He showed all eight of his teeth.

"Come here, little peanut." She pulled him into the bed. He immediately snuggled against her, and his warm body filled her with peace.

He lay still for less than a minute and then planted a kiss on her forehead. "Wake now?"

She chuckled. "Yes, I'm awake." She brushed his soft blond hair away from his eyes. "What are you doing here?"

In answer, he bounced on his knees with his hands on her shoulder. Soft conversation from the living room filtered through her bedroom door that Luke must have left open.

"Luke?" Eloise stuck her head in the room, grimacing when she saw him in the bed. "Sorry—we didn't mean to wake you." Eloise stepped in and pushed the door shut.

"There are worse ways to wake up." Hannah pulled the boy down into a tight hug until he squirmed off the bed. "What are you doing here?"

"I'll give you a six-foot ranting, raving guess." Eloise chuckled. "He wouldn't give us a moment's peace this morning until I suggested we all load up and come see you. He wanted to stay until you woke, but work was pressing. About an hour ago, we talked him into leaving us here for the time. It appeased him, momentarily." She sat on the edge of the bed.

"He told you everything?"

She nodded. "And Mr. Johanson was at the house when Zeke walked me home. You gave us a fright."

"What time is it?"

"Half-past nine at least."

"No!"

"Come—I'll help you dress, and you can have breakfast. I have cinnamon rolls—bakery leftovers from Zeke."

Hannah sighed. "You sure know how to pick 'em. Any other bakers available?"

"Only the one, but I know of a certain brickmaker who'd lay the world at your feet should you ask."

"Surely not." Hannah scoffed and raised her arms to slip into the skirts Eloise held up for her. "Not after last night," she muttered through layers of petticoats going over her head.

"I've never seen Tobias in such a tither, and that's saying something."

"He's very angry, isn't he?" Hannah slouched at the foot of the bed.

"Very." Eloise found the comb and worked it through Hannah's waves of long hair. "But once Charles is in custody, he's bound to calm down."

Luke climbed on the bed and crawled under the blankets, making a mole hole of them.

"I just pray Charles has enough self-preservation to stay away from the brickyard. If Tobias gets a hold of him first—" Eloise whistled. "He may forget to leave vengeance to the Lord." The tangles smoothed out, Eloise plaited Hannah's hair into a simple, thick braid. "There. That will be comfortable for a day of rest."

Eloise put the comb away, and she gathered the discarded dress and slippers from the night before and put them in their places. She dug Luke out of the bed and smacked him on the bottom. "Stay out, sir. You're making a mess." Eventually she quit her fussing and sat on the bed, resting her head on Hannah's shoulder with an arm wrapped around her. "You're awfully quiet."

"I'm going home to Des Moines and will let Mother do as she wills."

"Heavens, you're speaking nonsense. This isn't the Hannah Claire Benton I know. That Hannah would strap on her side-sword and do whatever it takes to weather this storm."

"He won't ever forgive me."

"Hiram? You're wrong about that too. He's out there now putting the lambs together in the little fence by the house, for no other reason than because he knows you like to play with them, even if he wants to lie to himself that it's for Luke's pleasure."

"Tobias hates me."

"You're mistaken." Eloise knelt in front of Hannah and took her limp hands. "I'm going to tell you a secret. I've been keeping it because I didn't want to spoil the surprise, but I claimed you as a sister weeks ago. I hadn't even met you when I put the two of you together. Call it a woman's intuition, the Holy Ghost, or just a plumb good guess, but when Tobias came out here to return your book—that he read first, by the way—the man whose days are filled to the brim with caring for us and pouring every ounce of energy into work spent his few stolen hours reading that horrid book."

Eloise shook her head, then squeezed Hannah's hands. "I knew the two of you were meant to be. He's not one to waste time on stories, but he did, because of you. And when we saw the two of you together, arguing and playing, laughing at nothing but each other . . . Hannah, look at me. Anybody with a lick of sense can see there's something special between the two of you, some connection, not to be spoiled lightly."

But that's what she'd done. She'd spoiled everything.

Eloise rose. "So take a deep breath, wash your face, eat a cinnamon roll, and you'll feel much better about the whole thing. Tobias will return sometime today. Who can say when, but at some point he'll have to fetch his family home. You'll see what I mean."

"But he was so angry." Hannah tugged on the end of her braid. "You don't understand. He wouldn't even speak to me."

Eloise pursed her lips. "Hmm. He does that sometimes. He's a man, Hannah. His brain can only take in so many thoughts at once." Eloise laughed. "He's so filled up with love for you and anger at Charles that he can't spare an extra thought to tell you about it."

"Stop it. It's worse than you know. We quarreled even before that. I was disrespectful and rude, and I said terrible, hurtful things I shouldn't have said."

"So you're human. Ask him about the ink pot I spilled if you want to hear about terrible, horrible things being said."

"Eloise, it's just not going to happen. We're not right for each other. I'm silly and a dreamer, and he's so . . . strong and determined. So focused."

"And in love with you."

Hannah flopped over on the bed and curled into a ball, hugging herself. "Eloise, he's not," she whined. "You really are mistaken. I'm a wicked child who deserves everything bad to happen to me. If this is the culmination of my sin, so be it. But will you promise to write to me? Once I'm home? I couldn't bear the thought of losing you too."

"No, dear. Because if you leave, you take my brother's heart with you, and I will never forgive you for that. Now get up. Sweet sugary bread awaits you. I honestly don't know how that hasn't tempted you out of this room yet. I would have been into my second one if I were you."

Hannah grinned. "You said Hiram put the lambs in Luke's fence?"

"Aha—there we have it. Come, have your breakfast on the porch, and we'll let Luke and the other lambs snuggle all your troubles away. When my sullen brother arrives, you can work out whatever nonsense you think has the two of you at odds."

Chapter 29

Tobias Franklin threw himself into work, even though every inch of his being wanted to be with Hannah. Charles had the foresight to send a note with Jonas in the morning that he wouldn't be returning to the brickyard. Tobias called on the sheriff to inquire about the matter and was told it had been handled. The outcome wasn't satisfying, and the whole affair was resolved by noon. Charles was invited for questioning, was repentant, and swore he would never intentionally harm a woman. Said he was caught up in the moment and was misled by her intentions. Because there were no other witnesses to the event and "the lady seems to be just fine," Charles was acquitted. A minor misdemeanor, a lecture, and a promise to behave.

Roy Swenson sauntered by, a grin on his face. The man was acting strange lately. How the man could pull night duty monitoring the kilns and then turn around and volunteer for extra shifts on the weekends had Tobias shaking his head. Roy must be saving up for something big.

A headache threatened, but Tobias had more important matters to attend to. Like an imminent betrothal. A surrogate mother for Luke was now the bonus to marrying Hannah, not the other way around. He'd been unable to think of anything all night but making Hannah his wife. If Charles had gone further, if he'd had his way . . . Tobias unclenched his fists and reminded himself that Hannah was all right.

If she were well and truly married, that would keep her out of trouble. A married woman would have the good sense not to walk off alone with another man. She'd be under his protection. Off the market, so to speak.

With his mind made up and the plan formed, Tobias switched gears and conquered every task at the brickyard with streamlined efficiency. His buggy was hitched to Dan by mid-afternoon. A mile into the drive to Hiram's homestead, he found Zeke walking along the road. He slowed for Zeke to hitch a ride.

"Thanks, old man," Zeke said, climbing into the seat. "I reckon we're going the same direction?"

"How'd you know where to find Eloise?"

"She's not hard to find, Boss. You know that as well as I do. I mean, if she's not home there's only 'bout three other places she'd be. I checked them, so that only left one other option. Plus, she left a note."

"She left a note where? She didn't go anywhere this morning."

"Yep. It was on your kitchen table." He held up a tiny scrap of paper. "See? It says, 'Zeke, with Hannah.'" He cleared his throat.

"Post Script: You are the most attractive man in the world, much stronger and smarter than my idiot brother. If you see him today, tell him he's an imbecile—"

Tobias palmed Zeke in the face, shoving his head against the back of the buggy.

Zeke flailed, trying to ward off Tobias's advances, but was laughing too hard to put up much of a fight. "Uncle! Uncle!"

"So," Tobias said after Zeke sat up and adjusted his ridiculous cowboy hat. "Need I remind you that you're pathetic?"

"Maim me and starve. At the very least, you'll be stuck with burned pancakes for life. Your choice."

When they arrived, there was no sign of anyone outside and Luke's paddock was empty. Tobias let himself in the farmhouse, and Eloise greeted him with a shushing motion, pointing to his old bedroom. "They're sleeping."

"Wake that boy, or he'll never go to bed tonight."

"But Hannah's with him, I know she needs the extra rest."

"How is she?"

Eloise rolled her eyes. "She's got it in her head she's returning to Des Moines."

Once Eloise noticed Zeke behind him, Tobias's chance of getting any more information from her was lost. The two went outside together, and Tobias made his way to the bedroom. He'd slept there long enough; it didn't occur to him that he was entering the room of a woman. A woman asleep on her bed with an arm draped around his son. Her long hair was pulled into a casual braid with wisps framing her face. She and the child slept in perfect peace. Yes, he could get used to this. If Tobias didn't marry her, Luke would miss her something fierce. It wasn't fair to the child to let Hannah return to Des Moines.

Unwilling to disturb them, he relaxed into the rocking chair near the bed. The one Hannah had occupied while keeping vigil over him the first night and the days that followed, full of reading and entertaining. For that's what she'd done. He would never survive a week of bed rest in anyone else's company.

Her sketchpad lay on the bedside table. Checking that she still slept, he leafed through the pages. Many of them were simple doodles of fairytale creatures. Some flying contraptions with excessive wheels and moving parts, often with dragon wings or fire bursting from a pipe. From the inside pocket of his jacket, he pulled out the ink drawings he'd found on his desk yesterday. A princess—a warrior princess—stood watch over the entrance to a cave. The other depicted an ogre bricklayer.

The second made him chuckle. A clear representation of himself, the beast wore Tobias's cap and his overall stature was similar. Of course, the dead giveaway were the words scrawled across the bottom of the page, *Mr. Togre Miser Franklin*. Perhaps he should be offended by the drawing, but if this was one way she processed anger while locked in an office . . . well, he'd accept it. He placed the ogre image back in his pocket and slipped the one of the princess in her sketchbook.

He paused in his perusal of the book when "Franklin" caught his eye. Most of the page was filled with sloppy squiggles and swirls, nothing of distinction, and yet the bottom was signed, "Forever yours, Mrs. Franklin."

"Find something of interest?" Hannah spoke softly, watching him from the bed.

He glanced at her with a hint of a smile and angled the page for her inspection. He knew she'd registered the *Mrs.* signature when her eyes grew wide before she squeezed them shut.

"Bugger," she whispered. "You wouldn't happen to have an eraser?"

"Fresh out."

"That was your letter to the chef. It seems I added an extra squiggle by accident. Would you believe it had nothing to do with my infatuation with the invalid in my bed?"

"I would not."

Luke hadn't stirred, and Hannah didn't move. While they were alone, mostly alone, he figured there was no better time to get on with it.

"Hannah," he said, closing the book and returning it to the table. "I'm ready if you're ready. To make it official. How'd you like to be Mrs. Franklin? We can have it done tomorrow."

She blinked. "Just like that?"

"I thought about it up-ways and down, and it's the best solution."

"Solution?"

"It would keep you safer first of all. As my wife, none of the men around here would ever have asked you to go outside with them, not to say that a rough character wouldn't try something if you were alone, but once we're married, you wouldn't need to come back and forth from here. You would stay at the house. My head's getting better every day, and with you at home with Luke, I'd have more time to focus on work without worrying about you or the rest of them. Luke wouldn't disagree." He chuckled. "As far as he's concerned, you're already his."

"No." She slid her arm over Luke's shoulder and turned on her back, staring at the ceiling.

"What do you mean, 'no'? I thought we had an understanding that this was what we were both working toward. In light of what's happened, why not go ahead with it?"

"As I recall." She bit off her words.

He hissed his breath between his teeth, already feeling the impending fight.

"Sir, the last conversation we had, in the daylight, spiraled very quickly out of hand with both of us yelling at the other and ended with 'fine' in acknowledgment that we were to yet discuss the terms of our *understanding*." She linked her fingers over her forehead.

He refused to raise his voice, and his words came out in hushed bursts of air. "You told me yourself that this is what you wanted, what you'd prayed for!" He sat on the edge of the rocking chair with his feet firmly on the floor. "You were the one who was afraid the only reason I showed up on your porch was because God forced me." He looked down at her and spread his arm wide. "Well, here I am. Asking."

Hannah snorted and lifted on her elbow, facing him. "There you are. Raising your voice—"

"I haven't."

"You just did. You want me to salute, like everyone else under your command? You remember everything so well, do you remember why I asked for what I did? I wanted to be free from a life of criticism and control. Shame on me for not doing proper research before I put in my formal request for a husband. I wanted freedom, Tobias."

"And you clearly can't be trusted with it for a single night on your own." His words were out even as he grappled to reel them in. They slammed into her and pain reflected in her face.

"I'm sorry." He buried his face in his hands. "I'm sorry. That was wrong of me. I shouldn't have said that."

Hannah extracted herself from Luke, who finally awoke and smiled at Tobias.

"Hannah, wait. I didn't mean it." He reached for her arm, but she speared him with a look of pure fire.

She bent near him to find her shoes under the bed and slammed the door when she left.

That did not go well. Not well at all.

He briefly considered if chocolates would have made a difference. There were ways of proposing marriage, wooing a woman to leave her family and to love and live for one man until she died, and then there was what he just did.

Clapping his hands together once, he nodded at Luke. "Well? You coming?"

He was undeterred. A big-mouthed fool, yes. But the path was still straight. Hope lingered. Namely due to the events of last night. Why did she insist on seeing him if not for the trust, friendship, and perhaps something more they had together? Johanson could have very well taken her home.

The evidence spoke for itself. Tobias was at least one notch ahead of any other man in Ockelbo.

Chapter 30

Tobias carried Luke through the house and joined the others outside. The balmy June day was perfection, aside from the mosquitoes that plagued them.

Luke climbed down the porch steps and ran to the enclosure that Hiram had built for him. He peered over the fence to see if there were any animals to play with. There weren't, but he was soon distracted by stomping on every dandelion between him and the porch.

Hannah avoided his gaze, and when Tobias stepped to the edge of the porch, she retreated inside.

Zeke and Hiram played a game of bag toss, and Eloise chased Luke to keep him from picking up the bags where they fell.

"What'd you do, old man?" Zeke asked, not even looking at Tobias as he tossed another bag, missing his mark by a foot.

"Whatever it was, you'd better go fix it." Eloise shot him a disapproving glare.

Hiram didn't join in the verbal assault, but he raised an eyebrow.

"I'm not the villain!" Tobias answered his accusers, but he sounded like a whiny child trying to avoid his lessons.

"Sundays are wonderful for a drive about the country," Zeke said.

"They're glorious." Eloise blushed. "How convenient that we have a Sunday every week, starting with tomorrow."

"Too bad we'll be so busy, Chipmunk." Zeke sighed dramatically.

Eloise matched his sigh. "At least we'll be working together on the float. And Luke will come with us."

"Agreed. We're sure to make more progress with him underfoot. What will Boss do with his free day tomorrow?" Zeke scratched his chin. "No work? No son to wrangle? The buggy at his disposal?"

Tobias leaned against the post with his arms crossed. He watched the game and ignored their meddling. Zeke showed no skill, but he was also smirking and winking at Eloise as often as watching his toss.

Hiram reclined next to Tobias against the porch railing. "How's the gash healing?"

Tobias grunted, running a finger against the tender line along his scalp.

"Let me have a look." Hiram moved aside the hair and poked at the wound. "Yep, that's a beautiful scar."

"It's time to go home," Tobias said.

"Nope." Zeke called from the yard before chucking a bag at Eloise. "We've already been invited and agreed to stay through dinner. It's too bad Hannah's in the house by herself. If only someone would offer to help her in the kitchen."

"Don't look at me," Eloise said to Tobias. "I'm very busy." She giggled and dodged another of Zeke's pathetic shots.

Hiram looked away. "I have chores to finish. Could use your help, Zeke."

"Bullies," Tobias mumbled. He shoved off the post and stalked into the house.

Hannah stood at the table chopping a pile of potatoes. She glanced at him, then resumed her work. The knife slid through the vegetables with a forceful *chop, chop, chop*. He pulled out a chair and sat across from her. She continued to chop and intermittently tossed the large cubes into a simmering pot on the stove. After watching the ominous blade slam against the board for several minutes, he drummed his fingers on the table in an upbeat *ratta-tat-tat* to accompany the downbeat of her rhythmic chopping.

"I like your hair in a braid," he said.

She paused, knife hovering a moment before beginning again. *Chop, chop, chop.* "Thank you."

"There's a lot of it." He leaned forward.

She paused again. "Potatoes?"

"Your hair."

"Oh."

"Must get heavy sometimes, piled on your head. All the pins."

Her lips tilted on one corner, almost as if she didn't want to acknowledge him but couldn't help it.

"I noticed you called me Tobias earlier. When you were mad."

She sucked her teeth. "You would have noticed that." *Chop, chop, chop.* "Did you hear anything else I said?"

"When you're finished with the massive knife, I'm ready to talk about it more."

"About there."

She kept chopping, and he kept drumming until she slid the lid over the pot.

It pleased him when she chose the seat next to him instead of across. "Hannah, I'm sorry for what I said to you in the bedroom. I was—am—hurt by your refusal, and my first instinct is to push back. Not helpful for my cause, I know. It was a terrible way to ask a woman to spend the rest of her life with me."

"Taking lessons from Mr. Darcy." She brushed the end of her braid against the palm of her other hand.

He wanted to pull out the tie and unwind the tresses. "Who?"

"Never mind—he's another Austen. We'll read it next."

That made him smile. Some of the tension in his chest dissipated, knowing she hadn't completely given up on him. "I didn't mind Mr. Knightley. Solid, practical man."

"You might hate Mr. Darcy."

"Then let's not meet him. Did we finish *Swiss Family*? I was in and out during that one. I can't recall if they got off the island."

"They did, but only Fritz and Franz chose to go to Europe."

"Oh, that's right. And Jenny."

"Naturally." Her voice was barely audible.

"Would you have stayed on the island?"

"Depends on who stayed with me, and if I felt safe. I can't even be trusted to make good choices in little Ockelbo. What would I ever do should I meet a deadly tiger?" Hannah trailed her finger along the weathered edge of the tabletop.

Tobias let out an exasperated breath. "Most of the time it's safe for a woman to take a step outside alone. It is not your fault that Charles attacked you. Charles did what he did because of who he is, not because of anything you did to bring it about."

"It wouldn't have happened if I hadn't gone out alone with him."

The self-loathing in her voice angered him. "You're alone with me right now."

"That's different."

"Mr. Johanson had two miles to have his way with you, and he was the perfect gentleman."

She shrugged.

He narrowed his eyes. "He *was* the perfect gentleman?"

"Yes, dearest. Truth be told, I don't think I interested him in the slightest."

"Whoa, how in the blazes?" He scooted his chair back and angled toward her. "No part of what you said makes sense."

Hannah cocked her head, finally looking at him. "Did you want him to be interested?"

Tobias walked his fingers over to her hand and covered it with his. "Everything about you is interesting. What kind of numb-skull banker is he?"

"I was preoccupied. You wouldn't have been interested in me either if I spent our first meeting preoccupied with thoughts of another man."

"You're wrong."

Her gaze unabashedly collided with his.

He nodded. "I would still be one-hundred-and-ten percent interested, only green as spring grass on top of it. I would then do everything in my power to sway you from your current mistake of male companionship and woo you my direction."

She blinked, breaking the spell. "And then you would ignore me for a week, snap at me for doing a job well done, lock me up because you forgot you'd spoken to me less than a minute prior, and let another man bring me to a dance." Her eyebrows shot up, and she went royal Emma Woodhouse on him. "Then what?"

He tapped his heel on the floor and waved a fly away from the cutting board. What could he say to fix this?

"You were so angry with me last night that you wouldn't even speak to me. Tobias—yes, there. You win. I said your name— what do you mean when you say you're going to court me? Am I free to explore other options as well?"

"No." He tightened his grip on her hand.

"Then show me that you're interested!" She yanked her hand away and tossed her braid over her shoulder. "I want to be with you. Do you hear me? Even after all your stupidity, you're the one I dream about, but if you don't start showing that you really care, I won't stick around much longer."

It was Maribeth all over again. She'd made similar claims, though she waited months to speak of it. The difference here was that he'd fight for Hannah. He'd strung Maribeth along with no real intentions. With Hannah, he was sorry for the time he'd wasted.

"I'll come for you tomorrow afternoon? We'll ride all the way out to the river? Enjoy the view?"

When she nodded, he found her hand and brought it to his lips. "Ah-ah-ah," she said.

He spoke while brushing his lips on the back of her hand. "Hands don't count."

She held her breath, and he smiled, loving her reaction. He slowly turned her hand and pressed his lips to the base of her thumb, and then moved them along the side of her wrist.

"Yep." He dropped her hand. "Hands count."

Hannah cast her eyes down and drew her hands to her lap. "I'm sorry for my disrespect in front of your men. That was wicked of me."

He ran a knuckle from her shoulder elbow. "I'm sorry for chastising about last night. I've said my share of hurtful things." She still hadn't relaxed and seemed to be avoiding his gaze. "Hannah, truly, I need you to tell me what's troubling you. I don't do well at reading minds."

"After what happened—with Charles—and you were so angry with me on the tails of our quarrel, I started to doubt if I really knew you. I want a life that's different from what I had before, but I was afraid you weren't pleased with me. Things have gone well between us, but maybe we've been lucky nothing else has occured? After all, has it only been three weeks?"

"It can't be." How could he feel this way about someone he just met?

"It's been three weeks. I know it feels longer." She waved a dismissive hand. "The first week was long. Tobias . . . in light of our temperaments, I don't want to live the rest of my life afraid of stepping the wrong way and finding a side of you I never knew was there. You say one thing and then turn to stone, and I can practically see the steam rising from you."

"I wasn't angry with you."

"Certainly you were."

"Darling, I was so enraged with Charles that I didn't trust myself to speak. I only had thoughts for your safety and justice for him. I proposed today not out of anger but a desire to have you with me always."

He wanted to be touching her but wasn't sure if he was allowed. "I insulted you from a place of pain over being refused. I wish those words had never come from my mouth."

"What about the days when I do something you don't like?"

"I was wrong." Unspoken excuses piled up. Frequent headaches from the concussion. Behind at work. Losing clients to competing brickyards. He'd been afraid. But none of those would heal the hurt he'd caused. The best he could do was show her that he wasn't always that man. That he could be better. And he'd spend every moment he had with her trying to show her how he felt.

"Forgive me? I admit I was upset with your show outside my office. That wounded my pride, but I understand your pain behind it. Will you let me be Boss at work? I can't let myself think of you and make bricks at the same time." He laid his hand on the table, inviting hers back into it. "How can I fix this?"

"Can we go on like this a few weeks longer?" She spoke tentatively. "Don't press me. Don't ask for more. I want to only play and have fun as much as I can before the summer fades."

"Can I sway you toward a future with me if I promise not to lock you in any more offices?"

She nodded.

"And you won't go off alone with anyone else?"

"Not even for stargazing."

He looked into her eyes, memorizing the curve of her dark eyelashes. Her long braid hung over her shoulder, and he pulled out the ribbon.

"Tobias?"

"Hmm?" It was difficult to pull his gaze from her hair as it slowly came undone.

"I know I spoke out of turn at the brickyard, and I was unwise. But you hurt me with your inattention last week. I don't want you to grovel, but I thought I'd signed up for picnics. Sunday drives. Chocolates. I expected surprise notes and serenades." She looked at him sheepishly. "I don't require all of that, but I need to believe you're interested in forever and not the convenience of today."

He leaned closer with his hand wrapped around hers on the table. Touching his forehead to hers, he breathed in her clean scent. "What's not convenient is a dad-blamed rule number two. Whoever decided we needed it is an imbecile. I hate him to my core."

She giggled, and it was balm to his soul. If she wanted a knight, he could be that, couldn't he? He closed his eyes. *Lord, guide my steps. If this is the beginning of forever, let us walk with you.*

So she wanted romance . . .

He smiled. Hannah was worth a little romance.

Chapter 31

"The blue or the brown? Blue or brown." Eloise held two tablecloth samples. "I like the blue best, just for looking, but half of my wardrobe is blue, and we might get sick of each other."

"Then go with brown," Hannah said.

"But I like the blue." Eloise ho-hummed and stood gazing at the options. "Maybe I should settle with the cream—then I can dress it up per the occasion."

"Leave them all, and we'll come back next week. Pray the angels sing to you in your sleep and clear up the whole thing. Come—we'll get a flag for Luke."

Eloise nodded and put the samples in the box on the counter.

Hannah swatted Luke's hand from undoing the bow on her yellow bonnet. "When do you meet Zeke for the parade?"

"About an hour." Eloise smiled. "You know I dread being up there and having everyone look at me, but he's so excited for it I didn't dare confess."

"You'll be fine."

Eloise shrugged.

"How's this for comfort? There will be so much extra noise and commotion, nobody will notice you."

"Better."

Hannah tucked her free hand around Eloise's elbow and pulled her away from the bolts of fabric in the mercantile. "Let's get a bite to eat before—" Her fingers dug into Eloise's arm as the air *whooshed* straight out of her. It took a moment to coax her lungs to expand. Heart pumping, Hannah swiveled and hustled them to the back of the store.

Eloise followed without a fuss. "What is it?"

"He's here. Charles Grady." Realizing what she was doing, Hannah stopped and prayed for courage. "No matter. This is my town too." She held Luke tightly against her chest. "Come along. We're going to go about our business as usual because we aren't afraid. What can he possibly do?"

Eloise reflected a look of sheer terror. "Or we hide in the corner until he leaves. That's what I choose."

They carried on in hushed voices, huddling in the corner. "Nonsense. He's nothing but a snake, and I'm not afraid of a little snake. He's a worm. A slimy, slithering worm with no backbone. Shoulders back, Eloise. There—chin up. Ready? Eloise, stop shaking your head. Whatever are you worried about?"

"Because I know him for the scoundrel that he is, and I'm your friend and his old boss's sister. It's uncomfortable, and I hate it."

"Sing 'Yankee Doodle.'"

"Now?"

"Yes, in your head, silly." Hannah waved her hand, conducting the first line and humming. "Bada, bum, bum, bum."

Eloise looked confused. "That's not 'Yankee Doodle.'"

Hannah laughed loudly. "Oh, dear—you're right. 'She's a Grand Ol' Flag'? Yes, that's what it is." She sang, "She's a grand ol' flag, she's a high-flying flag."

Charles was almost forgotten.

"That'll be fine. Go." Hannah waved her finger in the air. "Baaa-da, bum, bum, bum. Ba-da, dee-dee-doo-da." She pointed to the side of her head. "The rest up here. Now we march. Off we go. Eloise! Stand up straight. Blimey, child. How did you ever survive without me?"

Hannah led them boldly through the mercantile, marching past the aisle with Charles, and she didn't look his way once. If he took notice of her, she wasn't the wiser.

Bursting out into the bright morning sunshine, both girls breathed at the same time before releasing it with laughter. They quickened their pace and let Luke run between them to the bakery.

"Sweet rolls for my sweetie." Zeke passed three warm rolls over the counter to Eloise. "And a few to share."

Hannah snagged one before it fell to the floor and tugged on Eloise's arm. "No dreamy eyes. You can bask in his affection another time. We have work to do. Thanks, Zeke. We'll have her dolled up and ready for the parade straightaway."

"Have her back in an hour," Zeke called over the line at the counter.

The town was already beginning to fill with crowds for the Independence Day celebration. Eloise squeaked and jumped out of the way of a troupe of boys running down the boardwalk with tin whistles.

More school children flooded the streets, waving their hand-held American flags. The Fourth of July always knew to arrive on the hottest day of the year, and this was no exception. The wind even took the day off, along with most of the working class. Not a breeze came through to cool the back of anyone's neck.

Hannah slowed, eyeing treats and trinkets displayed on the booths that had popped up overnight. Lemonade, ice cream. Little bells, whistles, and drums. Flags. So many flags. Firecrackers.

"Don't buy anything," Eloise said. "Tobias will treat us later, I'm sure."

"Let's at least walk through the square. Everything is so festive. I love it."

An enlarged copy of the Declaration of Independence hung from a board in the center of the square near the bandstand. Next to it was posted the scheduled events of the day. An ongoing horseshoe tournament, a horse race, barbecue, parade. The band would perform soon and would set up again this evening for a town dance until the highly anticipated firework show after sunset.

"Eloise! Eloise!" A dark-haired woman about their own age came tearing through the grassy square.

Eloise laughed and opened her arms, catching her in a hug. "Oh, Jessica, how I've missed you." Eloise pulled back and waved

Hannah closer. "Jess, meet Hannah Benton. She's my new sister."

"No!" Jessica's mouth hung open.

"No." Hannah pinched Eloise's arm. "She means that we are *like* sisters."

Eloise tipped her nose in the air and shot Jessica a look. "She's in denial. She and Tobias have an *understanding,* whatever that means."

"Clearly, he tells you everything." Hannah extended a hand. "Hannah Benton. Pleasure to finally meet you, Jessica, and I hope you'll furthermore ignore anything she has to say about her brother and me."

"Jessica, he regularly buys her chocolates since she turned down his proposal." Eloise's eyebrows danced.

"Oh, this is serious. Tell me everything." Jessica linked arms with Hannah and Eloise, and the three, with Luke on Hannah's hip, went off to dress Eloise for the parade.

As much as Hannah tried to protest, with both girls determined to pester, it was a worthless cause. She fell quickly into their chatter, and Jessica's questions didn't subside until the subject was thoroughly resolved—yes, they had kissed, but not since the first time—yes, he was very good at it—yes, he bought her chocolates twice a week—yes, they were courting with the intent to marry—no, she didn't have a ring—yes, they went for long drives each Sunday.

Luke left a trail of sweet-roll crumbs all over Eloise's living room, but the girls were too busy braiding ribbons into Eloise's hair to give him any mind.

"Roy and I marry at the end of production for the year." Jessica shoved her hand under Hannah's nose.

"Why are you showing me your hand?"

"Do you see a ring?"

Hannah laughed. "No."

"Neither do I, but the wedding is months from now. I can hardly stand it. He manages to come out to the homestead at least once a week, but oh, how I miss him in between."

Hannah mumbled around the pins in her mouth. "Roy Swenson? I know him from the brickyard."

"Yes, head brickmaker. Working twelve-to-fifteen-hour shifts managing the kilns." She stuck her tongue at Eloise. "Tell Boss to let a guy have a few days off, why don't you?"

"By the end of October he's all yours," Eloise said.

"Hold still—almost done with this side." Jessica pinned a coil of Eloise's braid with a bright red ribbon weaved through it. "And you'll be Mrs. Eloise James in a month and plump as a mother goose by Christmas."

Luke tore down the boardwalk in front of Hannah, ignoring her calls to stop.

She lifted the front of her skirts and quickened her pace, but the rapscallion was a fast little bugger. "Luke Franklin! You come back here right now."

The tyke turned to her with an open-mouthed smile splitting his face, and he tripped.

Hannah winced and scurried the last few feet to catch him. They were almost to the corner where they were supposed to meet Tobias. Meeting his father with Luke in one piece was at this point her only goal. She scooped up the boy just as he released a tormented wail.

A stream of tears followed, and a smear of blood marred his lip. "I fall," he said. "I faaall."

"Yes, you did. You fell." Hannah steadied him on his feet and pulled her handkerchief from the cuff of her sleeve. "You ran away from Miss Hannah, and you did not obey. I will not go out with you anymore if I can't trust you to stay with me. It's not safe."

A pair of boots with brick-colored clay on the sides stopped next to her.

Luke recognized them as soon as she did and cried, "Dada!" Everything else he'd experienced so far this morning tumbled from the almost-two-year-old's mouth. In his halting words he tried to explain all they'd seen, and he pointed to the commotion around their huddle. He ended with "Bang! It loud."

Tobias picked Luke's cap from the boardwalk and straightened the tuft of hair that stuck up in the back before placing it on Luke's head. Their matching blue eyes and contagious smiles did funny things to Hannah's heart when Tobias gave his son this kind of undivided attention. "And you have a flag!"

Luke waved the stick in Tobias's face.

"Hurrah for the red, white, and blue." Tobias chuckled.

"Hoshoe, Dada?"

"I'll hold you." Tobias casually hoisted Luke to his shoulders. Hannah reached to intervene, but was too late.

"Don't fuss, woman." Tobias winked while throwing an arm over her shoulder. "Nothing but a bit of stiffness in the mornings. Dr. Hiram cleared me for duty."

"Mr. Franklin, please remember where we are." She wiggled her shoulders under his arm and looked around, wondering what people would think about his friendly display. "You've been be-having much too familiar lately, and you're bound to start tongues wagging."

He pulled her closer. "Like puppies. Another thing I hate about puppies. All those wagging tongues." He leaned in and spoke only for her. "Do you think all of these strangers know about our kiss?"

"They very well might." She worked very hard to keep a straight face.

"What do we say to that? What's that phrase you were using last week? 'Avast ye, something something, scalawag.'"

"Hush, darling." She gave up and broke into a smile. "Don't speak of what you know nothing about." Relaxing into his hold, she wrapped an arm around his waist.

He smiled but trained his gaze down the street. "If 3,000 bricks a day need three days to dry, seven to fire, and five to cool, how long before we've built the addition to the city hall?"

"Depends on how many bricks are needed for the addition."

"Trick question. The city isn't building an addition."

"But if they were, Franklin Brickworks would present the fin-est, most elegant bricks a city hall could ask for."

His smile deepened. "Aye, aye."

Hannah smirked. She knew her mother would throw a fit, and she didn't care in the slightest. Among the crowds, the noise, the excitement—nobody paid them any mind. For all they knew, she was his wife and Luke her son.

Mr. Franklin had been the doting beau since their latest argu-ment, but she still asked herself if his affection would last. Did he love her? Did he want to marry her of his own free will? Nowhere in Scripture did she find the answer to whether she should marry this man. Not a single verse. She couldn't know if she loved him for him, or for the excitement of the situation, or for the way he made her feel. How did one ever know for sure?

"Here they come." Tobias tugged on Luke's ankle, and the two looked down the street at the oncoming parade.

Hannah acknowledged that God used prayer as a means to communicate, but the decision to marry Tobias Franklin needed a bit more processing. When God delivered him to her porch, it may have been in answer to her first request, but God had been silent since.

She wasn't looking for perfection, for she could hardly expect more of a husband than she could give. Friendship they had. Passion was there. Was that love? Friendship and passion? Was love wanting his arm around her shoulder in the July heat despite the sticky sweat that clung to her back?

The band marched closer with trumpets blaring and cymbals clashing. Luke waved his flag from his roost on Tobias's shoulder. Tobias must have noticed her scrutiny because he turned his head down to her and smiled. She gazed into his eyes, only inches from hers, probably participating in the dreamy eyes that she accused Eloise and Zeke of. "Tobias, what is love?"

"Say again?" He shouted against the band and cheers that rose around them. He leaned his ear to her.

"What is love?"

He faced her again, eyebrows lowered. His eyes dipped to her lips, and his expression relaxed. His side clenched where her hand rested, and his rib cage swelled with a sigh, but he turned to watch the parade instead of answering.

Marry me, and I'll show you is what Tobias didn't say. *Spending hours alone with you each Sunday and still abiding by rule number two. That's love.*

With the band leading the spectators in cheers, "Hip hip hooray for America," it was poor timing for deep discussions. Someone jostled him from behind, and he took a step to catch his balance. Hannah hadn't turned her face away from his. She searched him as if she would find everything she needed there. The weight of what she might be searching for settled on him.

Greater love has no man than that he lay down his life for his friend. He focused on the parade though he no longer took notice of it, not with her stare drilling into him.

Love was getting up and going to work every day to provide for those under his roof. Love was holding Katie's hair out of the way while she emptied her stomach for the last two weeks of her life. Love was found at two in the morning, rocking Luke back to sleep for the fourth time instead of letting him cry and wake everyone else in the house. The pain of burying Katie. The joy of watching Luke take his first steps. Learning to navigate Eloise's moods and furnishing a safe place for her to heal.

He needed time to process this question and the questioner. He drew his hand across her back and down her arm until he found her gloved hand and intertwined his fingers with hers.

The rest of the day went along without any more surprise questions. Tobias and Hannah remained in each other's company the entirety of the day from the parade onward. Luke took his nap in Hannah's arms at the horse race of all places, dead to the exuberant shouts around them.

Anytime Tobias could get away with holding her hand, he did. If he sat next to her, he managed to have his knee against hers. At the table the toe of her boot put pressure on his. There was the unfortunate problem of the dance in combination with being the father of a toddler. His son needed to be in bed, and the days of counting on Eloise to stay home with Luke were over. Hiram joined them for supper at the house, so Tobias didn't even have the excuse of driving Hannah home.

"I'm sorry," he said to Hannah, leading her away from the others on his porch. "I'd keep you here with me if I could get away with it."

She shrugged. "Hiram is ready to go home anyhow. It's been a long day."

If tossing himself on the grass to throw a tantrum would change anything, he would do it. He resorted to whiny complaints in lieu of the kicking and screaming. "Why does Sunday afternoon only come once a week?"

"Something about God and sabbath and calendars."

"Will I see you before then?"

"I'll be at your house with Eloise, but unless you lift our brickyard visiting probation—" She shrugged as if not seeing him for a week was of no concern whatsoever.

"I'd feel better if you stayed away. Both of you."

"Why, if he's not there? It should be the one place where we know I won't run into him."

"Too many men, too many machines. For whatever reason, Charles got it in his head he could take what he wanted from you, and it started at the brickyard. Plus, you're distracting."

"To you or others?"

He wrapped his arms around her and tickled a giggle out of her. Not being allowed to kiss her propelled him to find other means of contact. She sighed and nestled into his chest. He leaned his back against the side of the house. "I don't think I'll ever get my fill of this," he said. "Just holding you."

"You never answered my question this morning."

He stood taller, knowing exactly what she referred to. "It's a whopper of a question."

"Love suffereth long, and is kind. Love envieth not, vaunteth not itself." She quoted 1 Corinthians against his chest.

"Is not puffed up, doth not behave unseemly."

"But love between a husband and a wife—I love my brother, but it's not the same."

"We didn't choose our family, you mean." Tobias held her shoulders at arm's length to look into her eyes. "Are you still worried about this choice? You said no to my offer of marriage, but you've not turned away."

"I—you know I think with my mouth open. I want to make sure we're doing the right thing. Passion and friendship? Is that enough?"

Tobias cupped her face. "How about joy? I'm a rotten man to confess this, but I felt a good amount of passion for Maribeth, yet we never talked like you and I do. The trust and friendship was never there. Zeke is my friend, but my heart doesn't skip and jump about when he enters a room. Just being near you is joyful." He laughed. "Like how we feel about Luke, but different."

"And when that joy runs out?"

"Says who?"

"Seems to be the way of things."

"Maybe they never had what we have."

"And what's that?"

Tobias gripped her shoulders. "A relationship built on honest friendship."

"I don't want to wait until Sunday to see you again." She bit her lip, and his heart stuttered.

"Thank heavens, me neither. Tell you what—if you can get to my house, I'll do my best to escape for lunch the entire rest of the week."

"I can do that. Will you do something else for me? Since we'll miss the band this evening, dance with me. Now."

"Mmm." Tobias slid a hand up her back, and he fumbled to clasp her hand without breaking eye contact. "My pleasure."

Chapter 32

Weeks later, Hannah made a face and mimed spitting. "Yuck. Don't eat that. Yuck, yuck, yuck."

Luke ignored her, and she dug her finger into his mouth, swiping along his cheek to clear out the chewed pieces of bark. "That's twice now." She called to Tobias, who reclined on their picnic blanket in the shade of the cedar shrub trees. "You aren't bothered that your son is trying to eat everything except his lunch?"

Tobias lifted his cap from his face to watch her struggling with the toddler. "Stop making him spit everything out, and he wouldn't be so hungry."

Throughout their attempted meal, Luke scampered about, and either Hannah or Tobias ran after him and returned him to the blanket. Sometimes, wonder of wonders, the child stayed nearby long enough for them to have a resemblance of a conversation uninterrupted. She and Tobias had managed to get together two or three times a week, though never long enough or often enough to satisfy either of them. Today he'd surprised her at the farm for a picnic.

"Bring him here." Tobias raised his arms without moving from the blanket.

Luke sprawled on Tobias's chest and sucked his thumb. "That's all right, buddy. I know that mean ol' lady won't let you eat the earth."

She lowered her voice, threatening. "Tobias . . ."

"She's right, you know. If you're going to grow up big and strong like your daddy, you have to stop trying to eat the sticks. It simply won't do." He went on lecturing in a soothing voice and adjusted Luke so he lay next to him in the crook of his shoulder.

It was a sweet image of father and son. Hannah's father had tended to spoil her, mostly by buying her things that Mother would never approve of like candy and books. But Hannah had no memory of being coddled so. No memory of summer picnics with her family. Her father allowed a kiss on the cheek before bed if he chanced to be home, and maybe he would look up from reading his medical journal and maybe he wouldn't. As she grew and was able to converse on the topics that interested him, a different relationship formed. They debated the latest medical practices, and he laughed at her questions and outlandish ideas. Outlandish, imaginative, ludicrous. Maybe that's why she continued in her fantasies; it brought a laugh from him when nothing and nobody else could.

Grasshoppers climbed up and down the stalks of grass and small white butterflies flitted about in the heavy summer air. Eloise's wedding was next Sunday. June and July had flown by, and Hannah was no more at peace with her parents than when she'd escaped. In every letter she sent home, she'd tried to convince them that an extension here with Hiram was necessary. After eight weeks of loveliness with Tobias, she knew she'd stay. How to convince them of her choice without losing the last connection she had with her parents? She did want freedom, but she didn't hate them. Without resorting to lying, she'd mentioned all the ways she was helpful to Hiram, and how she'd developed good friends in town. She touted the bakery, the dress shop, the regularity of the trains, and ease of long-distance communication.

In each reply her mother was more and more determined to refuse. In the last letter Mother threatened "to come myself and stay the final month of your holiday." Hannah thought it best not to mention it again.

"I want a puppy," Hannah said, squatting to watch an inchworm make its way across the butterfly weed. "I've never had a puppy, and I think I need one. Do you know anyone around here with a fresh litter?"

"No puppies." Tobias stuck his tongue out at Luke and wagged it back and forth until the boy giggled. "Who needs a puppy when you have a toddler?"

She held a hand to the inchworm, and it crawled right onto her finger, making its way along the back of her hand. "A little puppy with floppy ears." She stood and transferred the worm to the nearest branch of the cedar tree. "We'll name him something from one of our books we first read together. Maybe Austen for a boy, or Mr. Knightley." She giggled. "Can you imagine being stern with a puppy named Mr. Knightley? 'Mr. Knightley, did you soil this rug?'"

"We're not getting a puppy."

"Maybe Fritz would be a better name. We have a good supply of names to choose from. Huckleberry—though that might be asking for too much trouble. We'll just have to wait until we get the puppy and see what fits." Hannah flinched as a pinecone whizzed by, barely missing her face. She took a step back and narrowed her eyes at Tobias, who sat cross-legged on the ground with Luke. "Mr. Franklin, your uncouth behavior is unwelcome. That is no way to treat a lady."

"Neither is this." In one smooth motion he was on his feet and came for her. He hooked his arm around her waist and kicked her feet out from under her.

She squealed, falling to the ground, but he caught her at the last second.

His laughter filled the air when she struggled against him in a pathetic attempt to gain her footing.

She never quite appreciated the strength of a man until it was matched against her own. After a fair amount of laughing and feeble attempts at escape—surely they appeared that way to him, though she honestly gave it her best go—the wrestling match ended with her pinned beneath him on the ground with grass tickling her neck.

"Rogue," she said, gasping for breath under his weight.

"Dearest mine." He captured her hands above her head. "I don't think you understand how annoying puppies can be."

"But they're so soft and snuggly."

"They wet the floor."

She spoke slowly. "Soft and snuggly."

"They chew on the furniture."

"Big puppy-dog eyes that melt your heart."

"They cry during the night."

"You're crushing all my hopes and dreams. And me. You're like a massive boulder lying on top of me." She began struggling to get out from under him, pretending to suffocate.

"No puppies."

She scowled. "You're a killer of dreams. A giant tyrant with a mold-encrusted, flea-bitten spider for a pet."

"Thy nose is as the tower of Lebanon."

"What!" Hannah froze in her half-hearted struggle. "What about my nose?" Self-conscious, she frowned.

"You're not the only one who reads. Let's have another round."

"Get off me. I can't breathe."

He rolled to the side and lay on the quilt, eyes closed, hands resting on his chest. "How beautiful are thy feet with shoes, O prince's daughter!"

"Don't tell me you're quoting holy Scripture."

He smiled and continued reciting. "The joints of thy thighs are like jewels—"

"Mr. Franklin!"

"—the work of the hands of a cunning workman. Thy navel—"

"You're worse than a rogue."

"—is like a round goblet, which wanteth not liquor." He raised his voice over her continued protests. "Thy belly is like a heap of wheat set about with lilies."

"The lilies I don't mind so much."

He turned to her and grinned devilishly. "Thy two breasts are like two young roes that are twins."

She gasped. "Tobias Franklin, you stop that this minute. Those words were meant for a bride from her groom. Stop wiggling your eyebrows at me."

"If you call me a flea-bitten spider, then I'm allowed to compare certain parts of you to a baby deer. Rules be rules."

"But I'm not mentioning—" She shot her gaze along his stretched-out body, and heat rushed to her face. She clamped her mouth shut at just the idea of it.

He burst into raucous laughter at her embarrassment.

"Hey, where's Luke?" she asked, mainly to change the subject.

"He was just there piling up pinecones. It was his idea to try to hit you with one."

"Was it also his idea to wrestle me to the ground?"

"Yes." Tobias stood, adjusting his vest and straightening his cap. "Luke," he called.

"A lot of good that will do. He rarely answers me when I call."

"I know, but it makes me feel like I'm trying. Go that way, will you? See if he followed the sheep. I'll look around the trees."

"A puppy would come when it's called."

"If it's trained. After we find Luke, we'll get some treats and start training him. You train Luke to come, to stop chewing on things and wetting the floor, then I'll consider a puppy."

Tobias searched in and around the trees long enough without finding the blond-headed devil that he began to worry. He met Hannah coming down the hill, holding her skirts and walking with a slight jog to her steps. "No luck for you either?"

She shook her head. "He's not with the sheep, and I stood on the top of the rise and didn't notice anything. He couldn't have gone very far, but if he's simply sitting in the grass, we'd never see him."

Tobias turned in a slow circle. "We'll find him."

"Oh!" She squeaked. She pointed to the large cedar tree nearest their blanket. "Lord, have mercy."

In the uppermost branches, there was Luke, slowly making his way higher yet. Tobias started to sprint toward the tree, but Hannah grabbed his arm.

"Don't frighten him lest he fall."

"Fine, but if he's going to fall, I'd rather be underneath when it happens."

When they both reached the tree, the branches were so close together and so near the ground that Tobias couldn't get within five feet of the trunk. "How in the blazes are we supposed to get him?" Heedless of sharp needles and dry twigs that came at him, he shoved his way deeper into the mess of branches. Once he broke through the outer edge, there was slightly more room near the trunk. He saw how easily the little boy had made his ascent with the branches stair-stepping around the trunk like a ladder. But what came easily for a toddler was much more of a challenge for a six-foot man. Only a few feet from the ground and he knew he wouldn't be able to reach his son. The branches were too close together to allow passage, and they were already growing too weak to support his weight.

"Luke!" He broke off a dead stick that was the thickness of his thumb and tossed it out of his way. "Luke, stop!" Surely the boy had climbed as high as he could go by now. "Luke, can you come down? Daddy's here. It's time to come down."

Hannah spoke softly from outside the tree. "Tobias, he's stopped, but he can't get down."

"I see that. Are you praying?"

"Yes."

"Keep doing that. I'm going to see if I can go higher."

By now Luke looked down and began to cry. "Hoshoe, Dada. Hoshoe, Dada."

"I'm trying, son. Can you see me? Come back down. Move like you did going up, only backward."

Tobias stayed close to the trunk on each branch. His weight still proved to be too much when a branch snapped from under his boot. In doing so, it put all his weight on his handhold and then it snapped too. He hugged the trunk and stretched his toe until it found a branch below.

"Hannah, I can't go any higher."

"I see that. Are *you* praying?"

"Obviously." He spent some time doing just that while Luke continued to cry.

"Should I come up instead? I weigh half as much as you."

He looked down at her standing a ways from the tree so she could see them both from her vantage. After a moment he shook his head. "You'll never make it through with your skirts. These branches are so close together. You'll get caught for sure."

"I'll take it off."

"You'll take it—what?" He craned his neck around to see Hannah already fiddling with the side of her skirt.

"It's nothing you haven't seen hanging on the wash line all your life, pumpkin."

He sputtered. "But I haven't seen yours."

Luke cried louder but still hadn't moved from his perch.

"Come down, Tobias. He's frozen in fear."

When he'd scrambled to the base of the tree and fought his way through the jungle into the open, Hannah had shed her skirt and a mountain of petticoats. Standing only in her calico shirt-waist, pantaloons, stockings, and boots, she gave him a curt nod without making eye contact.

Chapter 33

Hannah ignored the gallant prince of a man who'd emerged from the base of the tree, heaving gulps of air as if he'd been fighting a mighty duel. She had to be the one to go up the tree. This was the only logical plan. Tobias was simply too big, and there wasn't time to find someone else. She'd climbed plenty of trees in her day when she still wore short dresses and long stockings. She could do this.

The cedar branches were prickly and caught in her hair and scratched her exposed skin. Only a tiny child would have been able to slip through unscathed. Focused on her task, she did a fair job of pushing aside the notion that Tobias M. Franklin had a full view of her half-dressed from the waist down in thin muslin pantaloons. Thankfully, she'd worn the skirt and matching shirt-waist today instead of a full dress. There'd be no taking that off without exposing the embroidered corset again. And though he'd seen it once, a wedding night was the only place she wanted to be undressed down to that.

Focus, Hannah. "I'm almost there, Luke."

He was near her reach, but the footholds had grown weak. With hands wrapped around the small trunk, she carefully tested the next step up, and then the other. "It's all right, baby."

"Hoshoe, Dada. Hoshoe, Dada." Streams of tears made rivers down his red face.

"Hannah," Tobias called. "Someone's coming down the road."

"Who?"

"I don't know; looks like a livery rental. Stay there. Likely they won't see you, and they'll keep driving."

"Your son is screaming like a banshee. How do you think they won't notice? Of all the rotten, lousy, ill-timed . . ."

Tobias snatched her pile of discarded clothing and wrapped everything in the blanket.

"We'll get you back to Daddy." She wrapped her hand around Luke's ankle, and he released a blood-curdling shriek, holding tighter to the tree. She spoke soothing words, and eventually he stopped crying and looked at her again. But he wasn't letting go. Hannah twisted around to look behind her at the buggy approaching. It was slowing down.

Cat's liver. "You could have at least tried to hide in the bushes," she mumbled to Tobias, who couldn't hear her and was even now approaching the buggy. From her height she couldn't see under the roof of the rig.

Luke whimpered again.

She whispered to him. "Remember when you were so quiet a few minutes ago? Daddy and I were looking and looking for you, and you were a sneaky little bugger because you were so quiet. Can you do that again? I'll be quiet with you. We'll both hide in the tree together. Won't that be fun?"

"Hoshoe, Dada." He opened his mouth like a big round O and began to wail, beginning with a low tone that rose higher and higher.

"Yep, very well. We can play Show-Everyone-Hannah's-Underpants. That's a very good game too. Here we go then. I'm going to help you get down." Hannah reached a hand to him. "Can I hold you? We're going to go down now." Hannah wrapped a leg around the trunk, hooking her knee to give her enough leverage to momentarily reach up with both hands to pry Luke away.

"Hannah Claire Benton, you get down from that tree this instant."

"Hush, Amanda. Let her get the boy."

Hannah groaned.

The distinct voices of her parents lectured her and each other over the sounds of Luke's continued wailing. She pursed her lips, for there was no time to change tactics, especially now that she was mid-work of prying Luke's fingers from his death grip on the trunk no bigger than his two hands could span.

One tiny hand claimed a handful of her hair, and then he flung himself to her.

When his full weight transferred, all twenty-five pounds of it, the small branch supporting her foot broke, and she cried out.

Her cry was echoed by the scream of her own mother.

Hannah didn't slip far. Thankfully, Luke had replaced his death grip from the tree to her and nestled to her chest with his arms and legs clinging to her. She caught herself with one hand around the trunk and inched down to a thicker branch.

Now what? Now she had the boy, but how could she climb down with only one free hand? For the moment, she held him and kissed the top of his head.

He relaxed his arms around her and stuck his thumb in his mouth.

"You, sir, are a troublemaker," she whispered. Still too afraid to look down at the three below, she considered staying here indefinitely. "Here's what we're going to do. You're going to take that thumb out of your mouth and hold on to me like your life depends upon it because it does. And then I'm going to let go of you and use both hands to get down."

He blinked his watery blue eyes and another tear dripped out.

"Don't look at me like some abandoned baby creature. You're the one who got us in this mess."

"Hannah!" Definitely her mother. "If you're planning to stay up there and avoid speaking to us, it won't work."

"Ready?" Hannah whispered again. "Hold tight, I'll start going down, and you can meet your new grandma and grandpa." And the thought didn't startle her. Instead, it gave her enough courage to take the next step down and the next.

Tobias would be there.

Mother was a beast, but she couldn't get away with half as much with Father standing near.

Hannah paused. There was still the matter of her attire. "Mr. Franklin?"

"I'm right below you."

"Oh!" With all the screaming and avoiding the calls from what must surely be her parents, Hannah hadn't heard Tobias come back to the tree. He stood within the over-crowded tent of the branches only a few feet below her now.

She lowered her voice. "I'm going to hand him down to you." She maneuvered Luke and held all his weight by his upper arm. Bending as far as she could go, she lowered him to Tobias's outstretched hand

"Got him." Tobias waited for her within the hidden confines of the tree until she scrambled down next to him. The branches were so thick with needles—and prickly ones—that they created a screen between them and her parents.

"I hate you," she whispered.

"I love you."

"Of course you do. I just saved your son from certain death."

"I love you."

"I hope you rot in a moldy dungeon. The next time I'm up a tree in my—" She wouldn't even say it but slapped the sides of her thighs. "—and my mother and father come sailing down the road, do me a favor and shoot me down yourself. I'd rather be dead by your hands than theirs."

"I love you."

Hannah stopped her whispered rant and glared at him.

He hitched Luke to one side and dug in his pocket. He held out a tiny circle of gold with a single blue pearl stuck into the band. "Hannah, be my wife."

Now? He does this here? "Rat's knees, Tobias. Don't ask me that right now." She pushed away his hand with the ring, careful not to look at it again. "I have approximately twenty seconds left of my life before Mother gets her hands on me. You'll be left a widower twice over."

"Listen to me, Hannah Claire Benton. I'm trying to help you."

"I don't need any favors."

They leaned close as they whispered in hushed tones. "You can walk out there as my betrothed, belonging to me, under my protection, an adopted mother to this child, or you can try to explain away a scandal that didn't happen."

"I'd rather be packed off to Des Moines." She huffed. "Just take Father off a ways so I can dress. If you're not at the house when I get back with Mother, it might go better for you."

His face softened. "I will not abandon you to her."

Hannah swallowed and breathed deeply through her nose. "Thank you." She tipped her head back to command the tears to stay away, resolved not to allow them to show themselves right now.

"Say you'll marry me."

"No!" She stomped her foot silently in the blanket of needles. "Stop ruining it."

"You're a bull-headed pig." They stood nose to nose with Tobias crouched low, straddling a branch. "Why are you digging your heels in about this?"

She would have backed up if there were room to do so. "I shouldn't have to spell it out for you, sir, because that will spoil the whole thing. But someday my daughter is going to ask how you proposed, and I don't want to lie to her. So stop ruining it, and do it right next time." Her finger waved under his nose. "Take a hint . . . I will not marry anyone because I'm obligated or for convenience sake or because a child needs a mother. Maybe I thought that would be enough a few months ago, but things have changed. I'll agree to marry you on the grounds of our friendship and delight in each other's company. Our commitment to living under God's law and grace forever and ever, to choose you every morning and to love that choice, will be a privilege, and if you can't get behind that, then find another woman to do your laundry." Blasted stinging in her eyes and a catch in her throat ruined her rant.

"I think you just said yes by accident." The fool man smiled and tucked the ring in his pocket.

"I didn't, and I currently still hate you."

"I choose you now and every morning."

"Don't grin at me like you've won some silly game because you haven't. I'm still the one about to be murdered, and I haven't forgiven you for it."

"You're the one who insisted on undressing to climb a tree."

"Because you had so many better ideas. Get on with you. Let's not give the evil queen anything else to fuss about."

He nodded. "Shields up, soldier."

Tobias covered Luke's face and led the troops, shoving his way to their certain doom.

Chapter 34

I'm still alive. Hannah's thoughts were all in a jumble as she served tea to her family. Though each minute that passed in her mother's company had her rethinking her bout of stubbornness with Tobias. He'd proposed how many times? The first in the buggy was a surprise and downright frightened her. The second in her bedroom was simply insulting, and the third . . . the third wasn't bad, especially on the tails of his confession of love. If he'd left it at that, she might have caved. Then he had to go and ruin the whole thing by trying to force her into it.

The teapot shook in her hand, and Hannah steadied her breath before she poured another cup. Even with Luke cradled in the other arm, Hannah didn't mind that nobody offered to take the pot from her. It gave her something to do. Mother, Father,

Hiram, and Tobias crowded around the table with one chair left open for Hannah when she finished serving. Tobias, bless him, didn't fuss about the tea when she knew he never drank the stuff.

"You believe the wool will bring a sustainable profit?" Father grilled Hiram on the ins and outs of their little farm.

"Enough to fill in the gaps. We have the garden, chickens. The pig we'll butcher in the fall, and the milk cow won't go dry for months yet."

Father accepted his cup from Hannah with a nod, his attention on Hiram. "You don't eat the sheep?"

"We may, but I'm working on growing the flock. Therefore, our main focus is the wool."

Tobias leaned forward. "There's talk of bringing a wool mill to Ockelbo."

"If it comes, it will provide a guaranteed buyer for our wool without the shipping costs, but in the meantime," Hiram said, "we'll send it to the factories in Lincoln or Omaha or sell a few bales to local wives in town who have their own wheels."

"You don't spin it yourself?" Father laughed and thumped Hiram on the back.

Hannah eased into her chair by Mother and across from Tobias, who thankfully hadn't tried to relieve her of her toddler shield.

Mother was exceptionally quiet. Since her tirade by the tree, which lasted until Hannah dressed and rejoined the men, she had put hardly two words together. It couldn't be Mr. Franklin's presence that quieted her, for she'd had no problem slandering him before. She stared at Luke, who'd given up fighting his heavy eyelids and fallen asleep.

Hannah knew Tobias was expected back at work, but he hadn't made any motion to leave. When had Luke ended up in her arms? *Oh, right.* As soon as she returned to the house, he launched himself from Tobias onto her. She adjusted the boy's head and let it rest in the crook of her arm.

Catching Tobias watching her, she offered him a hint of a smile, feeling uncharacteristically shy. She lowered her gaze, shutting out his handsome face. Now wasn't the time to get starry-eyed. Hannah smoothed Luke's hair, damp from sweat, away from his forehead.

"You have grass in your hair." Mother freed a long strand of prairie grass and twirled it between her fingers, interrupting the men's business meeting.

Tobias raised his cup and mumbled behind it. "Towers of Lebanon."

"Moldy dungeons," she breathed out.

Mother looked between the two of them and raised an eyebrow. "Both of you need taken behind the woodshed." She gestured to each of them in turn, waving the grass like a flimsy scepter. "Something is going on." With her full focus on Tobias, she asked, "What are you doing here?"

Tobias opened his mouth, but Mother interrupted before he could speak.

"Don't play with me." She smacked her fingers on the table with each proclamation. "Don't tell me a story. Don't make excuses. Don't, I tell you. Simply, don't do it."

Raising his eyebrows slightly at Hannah, Tobias questioned her. Hannah held her features in check and showed no trepidation whatsoever. He was on his own. She hated to leave him to the dogs, but there was nothing she could say. To defend him would push him in the fire, to deny their friendship was ludicrous, to claim it . . . ? Surprisingly, Hannah felt no fear, nothing but peace and a good amount of love. She trusted him. Trusted Tobias to take care of not only himself but her as well, whatever that meant.

He must have read her thoughts. "Mrs. Benton, Mr. Benton." Tobias nodded to each. "Your daughter and your son saved my life. When I suffered a traumatic head wound, Hannah had the good sense to see to my immediate needs, slow the bleeding, and wrap the wound. Pray." He smiled, and her heart swelled a little more. "Hiram put in the stitches and monitored my healing as I recovered. This experience threw us together. Hannah and my sister became friends, and the five of us, with my sister's betrothed, spend many delightful hours together."

Mother turned to Hannah. "This is the Eloise you speak of in your letters?"

Hannah nodded.

Mother clicked her tongue and stood from the table. "This is outrageous. You've regaled me with your stories long enough, child." She towered over Hannah. "I see right through you. Through and through. You've twisted this man around your finger, just like I knew you would. Thankfully, Nicholas and I arrived in time to put a stop to it before it was too late."

She turned on Hiram next. "We've come to take you home. Both of you. We won't allow you to throw away your life out here. Wasting your knowledge on sheep. Anyone can farm sheep. You were meant for more, Hiram. Stop moping about on the prairie and come back to the profession to which you belong. The reason for your dismissal has already been forgotten. Men get women pregnant all the time, but people tend to have short memories—"

"Mother, I didn't—"

"Tell him, Nicholas. We've met with the city medical board. They're willing to forget the whole thing. The fact the mother died has actually worked in your favor. You don't throw away years of training and money and time because of one mistake."

"Amanda, leave the boy alone." At her father's command, Mother snapped her mouth shut, but a look of pure hatred flared from her.

"Sit down."

She did.

"Let me handle it, Amanda." His steely gaze remained on her a moment longer before surveying the table. "I have leave from the hospital for two weeks. When we return, Hannah will be coming with us. I've secured you," he nodded to Hiram, "a position at the hospital in my wing. My staff will schedule your appointments. You show up for work and do what is asked. We need you to come home."

Hannah inwardly recoiled at the invisible cloud that grew and seeped outward between her parents. As if he could see it too, Tobias slowly stood from the table and walked around to Hannah holding out his arms for Luke. "I need to return to work."

"The man has a job." Mother sneered. "Even negligent fathers go to work. Fancy that."

Tobias's face reddened, but he held his tongue.

"I'll walk you out," Hannah said softly, cradling Luke against her chest.

He held the door open for her, and she held her breath until they were out of earshot of the house.

"I hate this." Hannah adjusted Luke. "I'm so sorry. I don't know why they're here. They didn't send any indication they were coming. Never, never, never would I have asked you to suffer through that. And it will probably get worse. Father is in a good mood, or he's simply behaving in front of you. Please, don't come to the house again because I can't bear to watch her drag you through the manure."

Tobias hitched Dan to his buggy, never once looking at her as she waited by the barn door. The muscles along his jaw tensed, and he kicked the wheel once for no reason whatsoever that she could see. His work done, he came to her, closing the distance in a few long strides. Instead of taking Luke, he wrapped his arms around her and the boy, burying his face in her neck.

"How?" He choked and tried again. "How are you here with me, untainted, beautiful, kind?" He lifted his head and gently cradled her face between his hands. "Perfect and wonderful." He seemed to be searching for something.

She was helpless to do anything but stare back into his eyes, and Luke's weight in her arms was forgotten.

Tobias leaned in, and her heart thumped wildly, anticipating the kiss to come. Instead, he rested his forehead against hers. His warm breath grazed her cheeks. "Promise me you'll be safe if I leave you here. My presence will only make it worse for you, I think. Stay near Hiram. You won't let them spirit you off during the night? Come to me or send word. I can move in with Zeke and let you stay with El."

Her laugh stopped his instructions. She didn't want to embarrass him with a fit of giggling else he think she was poking fun at him, but all the same, she couldn't stop her release of joy.

His big-brother complex was taking over again.

She turned and leaned into his chest. "Hush, dearest. Eloise and Zeke are getting married this Sunday, in four days. Please don't tell me you've forgotten. Let me deal with my parents. I've navigated this storm for two decades. They both have a lot of bark, but their bite is weak, especially now that I've moved out. Now that I'm here, aside from brute force, I don't see how they can make me return. Hiram and I are of age, Tobias. Legally, they hold no sway over what either of us do. Let them bluster about for a few days. You go home and lay low."

As he drove away with Luke in a knitted blanket on the floor of the buggy, Hannah experienced a momentary spike of fear. She envisioned running after him. Waving her hands in the air, calling him back. *Take me with you!*

He would do it. He would whisk her away to elope. They'd go together to the county seat to sign the marriage license. They'd be as one. Husband and wife.

From her periphery, before the dust on the road had settled, Mother marched toward her across the yard. *Shield's up, soldier.* Tobias's command made her smile. The peace that had been dancing around her the past hour settled on her again. *Lord, be my shield.*

There was nothing to fear in Mother. Even if the worst should happen and Hannah was hauled back to the city, God was sovereign. Was he not? He'd sent Dan to fetch Hiram after Tobias's accident. He'd sent Mr. Johanson to look for her and scare off Charles. He'd brought her to this place and if—no, when—he brought her out of it, it would be by his will.

Now, to honor her father and mother . . . when she was of age, and they were wrong. *Clearly.* If she went home with them, could Tobias not come for her? Eloping, running away, marrying in haste . . . compelling. Exciting. Fit for a story. But to sacrifice her family in the process? Unnecessary. A verse itched the corner of her mind from her reading in Psalms this morning.

"Come, Hannah." Mother stood next to her, holding out Hannah's bonnet and watching the retreating buggy. "Walk with me." It wasn't a request.

"Yes, Mother." Hannah waited until the last cloud of dust had faded from the road and turned to Mother, who looked at her curiously. She tied the ribbons and welcomed the shade. They started together toward the gate of the nearest pasture with the afternoon heat soaking into her shoulders. Once through the gate, they followed the fence. Grasshoppers whirred and took flight in front of them.

"You love him," Mother accused.

"I do." Hannah smiled at how easily the confession slipped out.

"Are you with child?"

Hannah was shocked speechless. She blinked, pausing in her walk.

"No, of course not." Mother waved a hand. "It would hardly be long enough to know for sure by now. When was your last monthly?"

"Mother," Hannah sputtered and caught up to her. "Mother, no. I'm not—I haven't. He and I aren't *together*."

Mother snorted. She held up the grass she'd pulled from Hannah's hair at the table. She'd been gripping it in her hand this whole time. "You often roll about in the prairie half-dressed?"

Hannah snatched the blade of grass and tossed it to the ground. "I haven't lied to you once, Mother. Why would I start now?"

"You don't have to lie to keep the truth from me. You've written a letter a week, each filled with tales of Eloise and shopping and the farm, and not once do you mention the handsome, blue-eyed man that fills your every waking thought."

"I knew you wouldn't approve, but I never lied."

"You were down to your drawers in his presence less than an hour ago."

Hannah nodded and quickened her pace along the pasture fence, the dry summer grass already packed down in front of her. "You saw for yourself the boy in the tree. We've been over this. Tobias was far too large to reach him, and there's no way I could have gotten to Luke otherwise."

"So you say, and I ask what distractions are so great that two adults lose track of a toddler prone to mischief?"

Hannah spun and confronted Mother. "I dare you to spend one afternoon with Luke without losing track of him at least once." Hannah breathed slowly and closed her eyes, willing herself to regain control of her tongue. *Lord, be my shield.*

Stay off the defense. Mother was not worth the anger. Again, the verse from this morning niggled in her mind, just out of reach. "I'm sorry, Mother. You're right, of course. Mr. Franklin and I were not paying him enough mind at the time. Luke does have a way of disappearing in a matter of seconds; therefore, we should have kept a better eye on him."

"Mr. Franklin is often here at the farm instead of at work?"

"No," Hannah said slowly, trying to avoid confessing he'd slept in her bed for a week at the start of the summer. "Usually our time together is reserved for a quick lunch in town, Sunday drives, or evenings with his family. Holidays. Today was a treat, and we're all busy helping Eloise and Zeke prepare for their wedding this Sunday."

"He is courting you."

"Yes, and when you get to know him, you'll see how wonderful he is."

"You're coming home to Des Moines in two weeks." Mother angled back to the house. "Show me to my room. I'm tired."

This was Hannah's home, her farm, her town. *Psalm 18:2.* The verse came together in her mind. *My God, my strength, in whom I will trust; my shield . . .*

She felt no anxiety, for she did have a God mightier than herself or her parents. "You and Father can take Hiram's room. He's on the second floor, but there's a large bed, full wardrobe. Thankfully, the house was partially furnished when he bought it. The other two rooms are empty upstairs." Hannah lengthened her stride to keep up. "I took the bedroom downstairs because the bed was already in place, but you'll like Hiram's room. The view from the window looks east. Same as mine. Deer usually come across the lower pasture in the mornings, and we keep the two gates open for them when the sheep are near the barn at night. We can put a pallet for Hiram in an empty room. I think you'll like it here, Mother. I've been in the habit of taking my coffee on the porch right away while the air is still bearable."

Mother walked with her head up, acknowledging nothing.

With only a slight hesitation, Hannah offered a flag of truce. "Will you come to town with me tomorrow? Eloise's dress will be done, and we're going to collect it from Abigail's Dress Shop. Remember the hat you bought when you were here last? Abigail's is next door. You'll love what they were able to do with Eloise's dress. She still had her mother's wedding dress from '52, and

Caroline Jenkins—she works with Abigail—is a fairy godmother with the needle. Caroline lives on a working orchard with her parents. Every fall once the apples are seasoned, they invite the church for an apple-picking festival, music, and games. It sounds delightful."

She trailed off and stole a glance at Mother, who hadn't sighed in annoyance or interrupted once during Hannah's chatter. "Mother?"

"You want me to come with you and Eloise for the final fitting of her wedding dress."

Hannah took her mother's hand. "I want you to accept that I have a life here."

"I want to lie down." Mother stomped up the porch steps, and Hannah rushed to open the front door.

Chapter 35

"Tobias, sit down. Luke needs to eat, and you're distracting him." Eloise tried again to bring Luke's attention to his dinner while Tobias paced across the small kitchen.

"She will be fine." Eloise softened her voice. "Running to her rescue is not required. Nobody expected them to simply show up, but we all knew by summer's end Hannah would have to do something to convince her parents to let her stay."

Tobias crossed the small kitchen once more until Zeke came behind him and put his hands on his shoulders. He aimed Tobias back to the table and pushed him to his chair. Tobias kept his heels off the floor and bounced his knees. "Tell me again."

Eloise sighed. "Amanda, Mrs. Benton, came with us to pick up the dress this morning, but she stayed out of the way, and Hannah was in good spirits."

"She didn't ask about me?"

"We were a little busy trying on dresses. Hannah had her hands full enough keeping Luke's fingers off the display while I changed. Amanda was quiet, almost nervous."

"Then how do you know Hannah doesn't want me to come to the farm and rescue her?"

"Because you told me she asked you not to! Just like you told her not to come to the brickyard. She hasn't shown up there, has she? Give her space. You'll see her Sunday. We're meeting again on Saturday to pick flowers for the wedding. You can't come with us because it will ruin the fun, and you're in charge of Luke all day because Zeke is making the cake." Eloise clucked at Luke to open his mouth for another bite. "Listen. I've got the rest of my things ready to move out Saturday afternoon, and Zeke's already moved into the house. Let me enjoy these last few days with you."

"What if she doesn't stay?"

"She'll stay," Zeke and Eloise said together.

"What if she doesn't want to? What if she decides she'd rather be in the city? There's a lot to offer in the city. She'll have access to shows and entertainment, shops, and exciting foods and books. What if she's been playing with us all summer and it's all a game to her?"

Eloise shot him a stern glare. "You don't believe that for a second. Shame on you. She's never once pined for the city. If that's how she felt you'd know it. She doesn't have a sneaky or deceitful bone in her."

"I've asked her to marry me three times, and she won't agree to it."

Zeke hissed. "Ouch—that's not good."

Eloise only laughed. "You're a goose. Of course she hasn't. You've yet to say anything sweet while you're about it." She puffed out her chest and lowered her voice. "'Marry me. Here's why you must. Or else.'"

Zeke laughed and punched Tobias in the shoulder. Or tried to. Tobias snagged his fist and twisted until Zeke came out of his chair, moving to the floor as he struggled to pull his hand free.

Eloise smacked Tobias's knee hard with Luke's spoon. "Boys!"

He released Zeke.

"Tobias, it's a terrible way to propose, least of all with Hannah. She's one of the few of us willing to go against your orders, so stop trying to tell her what to do."

"She tells you everything."

"Not everything but enough. She loves you, but she's not going to throw herself at you, escaping one cage to fly into another."

Tobias crossed his arms on the table and buried his head in the crook of his elbow. "I think I'm going to be sick."

"Oh, good grief. Zeke, take him for a walk. Tobias, Hannah loves you."

He groaned and mumbled into his arm. "Everything is falling apart. Just stay here, El. You don't have to get your own house." He angled his gaze across the table. "You're a rotten friend, Zeke. Why must you ruin everything? There's no reason you can't move in with us."

"Zeke." Eloise motioned her head toward the door.

Zeke's hands came under Tobias's arms, and he pulled. "Get up, old man."

Tobias slumped to the side, defeated.

"We're going to get pie. Pie makes everything better. You're buying, though. Now that I'm almost a married man with a mortgage, I'm broke. More broke than I was before, if you can believe it." He managed to get Tobias standing and slapped his pocket to check for loose change. "Before, I didn't have money. Now I have less than no money. But the house will be nice. You'll come visit, and I'll make you pie. For now, we'll let someone else make it. Off we go." Zeke fit Tobias's cap on his head and guided him through the house. "There he goes, out the door. Bye, Chip."

Tobias let Zeke lead him downtown. Mosquitoes annoyed them the whole way. He felt as if his world were closing in. The streets were mostly void of people, though families retired to their porches. For once, he kept his head down to avoid any greetings that may come his way. "I should go to her now. Confront her parents. Tell her she must stay."

"Blockhead, did you hear nothing we've been telling you? That is exactly what you're *not* going to do. She told you to stay away. If you love Hannah, you'll trust her."

"But what if she leaves me?"

"She's not going to leave you."

He stumbled like a drunk, and Zeke put a hand on his shoulder.

"You haven't met her parents." Tobias raised his hands with bent fingers like an attacking bear and swiped one across the air in front of him. "Her mother gets her hooks in you and digs down deep where it really hurts. One swipe, you're left open and bleeding. Hannah won't be able to fight against it. She'll be gone." He covered his face with his hands and groaned. "They'll take her away, and it'll be over."

Zeke stopped in front of him and squared up his shoulders. "Okay. Let's go that route since you're so keen on it. She goes to

Des Moines. Her parents tie her up, bound and gagged, and take her away. Then what?"

"Then I go after her." A surge of hope blew through him. "Des Moines isn't so far away. I could go after her! Zeke, I could kiss you. You're right! No, you're getting married Sunday. You're a villain. I could wait a few days until after the wedding. I owe you that much. But you'd keep Luke for me until I get back. You'd do that for me, wouldn't you? I'll go after her."

"And haul her back over your shoulder?"

"Yes." That's exactly what he'd do. If she left, he'd simply bring her back. Problem solved. He brushed a mosquito off his neck.

Zeke snorted. "What if you get there and she spits in your face and says, 'I never want to see you again. Go away'?"

"She wouldn't say that."

"No, she wouldn't—"

"—she'd say, 'Be gone from my sight, you wart-encrusted ogre. Return to your filthy cave where you belong.' Oh, blast, What if she leaves me on purpose and doesn't want to come home with me?"

"You're done. Stop talking." Zeke opened the door to Mike's, the saloon on Fifth Street. It was the most respectable of the three saloons. Drinks were served along the bar, but men also came for coffee and dessert. Checkers instead of cards. Tobias had closed many business deals around those tables. A haze of smoke clung to the ceiling. Jonas sat in the corner at the piano plunking out a lonesome tune.

Zeke led them around the edge of the room to a table in the corner and slapped Jonas on the back. "I didn't know you played. Give us something cheery. Boss needs a kick in the rear."

Jonas smiled at Zeke and sped his fingers through a scale before starting "The Yellow Rose of Texas." Tobias took notice of the other patrons and stood taller. He spotted two more of his employees from the brickyard.

"You brought me here on purpose," he growled at Zeke. "You knew I couldn't get away with sulking in public."

Zeke raised his eyebrows, playing innocent.

Tobias wanted to smack him.

"Pie," Zeke said. "I'm here for pie. Your sister can't cook a decent dessert to save her life."

"You work at a dad-blame bakery. You don't need pie from a saloon."

Zeke shrugged. "Watch your mouth, Boss. Callie's on her way."

A mousy girl with frizzy hair approached their table with a pot of coffee and two mugs.

Tobias drank his coffee without tasting it and did a fair job of ignoring Zeke's ramblings while he plotted how to rescue Hannah from her parents. He was on his second piece of pie when Zeke snapped his fingers under his nose. "You're not listening to me."

"You're a bag of hot air."

Zeke snatched Tobias's plate from him, confiscating the rest of his pie.

The bite on Tobias's half-raised fork fell to the table.

Zeke scooped it up, plopping it on the plate. "You need a plan, Boss. Sunday, Hannah shows up for church with her family. What are you going to do?"

"I'm going to clam up like a greenhorn and hide under the wagon."

Zeke rolled his eyes. "You're going to greet them like guests of honor and extend an invitation to Eloise's wedding. Hannah needs to know her parents are welcome. She's going to love you for it, and no matter how they treat you, you're taking the high road. And you're going to stop your fussing about it until then. Chip and I are only getting married once, and you're not allowed to ruin it. For Eloise's sake, you can't act like this. I'm counting on you to go all of Friday and Saturday with your shoulders back and head high."

Tobias nodded and slid his pie back in front of him. "How did you propose to El?"

"Oh, that was easy. We went down to the creek, skipped rocks for a while. When the timing was right, I sat her down on a nice dry log and knelt in front of her. Girls like that. Then I told her all the things I love about her, why she's so great, and asked if she wanted to be my wife."

"And she said yes, just like that?"

"She didn't say anything."

"Then how—"

"She was too busy kissing me to say much else, but boy-howdy, if you've ever been kissed the way your sister kissed me—"

"Ugh." Tobias pushed away the rest of his pie.

Zeke pulled the plate all the way to himself. "You done then?"

"How'd you know she'd say yes?"

The remainder of Tobias's dessert disappeared into Zeke's mouth. He raised his mug. After downing the last of it, he smiled. "I didn't, but I knew there was nobody else in this whole world I wanted to be with. Even if she tries to kill me with burned coffee on occasion, I went for it."

Tobias raised his hands in defeat. "But I've *went for it* three times."

"Did you get on one knee?"

"No."

"Did you ask nicely?"

"I think so."

"Did you tell her what to do and explain why she should marry you?"

Tobias sank his head on the table, careless of who saw him, and tried to block out Zeke's irritating face. "Everything that can go wrong for me has gone wrong. I'm giving up. Take it all. Just take the whole dad-blame wagon and push it over the cliff."

"We're miles from a cliff. If you're going down with the ship, can I keep the buggy? Tell you what—you pull it together through Sunday, and I'll drive you to the cliff myself."

Tobias grunted.

"You're not really upset about Hannah, are you?" Zeke asked quietly. "You have to know Eloise is going to be fine. Once she and I are married, all three of us are getting a fresh start. She's only going across town. I'm not taking her away from you and Luke. I'd move in with you if I thought it was the best thing, but it's not. Eloise needs a chance to have her own space again. Philip's death messed her up, and you know it. She's just now gaining confidence in herself again. Our own little house will be good, and we'll be at your place all the time. And until you and Hannah are hitched, she'll still keep Luke for you during the day. It's all working out as it should, so you can stop worrying about it."

The door of Mike's saloon flew open and banged against the wall. "Fire!" The alarm fell on every man in the room. Instantly alert and caught up in the mass exodus, Zeke and Tobias followed the crowd into the street. A fire at the beginning of August so long since the spring rains could sweep through every field in a hundred miles.

They all knew what to do.

Outside, a column of smoke visible in the twilight led them to the edge of town. Before he saw the fire, Tobias knew it in his bones.

Franklin Brickworks was in flames.

Chapter 36

Tobias charged to the front of the crowd. More and more people joined, buckets in hand, as the cry of "fire" spread through town.

The smoke grew thicker as they neared the field that edged the brickyard. A few men already manned a bucket brigade trailing from the pump to Tobias's office. The roof of the small building sported flames that reached several feet in the air. One of the three drying sheds was overcome and sent licks of flame to the next. Someone threw open the toolshed and handed out shovels. In the distance, the bells from the fire wagon clanged through town. Too late to save the buildings, but they would prevent it from turning into a prairie fire.

"Follow me." He called to those nearby and ran to grab a shovel. He started digging a trench twenty feet from the building in flames while others joined a line from the water pump. A swarm of men gathered by him. By himself he could do nothing. With an army of men working efficiently with him, a narrow firebreak soon took shape. He passed his shovel to another man and ran to see what else he could do.

Tobias tried to find a place in the bucket brigade or another job to help, but nobody was willing to surrender his place in line. He stumbled backward, hand on his head, watching the roof of his office collapse, shooting a volcano of sparks into the evening sky. Rivers of flames tried to make their way into the dry fields but were quickly checked by the mass of volunteers. Men stood ready with wet sacks and beat out the sparks that threatened the other machines or buildings.

The fires were now contained to the buildings on which they started. The office and one entire drying shed would soon be lost. The barn wall nearest the shed was blackened, but it had been snuffed before it took the rest of the building. As quickly as the call had been sounded, the emergency was contained.

He found Roy Swenson working the end of one of the lines, tossing bucket after bucket onto the roaring bonfire. Half the water evaporated from the heat before finding its mark. Black soot covered Roy's face and neck. Enough extra hands were available that Tobias pulled Roy from the line.

"What happened?" Tobias yelled above the noise of the cracking flames and the shouts of men.

"I'm sorry, Boss. I tried to stop it, but I was too late by the time I realized what he'd done."

"Who?"

Roy led him around the edge of the brickyard toward the kilns, avoiding the bucket lines and trenches. Then the fire marshal was there, barking orders at the volunteers. Tobias and Roy covered their mouths with wet handkerchiefs to filter out the ash and smoke that polluted the air.

One of the two kilns smoked twice as much as it should, and flames leaped from the iron door that stood open.

"How in the world?" Tobias adjusted the handkerchief over his mouth. "This was no accident."

Roy was the most experienced brickmaker he had on staff. He worked nights, alternating weeks with George. Not even an apprentice brickmaker would overheat the oven to the point of flames pouring out of the mouth of the kiln.

"No, sir." Roy crouched, coughing with his hands on his knees. "The mules are gone too, but we'll get them back. I came on for the night, checked the fires in each, and everything was running fine when I heard a noise in the barn. Pokey and the rest were putting up a fuss. Wary of rustlers, I hid in the shadows to check on them, but I didn't see anything amiss. Pokey was still kicking a ruckus, and when I went around the side, I found the barn door standing wide open. On closer inspection, every stall door was unlocked. One push and the mules could have walked free."

"If rustlers were after the mules, why would they set fire?"

"Right. Well, that's what I thought. I latched each of their stalls again and locked the barn. Kevin was still asleep in his cot. The old geezer hadn't heard a thing."

Heat poured on Tobias in waves from the inflamed buildings. There was enough wood on the roof feeding the fire that the brick walls fairly glowed like coals in a furnace. He raised an arm to block the direct heat from his face and turned slowly, surveying his company. At least a hundred men had arrived, and more still came running from town.

"This was started on purpose," Tobias said. "Whoever did this tried to set the mules free before the fire killed them." The roar and crackling drowned his words even as he said them. "This is a personal assault."

Roy studied him.

"What else do you know?"

"By the time I left the barn, I smelled the smoke. Oil had been splashed on a few of the buildings and set aflame."

Tobias searched his mind for anyone who could possibly wish him harm. "Charles Grady."

Roy nodded. "I can't prove it, but I believe I saw him running down the trail toward the creek. That's my guess. He's coward enough to try hurting you this way. There was nothing I could do on my own but sound the alarm."

"And he shoved the rest of the kindling and coal into the kiln while you were busy in the barn."

"Kevin woke up in time to let the mules out. We'll round them up tonight or tomorrow if we can find them."

Already, Tobias was tallying the numbers, bricks, payroll. Rebuilding. Setbacks. Lost contracts. Deadlines. Either letting men go or taking out a loan to cover the cost of rebuilding before he recouped costs. One drying shed lost and likely reduced to one kiln would cut their production almost in half until they rebuilt. The office building, he could do without, though the years of lost records was overwhelming to think about.

Not a few women and older children stood far back in the field, huddled in a group. Watching the destruction of years of work. And so many men. Old and young. Many of the willing, able-bodied volunteers stood around now that the mad rush had ceased. Buckets of water still flew to muddy the ground around the fire, but the main task was to ensure it didn't spread. The two buildings were already collapsing on themselves.

The image of Eloise and Luke nudged its way over his tallying. Hannah's smile and comforting touch. Picnics in a summer breeze. Zeke's cheeky grin. Loyal employees. Willing friends. God's continual provision.

Tobias shoved his hands in his pockets, and his finger slipped into the hard circle of gold he'd been in the habit of carrying for weeks now.

His laughter started softly. A small chuckle. A breath released. His shoulders soon shook with it, and he raised his arms wide and laughed long, sounding to all the world like a madman, but he wasn't. Not really.

Those nearest gave him odd looks, and a few backed away. Others took a step closer. From somewhere close, Zeke ran up to him. Probably one of the few who wasn't afraid of him and his delirious laughter over the evident destruction of his property. Tobias gripped Zeke's shoulders in both hands.

"I hated that massive desk." Joyfully, he slung an arm around Zeke's neck and turned him in a circle, showing off Franklin Brickworks by the flickering light of the bonfires. "Don't you see? It makes all the difference. I'm not in control of any of it, and I never was."

Zeke pulled Tobias's arm from around his throat. "You all right?"

"I'm perfect." Tobias's heart swelled just watching the men work together to pass a bucket down a line. "You probably have a verse for this, don't you?"

"It is only by the Lord's mercies we are not consumed?"

"Not that one."

Zeke didn't try to pull away from Tobias's grip around his shoulders. "Um . . . the Lord gave and the Lord hath taken away?"

"No."

"Jesus wept."

"Ha! Now you're being funny. Something happier." Tobias tapped on Zeke's forehead with his pointer. "There's a verse just beyond my grasp about God's thoughts."

"Isaiah 55? For my thoughts are not your thoughts, neither are your ways my ways, saith the LORD."

Tobias snapped his fingers. "That's it. That's the one."

"I'm not sure how that's exactly relevant."

Tobias sounded out each syllable. "I'm not in charge of anything." The peace that came with that statement was more than he'd ever felt before. Standing amid the destruction, he felt lighter. He stood taller as one by one the burdens he'd been carrying slipped off. He unloaded them brick by brick.

He released Eloise—acknowledged he was no longer, and never was, solely responsible for her well-being. Luke—the daily misgivings that he wasn't doing all he should as a father. Zeke—oh, Zeke, who was now as close as a brother. His guilt against Maribeth. The reputation he upheld in front of his employees and buyers, Franklin Brickworks as a whole. His standing in the community.

Then there was Hannah.

"I have something to do yet tonight. I need you to tell Eloise that I'll be home later. Don't get her all riled up about the fire. It's nothing. Nobody harmed. Nothing that can't be mended. Tell her good night and not to worry. I'll be home much, much later, and she's not to wait up for me, understand? And you're not to stick around either." He squeezed his soon-to-be-brother's shoulder. "A couple more days and she's all yours."

Zeke nodded and took off toward town at a swift jog.

Tobias walked slowly to the line of men still pumping water. He caught a splash of it with his handkerchief and wrapped it around his neck, cooling his skin.

"Thank you for coming." He greeted each man by name and shook their hands if they were free. Helped where he could. These were his people, his friends, his town. He had no doubt, not a single fear that he would be left alone to rebuild. With one announcement, most of these men would return to help clear the rubble in a day. It might take only a few more weekends to rebuild.

Thank you, Lord.

Gratitude was the only thing on his mind. Well, that and how soon he'd be able to see Hannah. She'd be pleased with a new window that opened in the office. And a new door—with a doorknob that worked properly. He'd stay here until the work was done, but then he'd speak with her. The peace on his shoulders was too big not to share with the woman he loved.

Chapter 37

Hannah flew.

She let the grass brush against her toes and grazed her hand over the soft tips as she flew over the prairie. Breathing out slowly, she pushed herself higher with the exhale. Her favorite dream.

She wasn't sure how this worked, but she always knew it to be a dream and yet somehow had to relearn how to fly each time. The pit of her stomach flipped as she dipped low, scattering a family of pheasants. A knocking in the nearby forest snagged her attention. She dropped to the grass and rolled over in bed, annoyed to be pulled from her dream.

The tapping on Hannah's window continued, and she snapped fully awake. All sorts of unsavory images flashed through her mind.

Someone tried to open her window.

Slowly she crawled out of bed and picked up her shoe. Holding it by the toe, she had the sharp heel ready to impale whomever or whatever was coming for her. Carefully and quietly, she crept to the window. In one swift movement she yanked aside the curtain just as the perpetrator managed to open the window a crack. She sucked in her scream, and it about strangled her. She brought her boot heel down on the fingers resting on her window ledge. A muffled curse followed, and the window dropped low again. Emboldened, she moved closer and found Tobias sucking his knuckle to his mouth, glaring at her in the moonlight.

She threw open the window, wincing at its screech. "Sorry," she hissed. "I thought you were a gremlin or a troll."

"Trolls live under bridges," he hissed back. "You didn't hear me tapping on the window the past five minutes?"

"I was flying."

"Of course you were." He shook out his hand and flexed the fingers she'd whacked. With the window open, the crickets' song flooded the house.

She waved her hand in front of her face. "You smell like a piece of raw meat that rolled out of a furnace and was left to rot a fortnight in the corner of the barn. What are you doing here?"

"Taking you on an adventure."

"I can't run away with you."

"We'll just walk around and talk."

"Right now? I'm not sure if that's worth getting caught."

"I wouldn't have come if I didn't think it was worth it. Will you come out? I want to get out of here before your parents wake up. You whisper louder than a donkey."

Hannah backed away from the window to find her other shoe. She hesitated, remembering she was in nothing but a nightgown. She couldn't go traipsing about the prairie in a nightgown. "Tobias, turn around."

Keeping an eye on him to make sure he didn't peek, she hurriedly pulled her sturdy calico work dress over her nightgown, not bothering with a corset, bustle, or petticoats. Her heart pumped in excitement at what she was doing. No time to second guess. Yanking on her stockings and her boots, she was ready.

She thrust her head and waist through the open window, and her long braid dangled over her shoulder. "Help me down."

Tobias's hands went to her waist, and she squeaked. With only two layers of cotton to separate, it was much too intimate. He jerked his hands away.

"Be quiet," he cautioned. "How're we doing this?"

"Back off. I'll climb out." She managed to get one leg out and then another until she sat on the ledge, hunched over with the top of the window eating into her back. She squeaked again when something hooked into her hair near the scalp. "I was wrong. Get back over here. Can you see where my hair's stuck?"

"I can't—it's too dark." His fingers felt along the side of the window frame, where she was thoroughly attached.

She winced. "I'm going to keep my head still. If you take out the braid, it should come free. Blimey, Tobias—you reek of smoke. Smoke and old sweat."

"Once you're released, I'll stand downwind." He chuckled. "On second thought, I'll go home and bathe. Come back in the morning." The dry grass crunched under his feet as he started to walk away and left her head still hooked on the window frame.

"Mr. Franklin!" She whispered as loudly as she dared. "Psst! Tobias! You will not leave me here."

He'd stopped a few feet away and turned back to her, laughing with arms crossed.

She twisted an arm and fumbled with the tie on the end of her thick braid. Slowly she pulled her head away from the edge, and the loose strands of hair came free. Gathering it up, she pulled her mess of hair over her shoulder and jumped from the window. She landed awkwardly with an *oomph* and fell to her hands and knees.

He lowered himself to the ground and sat cross-legged facing her. "I need to tell you about Katie."

Her stomach lurched. *Oh, dear.* Was it too late to climb back in the window? She'd known he'd been married before. He was a widower. He had a son. She knew about Katie. In theory. But she'd never asked, and he'd never brought her up. Somehow they'd enjoyed two months of blissful friendship without ever addressing the fact that he'd been married before. She brushed her hands and leaned against the side of the house. "You don't have to."

"I don't want to erase her. Pretend she didn't exist."

Hannah nodded. That was fair.

"But her ghost doesn't haunt me. When we marry, it will be me and you and Luke. Katie's memory is there. And I'd like to be able to share those memories with Luke, but she'll not come between us."

A firefly winked in the grass near her knee, and she cupped her palm over it.

"We've never talked about Katie," he said, "and I wonder now if we should have."

Hannah shrugged, uncertain of what to say. "Is this what you woke me up to talk about?"

He barked out a quiet laugh. "Not at all. I thought of it just now, and this needed to be addressed before I got to the other part."

"I think," Hannah said, choosing her words carefully, "the man I've come to know, Tobias M. Franklin, is who I want to be with. Katie was an important part of your life, but she's not here anymore." The firefly crawled onto her finger. "I don't want you to be afraid to mention her, but neither do I care to dwell on your past with her. Does that make me selfish? I can't hold it against you that you met her before me. Still, I'd like to think I'm the only woman who's ever caught your eye. Is that too vain of me?"

"As long as we both shall live, you'll be the only woman to catch my eye. Luke was too young to remember her, but I want to tell him about her when he's older."

"As you should."

Tobias smiled. Relieved. Something was different about him this evening. He was relaxed. The tension gone from his face and shoulders. He held himself lighter.

"Something else has changed, Tobias. Aside from smelling like a dead pig from the smoker, you're different. At peace. Sheesh, what are we doing sitting here? Tom and Huck would be sneaking down to the graveyard by now. Look at us, sitting and whispering." She raised her hand, and the firefly took off into the dark, blinking a signal to his friends.

"What is love, Hannah? You challenged me a month ago, and we both had answers that looked good on paper. God tells us over and over what it is, but until you've made a brick, it's not the same. I can explain the process to you. The machines, the tools, the molds, the drying process, kilns, how to regulate the fires. But that doesn't make you a brickmaker."

"I don't want to be a brickmaker."

"Shhh. I'm working up to my last proposal."

She curled in her lips and bit down, but unable to keep in the giggles, she snorted.

"Just wait—this one will be good."

"You're off to a great start." She held her side while hunched over with silent laughter. "Please, keep comparing love to bricks." She snorted again, trying her best not to laugh. "No," she whispered. "Don't come any closer. Stay downwind."

"Can you listen for once?" He sounded annoyed. "I'm telling you that knowing about something isn't the same as living and doing. We can read and know about love, but until we are truly loved or love ourselves, we can't know it. Dee and I spend days training new hires, and even then, I only have a few men who are really good at making bricks."

"Mr. Franklin, I hate to keep interrupting, but I think you've been at work far too long today. Even in the moonlight I can see you're filthy. You have soot in the creases around your eyes and hairline." He'd evidently splashed water on his face, but lines of soot or dirt still covered him. The bandana around his neck looked as if it had dried stiff, and his clothes were soiled and shabby. "Were you crawling around inside the kiln again?" Hannah took his hand and held it to the moonlight. "You've been at work until now? Since when do you work the night shift?"

He opened his hand to her, letting her run her fingers over his palm until he shivered. "Since someone set fire to the brickyard."

Hannah stilled. Roaming her eyes over his face, she searched for any sign that he was in jest. She didn't find any.

He closed his hand around hers. "I love holding you. The joy I have when we're together is part of the reason I love you. But by itself that's not enough. Commitment is part of love too. What was it you said? Deciding every morning to choose you and love that choice? I sulked all day, thinking you might leave me and what I was going to do about it. I'd decided to chase you to Des Moines and bring you back with me whether you wanted to come or not. But that's not love, that's—that's desperation and fear."

"Franklin Brickworks burned down?"

He lifted a shoulder. "Parts of it. I came to tell you I'm ordering a new doorknob for the office. I couldn't wait until tomorrow. I'll have at least three keys made for the lock and one will go to you. Just in case."

"Tobias, look at me. I'm trying to put this together, and you're avoiding the topic. Someone burned your office to the ground. On purpose? And you come here to tell me that you love me? Again?"

"Seems crazy, but yes. I watched Franklin Brickworks fall apart, and I won't have a moment's rest for weeks while we figure out how to rebuild, but it's nothing. I don't even care. I'm not worried one bit, because, Hannah, it turns out I'm not in control of anything. And it's the best feeling in the world." His carefree smile reminded her of Luke. "Last night, tonight, I was surrounded by a town full of friends willing to stand by me and set things right. I don't have to be in control of it because someone much wiser than me is taking care of it. He is sovereign and his thoughts are not my thoughts nor his ways my ways. Whatever he has planned for me is what I want, and I have the feeling he's not opposed to me rebuilding with you by my side."

The intensity in his eyes silenced her from any interruptions.

"Hannah, sweetheart, I want to be your husband. Not because my son needs a mother, not because Eloise is leaving, and not because you need a reason to stay in Ockelbo. I want to be your husband because when it looked like my world was falling apart, I laughed, knowing how pleased you'd be that I'm replacing the blasted doorknob for my run-down office!"

Tobias stood and pulled her up next to him. "Hannah, will you be my friend forever?" He brushed her loose hair behind her ear and ran his fingers through to the ends.

Hannah let out a shaky breath. This was the proposal she'd been waiting for. *Yes,* was on the tip of her tongue. She smirked for one last tease. "No."

He narrowed his eyes. "I forgot to get on my knees? Don't make me beg. I won't do it. This is my final offer."

"I refuse to marry a man who doesn't even want to kiss me."

"Doesn't wa—?" His whisper cut off as he saw her smile. Leaning down, he captured her lips in a chaste, quick kiss. "I was going to ask you to take a walk with me. But I'm afraid that's not a good idea if you're going to be breaking the rules."

"You needn't fear." She held a hand against her nose. "You really are repulsive."

In response, he grabbed her around the waist and pulled her against him. "Oh, yeah?" Her struggle was fruitless, and they wrestled together, both failing completely at keeping quiet. He bent and threw her over his shoulder. "Hold still, or I'll drop you on your head." He strode away from the house with her hanging down his back.

"You're a beast," she hissed, trying to wrap her arms around his waist and keep her hair out of the dirt. "Put me down, sir. I'll sic the dogs after you."

Twenty yards from the house, he put her feet on the ground and kept his hands at her waist. "You're a wild woman with your hair all around your face."

"And you're an ogre."

"Shoot. Your quaint depiction of me burned up in the fire. Togre Miser Franklin, wasn't it? Can I commission another?"

"Hmm." She rubbed a thumb along the scruff growing on his cheek. "You tell me what that M in your name stands for, and I'll think about it."

"No deal."

She shrugged and turned away. "I'll ask Eloise."

"Whatever she tells you, she's lying." He grabbed her elbow, spinning her toward him.

Hannah lifted on her toes and kissed him. Ignoring the smell of sweat and smoke, she pressed against him, demanding he kiss her back. She didn't have to wait long before he softened against her, and his hands gripped her shoulders.

He pulled back enough to speak. "You're cheating."

"Tell me what the M stands for." She returned to kissing him.

He angled his head and deepened the kiss, letting his hands trail down her back.

She knocked his cap to the ground and threaded her fingers into his hair, which elicited a groan from him. "Meriwether," he spoke against her lips, "Tobias Meriwether. There. Now take your hands off me, or I'm tossing you back over my shoulder."

"Tobias Meriwether Franklin." She disentangled herself from his arms and skipped backward, but he snatched her hand before she got too far away.

"Don't think you can always get what you want. Once we're married, that trick won't work. You'll be all mine."

"Let's not get married then." She laughed and ran along the path, leading him on a chase.

He caught her in only a few yards. They were up on the little hill by the road with the house still visible. The full moon lit their way, and mosquitoes buzzed. Hannah gasped as she looked down at the farm. A host of fireflies flickered around the house, in the pastures, between the barn, and through the grass. "It's so beautiful."

Tobias's hand was warm against hers when he slipped a ring onto her finger. "Can we get married tomorrow?"

"One step at a time." Hannah held her hand to the moon, but it was too dark to see the details of the ring. "Pray your heart out that my mother doesn't have a stroke when she sees this."

"What can I do? Should I come talk to them? Here—you can wait to wear it until you tell them." He took her hand to pull the ring off, but she curled her hand into a fist.

"Don't you dare. It's mine now, and you can't have it back, ever."

"Is that a yes?"

"Didn't I say yes? Surely I did at some point."

"Hannah." His voice rumbled from his chest.

She sighed and kissed him again, but he only brushed his lips against hers.

"You don't know what you do to me," he breathed against her neck. "I'm reinstating all the rules, or we'll be in trouble."

Hannah leaned against him and made him wrap his arms around her. Tilting her head, she gazed at the stars. "I've not seen them much this summer. The sun sets so late. It's stunning."

"What's your plan to bring your parents around?"

"I'm not sure yet. She's already got it in her head that she hates you." They stood in silence, enjoying the warm breeze of the night, the stars, the fireflies flashing around the farm. "Here's an idea. What if you bring Luke tomorrow and Saturday? You'll need to organize a plan for the brickyard and help Eloise and Zeke move into their house, and Luke will be out of the way here. Once she spends time with him, she won't be able to help herself. He's got a way about him. After she falls for him, it will be easier to accept you. You're sort of a packaged deal."

He grimaced. "You'd trust her with him?"

"I do. And I won't leave him with her. I promise. I'll just keep them together long enough for him to wrap his little fingers around her heart."

"You think it'll work?"

"It has to."

"Need help back in the window?"

Hannah laughed. "I'm better off going around to the front door." She pointed east where the smallest glimmer of light glowed across the horizon. "Run home before Eloise has a chance to worry about you."

Tobias kissed her hand and dropped it. "She'll be glad to know you finally agreed."

"You never believed I'd run away to Des Moines, did you?"

"Doesn't matter. I'm big enough to haul you home again."

Chapter 38

Hannah's eyes flew open. She lay atop her blankets in her nightgown. A gold ring banded her middle finger. Briefly, she wondered if it had been Katie's ring too. The sun glinted off the metal, and she smiled. It was the most beautiful thing she'd ever seen. A blue-gray pearl was set in the middle with two tiny diamonds on either side. She held it above her head and giggled as she stretched, not taking her eyes from it.

The creak of the rocking chair near her bed had her snatching her hand back. She yelped when she found her mother sitting there, calmly drinking a mug of coffee.

"Good morning, Hannah." Her mother clinked her cup on the nightstand. "I had half a mind to toss a pitcher of water on your bed. Have you any idea of the time?"

"Good morning, Mother."

"You often sleep in your long stockings?"

Hannah wiggled her toes.

"Never mind." She clipped out rapid-fire instructions. "Get dressed. We need to talk. I'm heating a pot of hot water for you because you smell of rotten smoke. Whatever have you gotten yourself into this time?"

I went running across the prairie with my best friend who worked for hours in the August heat putting out fires. I may have kissed him. It was delightful. Heavenly. Pure bliss. "Um. I—" Her chest sank with a *whoosh* of air. Instead of speaking, she swung her legs over the side of her bed and crossed the room for her brush. Attacking the long strands took over any conversation.

"Hannah, it's time you were told about your sister." Mother's voice was pinched.

Hannah stopped brushing mid-stroke. "I have a sister?"

"She died. I never meant to tell you, and your father and I haven't spoken of her in over twenty years, but the memory of her infant body has never ceased to haunt me." She walked to the window and stood gazing across the prairie, and all Hannah could do was force air in and out of her lungs.

Wisps of gray hair framed her mother's face. The rest was twisted in a fashionable yet practical knot behind her head. She held her shoulders back and chin up in the stern manner that Hannah was accustomed to seeing.

"What was her name?"

Mother shook her head, not taking her eyes from the distant hills. "We never named her."

"How could you—"

"Hush," she snapped. "Don't you dare speak of what you don't understand. I pray you never lose a child. But when you do, and your husband tells you to bury the thing and try again, that is what you will do."

Hannah clamped her mouth shut.

Mother ran her finger around the face of the cameo brooch at her neck and released a breath. "I was seventeen years old. Nicholas was older. You know this much. He was twenty-eight, already a surgeon of some standing in Chicago. Mutual friends introduced us, and it was love at first sight." She glanced at Hannah a moment with a smile that held no mirth. "I know what you're thinking, but I thought it was real. Real love. And real love made everything else in life fade in importance. Charmed my parents as well. Real love led me down a path that I couldn't turn away from. When we found out the baby was coming, we married only nine weeks after we first met." Mother twisted her own gold band, gaze still trained out the window.

"I knew I wasn't the only one in my group of friends to marry for such reasons. You'll find that's often the case. We had sinned against God, but our marriage could correct that sin. Or so I thought, but Nicholas had little time for me. He married me out of duty. Necessity. Covering up his sin. Our sin. This became apparent to me when I learned that he may not have married me otherwise. He took on more and more at work, and I was reminded of the pumpkin-eater's wife in that awful rhyme. 'There he kept her very well.' I was kept in a large house with plenty of servants. A cook, a maid, a coach. Everything I could want was at my disposal. Chicago offered endless entertainment for me."

Hannah stood across the room, unsure of what to say. Mother's tone lacked inflection. Was she as unfeeling as she sounded?

"She was born premature, a stillborn. Nicholas entered surgery within the hour. A mangled leg from a factory accident required an amputation. The screams of that man covered any tears that I might have shed. I went home. No longer a mother and hardly a wife. He didn't love me. He'd never loved me. Don't you see? Men don't need a wife. They need a cook, a maid, and someone to warm their beds."

Oh, Mother. No.

Mother glanced at Hannah with raised eyebrows as if reading her thoughts. "Oh, I don't hate him for it. He can't help that's how he is. He doesn't hate me. He's not a brute. He did what he thought he must do. He tried to do right by me. We were young and foolhardy. But I asked myself for years if it would have mattered if she'd lived."

Hannah hugged herself and stared at her mother by the window.

"When you and Hiram came along a few years later, I thought it would be enough to fill my days. Nicholas moved us to Kansas City, then to Des Moines. Like he could run from me even while dragging us with him. He treats you like a pet. A little pet to coddle and play with and send on your way when he's done."

"Oh, Mother—"

"I don't mean to speak ill of your father. He's worked very hard to be where he is now. He is one of the most skilled surgeons of our time. When he goes after something, he gets it—there's a certain drive about him that I admire. But there's a wedge between us. Perhaps we blame the other for being shackled together."

Mother sighed and closed her eyes, looking as if the oppression of every decision she'd ever made was still pushing her down, grabbing and pulling, forcing her to struggle against its weight.

"So. Now you understand why I've done everything the way I have to keep you from marriage. I've done my best to save you from this life. Your father has means enough to provide for you and has set aside enough to keep you secure after he's gone. I left you to your own devices for a few weeks, and you're already too far lost to me."

Hannah had never once seen her mother cry. She hadn't thought she was capable of it. Her mother covered her mouth with her hand and didn't make one noise to betray herself, but first one, and then two, and three tears slid down her cheek.

She lingered at the window, and if it were anyone else, Hannah would have hugged her by now. It was all so strange and surreal. This wasn't her mother baring her soul, trudging up long-buried pain and years of bitterness. Her mother didn't cry. She didn't feel things like normal people.

"Yesterday, I knew that once Mr. Franklin was bored with you, your life would be an endless cycle of trying to both please and avoid him." Mother wiped a finger under her eye and cleared her throat. "I'd hoped for better things for you. You could find a good position in Des Moines high society without a husband. You would have the time to run committees and organize charities. Hannah, you have enough drive to influence local politics. There was no reason for you to seek a husband."

The handle of the brush bit into Hannah's hands. When she turned to set it on the nightstand, it slipped and clattered to the floor.

As if remembering Hannah was still in the room, Mother turned swiftly and came to the bed. "Sit." She patted the quilt once. That was more like the mother Hannah knew. The commanding one who never asked twice and demanded immediate obedience.

Hannah sat in such shock that thoughts and replies eluded her.

Mother put her hand on Hannah's forearm and tugged until Hannah relinquished her hand to her, exposing the ring. Even under her mother's scrutiny, Hannah had trouble repressing the burst of joy that washed over her just seeing the band on her finger.

"He's right about one thing, child. You whisper as loudly as a donkey." She scoffed at Hannah's expression. "Innocent darling, you've never been able to get away with anything your father and I didn't know about." She tossed Hannah's hand to her lap. "Now, we don't have much time. Your father won't want to delay the trip home. Two weeks minus a day will be enough to commission the dress, and I'm sure Nicholas will gift a large sum toward rebuilding the brickyard as a wedding present."

Finding her voice, Hannah blinked. "You both? You aren't angry?"

"Child, we heard everything. Every last word until he took you away from the house, and if you hadn't remained in sight, be assured we would have gone after you. Your father is on his way to town to speak to the sheriff about the fire."

"But why—how? I don't understand."

Mother almost smiled. The muscles needed warming up, but Hannah was sure that's what her mother attempted. Mother opened and shut her mouth multiple times. Someone had taken her mother and replaced her with a woman who didn't know what to say.

Releasing a shuddering breath, Mother dashed away another tear, clearly embarrassed. She spoke softly, almost as if she were afraid to say the words out loud. "Friendship, Hannah. Last night I overheard a conversation between friends." She procured a handkerchief and dabbed at her nose. "Nicholas and I made our choice in fear. Desperation and fear. Isn't that what Mr. Franklin said?" Mother covered her face, and her shoulders shook. Hannah patted her awkwardly on the knee and wished for Hiram to burst in and save her any minute.

Like the dust thrown around the yard during a windstorm, Hannah was assaulted with a swirl of emotions. Too many to process all at once. Her mother's stoic demeanor had crumbled. Hannah had a sister? Mother and Father overheard Tobias's proposal and they . . . approved?

It didn't take long for Mother to find her voice again. "Come. We have much to do. We'll go to town straightaway and see about the dress." She was across the room and opening the door before Hannah choked out a response.

"Mother, wait. I—I can't today. Eloise is getting married. Tobias's sister. And I promised to watch Luke today and tomorrow so she could finish moving into the house. The wedding is Sunday. In two days. Will you—would you and Father come?"

"Gracious, no. Whyever would we do a thing like that?"

"Because you're my family, and Eloise and Zeke, Tobias and Luke are soon to be my family."

Mother's eyes narrowed, and her gaze flitted about the room, dancing from the window to the bed and finally slamming into Hannah again. "Very true. The water will be hot by now. Bathe and dress quickly. We'll fetch the boy and bring him with us while we run errands." A curt nod finalized her plan. "I hadn't considered the boy. Luke, you say? He needs a mother. You will show me Eloise's house. Perhaps we can be of service. Up, child. Up, up. We have much to do. The boy won't be underfoot with three women to manage him."

Chapter 39

Flat on his stomach, Tobias peered under the sofa. Wooden blocks, toddler stockings, and a spoon blocked his view, and he shoved them aside. He grunted when Luke jumped on his back.

"Not now, Luke. Get off."

Luke squealed and pulled at Tobias's shirt. A knock sounded at the door, and Tobias flinched, crashing his head against the bottom of the sofa. "Get off!"

Luke tumbled to the floor and began to wail. His eyes filled with tears, and he crawled away. He fought when Tobias reached for him but soon changed his mind and snuggled close. Immediately his cries cut off when he found his thumb, but crocodile tears already dripped from his chin.

"I'm sorry I snapped at you," Tobias murmured. "But I can't play right now." With Luke hooked under an arm, he swept the pile of clutter back under the sofa, then made his way to the door.

Hannah's glowing face greeted him. "Good mornin'."

Tobias flashed her a smile.

She ducked her head, scraping the toe of one shoe behind the other.

"What are you doing here? I thought I was coming to you."

Luke reached for her, and she took him into her arms.

"I missed you," Tobias said.

She looked up with a flirtatious smile. "Flatterer—it's been less than six hours."

He winked. "Honest truth, it's been six too many."

Luke placed his hands on her cheeks and pulled her face to his until he giggled.

"I think someone else missed me too." She kissed the boy on the nose.

"We're both hopeless without you." Tobias came outside and pulled the door shut behind him.

She ran a finger along his freshly shaved chin, her ring catching the light. "You smell nice."

"Why, thank you." He captured her hand and kissed her fingers. It was then he looked past Hannah and noticed the rented buggy sitting in the street. Mrs. Benton sat on the bench, watching them. Tobias raised a tentative hand in greeting.

"There's been a change of plans," Hannah said, following his gaze.

"Is it bad?" Tobias said in a low voice.

"She wants to take you to breakfast, and then we have business to attend to without you. Where's Eloise?"

"She went over to the house right away this morning. Zeke works today and tomorrow yet, so she's trying to get everything set up that she can on her own." Tobias's stomach growled. "Breakfast sounds delightful." He offered his arm in an effort to disguise his weakening courage at sharing breakfast with her mother. "Shall we?"

"I think you're forgetting something," Hannah said.

"Hm?"

Her eyebrows shot up before she burst into laughter. Gently, she tapped her foot on his stocking. "You have one lost shoe."

Zeke's specialty sat before Tobias. A cinnamon roll as big as his face. But for once, Tobias wasn't sure he could eat it. Amanda Benton hadn't ceased bombarding him with questions since he squeezed into the buggy next to her. He was beginning to see that he was lucky she even handed over the literal reins. Next time he'd walk.

"Mother," Hannah insisted. "Let the man breathe."

"You've always lived in Ockelbo?" Mrs. Benton stared at him over her coffee, which was almost empty, though he wasn't sure how she managed the time to drink it with the artillery she fired.

"Mostly. I was too young to remember anything else from before."

"Hannah remembers Chicago," Mrs. Benton said. "Why did your family settle here?"

He nodded. "Pa worked as a wagon train guide before I was born. He'd seen enough of the country, and they settled here when the town was first founded."

"Though you're not Swedish."

"No, ma'am."

Hannah's fingers brushed against his leg under the table, and he flinched involuntarily. Without taking his eyes from Mrs. Benton, he brushed Hannah's hand away. It was hard enough being interrogated by one Benton woman. He didn't need the other distracting him.

Mrs. Benton turned her focus to Luke, who sat in Hannah's lap. She put her cup down and reached for him. "Come here, child. Will you sit with me?"

Luke paused in his work of stirring Hannah's coffee with the fork he'd snatched from her earlier. He bounced in Hannah's lap and then tossed himself toward Mrs. Benton.

Tobias wasn't sure if he should protect her from his son or the other way around. He moved his free hand back to Hannah under the table and floundered until he found hers. She glanced at him and smiled. He was as nervous as a mouse slinking across a field full of circling hawks. And about as exhausted. He'd had about two hours of sleep on the sofa before this bundle of joy leapt on him this morning.

Luke stood on Mrs. Benton's knees, and she held him away from her at arm's length. The two looked at each other. Sizing up the other. Luke pointed a finger at Mrs. Benton's cameo pinned at her neck.

"That's your great-great-grandmother's brooch. From Spain. You mustn't touch it. If you behave yourself, I'll let you hold it someday when you're older. But not today."

Luke popped his thumb in his mouth and stared at her.

"Hmm. Mr. Franklin, you let him suck his thumb whenever he pleases?"

"I do." His grip on Hannah's hand grounded him; otherwise, he would have swept the child off her lap to rescue him.

Mrs. Benton studied Luke for an agonizing minute. "Well, then." She turned Luke to sit across her lap. He curled into her as if he could hear Tobias's silent pleas to make a good impression. She snapped her gaze toward Tobias and Hannah. "Eloise marries Sunday. Two weeks is too long to wait for yours. Hannah and I will see about the dress today, and the rest is nothing." She waved her hand at an invisible fly. "You will marry next Friday or the day before, and that will leave a week for your honeymoon before Nicholas and I return to Des Moines. We'll keep the boy."

His mouth parted, but there were no words. First, he needed to tell her he could make his own decisions. What kind of marriage would this be if he started off by letting his mother-in-law control everything before he was even married? And a honeymoon to boot? He'd never considered such a thing. Work wouldn't allow it, and Luke was an ever-present tag-along . . . no, a honeymoon wasn't necessary. On the other hand . . . days alone with his new wife? Friday or the day before to have Hannah as his own? To bring her into his home to stay?

"That's a very good idea," he heard himself say. "Thursday works well for me." He stuttered and looked at Hannah. "If—if that's all right with you, dear?"

"I believe I could clear my schedule for Thursday." She failed at keeping a straight face. "It works as well as any other day."

It was a relief to finally escape the women and face the demands of the brickyard. Tobias looked forward to next Thursday, but he could do without the hubbub that would take place before then.

Still mulling over the conversations of the morning, he walked all the way to the middle of the brickyard before he registered his surroundings. There stood Nicholas Benton next to a pile of new lumber, commanding Tobias's men about. A crew shoveled the debris of the drying shed and cleared the lot to rebuild. A spike of irritation shot through Tobias when he saw his foreman, Dee Williams, in conference with Mr. Benton.

"What's going on?" Tobias asked, forcing himself to keep the accusation from his tone.

"Ah, good." Mr. Benton barely glanced at him. "Williams and I agree that this tragedy has presented us with the opportunity to easily expand the drying shed. We'll make it at least fifty percent larger." He patted Dee on the shoulder in dismissal and turned to Tobias. "Now, about the office. Rebuilding from brick again is a worthy idea. Looks good to buyers, sets a proper tone for the area, but you don't currently have the resources for it, and it would be a fool business plan to take bricks from signed contracts. But I was thinking of expanding it as well. Provide a second story for your foreman, timekeeper, or anyone who has use of it. A balcony on the second floor provides a view of the whole yard. Overseeing the operations from there would be a treat for the eyes."

Tobias wanted to argue again, but everything the man said sounded wonderful. He couldn't afford these expansions though. He would barely be able to cover wages after last night's loss until the next shipment of bricks went out.

"Think on it. Think on it." Mr. Benton stepped closer. "About the other matter. Charles Grady? Your sheriff is dragging his feet about moving against him. Lazy man, I'd warrant. No matter I've wired a friend, Detective Monroe, and he'll be here by the afternoon. He'll track him down and see that he's brought to justice. If Grady isn't our man, Monroe will weasel the truth out of the situation."

Mr. Benton didn't even know how much Charles had hurt this family. How would he react if he learned Charles had accosted his daughter?

"Amanda said she's planning the wedding and not to bother her. Fine by me. We've much to do to stay out of her way." Mr. Benton turned slowly, taking in the scene while Tobias stood dry-mouthed, grateful, and annoyed at the same time. "Much to do indeed."

Tobias loosened his voice and nodded to the wagon of lumber. "Where'd that come from?"

"I ordered it this morning straightaway. We'll need more, but it's enough to start."

Calculations of the costs and bills and overextended credit filled his mind. Mr. Benton interrupted his feverish thoughts with a low voice.

"Excuse my liberty. I extended your credit at the mill since I didn't think you'd appreciate my charity on the matter, but Hannah comes with a dowry. She's not aware of it, though. We didn't think it wise to mention it before. I set up a fund for her when she was born. I think you will be pleased with it. Once you marry, the funds will be at your disposal. Consider this a gift from your wife with more to come."

My wife.

His ears burned each time they heard the phrase. Mutely he nodded at the barrage of information. Eloise was moving out and marrying Zeke on Sunday. Hannah would become his wife and mother to Luke next Thursday. His mother-in-law was already running his personal life. His father-in-law was taking over his work life.

God must find pleasure in making his point solidly heard. *Do you trust me? Do you trust me when you're out of control? Can you let me take care of you?*

"I think." Tobias swallowed. "I think you have things well in hand. If you don't mind, my time could be better spent somewhere else today."

Mr. Benton listened with hands clasped behind his back.

"Um, make sure Kevin doesn't overdo it. You can send an order to Anderson's Bakery for lunch—we have an account. Send George out for any missing mules . . ."

Tobias found Eloise in her new little house. She at in the middle of the living room with her knees pulled up and her head buried in her arms. Sobbing.

"Hey." Tobias sat beside her and gathered her into his arms. "I'm here, El. I'm here."

She pressed against him, and he dug a clean handkerchief out of his pocket. He'd learned to always have a spare for her or Luke.

"I can't do this, Tobias. What if I'm making a terrible mistake?"

"Do you love him?"

"With all my heart."

"Then what's the problem?"

"I don't want to leave you and Luke alone." She blew her nose. "And what if something happens to Zeke or you or—" She cried through the rest of her doubts.

He pulled her to her feet. "Hush, now."

He held her close with one hand against her back and the other cradling her neck, and he swayed until she breathed normally. He softly sang "Guide me, O Thou great Jehovah" and danced her around the empty living room. "Pilgrim through this barren land. I am weak, but Thou art mighty; hold me with Thy powerful hand."

She didn't sing, but she began to hum through the rest.

"Bread of heaven, Bread of heaven, feed me 'till I want no more . . ." He slowed and held her close again. "Here's the thing, El. I'm getting married next week, and as much as I love you, I most surely love her more. It might be uncomfortable for you to stay at the house with us because there's going to be so much kissing. And as much as I like you and Zeke, you'll be doing your own fair share of kissing, and I might throw up if I have to watch."

The sweet sound of his sister's giggle was his only answer. "Hannah finally said yes."

Tobias blinked. "Oh." He furrowed his eyebrows. "Well, she's wearing the ring."

Eloise laughed harder. "Finally."

He shook his head, smiling. "And I have a set of in-laws that will scare you to bits. The sooner you're under Zeke's protection, the better."

"They can't be that bad."

He whistled. "Not for you they won't be." He hugged her one last time. "Pray for me, El. I think God is seeing how far I can stretch. Dry your eyes. We have work to do." He chucked her under the chin. "My company burned down, and God sent someone else to take care of it. I really, and I mean really, want to fight the whole lot of them, but I've decided to hang out with you instead. Now, tell me what to do. My whole day is yours. Let me be whatever you need today and tomorrow. Then I'll walk you down the aisle and send you off in peace in exchange for a lifetime supply of baked goods. From Zeke, not you. To be frank, please don't bake me anything. Ever again."

Chapter 40

"How do I look?" Hannah spun in a slow circle Thursday evening in her bedroom, modeling her wedding gown with only Hiram for an audience. Mother had left her for one blessed moment to get herself dressed.

Hiram squinted, turned his head one way and then the other as she held up the folds of her white satin gown trimmed with lace and eighty-seven pearl buttons. He raised both hands as if weighing two similar objects on a scale. "Ehhh, I wouldn't be ashamed to be seen with you."

Hannah pressed her hands to her stomach. Mother had cinched her in too tightly. "I'm going to be sick."

"Don't, I've only got one suit."

"Hiram, what if—what if it's all a terrible and delightful dream?"

"Then it's a powerful one if it's brought Mother and Father and me into it as well. Keep dreaming through today, and you'll wake up a married woman."

"You're going survive with them? Without me?"

"I'll keep busy."

"You aren't going back with Father?"

Hiram snorted. "He'll figure it out soon enough. He can't snap his fingers and make me jump when I own the farm, the sheep, and the garden. What's he going to do, sell it from under my feet without me knowing?"

"He might." Hannah fiddled with Hiram's vest.

"I haven't seen either of them much this week. Mother's organizing the troops for the wedding, and best I can tell, Father's playing contractor at Franklin Brickworks."

"I don't know where Father's been, but I'm ready to jump into a convenient marriage with a handsome stranger just to escape Mother."

"You don't mean that. That's not what this is, is it? Say, what's gotten into you?"

"Mother's kept me so busy, I haven't seen Mr. Franklin since Sunday, and I'm going mad—that's what. Eloise's wedding was a dream. Perfection. A small affair of family and friends. Intimate. Comfortable." She heard her own voice rising in pitch. "Oh, blast. Hiram, why couldn't my wedding be like that?"

He took her shoulders and gave her a little shake. "Because you're Hannah Claire Benton, a warrior princess who commands her subjects to pay homage to her as she unites her kingdom with another."

"You think so? You don't think Tobias has run off sometime between Sunday and now, has he?"

"He'd be a fool to leave his queen."

"Why am I so nervous?"

"I'll saddle Speck and run to town before you to check in on the groom. I'll signal to you when you arrive that all is well."

Before Hannah could answer, Mother breezed into the room. "Father is hitching the buggy. Let's be off."

"I'll ride separate," Hiram said.

"You'll sit with us. We'll arrive as a family."

Hiram had the courage to smile at their mother. A small act of rebellion on his part. "I have other business to attend to."

She sputtered. "Hiram Benton, what could possibly be more important today of all days than your sister's wedding? You come back here this minute. Don't walk away from me."

He returned as commanded and surprised his mother with a kiss on the cheek. He winked at Hannah and strode out the door. Mother was left muttering about ungrateful and disobedient children before she snapped her gaze to Hannah. "Turn."

Hannah did.

"You'll do very well. Let's be on our way."

Tobias shook hands with so many people, he'd stopped seeing them. It looked as if half the town milled about the Jenkins's orchard. A couple hundred at least. Everyone from church, the brickyard, friends, and friends of friends. All he'd done was pass the word about the day and time, and Amanda Benton took care of the rest. Somehow she'd managed to hire tables built and loaded them with a variety of mouth-watering pastries. Jugs of cider, lemonade, tea, and water filled one table by itself. The band would set up afterward for a dance, and ropes strung with lanterns hung between poles near the wooden platform.

Hannah was liked wherever she went and had a knack for drawing people to her. Hannah's mother was another force entirely. She spoke and men scraped and bowed to do her bidding out of fear.

Tobias tugged the collar of his shirt again and wiped his hands on his jacket. The August humidity smothered them like a damp blanket. "Where's Luke?"

Zeke scanned the crowd nearby before answering. "I don't know, but you have to stop asking me. Chipmunk said she'd watch him, so she'll watch him."

"I think I'm going to be sick."

Zeke laughed. "You won't. As soon as you see her face, everything else will melt away."

"It wasn't like this with Katie."

"Was Katie's mother scary?"

"You're scared too?"

"Land sakes, Boss—everyone's scared."

Tobias felt somewhat better at that. "You don't think she's changed her mind, do you? Hannah didn't run off, did she?"

"You're an idiot."

"Distract me. You owe me that much."

"Did I ever tell you how Eloise and I first met?"

Tobias rubbed a hand over his face "She said you bumped into each other in town. What's there to tell?"

"She lied."

"Eloise doesn't lie." Tobias continued to search the road, looking for any sign of Hannah's buggy coming from the farm.

"Did she tell you I came across her in the creek soaking wet wearing nothing but her, ah, unmentionables?"

Tobias turned on Zeke.

Zeke eased backward. "Now, wait a minute, Boss." He tripped another step back as Tobias advanced. "She and I are married now, so I've seen a lot more."

Tobias took a swipe at him, and Zeke jumped to the side. "Seen a lot more? Watch how you talk about my sister."

"It was an innocent accident." Zeke bumped into a pear tree and angled around it. He laughed, but it was a high-pitched, nervous laugh. "You asked me to distract you. Is it working?"

Tobias growled low in the back of his throat, tension coiling around his chest.

"You should be thanking me. See how confident you are now? Look at you, asserting dominance. That's the Boss we all know and love."

A branch full of hard, unripened pears blocked his view. Tobias snapped one off the tree and shot it at Zeke.

"Ow." Zeke yanked his hand from the trunk, shaking it. "Oh, look—there's Hiram."

Tobias turned, and Zeke ran off.

Hiram strode toward him at a fast clip. "Hannah wants to know if it's too late to elope."

"Ask your mother. She's running the show."

"You have everything you need?" Hiram tucked his hands in the pockets of a well-pressed suit. Mrs. Benton had dragged them both to the tailor last Monday.

"I think so." Tobias wiped the sweat from his forehead. "Bags are packed, and Luke's going home with Eloise. I still can't believe we're leaving."

Guests were filling the chairs as sunset approached. "Hiram, we've been firm about this, and we're trusting you to keep it that way. Amanda can visit all she likes, but she's not to take Luke home. We'll only be in Omaha. You can send a telegram anytime to our hotel, and we'll be on the next train home."

"So you've said. I'll look out for him."

"Shield Eloise if you can. I don't want her in the middle of that. Dee's handling the brickyard next week with your father, I suppose. He's everywhere I turn. It makes me jumpy." He jiggled his shoulders and looked around. "We're all set. Just waiting on my bride."

"She'll be here any minute. Anything you need right now?"

"A bucket of cold water to dump over my head. It's hot as . . ." Tobias stalled and pulled at his collar.

"A lake of burning sulfur?"

"Something like that."

"The wind never blows in August."

"No, sir, but it'll suck the life out of you from October to March. In August it goes on holiday. If it visits, it'll bring a tornado. I guess we should be thankful for the stillness." Tobias considered the vast blue sky, currently spotted with cotton puffs of clouds.

"Say, how old are we anyway?" Hiram knocked him on the shoulder. "Standing here gabbing about the weather."

"My hands won't stop shaking. How's Hannah?"

"See for yourself soon enough." Hiram motioned to a buggy on the road. "It's time."

"She's here." Tobias drew a slow, healing breath. He spoke to Hiram without taking his eyes off the approaching team, not wanting to miss a glimpse of her. "Fetch Pastor Bernas, will you? Let him know we're a go."

Hannah had dreamed of this day since childhood. How she would do her hair, what her husband would say, what she would say. Where and when, what, how, who. *Everything.* Of course, the reality wasn't like her dreams. There was only Tobias Franklin, and he was more real than any dream she'd ever had.

Father handed her from the buggy, but her attention snagged on Tobias across the orchard. He stood alone in the shade of a pear tree, looking at her with a slight smile. When she met his gaze, his smile grew until he appeared to laugh, but he was too far away to know for sure. He chucked something behind his shoulder and took a step toward her.

Mother was speaking. Hannah noticed her parents only when Father stepped into her line of sight. "It's not too late to change your mind," he said.

She exhaled with a laugh. "It was too late the moment his whirlwind of a son spilled my trunk at the train station."

Father said something else, but Hannah didn't register his words. He waited with her by the buggy, practically holding her from running off. Within minutes, everything was in place.

Tobias stood with Pastor Bernas, and everyone else was seated. They'd timed it perfectly. As the sun grazed the horizon and began sinking its way into the prairie, a hush fell upon the orchard while the heart-aching pull of a single fiddle soared into the evening. They had roughly half an hour until full darkness. It was time. Father squeezed her hand that rested on his arm and took the first step.

Tobias held his wife, and they hardly danced anymore, only swayed. The last song had ended minutes ago, and the band was packing up, going home. His mother-in-law strode from one end of the orchard to the other, overseeing the clean-up crew. Luke had long ago fallen asleep, and Eloise sat with him under a tree. The lanterns around the platform moved ever so slightly in the barest breeze.

"I'm in a dream," Tobias said. He felt, more than heard, Hannah's small laugh through his hand on her back.

"I've already checked," she answered quietly. "Kiss me again, and we'll see if I wake up."

He brushed his lips across her cheek. "That's exactly what you might say in my dream."

"Mmm," she all but purred. "You have nice dreams."

Tobias caught Zeke's signal from the side of the platform. He nodded once and eased Hannah away. "I bought you something. A wedding present." He slid his hand down her arm to link their fingers.

Hannah froze, and he knew she'd seen it. Next to the platform in a small open-topped crate was an eight-week-old black-and-white mutt. With a squeal Hannah released Tobias's hand.

She bent over the crate and crooned to the little animal. "Hello, dearest. Oh, he's sleeping. What a precious creature. Oh. Oh. Oh. Feel how soft." Gently, Hannah picked him up and held the puppy under her chin. "What'll we call him?"

"He's your puppy. Call him whatever you want, provided I won't feel dumb yelling it around town when he runs off."

"He'll be a good boy." She stroked the puppy's head. "Won't you, boy? You won't ever run off." His wife squinted, thinking. "Darcy . . . Knightley . . . Victor."

"Don't overwhelm him with too much class. Go with something carefree."

"Tom . . . Huckleberry . . . Fritz."

"Fritz will do."

"Fritz. A worthy name. You'll be a good helper around the place, won't you, dear? Oh, I'm going to cry. He's so soft." She switched to baby talk. "Yook at him, oh, baby. Feel his wittle ears."

Tobias smiled. He wasn't interested in the puppy. He was too busy gazing at Mrs. Franklin.

She must have noticed his silence, for she looked at him, eyebrows drawn together. "What?"

He pulled her closer. "Are you ready?"

"For what?"

"For forever."

She closed the distance with a kiss. "Forever and ever."

A Special Letter of Acknowledgments

Dear you,

I'm #sorrynotsorry if you missed your bedtime waiting to find out if they were going to kiss already. I hope you laughed a lot, cried a little, and glory to God if you learned anything and were encouraged.

I totally need to acknowledge all the people who helped turn these words into a book. All of you. I'll mention some below, but of course, there are always more!

My American Christian Fiction Writers critique group helped nudge *Wildflower* from a "pretty good" story to the gem that it is and introduced me to my elite editor, friend, and author, Megan Schaulis. Just wow, Megan. You added seasonings, trimmed the fat, and fixed those troublesome farthers/furthers. I love when you say, "Tobias would have said…" or "Hannah needs to…" because you knew them so well. I confess, I was usually annoyed with "Action needed here. What is she doing?" I don't know! Okay? My only disappointment is that my Tobias and your Zadian will never meet. Unless Z's world invents a time machine? For now, we'll leave them be and not speak of such things.

Mary Connealy, Sharee Stover, and Dawn Ford, I'm so grateful to count you as friends. You welcomed me to your table, and I was immediately at peace in a big new world.

Robin, Michelle, and Mom were my first draft readers. I know Stephen King says to write the first draft with the door closed, but . . . Robin, I'd like to keep that door open to you every time. I'll forever write stories without "all the boring parts" that I know you'll just skip. There's nothing like a sister to tell you that you're amazing and that the chapter stinks in the same breath.

Mom, thanks for laughing your way through Tobias's third and fourth proposals. It was a joy to see it come to life through you.

Thank you, Heather, my bosom friend, for naming Dan, the dappled gray. Who knew naming a horse could be so much trouble? The final wedding scene and the puppy are your fan fiction come to life. I hope I delivered. I gave Caroline Jenkins your hair since you named her as well. You're welcome. And you'll be pleased to hear nobody ever calls her a ginger. Yet.

Danae, thanks for your willingness to talk storyline. You continue to answer the phone even when you know I'm going to launch straight into out-of-context plot holes for you to fix. You're everything a writer's friend could be. There will never be enough time to write all the amazing stories we've plotted together.

Reuben, in this economy and after the wolves came, I had put *Wildflower* aside. Then I busted out the last 50,000 words because of you. Thanks for taking my stories seriously and talking through my characters' issues when, you know, it's a girly book. Writing the final scene in your living room, legs crossed and sunk deeply into your larger-than-practical couch, with no care in the world but lifting a cup of way-too-strong coffee to my lips, was the perfect way to celebrate the completion. I've rarely felt the sense of peace as I did that weekend in Dallas when my massive project was "finished" and you drove me places and bought me food. (Though I'll take my blueberries in a dish next time, please. Thank you.)

Hey, kids—I'm sorry this took so much of my time. Someday you'll read *Wildflower* and smile. Jasmine, I cried sweet tears when I found a copy of *Bluebird* hidden under your pillow before you could read. Do you remember our brainstorming sessions at dinner? "What funny things could happen to Hannah?"

Except for "morning time!"—that was for Grams—there is nothing in Luke that isn't a direct impression from one of you kids, namely my sons, rapscallions all three.

Peter, you were the toddler in the tree. You went up and could not come down. I climbed up the prickly cedar tree on our prairie with needles poking my neck and scratching my arms. When I reached you, you flung yourself into my arms, and I somehow climbed down with one hand. It was difficult. Eventually I clung to your wrist and lowered you as far as I could and dropped you. You fell into your big brother's arms below. So that thing at the beginning that says it's all made up? Well, that bit was sort of real.

At the time I thought to myself, "This would be difficult in a dress. Impossible, I think." It was the *eureka* moment I needed for the rising climax and answered the question "What's the worst possible thing that could happen to Tobias?" Originally, Hannah climbed the tree, but Luke fell and broke his leg—a compound fracture. I wrote 3,000 words of that storyline. It was intense. I cried. Tobias carrying Luke, stony resolution, knowing his son would lose his leg. Hannah ran along ahead and found Hiram because ain't nobody going to Dr. Farley again. Mary Connealy and I discussed the possible options for repairing a compound fracture in the late 1800s, but it wasn't looking good for Luke.

You know, I'm just not that wicked of an author yet, and in the end I couldn't break Luke's leg. I reminded myself I was writing comedy and thought, "Hmm—what's the worst possible thing that could happen to *Hannah* at this moment *besides the horrendous event of a compound fracture in the 1800s resulting in death or loss of limb?*" Obviously Mother and Father Benton arriving out of nowhere while Hannah's literally up a tree in her underwear. (The author rubs her hands together and giggles mischievously.) Much funnier than breaking bones, and still terrible in its own way.

More importantly, kids, I want you to understand what marriage can be. I hope Ben and I have shown you an example of commitment and joy in our love for each other and for you. I pray that when you grow up, you'll be surrounded by friends who love you as my characters love each other, faults and all.

Ben, as I type this, you've started your tenth year of teaching middle school, and we've not seen much of each other in the past two weeks. *Wildflower* is for you. Every scene, every chapter, you were on my mind. How could I tell a story of two friends falling in love and not think of you? Tobias is not you, but he is similar in many ways. His love for Luke is yours, and his commitment *and joy* are yours. The tuft of hair that sticks up in the back is yours.

My goal from the beginning was to show two realistic people with flaws falling into friendship and then love. I asked, "If they're friends, if they love each other, can there still be conflict?" I've learned that it's quite possible. Thanks for loving me through conflict. For being that safe place where I can retreat.

This is my gift to you for our fifteenth wedding anniversary. Sorry it's a few months late. I tried, but things happened. As with *Bluebird,* a "Well, I didn't hate it," from you would suffice. Bless you, but I *will* take my chances with the flea over the tiger. Always. Thanks for standing up with me—and against me when it's warranted.

When I was stuck and trying to work through Hannah's doubts, I asked you, "What is love in a marriage? Commitment and . . . ?" You told me, "Joy."

Your answer shaped the entire theme of this book.

Happy anniversary. Forever and ever, I love you.

Tasha
August 11, 2022

About the Author

While at York University completing a B.A. in English, and English education with a minor in theater, Tasha married her best friend. Now, instead of analyzing Shakespeare's plays, she writes with hope and humor to encourage and entertain. Although she spends a good deal of time typing words, washing dishes, cooking for six, sewing, and folding laundry, her favorite thing is family. They give her the kind of love people write books about.

Made in the USA
Coppell, TX
31 July 2023

19821874R00239